D1356849

District
Rotation Plan
no. 3

THE TIME OF SINGING

THE TIME OF SINGING

Elizabeth Chadwick

sphere

SPHERE

First published in Great Britain in 2008 by Sphere

Copyright © Elizabeth Chadwick 2008

The moral right of the author has been asserted.

*All characters and events in this publication, other than those clearly
in the public domain, are fictitious and any resemblance to real persons,
living or dead, is purely coincidental.*

A CIP catalogue record for this book
is available from the British Library.

ISBN 978-1-84744-097-6

Typeset in Baskerville MT by Palimpsest Book Production Limited,
Grangemouth, Stirlingshire
Printed and bound in Great Britain by
Clays Ltd, St lves plc

Papers used by Sphere are natural, renewable and recyclable
products, made from wood grown in sustainable forests and
certified in accordance with the rules of the Forest Stewardship
Council.

Mixed Sources
Product group from well-managed
forests and other controlled sources
www.fsc.org   Cert no. SGS-COC-004081
© 1996 Forest Stewardship Council
FSC

Acknowledgements

I'd like to say a brief but heartfelt thank you to the people behind the scenes, who have kept the ship afloat during its journey across the ocean between the first word and the last.

In the publishing profession I'd like to thank the editors and the rest of the team at Little, Brown – Barbara Daniel, Joanne Dickinson, Richenda Todd, Alexandra Richardson, Emma Stonex and Rachael Ludbrook. As always, my thanks go out to my agent Carole Blake, her assistant Oli Munson, and the rest of the staff at Blake Friedmann for all their hard work on my behalf, and their friendship. Who says you can't combine work and pleasure?

On the domestic front, as always, I send my love and gratitude to my husband Roger. It has been a bit strange having a husband with the same name as my hero for this novel. Two very different men, eight hundred years apart – and I know I have the better deal re the house-work and ironing!

A warm thank you, too, to Alison King, a special friend with an exceptional gift.

On the writing front (as opposed to the publishing)

I want to thank the members of the RNA for their support and friendship down the years. The same goes for the list members of Friends and Writers and Penman Review. You colour the world and help me to keep both oars in the water!

Arise my love, my fair one,
And come away;
For lo, the winter is past,
the rain is over and gone,
the flowers appear on the earth,
the time of singing has come.

The Song of Solomon

Selective Bigod Family Tree

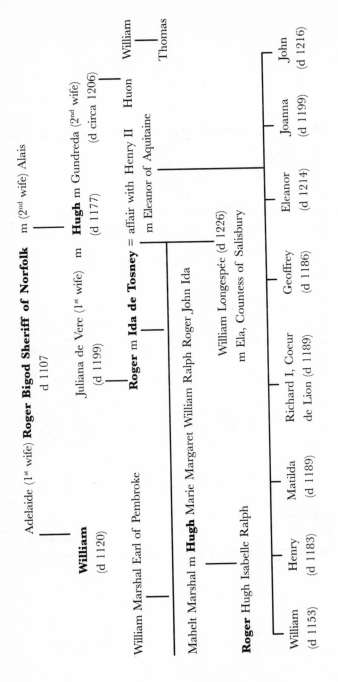

Settrington
York

Hunstanton   Cromer
                        Great
                        Yarmouth
Nottingham   Norwich
Leicester   Thetford
              Bungay   Framlingham
Hereford   Bury St Edmunds   Orford
Woodstock   Dovercourt   Ipswich
Chepstow Oxford   London
Pembroke
        Windsor
Salisbury   Greenwich
        Winchester

WYE

Miles
0   50   100

1

Framlingham Castle, Suffolk, October 1173

Roger woke and shot upright on a gulp of breath. His heart was slamming against his rib cage and, although the parted bed curtains showed him a chamber sun-splashed with morning light, his inner vision blazed with vivid images of men locked in combat. He could hear the iron whine of blade upon blade and the dull thud of a mace striking a shield. He could feel the bite of his sword entering flesh and see blood streaming in scarlet ribbons, glossy as silk.

'Ah, God.' He shuddered and bowed his head, his hair flopping over his brow in sweaty strands the colour of tide-washed sand. After a moment, he collected himself, threw off the bed coverings with his right hand, and went to the window. Clenching his bandaged left fist, he welcomed the stinging pain like a penitent finding comfort in the scourge. The wound was not deep enough to cause serious damage but he was going to have a permanent scar inscribed across the base of three fingers. The soldier who had given it to him was dead, but Roger took no pleasure in the knowledge. It had been kill or be killed. Too many of his own men had fallen yesterday. His father said he was useless, but it was a habitual opinion and Roger no longer felt its impact beyond a dull bruise. What did abrade him were the unnecessary deaths of good soldiers. The opposition had been too numerous and his resources insufficient to the task. He looked at his taut fist. There would be a lake of blood before his father's ambition was done.

To judge from the strength of the daylight he had missed mass. His stepmother would delight in berating him for his tardiness and then comment to his father that his heir wasn't fit to inherit a dung heap, let alone the Earldom of Norfolk when the time came. And then she would look pointedly at her own eldest son, the obnoxious Huon, as if he were the answer to everyone's prayers rather than the petulant adolescent brat he actually was.

Framlingham's bailey was packed with the tents and shelters of the mercenaries belonging to Robert Beaumont, Earl of Leicester – an ill-assorted rabble he had plucked from field and town, ditch, gutter, weaving shed and dockside on his way from Flanders to England. Few of them were attending mass to judge by the numbers infesting the inner and outer wards. Locusts, Roger thought with revulsion. By joining the rebellion against King Henry and giving lodging and support to the Earl of Leicester, his father had encouraged a plague to descend on them, in more ways than one. The plot was to overthrow the King and replace him with his eighteen-year-old son Henry – a vain boy who could be turned this way and that by men skilled in manipulation and the machinations of power. Roger's father had no love for the King, who had clamped down hard on his ambition to rule all of East Anglia. Henry had confiscated their castle at Walton and built a strong royal fortress at Orford to neutralise their grip on that part of the coastline.

To add insult to injury, fines for earlier insurgency had gone to assist the building of Orford.

Turning from the window, Roger sluiced his face one-handed in the ewer at the bedside. Since the tips of his fingers and his thumb were free on his bandaged side, he managed to dress himself without summoning a servant. From the moment he had been capable of tying his braies in small childhood, a fierce sense of self-reliance had driven him to perform all such tasks for himself.

On opening the coffer containing his cloaks, his eyes narrowed as he noticed immediately that his best one with the silver braid was missing. He could well guess where it was. While donning his everyday mantle of plain green twill, his gaze lit on the weapons chest standing against the wall. Last night his scabbarded sword and belt had been propped against it, waiting to be checked and cleaned before storage, but now they were gone. Roger's annoyance turned to outright anger. His sword had been a gift to him from his Uncle Aubrey, Earl of Oxford, at the time of his knighting. This time the thieving little turd had gone too far.

Jaw clamped, Roger strode from the chamber and headed purposefully to the chapel adjoining the hall where mass had just finished and people were filing out to attend their duties. Roger concealed himself behind a pillar as his father walked past deep in conversation with Robert, Earl of Leicester. They were an incongruous pair, Leicester being tall and slender with a natural grace and good humour, and his father with a rolling pugilistic gait reminiscent of a sailor heading from ship to alehouse. His paunch strained the seams of his red tunic and his hair hung in oiled straggles, the colour of wet ashes.

Roger's stepmother Gundreda followed, walking with Petronilla, Countess of Leicester. The women nodded

3

graciously to each other, smiling with their lips but not their eyes. There was little love lost between them, even if they were allies, for neither woman possessed the social skills upon which to build a friendship and Gundreda was resentful of Petronilla's superior airs.

As they moved on, Roger's seeking gaze struck upon the flash of a lapis-blue garment and a twinkle of silver braid as his half-brother Huon swaggered out of the chapel, one narrow adolescent hand clasping the buckskin grip of a very fine sword. A little behind him traipsed Huon's younger sibling Will, fulfilling his usual role of pasty shadow.

Roger reached, seized and swung his half-brother around, slamming him against the pillar. 'Have you nothing of your own that you must resort to thievery of everything that is mine?' Roger hissed. 'Time and again I have told you to stay out of my coffers and leave my things alone.' Taking a choke-hold on the youth's throat with his good hand, he used his other to unhitch the sword belt with a rapid jerk of latch and buckle.

Huon's down-smudged upper lip curled with contempt, although his eyes darted fearfully. Roger noted both emotions and increased the pressure. 'I suppose you wanted to parade before my lord of Leicester and show off a sword you're too young to wear?'

'I wear it better than you!' the youth wheezed with bravado. 'You're a spineless coward. Our father says so.'

Roger released his grip, but only to hook his foot behind Huon's ankles and bring him down. Straddling him, he dragged the purloined cloak over his half-brother's head. 'If there's a next time, you'll wear this on your bier,' he panted, 'and my sword will be through your heart!'

'Huon, where are y—' Gundreda, Countess of Norfolk, had turned back to find her lagging son and now stared at the scene with consternation and fury. 'What do you think you're doing!' she shouted at Roger. 'Get off him; leave him alone!' She forced Roger aside with a hard push, the full weight of her body behind it.

Choking and retching, Huon clutched his throat. 'He tried to kill me . . . and in God's own house . . . He did, Will, didn't he?'

'Yes,' Will croaked as if his own throat had been squeezed. He refused to look anyone in the eye.

'If I had intended to kill you, you would be dead now!' Roger snarled. He encompassed his stepmother and his half-brothers in a burning glare before flinging from the chapel, his cloak over his arm and his scabbarded sword clutched in his good fist. Her invective followed him but he ignored it for he had become inured to that particular bludgeon long ago.

'I didn't have enough soldiers,' Roger said to his father. His sword hung at his hip now, its weight both a burden and a support. A man shouldn't have to wear a weapon to bolster his confidence; he should be at ease within his own skin, but Roger always felt off balance in the presence of his sire. The Earl had called a council of war in his chamber; Robert of Leicester and all the senior knights were present to observe whatever humiliation Hugh Bigod chose to mete out to his eldest son on the scathing edge of his tongue.

'There is always an excuse, isn't there?' Hugh growled. 'I could give you an entire army and it still wouldn't be enough. I daren't put weight on you because you're not strong enough to bear it.'

Roger made a throwing gesture and felt the wound on his hand smart like a wasp sting. 'You don't give me the tools to do what you ask of me. You don't trust me; you don't give me credit for what's due; you don't—'

'Credit!' Norfolk bared a palisade of teeth yellowed by more than seventy years in the gum. 'I'll give you credit, boy. For losing experienced men we couldn't afford to lose, and letting good ransom money slip through your inept fingers. You've cost us at least a hundred marks, which is more than your hide's worth. How much more credit do you want?'

Roger swallowed, feeling sick. He sometimes thought that his own death would be the only coin to satisfy his father. Whatever he did, it would never be right. Yesterday they had seized and destroyed the castle of Haughley, taking pledges of ransom from the knights and turning over the rest of the garrison to the butchery of Leicester's Flemings. Roger's task had been to secure the postern, but his father had given him insufficient men for the assignment and some of the defenders had managed to break free, killing several of Roger's soldiers in the process.

'The young men of today aren't as hard a breed as we had to be, Hugh,' said Robert of Leicester, who had been watching the exchange between father and son with shrewd speculation. 'Let it rest. At least he didn't run. I am sure we can still find a position for him that will be useful to us.'

'Aye, following the dung cart,' Hugh sneered. He pointed to a bench. 'Hold your tongue, boy, sit and listen and see if you can keep more than fleece between your ears.'

At five and twenty, Roger had left boyhood behind long ago – on a warm summer afternoon, aged seven, locked in the solar, watching distraught from the window as his mother departed her annulled marriage to his father and rode away to a new life with another husband. Within the week, Gundreda had replaced her at Framlingham

6

and nine months later had produced Huon. His father had never once called him 'boy' in affection; it was always an insult or a put-down. As a child, he hadn't understood, but maturity had brought knowledge. It was about power; it was about keeping the young stag down . . . and it was about punishment. His mother had escaped, but he hadn't, and he was her proxy. Everyone said he was like her in his way of seeing the world, and in his father's lexicon, such a trait was unforgivable.

Eyes downcast, Roger stepped over the bench, sat down and folded his arms. The fingertips of his right hand sought reassurance in the feel of the solid iron disc of his sword pommel.

Leicester said, 'Haughley is no longer an obstacle, but the keep at Walton still stands and so does Eye.'

Hugh grunted. 'Eye's damaged and the garrison won't venture beyond it. The same goes for Walton. We should strike into the Midlands while Henry is fighting in Normandy and the justiciar is occupied chasing the Scots. Once Leicester's yours, we can push north-west and join Chester.'

Roger bit the inside of his cheek at the not-so-subtle hint in his father's words that Leicester should move his army to his own lands. The Flemings were denuding Norfolk's supplies at a terrifying rate and had already started to strip the hinterland with their foraging parties.

'Quite so,' Leicester said. A hard smile curved his lips. 'I wouldn't want to outstay my welcome, but I'll need provisions.'

Roger saw his father's gaze narrow. 'I have no more to give. My barns are down to the last sheaves and the hayricks are sweepings. I'll have to buy in more for the winter at God knows what price.'

'Then let our enemies provide it. The abbey at

Edmundsbury is well stocked, so I hear, and the Abbot is no friend.'

Hugh rubbed his jaw, considering, his fingers rasping on his stubble. He threw a sneering glance at Roger. 'Pigsticking,' he said with a humourless grin. 'Do you think you can at least manage that?'

Roger returned his father's stare. 'You want me to run off pigs and burn villages?'

'For a start. If you prove capable, I might think about promoting you, but foraging is all you are worth at the moment. You have my leave to go.'

Roger jerked to his feet, his chest hot with anger. How easy it would be to draw his sword and use it, to rage like a wild bull. Easy – and pointless. 'Edmundsbury,' he said stiffly.

His father raised one eyebrow. 'Not superstitious about the Church, are you?'

Since the last King's son and heir had died after raiding the lands of the abbey of Saint Edmund, Roger might have answered with veracity that he was, but knowing his father expected such a response, he didn't rise to the bait. 'No, sire, but we are vassals of the abbey for three knights' fees and I have always honoured the Church.'

'And do you not honour your father also?' Hugh leaned a little forward and clenched his fists. A seal ring gleamed on his bleached knuckles. 'I will have your obedience – boy. My other sons do not shirk their filial duty and question my authority.'

Roger gritted his teeth, performed a perfunctory bow to his father and the Earl of Leicester and strode from the room, his control hanging by a thread. Reaching the safety of his chamber, he threw himself down on the weapons chest and covered his face with his hands. It was too much. He wasn't just at the edge of a precipice, he was over it and scrabbling to hold on by his fingertips while above him his father prepared to stamp on his precarious hold and send him into the void.

The pattern of light through the open shutters dulled as clouds crossed the sun. A mouse ran across the floor and disappeared into a hole chewed in the side of a pallet propped against the chamber wall. Roger roused sufficiently to go to the ewer, splash his face and rinse the taste of the meeting from his mouth. He drew his sword and looked at it. There were nicks that needed honing out, and the edge required sharpening after yesterday's work, but it still had a beautiful, clean balance. Life should have that balance too, but it didn't. Down the fuller, the faint, gold gleam of latten picked out the letters INOMINEDNI. In the Name of the Lord . . .

A shadow darkened the doorway and he looked up to see Anketil, one of the hearth knights, standing there. 'Sire, there is news.' Anketil's Nordic-blue eyes fixed on the sword in Roger's hand and then on Roger himself.

'Good or bad?' Feigning nonchalance, Roger returned the weapon to its scabbard.

'That depends on how you take it. De Luci has made a truce with the Scots. He'll be turning south towards us now.' He gestured with his thumb. 'Messenger's just gone in to your father and the Earl of Leicester.'

Roger didn't suppose it would change his own orders except to make them more urgent. Leicester would have to move imminently if he was going to secure his castle.

Anketil gestured towards the scabbard. 'Saw your brother wearing it this morning in chapel,' he said. 'It didn't suit him.'

'He won't have the opportunity again.' Suddenly Roger's mind was clear and the decision so easy it was like throwing away a piece of used, scratched parchment and drawing forward a fresh, clean sheet, unmarked by the pricking tool. 'Assemble the men,' he commanded. 'Tell them to sharpen their swords and ready their equipment. Make sure the horses are well shod and that everyone has arms and provisions sufficient to his needs.' As he gave the order, he felt as if something that had been crushed and packed down into a tight corner was expanding, rising, filling with light and air.

Anketil eyed him keenly. 'Where are we going?'

'The abbey at Edmundsbury,' Roger said with a mordant smile.

2

Abbey of Saint Edmund, Suffolk, October 1173

In the guest house at the abbey of Saint Edmund, Roger bowed his head and knelt to his maternal uncle, Aubrey de Vere, Earl of Oxford, and to Richard de Luci, justiciar of England. 'I offer myself in the King's service,' he said, 'and I yield to his will.'

De Luci, a hardbitten warrior and statesman whose loyalty to King Henry was unshakeable, studied Roger dispassionately. 'Be welcome,' he said. 'The more we have to swell our numbers the better.' He gestured Roger to rise and take a seat before the hearth. A chill wind rattled the shutters and whistled under the door, making Roger very glad of his fur-lined cloak. The abbey grounds swarmed with the troops of the royalist army, their tents a patched and campaign-worn village of canvas. The commanders and their knights were preparing to bed down in the guest hall and sundry chambers – wherever there was space for a man to roll himself in his cloak. The town and abbey precincts were already bristling with refugees, driven from their homes by the depredations of Leicester's Flemings and huddling in what shelter they could find. Many of the displaced had grim stories to tell of pillage, murder and rape. Roger tried not to think of how close he had come to adding more of the same to their tally and prayed for forgiveness and God's guidance to do the right thing.

De Luci sat down beside him. 'In truth, I am surprised to see the heir of Hugh Bigod in my camp,' he said. 'What brings you here to us?'

Roger leaned towards the fire and folded his hands between his knees. He rubbed his thumb over the bandage and felt the pain spark. 'If you want the simple truth, I am here because of my father.'

De Luci raised his brows and glanced at de Vere.

'Your father?' De Vere's hawkish features creased in puzzlement.

'I didn't want to follow his path,' Roger said. 'All my life I have striven to obey him and do my duty as a son, but when he asked me to raid the lands of Saint Edmund, I realised I could follow him no further without damning my soul.'

De Luci gave him a hard stare. 'How do we know this is not a ploy hatched by your father to ensure the Earl of Norfolk has a foot in each camp?'

'You do not, my lord, apart from my word of honour.'

'Which is not the same as your father's word of honour,' his uncle remarked sardonically. 'Men shake his hand and then check to see that the rings are still on their fingers.'

'No, my lord, it isn't.' Roger was too intent and serious to respond to his uncle's acerbic humour. 'He sent me to raid the abbey's lands and I came to you instead.' His mouth twisted. 'I won't return to him whatever happens; that part of my life is finished.'

De Vere and de Luci exchanged glances again. His uncle signalled a squire to pour wine for Roger. 'How many men does Leicester have with him?'

'Skilled, or rabble, my lord?'

'All told.'

Roger took the cup and gave them the information they desired. It wasn't betrayal. It was strategy and proof of good intent. 'They outnumber you four to one, but from what I have seen, your men are better organised and equipped.'

De Luci pinched his upper lip and gave Roger a long, considering look. 'Come with me,' he said.

Alert with tension, Roger followed him from the guest hall and into the great abbey church of Saint Edmund. The smell of incense fragranced the air and the encroaching night was illuminated by the soft glow of lamps and islands of clustered candlelight leading the way down the massive nave. Beyond the choir at the eastern end of the great church stood the shrine of Saint Edmund, the Christian East Anglian King, martyred by the Danes three hundred years ago. A gabled canopy embellished with panels of beaten silver and coruscating with precious stones covered the tomb and reflected the light from candles and altar lamps as if the surface of the metal was running water upon a bed of jewelled pebbles. Standing in a filigreed socket at the side of the saint's tomb was a banner, its saffron silk gleaming in the light from the altar lamp. Gold and red tassels hung from the tabs attaching it to its pole and embroidered in the centre of the silk was a red crown, pierced by arrows.

'This is the standard of the ancient rulers of this land,' de Luci said. 'Edmundsbury was once their seat, as you must know. Your uncle was intending to bear this banner into battle, but perhaps he can be prevailed upon to relinquish the responsibility to another of his kin.'

Roger's hair prickled at his nape and rose on his wrists. He flickered a glance at de Luci, but there was no censure in the justiciar's eyes, no contempt or pre-emptive expect-ation of failure. 'My lord, I will willingly bear it in his stead – if you and he will permit it.'

De Luci clapped a firm hand on Roger's shoulder. 'It is for the saint to decide. But since you are here before his shrine, and not robbing his lands at the point of a sword, I would say he has already spoken.'

Roger stared at the banner. Gold filaments on the top tassel caught in a movement of air and gently wafted. 'My lord, I beg leave to pray.'

De Luci nodded. 'As you wish. When you are ready, seek me out.' He left, the soles of his shoes making no sound on the chapel floor. Roger breathed deeply, inhaling the scents of the church, seeking spiritual calm. His father had scorned Roger's need for moments like this, alone with God. He said that lingering in churches was for monks, foolish women and men with addled pates, but Roger valued the time in which to be tranquil, to set all in order with his maker and to gather mental strength. His opinion of what addled a man's pate had never been the same as his father's.

He closed his eyes and, as he prayed, the darkness behind his lids yielded to the image of the banner surging in a stiff breeze and his hand gripping the shaft. Beyond it he could see Framlingham ringed by flames. Further back still, and scarcely glimpsed, new towers rose out of the ashes and he could not tell if the red and gold dancing along the battlements was his family's banner, or the destruction of fire.

Gundreda, Countess of Norfolk, watched her husband making final preparations to leave with Leicester's army, and knew she had to act, because this might be her last opportunity. He was well past seventy years old, even if he was still hale and strong. There was no certainty he would return from this foray. She knew from the way he was stamping about with a complexion as red as a boiled crab's that she was chancing his temper, but a slap or a kick was a risk she would have to take if she was going to secure her sons' inheritance.

'I knew Roger would do this to you,' she said. 'You've never been able to rely on him and now he has proven his worth by turning traitor.' She studied him from beneath her lids to gauge his response. On receiving the news that instead of raiding the lands of Saint Edmund's abbey Roger had taken a contingent of knights and serjeants loyal to him and declared for King Henry, Hugh had swiped all the silver cups off the sideboard, torn down a hanging and smashed a footstool against the wall.

He glowered at her. 'Why should you put your oar to rowing the boat, woman? He's the misbegotten son of a whore; I already know that without you telling me.' He put his foot up on a coffer to tighten the fastening on one of his spurs.

Gundreda folded her hands in her lap and looked at them rather than at him, so she would not appear too assertive. He only liked assertiveness if he could beat it down and dominate it. 'Because, husband, if he is the things you say, he should not be your heir. You have two loyal sons at home who are worth twice his mettle, and they do not defy you.'

He finished the adjustment to his spur and stood straight again, short legs planted wide in a dominant pose. The first time Gundreda had laid eyes on him, she had been reminded of a stocky bull-baiting dog, and the years had exaggerated the characteristics, even down to the pendulous jowls. 'I will decide who inherits what,' he growled. 'I'll not have you meddling.'

15

'No, my lord, but might it not be wise to settle the matter before you leave?'

'Lest I die?' He curled his lip at her and sour amusement gleamed in his eyes.

'It would do no harm to state the terms of your will, so that all can be sure. Do you really want to see Roger follow you as Earl of Norfolk? He tried to kill our son in the chapel over nothing – a boy's prank.'

He arched a shaggy eyebrow. 'Indeed, but that begs the question: why should I bequeath my earldom to a callow youth who cannot hold his own?'

Gundreda dug her fingernails into her palms, knowing he was deliberately baiting her. She also knew that making him think about anyone being Earl of Norfolk other than himself was akin to pushing a boulder-laden cart uphill. 'I am saying you should not leave it to someone who has failed and betrayed you. You annulled the marriage to his mother.' She gave him a sly, hopeful look. 'A court of law might consider him a bastard.'

Hugh laughed as he picked up his cloak. 'You are optimistic, woman. Juliana's the sister of the Earl of Oxford and the daughter of a de Clare. Even a room full of gold wouldn't be enough to sway a lawyer in that direction.'

'But . . .'

'I'll think about it when I return,' he dismissed. 'Now do your duty and come and see us on the road.'

Gundreda struggled to hold down her frustration and impatience. She too wanted to scream and hurl a stool against the wall because she hated being trapped and powerless, a victim of his whim. She followed him from the room with clenched fists.

Her eldest son was waiting in the ward for his father, whom he was accompanying as a squire. The sight of him wearing a padded tunic, a long dagger at his hip, made her quail with fear. The beard he had recently begun cultivating edged his jaw in a sparse, soft fuzz. She was afraid for him but dared not show it, and she was ambitious too. If she had her way, he and not that faithless runt Roger would be the next Earl of Norfolk. Gundreda embraced him, but he stiffened and drew back, far too full of masculine hubris to permit such a display in public. The lines between his brows mirrored his father's and would one day be fixed in his flesh as a permanent brand of paternal heritage. Abruptly he turned from her to his horse and mounted up, putting himself safely above her.

Petronilla of Leicester set her foot in the stirrup and swung astride like a man. The full skirts of her gown allowed her such leeway and she was wearing men's hose and braies beneath. Gundreda was shocked at such brazen behaviour. At least she knew how to behave in a manner befitting her sex and status.

As Petronilla collected her reins and turned her horse, a large sapphire ring flashed on her middle finger. She had been flaunting it under everyone's nose throughout her overstayed welcome at Framlingham and Gundreda hoped with vehemence that she'd lose it.

The last baggage cart rumbled out of the bailey, stacked with barrels of arrows, hides, nails, coils of chain, snakes of rope and lengths of timber, and Gundreda heaved a sigh of relief. Signalling the porter to shut the gates, she began chivvying the servants into clearing up the detritus left by their 'guests'. Her younger son Will stood rumpling his hair and gazing after the baggage train until the sight was cut off by the closing gates.

'There's no use moping,' Gundreda snapped. 'You are too young.'

Will shrugged his shoulders. 'I'm not moping,' he said. 'I was just thinking it might be peaceful for a while.'

Gundreda said nothing but her expression was hard with discontent. While she didn't want both her sons riding off to war, Will's lazy preference for the easy life was a source of irritation and concern. 'It does not mean that work stops,' she snapped. 'Do not think this is an excuse to shirk your obligations. Indeed, with your father and brother gone, you'll have more to do.'

'Yes, Mother,' he said in a bland voice.

Frustratingly, Gundreda could not tell if he was acknowledging his duty, or merely paying lip service in order to escape. Will was like a soft, down-filled cushion. No matter how much you hit it, you never made any impact.

The wind sweeping across the North Sea from Flanders was bitter – a leaf-stripping gale with an edge that brought an ache to the jaw and teared the eyes. An hour since the scouts had reported that Leicester's army was approaching the river crossing to the north of the abbey and they were at least eight thousand strong. As Roger had told de Luci, Leicester's force outnumbered theirs four to one, but the bulk of the troop consisted of hired Flemings, few of whom were skilled with weapons.

Roger gathered the reins at Sorel's neck and set his foot to the stirrup. He had confessed his sins and received absolution. He was calm, determined, and prepared. He knew what he had to do, both for himself and the men depending on him.

His uncle, fully armed in hauberk and helm, handed up to him the banner of Saint Edmund. Earlier, Prior Robert had formally presented it to Roger in church with his blessing. Now the responsibility was his alone and the knowledge was strength rather than a burden as he untied the binding cord and unfurled the tasselled silk to let the red and gold colours snap in the wind.

'The scouts say your father is riding with the Earl of Leicester,' his uncle commented without inflection.

'He has chosen his path and I have chosen mine,' Roger replied, matching the other man's impassivity.

'And if they meet?'

'Then he may do as he pleases, but I won't back down.'

His uncle studied him closely, and whatever he saw satisfied him for he gave a brusque nod. 'Indeed, nephew, today will tell who is the stronger man.'

'I hope I am, sire.' Mouth hard with resolution, Roger fastened his ventail to protect his lower face.

His uncle turned to his stallion. 'That is not enough,' he said. 'You must know you are. They mustn't cross the bridge. We have to stop them here and drive them into the marshes.'

Roger's voice emerged muffled by leather and mail. 'They won't prevail, sire.'

'God help us all if they do. De Bohun's going forward with the knights. My lord de Luci wants you to take that standard and lead out with the heralds.'

Roger's chest swelled with pride and apprehension. He gripped the haft of the banner of Saint Edmund and heeled Sorel in the direction of de Bohun's contingent, which consisted of three hundred knights in full mail on well-equipped warhorses. There were serjeants too with armour of leather and padded linen, and mounts of lesser quality. Here and there Roger saw footsoldiers armed with old-fashioned English round shields that had probably been handed down father to son through several generations and stored away in the rafters for eventualities such as this one. The weapons among the local militia were of

19

the to-hand variety: wolf spears, slings, scythes and pitchforks.

The heavy rain of the last two months had made the ground muddy at best and much of the meadow adjoining the swollen river was a bog. The river Lark was running in spate and the only way forward was over the bridge.

Roger joined the front rank of de Bohun's knights and faced the road, his heart pounding in full, solid strokes and his belly churning. There was no retreat from this and if he died in battle, so be it. He was done with turning the other cheek.

The scouts came galloping back to their commanders to report that Leicester's army was sighted, but was spread out and straggling rather than holding tight formation as his troops strove to find solid paths through the mire. Those in the vanguard were churning up the ground and hampering the men following behind, but still it was a formidable array. Roger glanced round and saw his uncle drawing up to support de Bohun's left flank, while de Luci took the right. Everything became still on the edge of the storm and Roger felt the electric moment prickle through his veins.

Fixing his gaze forward again, he saw Leicester's banner and the glitter of mail worn by the better protected knights – men with whom he had recently sat at meat in Framlingham's great hall and who were now his enemy. He raked his gaze across the field, searching for yet more intimate prey, and finally located the saffron and red Bigod standard at the back, close to the baggage detail. Wily bastard, Roger thought, shaking his head. His father was near enough to give the impression of support, but had left himself room to flee if necessary.

De Bohun raised his sword to de Luci and de Vere, who saluted in reply; the heralds blew on their hunting horns, signalling the attack. As de Bohun spurred his stallion, Roger pricked Sorel's flanks and roared his own battle cry: 'Saint Edmund! Saint Edmund!' Anketil at his left shoulder, he spurred towards Leicester's knights who were galloping to meet the royalist charge. One of their number hurtled straight at him, spear levelled, clods of moist earth showering from his stallion's hooves. Roger adjusted his shield and twitched the rein so that Sorel canted to the right. The knight tried to turn, but was taken by the warrior on Roger's left. Roger lifted the banner, raised it on high and planted it in the heavy soil with a deep thrust, the energy shivering up his arm and neck and into his skull. Then, right hand free, he drew his sword.

For all his father's antipathy towards him, Roger had received a thorough grounding in weapons skills, and of his own talent he excelled at swordplay. Men saw his slender build and underestimated his tensile strength, his speed and his balance. Now his blows bore the force of anger, but he controlled and contained the blaze within him. He had seen men become white-hot with battle rage and usually they died. When it was kill or be killed, you had to know what you were doing if you wanted to survive. Building up a steady rhythm, he and Anketil wove through the battle as if performing the steps of a deadly progressive dance, engaging partners and, as each partner fell away, moving on to the next and the next. Roger uprooted the banner and planted it again and again in each new place he chose to dance. His sword blade developed a pattern of random scarlet swirls and the blows absorbed by his shield scuffed the blazon to a smudge resembling the heart of a fire. Sorel's chestnut hide darkened to the colour of raw liver, but not for a moment did Roger slacken his momentum.

Leicester's core fought back hard, but the edges were weak and began to crumble and collapse, and without that support, the backbone disintegrated under the continued onslaught. The weight of numbers was all surplus flesh devoid of muscle and will. Suddenly Roger found himself bereft of a dancing partner. Leicester's knights were disengaging, fleeing, throwing down their arms, surrendering. The Flemish mercenaries, earlier so bold, turned tail and were pursued by de Luci's infantry and the local militia brandishing their scythes and pitchforks. Teeth bared, air rasping in his throat, Roger uprooted the banner of Saint Edmund again and rode hard for the baggage wains and pack ponies, intent on reaching them before they were robbed.

Deploying his men with a few sharp commands, Roger secured the Earl of Leicester's baggage supplies, seeing off would-be looters and scavengers with the voice of authority, backed up by the sharp end of lance and sword. In his peripheral vision he noticed a string of laden pack ponies trotting back the way it had come, escorted by several serjeants. There was no sign of the Bigod standard but Roger recognised the men by their familiar red and gold shields. Leaving Anketil to guard the baggage, he gathered a handful of knights and spurred in pursuit of the escapees. Sorel was tiring, but was still faster than the laden ponies, and the Bigod soldiers could not guard them and fight at the same time.

'Go!' Roger bellowed to his father's serjeants as he overtook them and slewed Sorel across their path, sword drawn. 'I grant you your lives but leave the baggage. Otherwise let this field be your grave.'

The men hesitated, eyes darting.

Roger unfastened his ventail and addressed their leader, while beneath him Sorel sidled and pranced. 'Torkil, you know me. In Christ's name, man, see sense and save your-selves. I don't see my father hanging back to defend his baggage, do you? I will kill you if I must and that is no idle threat.'

The serjeant licked his lips and glanced at his companions. 'Lads,' he said and, dropping the lead rope on the foremost pack pony, dug his heels into his gelding's flanks. Roger watched the men gallop off. If they survived this rout and had any sense, they'd seek employment elsewhere than at Framlingham. Grasping the rope that Torkil had dropped, he handed it to one of his knights and returned to the baggage line.

De Luci had pursued the fleeing Earl of Leicester and his wife, trapping them against the banks of the spated river Lark. The Countess, clad in a hauberk as if she were a man, had pulled off her fine rings, including her precious sapphire one, and tossed them all into the river so that her husband's enemies should not have them. She and Leicester were brought to the baggage camp and placed under close guard in Leicester's wain, Petronilla having first been relieved of her mail shirt and her long dagger.

As Roger dismounted from Sorel, Aubrey de Vere walked up to him and clapped his shoulder. 'You fought well,' his uncle said with a smile of acknowledgement for a deed well accomplished. 'Today you have redeemed the honour your father has sold. You have become your family's future.'

Roger swallowed and said nothing. His uncle's words settled upon his shoulders like a thick cloak, but for the moment he couldn't decide whether they were a protection against the cold, or something that was going to smother him.

3

Castle Hedingham, Essex, July 1174

Juliana, former Countess of Norfolk, now Lady Maminot of Greenwich, gazed at the slender young man standing uncertainly in her chamber doorway. Dear Holy Mother, her son looked nothing like the image she had carried in her mind these last five years. Gone were the final vestiges of boyhood softness and in their place was a man's hard strength of bone and a soldier's burnish.

'Roger!' Rising from the window seat where she had been working at her embroidery, she hastened to him with one arm outstretched.

He hesitated, then took her hand and knelt to her in formal greeting. 'My lady mother.'

Juliana looked down at his bent head. His hair was cut short for wearing under a helm, but was still as she remembered: fine-textured but plentiful and the soft brown of shadow-darkened sand. A lump tightened her throat and surprised her for she never cried. Not even when his father had done things to her no woman should have to endure. 'There is no need to stand on ceremony with me,' she said and raised him to his feet. She was tall for a woman and his height was only a finger length above hers, although he had a goodly advantage over his father. Hugh had hated the fact that she was bigger than he was and counted it one of her many transgressions. 'Let me look at you.'

He stood calmly under her scrutiny, but a flush rose from his throat into his face. The stubble of what would be a strong beard if he let it grow gave outline to a square chin and mobile, well-shaped mouth. His eyes were a mingling of grey on blue, and they too reminded her of a north coast seashore. Perhaps that was where his essence came from, blown into Framlingham on the stormy night of his conception, for there was little of Hugh to see in him. She noted that he wore both sword and spurs and although his tunic and person were clean, an aroma of hot horse clung to him.

'It has been too long,' she said, 'far too long.' Reaching out to touch the side of his face she thought with regret of all the years that might have been and never were. Hugh had banned her from seeing Roger after the annulment and Walkelin had made it clear that Hugh of Norfolk's spawn was not welcome at Greenwich. Hedingham, the abode of Juliana's brother, Aubrey, Earl of Oxford, was neutral territory and a place where mother and son could meet on rare occasions like this.

'Have you travelled far?' She signalled a loitering servant to bring wine and drew him to the window seat where she had been sewing.

'From the King's camp at Sileham.'

'Ah.' She waited while the attendant fetched cups and a platter of spiced marrow tarts. 'You are with the King then?'

'Yes, madam.' He drank some wine and ate one of the tarts. She suspected that he was ravenous, although he was being politely restrained – unlike his father. Control,

25

she thought. He had that from her . . . and his ability to be still in the storm. She had heard about his prowess at the battle of Fornham in the autumn. Aubrey said the victory had been overwhelming despite odds of four to one and that Roger had borne the banner of Saint Edmund into battle and fought out of his skin.

'Your father . . .' She stopped herself with a sip of wine. There was no point in being corrosive; it was in the past and she would never vent her spleen on her son. She had heard that following the defeat at Fornham, Hugh had bought off the justiciar and paid a thousand marks to make a truce. Whatever his claims of persecution and impoverishment under King Henry's rule, he remained one of the wealthiest men in the kingdom. Being what he was, her former husband had used that truce to make his own pacts with the Flemish. More mercenaries had arrived, better trained this time, and he had taken them to Norwich and sacked the city. As usual, he had over-reached himself and underestimated the King. She had daily cause to be glad her marriage to him had been annulled, even if she was no longer a countess. Let Gundreda have those gauds and suffer Hugh's brutish demands. Her one regret was losing her child.

'. . . has dug his own grave with his shovel of greed, and perhaps mine with it,' Roger said grimly. 'He's been commanded to submit to the King and he must because the rebellion has failed and there's no one left to stand beside him.'

Juliana knitted her brows. 'Why do you say he has dug your grave too? Surely the way you have fought in the King's service this past year will stand you in good credit?'

'The surrender terms are punitive. My father's treachery cancels out my loyal service to Henry. Burning Norwich was the final straw. The King won't leave him the where-withal to rebel again.'

'And the terms are?' She looked at him over her cup, striving to appear detached and serene.

'He is to send all of his mercenaries back to Flanders and he is to pay another fine – I don't know how much, but it won't be small . . .'

She waited, knowing there was more because what he had said thus far was surmountable.

'The King intends to raze Framlingham.'

Juliana's brows arched towards the fluted edge of her wimple. 'What?'

'All the defences are to be destroyed.' He gave her a sick look. 'Henry's employing the carpenters even now and he's put the work into the hands of Ailnoth his senior engineer. Bungay's threatened too, although Henry hasn't decided yet. Certainly he'll garrison it with his own men. He's also going to withhold the third penny of the shire and exercise distraint on goods and chattels.' His eyes were storm-grey now. 'By his lights he's being generous. He's allowing my father to remain Earl for his lifetime.'

Juliana bit her lip. This was bad news indeed. 'For his lifetime?' she repeated.

He nodded. 'And then the King renegotiates with his heirs, and that means he could withhold the right to the title of earl, and the revenues that go with it. My step-mother . . .' His expression twisted. 'My stepmother is angling for what is left of the inheritance to go to my half-brother.'

Juliana was appalled. 'That will never happen!' She stiffened with indignation. 'You are Norfolk's rightful heir!'

'I have the better claim, but it won't stop her from bringing her demands to court.' His gaze was bleak. 'There will be a fight every whit as bloody as a trial by combat.

27

She will try to claim the invalidity of your marriage to my father, and say that I am bastard-born.'

Juliana's eyes flashed. 'Then she will find herself pitched against the might of de Vere. How dare she!'

'Because she wants the best for her sons – or at least the best she can salvage.' He drew himself up. 'It's my battle to fight, and I will deal with it the best I can. I am not a fool. I will come for help if I need it.'

'And it will be given. I have always regretted—' She compressed her lips. She could tell by the way he was attending studiously to his wine and not meeting her gaze that it was too late for all that, and men as a rule did not deal well with such conversations. 'I want the best for you too,' she amended, 'more than salvage, more than crumbs.'

'For the moment my father is still alive,' he said abruptly, 'and may yet live for many more years. It's rumoured he's withdrawing to the court of Philip of Flanders.'

'You think it true?'

He gestured assent. 'I do not suppose his pride will let him stay in England.'

'And your stepmother?'

'I understand she will dwell at Bungay with the younger son, although the older one may also exile himself in Flanders to prove how dutiful he is.' The flat tone of his voice revealed what he thought of that particular notion.

'And you, my son?' she asked. 'Where will you call home?'

'If my father does go into exile, I will go to Framlingham.'

'Even if there is nothing there but grass?'

Now he did meet her gaze, and his eyes were as hard as sea-tumbled flints. 'You can pitch a tent on grass,' he said. 'You can use it to feed a horse; you can build again.' After a moment he reached for another tart.

She studied his hands: the firm fingers; the thumbs that curved away from the upright like her own. They weren't large, but they had symmetry and strength. A new scar, campion-pink, inscribed the base of three fingers on his left one. His skin was tanned to the start of his tunic cuffs, and dusted with fine gilt hair. She remembered when she had held the hands of a little boy. White, unmarked, soft, their story unmapped beyond fine sketch lines on either palm; sometimes grubby from childhood play in the dust. She would take them between her own and wash them clean in the ewer with fine soap of Castile. Now they were the hands of a man – scarred, experienced, no longer a mother's to hold, but caught in the waiting moment before they grasped a wife's, or were themselves grasped by the tiny, dependent clutch of the next generation. 'Yes,' she said. 'I understand. If you don't believe you can start again, where do you go indeed?'

Roger came to Framlingham Castle ahead of Ailnoth the engineer and his demolition team. The sun was low on the horizon and a hot summer day had drenched the land in heat so that the soon-to-be-demolished palisade timbers gave off a haze of stored warmth. Roger handed his horses to a groom and had an attendant take his baggage roll to the hall, where he had also directed his small entourage. Then, with only Anketil in tow, he mounted the wall walk and faced the sunset.

He had spoken to his mother of pitching a tent, and indeed had been prepared to do just that in order to claim his inheritance, but in the event, Henry had shown a glimmer of mercy. Tomorrow the destruction would begin, but Ailnoth and his crew had instructions to leave the stone great hall and chapel standing, and the kitchens, byres and utility buildings. What was to be destroyed were the battlements, the gatehouse tower and guardrooms, the earthworks and defences – everything that had made Framlingham a stronghold. But at least he had a place to live.

His father had not stayed in the royal camp beyond making his formal surrender. Having agreed to all the terms in a voice devoid of emotion, he had departed, intent on taking ship for Flanders with his mercenaries. He hadn't spared a single look for his eldest son, as if by refusing to acknowledge his presence in the King's campaign tent he could wipe him from existence. All Roger had seen was an old man, deflated, beaten, almost used up, but still existing on the dregs of his bitterness and venom.

'My father wouldn't stay to see all this pulled down.' Roger pressed the flat of his hand against the sun-warmed oak, now in shadow. 'But someone has to bear witness. Someone has to watch it all come down and face the consequences.' He looked round at Anketil, resolution firming his jaw. 'Someone has to rebuild.'

'Sir?'

'You fall over, you get up again,' Roger said. 'This was my father's castle. The next one will be mine.'

4

Windsor Castle, September 1176

Ida de Tosney studied the wall hanging in the chamber, admiring the way the embroiderer had combined two shades of blue thread and mingled it with green to depict the river where the hunting party in the picture had paused to water their horses. She imagined how she would work such a scene, perhaps adding a line of silver to the water and a fish or two. She loved planning embroideries and although she had but recently turned fifteen years old, she was an accomplished needlewoman.

Her rose-coloured gown was embellished with vine-leaf coils of delicate green thread at the sleeves and neckline. Small clusters of garnet grapes adorned the scrollwork, and the outline borders were worked with seed pearls. The belt, double-looped at her waist, was of her own weaving, and it too was decorated with pearls, for she was an heiress and these were her court robes, especially made for her presentation to the King whose ward she was. Beset with anxiety, she had imagined the moment a hundred times, envisaging her curtsey, the rise and the step back. She hoped that if he spoke to her, she would be able to make an appropriate answer.

Her maid Goda twined gold ribbons through Ida's thick brown braid, whilst Bertrice tweezed Ida's eyebrows until they were shapely arches and Ida tried not to flinch.

'You have to look your best for the King,' Bertrice said with a practical nod. 'If he likes you, he'll deal well with your wardship and find you a good husband.' She patted a moist, lavender-scented cloth against Ida's brows to remove any redness, and then smoothed the area with a gentle fingertip.

'Perhaps you'll even find a husband today, among the courtiers,' Goda said, optimistically. 'It wouldn't do to look ungroomed, would it now, young mistress?'

Ida blushed and made herself stand still while the women completed her toilet. She knew they were anxious she should please the King, because it reflected on their care of her. She wanted to please the King too, for her own sake as well as theirs; and, as they said, some of the men looking on might be in search of a wife. Although still innocent of the world, Ida had begun to notice the assessment in men's glances – the way their eyes lingered on her lips and her bosom. Such attention created a warm glow in her solar plexus even while it scared her. Something told her that here was power and here was danger, and both were frightening new territory.

An usher arrived to take Ida to the great hall where, together with other wards and supplicants, she was to be presented to the King before dinner. Goda gave a few final tweaks to Ida's gown and draped a midnight-blue cloak at her shoulders, fastening it with two round gold clasps. 'Good fortune, mistress,' she whispered.

Ida gave her women an apprehensive smile as they curtseyed to her. Taking a deep breath, she followed the usher from the room.

In the great hall she was bidden to wait with a group

of others, all clad in finery and glowing from recent ablutions. Ida, being the youngest, apart from an adolescent youth who was a royal ward like herself, had a place near the end. The smell of rose water, tense sweat and new woollen cloth filled Ida's lungs each time she drew breath. She clasped her hands in front of her so she would not be tempted to fidget as some of the others were doing, and kept her eyes modestly lowered, although now and again she peeped from beneath her lids to see what was happening around her.

Trestle tables had been set up for the main formal meal of the day. On the dais, the board was covered by a cloth of embroidered white napery and the dishes, cellars and cups standing upon it were of silver gilt, some of them inlaid with gemstones. Two pantlers were busy carving oblongs of bread into flat trenchers for holding meats in sauce, and other servants were bringing jugs of wine from the buttery to a side table. Despite feeling anxious, Ida still managed to be hungry. She hoped her stomach wouldn't rumble when she had to curtsey before the King.

When Henry finally arrived, he breezed into the room as if blown by his fanfare and the group scarcely had time to curtsey and kneel. His auburn hair was cropped close to his head in a practical manner, unadorned by oils or crimping, and his clothing was commonplace in comparison to those of his supplicants and guests. If Ida hadn't been forewarned about his preference for practicality, she would have mistaken him for an attendant, and his marshal, bearing a golden rod of office and wearing a sumptuous scarlet tunic, for the King.

Glancing upwards through her lashes, she watched Henry arrive at the presentation line and begin moving along it, pausing for a brief word to each person. His voice had a harsh edge, as if he had been inhaling smoke,

33

but he spoke well and pleasantly and had a way of putting people at their ease. Although he had bounced into the hall, she thought he was limping a little now and wondered if his shoes were pinching him. She noticed a scratch on the back of his right hand that looked as if he'd had a tussle with a dog or a hawk. Numerous rings adorned his fingers and she had seen him take a couple off and present them to others in the line as gifts. She supposed he must have a coffer full of them for such events. Certainly, he wasn't wearing the rings to show off the beauty of his hands which were rough-skinned, as if he'd been engaged in manual labour all day.

His glance flickered to her as he spoke to the youth standing at her side. Ida, looking up at that same moment, was briefly snared in a stare as bright as sunlit glass. Hastily she dropped her gaze, certain he would think her rude and mannerless.

'Ida de Tosney,' said the marshal. Ida curtseyed again, keeping her focus on the minute stitches in the hem of her dress. Then she felt a forefinger beneath her chin, tilting it up.

'A most graceful curtsey,' Henry said, 'but I would have you stand straight and look at me.'

Ida summoned her courage, did as he asked and was again caught in that predatory crystal stare.

His finger moved, to touch one of her gold cloak clasps. 'Ralph de Tosney's little girl,' he said softly. 'When last I saw you, you were a red-cheeked babe in your mother's arms, and now look at you – grown enough to have a babe of your own.' His eyes followed his words up and down her body and heat burned Ida's face. 'But still red-cheeked,' he added with a smile.

'Sire,' she whispered, feeling embarrassed and frightened. The looks she had received from young men in

34

passing were as nothing compared to the way the King's gaze was devouring her.

'Your modesty becomes you,' Henry said and moved to the youth at her side, but he cast a lingering look over his shoulder.

Quailing with embarrassment, Ida awaited a dismissal that did not come. There was still time before the dinner hour and the King wanted to speak further with his wards and charges. He had a chair fetched and a fine cushioned stool which he bade Ida set under his left foot.

'The pains of old age,' he told her with a wry smile. 'I would have the sight of your youth and beauty take them away.'

'Sire, you are not old,' Ida said politely as she arranged the footstool to his liking, which took several attempts. She had to touch and lift his leg, which was an intimate thing to do, and all the time she was aware of his scrutiny and was embarrassed. Having performed the duty she started to retreat to an unobtrusive place at the back of the gathering, he would have none of it and beckoned her to stand at his side. 'Be my hand-maiden,' he said.

Ida saw some of the experienced courtiers exchange knowing glances and their looks tied her in knots. Henry engaged the rest of the group in conversation, but now and again he turned round to her with a glance or a gesture. She responded with tentative smiles but felt the strain at the corners of her mouth. She hated being singled out. As always when faced with things that worried her, she turned her mind inwards to embroidery. Fabric of gold damask silk covered the footstool with an exquisite diamond lozenge pattern. She began assessing how to recreate it on a rectangle of tawny wool she had in her sewing casket.

'You are lost in reflection, little Ida,' Henry said with amusement. 'Tell me what deep thoughts you hold in your head.'

She reddened and darted a worried glance around at the rest of the gathering. What must they think of her? 'I . . . I have no deep thoughts, sire,' she answered tentatively. 'I was only thinking about the pattern on your footstool and how I would work an embroidery of my own.'

She saw laughter fill the King's eyes before she lowered her own. Now he would mock her, and indeed he did, but with kindness and a note in his voice that made her shiver. 'Ah,' he said, 'if only all the women I have known had minded their needle, perhaps I would be a less haunted man today.'

'Sire?'

'No matter.' He shook his head. 'You remind me, Ida, that there is still innocence in the world and gentle moments remaining in life – and that is one of the rarest and most difficult things anyone could do.'

Ida saw sadness in his eyes and, despite her discomfort and unease, it awoke her compassion. His words lit a small flicker of warmth inside her too to think she had given him something others could not.

A courtier mentioned a piece of gossip he had heard – that Hugh, Earl of Norfolk, had taken the Cross and departed for the Holy Land with the Count of Flanders.

Henry's jaw dropped in astonishment, then he gave a short bark of laughter and clapped his hands on the arms of his chair. 'Hugh Bigod a crusader? Now there's a sight I'd like to see!'

'That is what I heard said, sire.'

'God's blood, the old bastard must be four score years by now!' Henry gave a vigorous shake of his head. 'It's a long way to go in order not to have to return to England and face me and his ruins!' He smiled at Ida and brushed his hand against her skirt as he spoke.

She wondered if she was supposed to nod agreement or make a witty comment. Uncertainly she said, 'Sire, perhaps he has gone on crusade for the benefit of his soul.'

Henry snorted. 'Hugh Bigod has no soul. If he ever had one, he traded it to the highest bidder years ago.' He waved his hand in dismissal. 'If the rumours are true, let the Saracens have him, but from what I saw of the Earl's condition at Sileham, I doubt they'll be granted that pleasure.'

A steward bowed before him and informed him that the meal awaited his pleasure to dine. Henry gestured acknowledgement and bade Ida lift his foot from the stool and assist him to rise. He leaned on her and for a brief moment his hand rested at her waist and his gaze plundered her bosom. 'We will talk again,' he said. 'I have enjoyed your company and I would not have you hidden away to bloom out of my sight.'

As he left to take his place at the high table, Ida curtseyed to him and concealed her hands beneath her cloak, so that no one would see them shaking.

That night as Ida was about to retire, John FitzJohn, the King's marshal, came to the door of the women's chamber with the message that the King desired to talk to Ida about the matter of her wardship and marriage.

Ida's women swiftly began dressing her again, because one did not deny a royal summons, especially when delivered by an official of the marshal's stature – even if it was at night when most of the court had retired.

'Well,' Bertrice said breathlessly as she retied the lacings on Ida's gown, working swiftly from armpit to hip, 'you seem to have snared yourself a king.'

Ida shivered. She didn't feel like the one doing the snaring. 'What am I to do?'

Bertrice fastened the ends of the laces. 'Treat it as an opportunity. He hasn't had a mistress since Rosamund de Clifford died in the spring.'

Ida stared at the woman aghast. 'You are saying I should yield to him!'

Bertrice's eyes were knowing and shrewd. 'My love, unless you want to spend the rest of your life wedded to some dolt chosen out of his displeasure at your refusal, you will do as he bids you tonight. And then you can have whatever you want for the asking. A woman who has a king's favour is a power to be reckoned with.'

Ida thought she was going to retch. 'If I had known, I would have dressed in my drabbest gown and not washed for a week.' She looked reproachfully at her women, for they were the ones who had stressed the need to make an impression. 'He wouldn't have noticed me then.'

'Oh, I think he would, my sweet. Pure gold is always pure gold.' Bertrice fetched a comb and with swift strokes worked Ida's oak-brown hair into a sleek skein before rebraiding it with silk ribbons.

'If the King commands, you must do his bidding,' Goda said. 'Bertrice is right. If you do as he says, you will have power from this.'

Beyond the door a masculine throat was impatiently cleared. 'When you are ready, my lady,' said the marshal.

In her mind's eye, Ida imagined hiding under her bed or absconding out of the window, but in reality there was no escape. Perhaps he really did want to talk about her wardship, she thought, clutching at straws. Taking a deep breath and raising her head, she went to the door. The marshal bowed to her, holding his golden rod of office as he had been holding it earlier that evening, his expression carefully impassive.

'Am I to bring one of my women?' she asked tentatively.

'No, demoiselle, that will not be necessary.'

He had a youth with him who lit their way by lantern along corridors and up and down stairways to the royal apartments. The marshal was tall and moved with a soldier's long stride so that Ida almost had to run to keep pace with him. 'It is very late,' she said, and received no reply. She looked over her shoulder, but the way behind was pitch dark beyond the dull halo of lantern light. There was nowhere to run. 'Please . . .' She caught at his sleeve.

He slowed and stopped, but not because of her. They had arrived at a guarded doorway. 'Demoiselle,' he said, and gently removed her hand from his arm. 'The King greatly honours you by this summons. No ill will befall you.'

How many times had he done this before? Ida might be innocent, but she was not entirely without knowledge. The King's ushers and marshals were responsible for regulating the royal concubines. It was their duty to control the hidden underbelly of court life. But she wasn't a concubine; she was the King's ward – an heiress. How many other heiresses and wards had trodden this path at the marshal's side in the dark watches of the night? He said she was to consider herself honoured, but it didn't feel like that. It felt sordid, clandestine, and terrifying.

The marshal banged his rod on the door, then opened it and ushered her before him into the chamber, his hand firmly but gently at her back, propelling her forward. 'Sire, the lady Ida de Tosney.'

Seated on a settle-bench before the hearth, Henry

glanced up from a sheaf of parchments loosely stitched together at the top. 'Ah,' he said and beckoned to Ida with the hand not holding the documents. 'Come, mistress, sit with me.' A nod and a glance were enough acknowledgement to dismiss his marshal who bowed quietly from the chamber. Ida's gaze flew around the room, but there were no servants; no other guests. She was alone with the King. With great reluctance, she came to perch on the end of the bench and folded her hands in her lap. She wondered if the documents he was perusing were concerned with her wardship. Perhaps he was reminding himself of what she had in dower.

Henry gave her a long look that dissolved her stomach. Setting the documents aside, he rested one arm along the back of the bench and stretched out his legs. She saw that the toes of his boots were scuffed. 'There is no need to be afraid of me,' he said. 'I won't hurt you.'

'No, sire.' She pressed her knees together.

He chuckled softly. 'You don't believe me, do you? Your lips say one thing and your eyes are filled with all that you deny . . . No, don't look down. You have beautiful eyes, brown as hazelnuts.' He leaned forward and stroked her cheek with his forefinger. 'And skin like the petal of a rose.'

'Sire, I . . .' She tried not to recoil.

'I know what you are thinking. You don't want to be here, do you?'

Ida swallowed, afraid of saying the wrong thing. She struggled to make her mind work through the paralysis of fear. 'The lord marshal said you wanted to talk to me about my wardship?'

'Ah, your wardship.' His hand had moved down to play with her braid. 'You are an heiress, Ida. You will have suitors aplenty, keen to get at your lands and take a healthy young wife on which to breed their sons, hmm?'

40

She flushed at his barnyard forthrightness. 'I do not know, sire.'

'Oh, not at the moment, you do not. You have scarcely arrived at court, but soon they will come, and they will be eager. Ralph de Tosney was a man of standing, and your mother was a Beaumont.' He moved his fingers reflectively up and down her braid, but always travelling lower until he reached the tassel at the end which was level with her breast. 'You have lands; you have youth, and beauty and innocence. A prize indeed and one I am minded to keep for myself.'

Ida's gaze widened. She tensed to spring to her feet. 'Sire, you would ruin me.'

Henry gave a lazy smile. 'Indeed I would, for all other men after me, my dear, but not in the sense you mean. My attention will make you an even greater prize in the eyes of those vying for my wealth and favour.' He indicated a rock-crystal flagon standing on a coffer. 'Pour us some wine, there's a good lass.'

She was glad to escape to the task but her hands were shaking and it was difficult not to spill the wine which was as red and dark as vein-blood. She was aware of Henry's scrutiny and it made her want to cross her arms over her body.

When she returned to him, he stood up and set his hand over hers. 'You would not make a good cup-bearer in the hall,' he said with amusement.

Ida's chin wobbled. Henry took the wine from her, set it down on a chest, then turned back to her. 'Ah, here now, lovely, don't cry, don't cry. Hush. It's all right. I won't hurt you, I swear I won't. I only want to . . .' The last word trailed off as he unpinned the round brooches closing the neckline of her gown and pushed the garment off her shoulders. Then he unplucked the ties of her chemise

41

and did the same again, so that she stood before him, naked to the waist, shivering.

'Sweet,' he said. 'So young and innocent and sweet. You do not know what you do to me . . .'

Ida lay in Henry's bed, her limbs upon scented cool linen, her body covered by soft clean sheets and a coverlet of wine-red silk embroidered with a peacock design. Tears leached from beneath her lids and she swiped them away on the heel of her hand. There was a burning pain between her legs and a dull ache in her pelvis.

Henry sat on the bed, gazing at her with heavy, sated eyes and tenderness in his expression. 'Come now,' he said. 'No tears. It wasn't so bad, was it?'

Ida swallowed. 'No, sire,' she whispered. The deed itself had been strange and uncomfortable, but she had set her teeth, told herself that this was the King and she had no choice but to obey his will. She had endured and she was still alive – in body at least.

'Then why do you weep? It is a great honour I do you, sweeting. You are like a bride to me; the King's virgin bride, hmm?' Gently he pushed a strand of thick brown hair away from her face.

'But to me, it seems like dishonour,' Ida found the courage to whisper. 'People will look at me and call me whore. My good name is gone. I will not come to my husband a virgin.' She swallowed against the painful tightness in her throat and tears spilled over her lids.

'Ah, sweetheart, no!' Henry gathered her in his arms and brushed her wet face with the side of his thumb. 'No one will think that of you. You are mine. You are the King's, and the King only ever has the best. If anyone dares to cast a wrong glance or missay you, I will have them horse-whipped, but it will not happen, I promise you. Your worry is to your credit, but it is needless. I look after those who are mine to me. You will hold your head high and be proud.'

He made her sit up and brought her wine with his own hands, poured out like blood from the flagon. Then he took a ring from his coffer – not one of the gauds he had been distributing earlier in the day to all and sundry, but a fine piece of jewellery set with a balas ruby the size of a large man's thumbnail. 'Wear this for me,' he said. 'And thus people will know the value I set on you, and that you are mine.' He placed it on her heart finger, where a wedding ring should go, and then he kissed her cheek and her mouth.

Feeling the wiry softness of his beard and the slightly damp imprint of his lips, she shuddered.

'Ah, Ida, your power is not knowing you have it,' he murmured.

When she had finished the wine, he helped her to dress, rolling her silk stockings back up her legs, tying her garters, kissing the soft inside of her thighs above the fastenings and below the smears of blood and semen. He gave her a collar of ermines to wear at her throat as another symbol of his royal possession.

'There,' he said, stroking the fur and then her neck. 'That will keep you warm for me until our next meeting.'

Ida was unaware of leaving his chamber, of putting one foot in front of the other as the marshal returned her to the women's chamber. Goda and Bertrice fussed around her, but she stood like a stone beneath their ministrations and would not speak. All she wanted to do was sleep, to shut out the world and descend into oblivion where she didn't have to think or feel.

5

Four days later, having been summoned by the King twice more, Ida began her flux, and was utterly relieved that Henry's seed had not taken root. Bertrice, who was knowledgeable about such things, told her to rinse her woman's passage in vinegar before she went to Henry because it discouraged conception. Ida knew that preventing pregnancy was a sin but in fornicating with the King she was already beyond a state of grace and the notion of quickening with a child filled her with fear and shame.

At first she was wary about leaving her chamber, thinking that everyone would be staring at her with the word 'whore' on their lips, but the attention she received although speculative was mostly sympathetic. A few glances were admiring; occasionally there was pity. The King's officials treated her with deference. If there were smacked lips and knowing gestures, no one did so to her face or in her presence. She was the King's mistress; she wore his ring on her finger, his ermine at her throat, and, as Henry had said, his interest in her was a bright halo of protection.

More gifts from Henry came her way. Rich cloth for

gowns, dainty gilded shoes, hose of the sheerest silk, ribbons, rings and brooches. Henry liked to have her sit in his chamber of an evening, where she would embroider, or weave braid on her small loom, and he would watch her with an indulgent smile. Having something on which to focus, something she could do well, helped Ida to overcome her anxiety, and Henry seemed to find contentment just by having her there as a background comfort. He liked her to massage his shoulders or rub his feet and sing to him. Often she would receive the summons to his chamber and all he would want was the consolation of company and a soft feminine presence that did not demand intellectual concentration. On the occasions he did want to bed her, Ida submitted to his demands, compliant, if not eager. Becoming accustomed to what he expected and what to expect herself, her apprehension diminished. As familiarity grew, she was even a little gratified to feel the power of being the pleasure-giver.

As the weeks and months progressed, Ida began to feel a certain affection for Henry. He had an endearing way of rumpling his hair when he was thinking, and since she frequented his private chamber late at night, she saw the vulnerabilities he did not expose to the court. Some months before taking Ida to his bed, his mistress Rosamund de Clifford had died in childbirth and the baby with her. Henry was reticent on the matter, but from the bleak and painful little that he said, Ida understood that her death had left a hole in the fabric of his life that no one was ever going to fill. She herself was a pale substitute – a faint flicker of warmth to ease the coldness in the void.

As her position became established, supplicants began offering her bribes to intercede with the King on their behalf and gain his ear. Ida was shocked and astonished the first time a merchant presented her with a length of scarlet silk and asked her to help him build up a clientele among members of the court. Not knowing what to do, but deciding that honesty would serve her best, Ida took the fabric and showed it to Henry, who laughed aloud and, kissing her, told her what a darling she was.

'Keep the silk,' he chuckled, 'and recommend him, because it will make more patronage for you, and you deserve a reward for your freshness and honesty!' Wrapping a coil of her hair around his knuckles, he added, 'Whatever you are given, though, always bring it to me and tell me who gave it to you and what they want in exchange. Let me decide what is to be done.'

Ida nodded, feeling relieved and pleased. She had negotiated her way through a new and difficult situation and, to judge from Henry's response, had done the right thing.

In early March, six months after her presentation to Henry, the court settled again at Windsor. On the cusp of spring, winter launched a rearguard assault. A bitter north-easterly wind hurled flurries of sleet against the tightly closed shutters and extra candles had to be lit to banish the gloom. Sitting in a window seat, glad of the sable-lined mantle covering her gown, Ida played dice-chess with Henry's youngest son, John, who had recently turned eleven years old. He was a quick, intelligent child with a vibrant smile and a misleading air of innocence masking sly cruelty. He couldn't be trusted; he was apt to cheat in order to win, which was why people were reluctant to play with him. He had cornered Ida in the window seat before she could make her escape. Ida didn't like John, but she did feel sorry for him and it was not in her nature to rebuff a child. Queen Eleanor his mother was under house arrest at Salisbury for her part in fomenting the rebellion of three years ago, and John seldom saw

46

her. His brothers were already grown men with their own entourages and concerns and, as the lastborn child, his inheritance was an uncertain one.

Looking up, having cast his dice and made his move, John's hazel glance followed the progress across the chamber of a sombrely dressed woman with two young men trailing at her heels.

'Gundreda, dowager Countess of Norfolk, and her sons, come to pay their respects to my father,' John announced. A sardonic gleam, older than his years, kindled in his eyes. Politics and intrigue were as much a part of him as his father's build and his mother's colouring. Bred into him, blood and bone.

Ida glanced across. 'You know them, sire?' The Countess Gundreda was her second cousin, but she had never met or spoken to her.

John shook his head. 'Only of them. They attempted to speak with my father earlier this morning but he was too busy. I heard her trying to wheedle John Marshal into letting her past the ushers, but he refused.'

Ida remembered hearing that Gundreda's husband, Earl Hugh Bigod, had died in Flanders. The rumours several months ago about him taking the Cross had been true but, despite his oath, he had never set foot beyond Saint-Omer, his health being too poor. His widow wore hard lines between nose and mouth corner and her eyes were full of watchful suspicion, but no grieving. Her older son was about the same height as Henry, with a pale complexion. A yellow beard fuzzed a prominent jaw, and he had the same wary gaze as his mother. The younger one, dark of hair, slouched in his wake, his belly hanging over his tunic like a lump of dough.

'I don't think my father will be very interested in her,' John said with a sneer. 'Not unless she's got something

47

good to bargain. She's got a face to curdle milk and a body like a sack of turnips.'

Ida pressed her lips together and didn't give John the pleasure of a shocked response, because that was what he wanted. She threw the dice, moved her piece, and put him in a difficult position. He scowled at her and she knew she had committed the error of not letting him win. Where Henry would have laughed and called her a clever girl, John narrowed his eyes. 'Still,' he said, 'at least you won't have to worry; you'll still be my father's favourite mattress, I'm sure.' He swept the pieces to one side of the board so that no trace of their former positions remained, rose to his feet and stalked off with the air of someone who owned the world.

Seething with fury and humiliation, Ida carefully returned the pieces to their casket. Whatever hurts in his own life he was compensating for, he had no right to say those things to her. She would not stoop to John's level and carry tales to Henry, who would likely laugh anyway and call them no more than a boy's impudence, but she vowed that from now on she would avoid the youth whenever possible and feel sorry for him no longer.

'May I join you, mistress?'

Looking up, Ida found herself being addressed by the dowager Countess of Norfolk. Her sons were no longer at her side, but had drawn off to talk to some other young men and warm themselves at the hearth.

Ida rose and curtseyed, then sat down again, making room for her kinswoman. 'The lord John told me who you were.' Swallowing her anger, she concentrated on her companion.

'Did he?' Gundreda's nostrils flared. 'News travels fast.' Her nose was arched at the bridge and the skin was shiny as if the bone was about to break the surface. Her lips were thin and dry, her cheeks showed fine thread veins. Defying the slow ruin of the years, her eyes were a rare, clear green, like window glass, and would have been beautiful if the expression in them had not been so bitter.

A few months ago Ida would have blushed with chagrin, but she had grown a thicker skin since then. 'I am Ida de Tosney, the King's ward. We are kinswomen through my mother, I believe.'

Gundreda inclined her head. 'I am pleased to make your acquaintance, although I do not know your family, even if I have heard of them. You have a brother, do you not?'

'Yes, my lady. In wardship too, but in Normandy. I haven't seen him in several years,' she added with a wistful pang.

'Let us hope he has less trouble claiming his inheritance than I and my sons,' Gundreda said acidly.

'I am sorry for your loss,' Ida murmured into the taut silence, seeking the right thing to say but unsure of her ground. 'I pray God will succour you.'

Gundreda of Norfolk gave her a pinched look. 'It is not God's succour I need but the King's – and his justice.'

'I am sure both will hear you, my lady.'

'I am the dowager Countess of Norfolk, you would think so.'

Ida noticed how Gundreda's hands imprisoned each other in a tight grip, left over right. Her thumb rubbed repetitively over a heavy gold ring on her wedding finger and the tension in her clenched jaw made visible hollows in her cheeks. Concerned, Ida set aside her sewing and personally fetched her kinswoman a cup of wine rather than summoning a servant.

'They say your husband died having taken the Cross.' She tried to offer comfort as Gundreda thanked her for the drink and sipped. 'Surely he is in heaven now.'

49

'The whereabouts of my husband are of no interest to me,' Gundreda said coldly. 'He was a bastard from the start of our marriage to the end and if his eternal home is hell, then may he rot there in torment. What does concern me is my dower and the inheritance due to my sons. It is too easy to cheat widows, heiresses and wards out of what is theirs by right.' She glanced towards the young men by the fire.

'I hope you will be successful, my lady.' Ida was inwardly shocked by Gundreda's corrosive attitude. How could anyone speak in such a fashion of another person?

A severe-featured man with a greying beard was looking in their direction. His mantle was lined with squirrel fur and his tunic was the expensive blue-black of over-dyed woad. Ida did not know Roger de Glanville well, although she recognised him. He was one of the officials serving the administrative side of the court. An older brother, Ranulf, was employed in a similar capacity, and a younger one was the castellan of Henry's keep at Orford.

'My lawyer,' Gundreda said. 'You will excuse me.'

Ida watched her go to the man and speak to him, before leaving the room with her hand on his sleeve. The quality of the gesture made Ida thoughtful. Gundreda's sons followed, reminding Ida of hounds trailing after their owner. The older one flashed her a glance in which she saw speculation mingled with what she now recognised as a predatory glimmer. It was unsettling, but she no longer blushed at such looks. Six months of dwelling in the eye of the court had taught her a great deal about men and more than a little about herself.

That evening at her prayers, she said one for the soul of the Earl of Norfolk and another for Countess Gundreda and her plight.

* * *

50

Two days later, Ida was in the hall when the Countess approached her again. This time Gundreda's lips wore a forced smile and her eyes were as hard and bright as peridots.

'Have you been able to see the King, madam?' Ida asked politely.

Gundreda nodded. 'Master Glanville has spoken to him at length on behalf of me and my sons.' She glanced towards her offspring, who were occupied with some new acquaintances they had made among the squires. Ida looked too. The older one's shoulders were thrown back and his chest was puffed out like a cockerel's as he boasted about something or other.

Gundreda shifted position so that she was hemming Ida into the corner, cutting her off from the hall. It was a dominant, almost masculine ploy, and disquieted Ida. 'I have heard,' Gundreda said, 'that you have a certain – shall we say – influence with the King?'

Ida's cheeks burned. 'My lady, whoever told you so is mistaken. I have no influence with the King at all.'

Gundreda arched her brows. 'I have it on good authority that he dotes on you and you are one of his favourites.'

'People always exaggerate.' Ida folded her lips together, feeling acutely uncomfortable.

'Even so, there must be a grain of truth in what is said. There always is.' Gundreda sighed and suddenly looked worn out rather than intimidating. 'You were kind to me earlier. I would not impose on your goodwill and kinship, but if you can find it within you to help me, I ask you to intercede on my behalf. I only want what is mine by right of law. As another woman, I hope you will understand.'

Ida looked down at her hands, at her trimmed pink nails and the gold rings Henry had given to her. Her initial thought was that if the lands were Gundreda's by

51

right, she would receive them, but she knew now from bitter experience that life was not fair. Gundreda of Norfolk had to fight for her advantage with whatever weapons came to hand. 'I will tell him,' she said. 'But I have no influence upon his decisions – truly.'

'Even so, I am grateful. I will not forget.' Gundreda leaned forward, kissed Ida on both cheeks with her dry, cold lips, then left. Soon afterwards, a servant approached Ida and presented her with an exquisite wooden box, enamelled with scenes from the miracle of Saint Edmund in rich colours, including the vastly expensive vibrant blue of ground lapis. 'My mistress the Countess of Norfolk begs you to receive this gift as a token of her esteem,' the man said.

'Thank your mistress and tell her that I esteem her too,' Ida replied with formal courtesy. Feeling a frisson of unease, she sprang the lock with the small bolt key provided and opened the lid. Framed in swirls of gleaming red silk was a silver-gilt goblet patterned with a design of oak leaves. Amethysts as dark as blackberries glowed around the base, their power protecting from poison whoever drank from the cup. Ida suspected that both the box and the cup were valuable well beyond anything she was going to be able to do for Gundreda.

Ida smoothed her oiled hands over Henry's shoulders and back. He had a barrel-shaped body and was a little corpulent around the gut, but his skin felt good under her fingertips and the freckling reminded her delightfully of the speckles on an egg.

As she worked, he took the silver cup from its box and examined it in his rough hands. 'Well, well,' he said with a rumble of laughter, 'the dowager Countess is selling off Hugh's baubles to bribe her way to riches. Crafty vixen.'

'Sire?' Ida suspected from Henry's tone of voice that

he wasn't going to be sympathetic to her kinswoman's cause.

He twisted to look at her. 'This cup's from a set I gave to Hugh Bigod in the year I became King. Fashioned on the Rhine. My mother had them made when she was Empress of Germany. I'll warrant the box is something to do with the knights' fees the Bigods owe to the abbey at Edmundsbury. Wouldn't surprise me if it had been misappropriated from the abbey itself.'

Ida gave a mute shake of her head to say she didn't know.

He gave an amused grunt. 'Do you like your gift?'

Ida pondered. 'I can see it is worthy and handsome,' she said, 'and I understand that both are valuable and the cup would look very magnificent on a sideboard or table, but glass is prettier and finer.'

She felt him laugh. 'Prettier, yes, but more fragile and not so much use. You can't melt down glass when you become short of funds and if you drop it, that's the end. Not much you can do with a few shattered pieces.'

'So that would make glass the more precious?'

'And the less practical, my sweet. Give a king silver gilt any day.' He grinned playfully. 'I'll exchange this one for a glass cup if you want.'

Ida shook her head. 'It's a gift from a kinswoman, I'll keep it.'

Henry threw back his head and roared. 'A diplomatic way of saying that while you yearn, you're practical enough to know the true value of things in life.'

'I am learning,' Ida replied demurely.

'Learn all you wish, but do not lose your innocence because that is a treasure beyond price and everyone will try to be near you because you have it, and steal it from you if they can.'

Ida thought that Henry had been the first one to do that, but she didn't say so aloud. They both knew it, and he had just as good as admitted his own part. 'Are you going to give Lady Gundreda's son the earldom?' she asked after a moment.

Henry grimaced at the notion. 'My sweet, one Hugh Bigod is enough for any man to suffer in a lifetime. The old bastard's dead. I'll think twice or even three times before I replace him with another of the same blood – even if she did offer me a thousand marks to recognise him.'

Ida oiled her palms, smoothed them over Henry's shoulders and began to knead again. His groan of pleasure vibrated through his flesh and into her fingertips.

'I'm tempted to take it,' he said, 'but the older son is the proven soldier and administrator . . . still a Bigod though,' he added with a slight curl of distaste.

Ida stopped rubbing. 'So the Countess's son is not the oldest?' she asked with surprise.

'You thought that he was? Ah, I suppose there's no reason you would know better and she wouldn't tell you. Hugh of Norfolk has a son, Roger, from his first marriage to Oxford's sister. In fact he's here now – arrived just as the gates were closing, so I was informed. I've warned the marshal to be on his guard lest family affection grows a little too warm.' His eyes sparkled. 'I wonder what he'll offer me for the right to his father's earldom. Certainly not any of those cups, because his stepmother appears to have appropriated them.'

'Why, if he is the oldest son, is he not the heir?' Ida asked.

Henry shrugged. 'He is, but his father annulled his first marriage, and the new Countess is trying to prevent him from inheriting so that her own son may claim the earldom. She wants Roger to be declared a bastard.'

54

Ida made a soft sound of dismay. She didn't want to think Gundreda had played her for a dupe. 'What are you going to do?'

Henry looked thoughtful. 'Despite her efforts, Roger Bigod will remain legitimate. He's the Earl of Oxford's nephew and his great-uncles are de Clares. I'm not about to meddle with that. I suspect Gundreda knows she can't win on that score, but what she can do is claim a large portion of the inheritance for her son if I am so minded to bestow it. Her eldest boy has a good claim on the lands his father acquired during his term as Earl, and they're a substantial part of the inheritance – most of the Yorkshire estates for a start.' A calculating note entered Henry's voice. 'I'm not inclined to give it to either party. The father was a treacherous whoreson and blood will out. Roger might have fought for me at Fornham, but to do so he deserted and denied his own father.'

Hearing the censure in his tone, Ida took heed. She knew the fact that his own sons had rebelled against him had created an unhealing sore spot in Henry's soul. That the Queen had joined their defiance had deepened his distrust and increased his cynicism. 'You must do as you see fit, sire,' she murmured.

He turned round and kissed her. 'Indeed I must. And what best serves my kingdom too. You're good for me, girl, do you know that?'

Ida gave a modest smile and lowered her eyes. Henry tilted up her chin and kissed her again. 'Don't change,' he said with sudden intensity. 'Don't ever change.' He handed the cup back to her. 'Here, put it away and keep it somewhere safe.'

Ida shook her head and laughed. 'Sometimes, sire, I feel like a magpie with a coffer full of shining things.'

Henry gave her a look both bright and slumberous.

'Never a magpie.' He reached for her. 'Your breasts are like swansdown.'

Ida sat at the dining board among the ladies of the royal household. Although of rich fabric, her gown was modestly cut with neat, understated embroidery and her hair and throat were entirely covered by a linen wimple. Henry's gold and ruby ring shone on her heart finger and to initial appearances she resembled a respectable young goodwife rather than the latest royal concubine.

Her immediate companion at the board was Hodierna, who had once been a wet nurse to the King's son Richard. Her own son, suckled at the same time as the royal nursling, was now at study in Paris. Ida enjoyed Hodierna's company, for she was a warm, maternal woman, sociable and garrulous, but trustworthy too, and Ida found herself telling her about her meeting with Gundreda of Norfolk and what Henry had said about the situation.

'Always hard for a woman to claim against a man,' Hodierna said, 'and I reckon the Countess thinks she's owed some recompense for the life Hugh Bigod led her. Can't say I blame her for that. It's a pity she's taking it out on the first son though.' She nodded in the direction of a group of men sitting at a trestle to the right of the King. 'There,' she said. 'That's Roger Bigod in the blue tunic, second on the left.'

Ida glanced surreptitiously at the man Hodierna had indicated, who was talking to the Earl of Oxford. His head was turned away and all she could see were thick feathers of golden-brown hair and a gesturing fine-boned hand. He nodded to something that Oxford had said, and then faced forward to pick up his wine so that for a moment Ida caught a glimpse of his features: high cheekbones, long mouth, square jaw. His expression was tense and watchful and Ida quickly dropped her gaze to her meal lest she be caught looking at him.

'He'll be at court a great deal while he is fighting the dowager Countess through the courts for his earldom,' Hodierna said.

Ida attended to her food and feigned disinterest, although her curiosity had been piqued, especially after her discussion with Henry this afternoon. She continued to give Roger Bigod swift little glances. He too was looking round, but he made no direct eye contact with any of the women at the trestles. His gaze was observant and assessing, constantly on the move as if on the lookout for danger. She wondered what colour his eyes were.

'He has no wife, nor is he pledged to marry,' Hodierna remarked, 'but I expect plenty of fathers will be making enquiries. Even with his lands in dispute and the defences at Framlingham destroyed, he's still worth consideration.' Her tone was bland, but Ida took things less at face value these days, even with those whom she trusted. Hodierna was telling her that Roger Bigod, despite his circumstances, was a good catch for someone.

Roger entered the King's private chamber, knelt before Henry and bowed his head. Henry leaned forward, took Roger's hands in his and bestowed the kiss of peace on him. 'I was sorry to learn about the death of your father, God rest his soul,' Henry said.

They both knew it was a platitude; neither man was sorry at all. 'It was as he chose, sire.' For a moment Roger's vision filled with the image of his father's sealed lead coffin being placed inside the tomb at the family foundation of Saint Mary at Thetford. Whether his soul would lie in peace was a different matter. Certainly, there was little for the living.

57

'I am pleased to see you at court,' Henry said. 'You have been too long absent.'

'Sire, I have been busy on my lands,' Roger answered, putting a slight emphasis on the 'my'. 'There has been much to do.'

Henry rubbed his chin and considered him with thoughtful leisure. Roger remained stoical under the scrutiny. He had felt sick to realise that his stepmother and half-brothers had arrived at court before him and used the advantage of time to make the first plea. They had been staring across the hall at him earlier with a mingling of hostility and smugness.

Henry signalled a chamberlain to pour wine and gestured Roger to sit on the bench before the hearth. 'Your stepmother has offered a fine of a thousand marks for me to find in her favour on the matter of your father's lands,' he said.

Roger took the cup, hoping the contents were better than the usual sludge Henry served to his guests. 'I have always known my father's wife would dispute the inheritance, sire, and I deny her claim to the utmost. The lands are mine by right as the eldest son. If provision is to be made for my half-brothers, then let it be out of their mother's estate. Whatever my father acquired in his lifetime is due to me, not them.' Taking a tentative sip, he discovered his hopes in respect of the wine had been in vain.

'I am not unsympathetic to your plea,' Henry replied, 'but the matter needs examining in more detail before I can give a decision.'

Behind a neutral expression Roger wondered if 'more detail' was a euphemism for more bribes. Presents and gratuities served to grease the wheels of court life, but Roger had no intention of setting himself up in competition with his stepmother and beggaring himself whilst Henry rubbed his hands.

Henry leaned back in his chair, one shoulder pressed into the corner, arm braced, hand gripping the finial. 'What I can say for certain, and this the Church endorses, is that you are of legitimate birth, but it does not entitle you to the entire inheritance and your stepmother still has grounds for dispute.'

Relief coursed through Roger. That at least was something, although in truth he hadn't expected to fail on that score.

'While the issue is being deliberated, the title of earl has to be withheld, and the third penny of the shire.' Henry's gaze narrowed. 'To be blunt, it is not within my interests to grant preference and promotion to a family whose titled lord betrayed me at every turn.'

Roger's breathing quickened. Even though he had been prepared for this moment – because Henry was hardly going to return privileges and revenues with an open hand – the words were like a blow to the midriff. 'Sire, I am not my father. I have served you in good faith since the battle at Fornham and done all you have asked of me.'

'Yes, you have,' Henry replied tepidly, 'but in so doing, you have also been serving yourself, and that seems to be an overweening family trait. You abandoned your own father, and that tells me you have the capacity within you to bite the hand that feeds.'

It was another blow, this time at groin level. Roger's jaw tightened. 'Sire, given the choice between treason to my King and disloyalty to my father, I chose the lesser dishonour. What would you have had me do?'

'Perhaps, too, you gambled on which would be the greater benefit to your future.' Henry's lips curved in a wintry smile. 'Thus far I am pleased with your loyalty,

but like good bread it needs a second proving. Before I
entrust anything to you, I need to know you will be steadfast. It is not good enough for you to swear you are. I
need proof.'

Roger suppressed the comment that proof would only
come from shouldering the burden. 'By whatever means
you ask I will give you that proof, sire,' he said instead,
holding his voice steady and keeping his posture relaxed.

Henry pressed his forefinger to his lips, considering. 'So
be it,' he said at length. 'Your stepmother's claim must
be carefully examined before I can come to a judgement
and, in the meantime, loyal service will do you nothing
but good. I will keep and cultivate your presence at court
and you will do me homage tomorrow for those of your
father's lands that are not in dispute.'

'Sire,' Roger said. He recognised that his audience was
over and this was as much as he was going to get from
Henry at this stage.

As he returned to the hall, he pondered on what Henry
had and had not said. Matters could be considerably better,
but he was philosophical. They could be worse too. At
least Framlingham was secure, as were his interests at
Yarmouth and Ipswich. Heaving a sigh, Roger mentally
braced his shoulders. There was leeway for optimism, but
he was going to have to toil like an ox for any reward.

In the hall, a group of women were singing a joyful
song about the delights of springtime to entertain themselves and others. Roger paused to observe and listen
while he recovered his equilibrium. The piece was one
he vaguely knew with a poignant chorus line and some
intricate tonal work in the verses and as he absorbed
himself in the patterns and pleasure of the music, he
started to relax.

His Uncle Aubrey joined the gathering of listeners and,

standing beside Roger, arms folded, asked under cover of the singing how the interview had gone.

Roger told him. 'It was not what I hoped for,' he said, 'but it was what I expected.'

De Vere looked thoughtful. 'The race is not always to the swift. You have the stronger case. Bide your time and you'll yet have all.' He laid a supportive hand on Roger's shoulder.

Roger nodded and looked equable, but beneath his calm exterior, his impatience simmered like a pot close to the boil. He had a feeling he would have to bide that time for years rather than weeks or months, and that permission to rebuild Framlingham's defences would be like obtaining blood from a stone.

Making a deliberate effort to settle down, he focused on the singers and noticed several young women who were as easy on the eyes as their voices were on the ears. A tall girl with a tilted nose held the notes with pure strength. Beside her a plump young woman warbled with her eyes closed, a stray tendril of blond hair tickling the side of her face. At the end of the semi-circle of women, a slender girl clad in a gown of green wool attracted his gaze. She had melting eyes of hazelnut-brown, arched dark brows and a dimpled smile as she sang in a clear, sweet voice. At the chorus, the singers had to clap and turn to the left and then the right and she performed the moves with a sparkle and a laugh.

'Lovely girl,' his uncle said and ran his tongue around the inside of his closed mouth. 'Ida de Tosney – Henry's new young mistress and very dear to him.'

Roger was a little shocked because the innocent joy in her face and movements sat at odds with the notion of her sharing the King's bed. There was nothing of a concubine in her mien.

'She's not one of the regular whores,' his uncle added. 'She's one of his wards.' He lifted a sardonic eyebrow. 'An heiress but, like yourself, Henry is considering her future while holding it in abeyance.'

Roger was quick enough to absorb the meaning within his uncle's remarks. Ida de Tosney belonged to Henry and a wise man would keep his distance. Not that approaching her had been on Roger's mind. He liked women and had the same urges as any healthy young male, but he was also self-contained and wary of the court butterflies.

Dismissing Ida de Tosney from his mind, he murmured to his uncle and headed to the latrine to empty his bladder of Henry's vile wine. Task accomplished, he turned to leave but found his way blocked by his half-brothers and Gundreda's lawyer, Roger de Glanville. Roger's heart started to pound but he held his gaze steady and kept his head high. He was accustomed to games of intimidation; his father had taught him well.

'Was a thousand marks all you could offer the King by way of a bribe?' he scoffed at Huon, striking first and feigning amused contempt.

Huon flushed. 'I doubt you could offer him better.'

Roger shrugged. 'We shall see.' He made to push past and Huon stepped to bar his way, but did not complete the manoeuvre. De Glanville leaned against the outer wall in watchful silence, observing but not taking part, and Will hung back looking anxious and biting his lower lip. 'Oh, for Christ's sake, either piss or put your cock in your braies,' Roger said scornfully.

Huon whitened. Roger fixed his stare on de Glanville. 'Or perhaps you are waiting for someone else to piss for you. That's more in keeping, isn't it?'

Huon seized Roger's arm. 'You'll not win this,' he spat, his voice saturated with loathing.

'Watch me,' Roger retorted. Shrugging himself free of Huon's grip, he strode out of the latrine alcove. His heart was banging in his ears and he felt nauseous. He had no doubt that Huon would be doing just that – watching him and it made the space between his shoulder blades prickle as if he'd fallen in a patch of nettles.

Gundreda frowned at the chemise she had just picked up off the returned laundry pile. There was a tear in one of the seams that hadn't been there before it had gone to the washerwoman and still a hint of grime at the cuffs. Why could no one ever do a job properly? The bread at court was either undercooked or burned, and the wine undrinkable. The mattress last night had bounced with fleas. She felt like throwing up her hands and retreating to Bungay, but she couldn't. There was too much at stake. And now the ripped chemise on top of all else. She wanted to weep and scream and swear and stamp, but it would all take too much effort.

The sound of a male throat being cleared made her look up. Roger de Glanville was standing in the doorway, his fist clenched against his lips. She didn't know whether to welcome the distraction or be irritated by it.

'Countess, I would have a word, if it please you,' he said.

It made a difference to be addressed with courtesy, she'd give him that. Heaving a sigh, she gestured at the pile of linens. 'I shouldn't have paid the laundress until I'd looked at these. Why is it so difficult? Do I ask too much?'

'My lady, of course you do not.'

She heard the placatory note in his voice and knew he was humouring her, but at least there was compassion in his eyes – something she had never seen in her husband's.

In twenty years of marriage, she could not remember a single kindness from Hugh. 'No,' she said. 'You do well to remind me.' With a sigh she gestured wearily to her maidservant. 'Put these in the coffer, and make sure you scatter fleabane between the folds.' She looked at de Glanville. 'A word about what?'

'About the future.'

'What of it?'

'This dispute over your son's inheritance may not be resolved for months or years. You will need an advocate at court to fight your case and make sure it does not become buried.'

Gundreda gave a harsh laugh. 'You tell me nothing I do not already know.'

He stroked his moustache. 'Your stepson is a determined young man.'

'He is nothing!' She spat the last word. Ever since arriving at Framlingham as a shrinking unwilling bride, she had felt little but antipathy towards Roger. Her early overtures to him had been rebuffed with angry tears and outbursts of rage. It wasn't her fault that his parents' marriage had been annulled and his mother sent away, but he had blamed her nevertheless and she had possessed neither the time nor inclination to deal with his hostility. She couldn't help it that she wasn't the sainted Juliana. When she complained to her new husband of his son's behaviour, Hugh had predictably thrashed the boy black and blue, and Roger had blamed her for that too. Their mutual dislike had continued on a subdued level. Roger persisted in his rejection by ignoring her and keeping his distance. Once her own sons were born, her impatience with his attitude had hardened. He was the cuckoo in the nest; the child who stood between her own offspring and their rightful inheritance. And thus it remained.

64

'In your eyes perhaps, but the King will confirm his legitimacy and his right to Framlingham, and there is nothing I can do about it.'

Gundreda had been prepared to hear as much, but it still added to her feelings of frustration and misery. 'Then what can you do?' she snapped. 'I was told you were the best. Was that an idle boast?'

He sighed and gestured her to sit down. 'My lady, I—'

'Countess,' she said sharply.

He gestured again and, after a moment, she did his bidding, but made it clear that it was a concession.

'Countess, it is not an idle boast,' he said firmly. 'You will find no better legal advisers at court than me and my brother Ranulf. He is high in the King's favour and likely to become the next justiciar, but neither of us can work miracles.'

Gundreda eyed him narrowly. 'What of the acquisition lands? I suppose you are going to tell me there is nothing you can do there either?'

He gave her a meditative look. 'The King will hold them himself for the time being, while the dispute is being considered, but there is a chance he can be persuaded to give them to your sons.'

'And for how long is the "time being"?' she asked.

'That I cannot say, Countess, but I will continue to lobby him.' He sat down beside her, hesitated, then said, 'I have a proposition to put to you, which will benefit both of us, I believe.'

The way he looked at her sent a ripple down her spine. 'What kind of proposition?'

He cleared his throat. 'I am a second son, but not without prospects and I am well employed at court. My family has influence in East Anglia and I believe if we were to marry, it would be a sound match. I have witnessed and admired your fortitude and I think we would do well together.'

Gundreda had to choke down laughter, knowing that if she began, she would never stop, and she did not want him to think her mad. 'Why should I ever want to marry again?' she demanded. 'Once was too much.'

'Because it will make you better able to stand against the gale,' he said. 'Because it will be more effective for me to argue the case from a marital point of view. You will not be permitted to remain a widow. Someone will ask the King for you and he may turn out to be of the same ilk as your former husband. There are many such men about, but I am not one of them.'

Gundreda eyed him suspiciously. 'What is in it for you?' she demanded. 'No one weds without advantage to themselves.'

'Indeed not. You would bring a marriage portion in East Anglia and a link for my family with the Earls of Warwick. If I can win the acquisition lands, then who knows what else we might gain?'

She arched her brow. 'How do I know I can trust you?'

'You don't,' he replied with candour, 'but the same goes for anyone. If I have a vested interest in obtaining the estates for your son, I will be the more likely to keep pushing the cart. It will be to our mutual advantage.'

'I am beyond child-bearing age. You will have no heirs from me.'

'That matters not. I am a younger son; I have brothers to carry the line.'

'And if I refuse?'

He gave a faint smile. 'Then it was worth the asking . . .' He hesitated. 'Forgive my boldness. You have beautiful eyes.'

Beyond all sense, beyond all cold reason, it was his last

66

words that fixed the decision in her mind like lead tracery securing expensive green glass in a window. No man had said anything like that to her before. Hugh would rather have beaten her than pay her a compliment. She could feel heat seeping into her cheeks as if she were a foolish girl with a head full of dreams. 'I will have to think on the matter,' she said, shielding herself, but knowing her defences were in ruins.

'Of course, but I hope you will do me the honour.'

He left then with a grave little bow. Standing in the poky, dusty chamber, Gundreda felt tears well in her eyes and spill down her face.

'Countess?' said her maid in concern.

Gundreda wiped her face on her cuff. 'I've changed my mind,' she said. 'Fetch the laundress back and give her that shift. I want it washed whiter than driven snow, and see to it that the seam is repaired too.'

6

Winchester, August 1177

Seated on a sun-warmed bench in a corner of the courtyard, Ida reached into her sewing basket for her embroidery. She was working on a footstool cover with a design of fern leaves and small scarlet pimpernels. She had stitched a small brown hare in one corner, peeping out from the midst of the foliage, and a seeking hound in the other, and was delighted by the effect. Beside her, Goda kept her company, hemming a chemise.

Henry was confined to his chamber, suffering from an abscess on his leg. Some years since, a Templar's horse had kicked his thigh, damaging the bone, and every now and again, the old injury flared into a pus-filled wound. His physician had ordered him to rest, insisting that the leg be poulticed and propped up on cushions to aid drainage. Henry had intended sailing for Normandy to deal with pressing affairs, but until the wound healed, he had no choice but to remain in Winchester; thus he was not only feverish, but grumpy too. He was in no mood for bed sport, for which Ida was glad, but she knew she might be summoned at any moment to adjust his footstool, plump his pillows, sing to him, or just sit in his chamber. For the moment, however, she had the freedom to bask in the sunshine and enjoy her sewing.

Hearing the sound of hoof beats, she looked up from her work and saw Roger Bigod trot into the courtyard with a couple of companions. He dismounted in a lithe, balanced motion and her breath shortened as he laughed at a remark cast by one of his companions. In the time he had been at court, she had seldom seen him in a light mood and his smile was a revelation. His expression bright with enthusiasm, he ran his hands over the courser's neck, chest and shoulders with firm competence. Watching and listening, Ida realised the grey wasn't his, but he was inspecting it for one of the others and the entire group was deferring to his expertise. He picked up the grey's foreleg to examine the hoof before setting it down and standing back to study the entire animal, a frown of concentration between his brows.

'I hope my lord Bigod turns round before the hole you are boring in his spine becomes visible to all,' Goda said, a warning note in her voice.

Ida guiltily transferred her gaze to her sewing. 'I don't know what you mean.'

Goda shook her head. 'The moment he appears, you fix on him as if you are starving and he is your sustenance.'

Ida was mortified. 'I don't!'

'Perhaps I embellish a little, but there is hunger in your look, even if you do not acknowledge it.'

Ida bit her lower lip and didn't answer because Goda was right. She did find Roger Bigod attractive.

'Still,' the woman said, 'I reckon you're safe because he's one of those men who doesn't notice what's in front of his eyes where women are concerned – or chooses not to. He doesn't engage with the ladies at court, whatever their standing.'

That was true, Ida thought as she poked a new thread through the eye of her needle. Roger Bigod, from what she had seen, was mostly a quiet observer of the evening entertainments, usually on the periphery, sometimes joining in, but always with caution. That was why watching him now, in his element, was such a revelation to her. She wondered a little mischievously what he would do if she attempted to draw him out. It would, of course, be playing a dangerous game . . .

'That brother of his, though . . .' Goda interrupted her thoughts. 'I'm glad he's gone from court.' She shuddered.

Ida grimaced. Gundreda's eldest son had already gained a reputation among the ladies at court for being un-mannerly and rough. Hodierna said he was like his father, the old Earl of Norfolk, who had been a discourteous boor too, expecting everyone to cater to his whims and foibles and cornering the serving girls to pinch and fondle them should the opportunity arise.

Huon and his brother had left shortly after their mother's marriage to Roger de Glanville. Ida had attended the wedding, which had been a quiet affair conducted in the royal chapel at Marlborough. Both parties appeared pleased with the match and the sons had seemed accepting of their new stepfather. Gundreda had returned to Norfolk, but de Glanville remained at court and Ida frequently saw him speaking to other lawyers and clerks, or toiling over pieces of parchment in window embras-ures, working upon his wife's disputed inheritance. Knowing Henry's opinion on the matter, Ida suspected it would be a long time before a decision was forthcoming – if ever.

Roger and his companions moved off to the stables, still engrossed in their discussion about horses. Ida bent her head over her embroidery, but when the group had gone past, she looked up and followed the graceful motion of Roger's walk.

Roger picked up the skewered fruit, warm, soft, and dripping with a glaze of wine and honey, and did his best to eat it without getting drips on his tunic and runs of sticky juice up his sleeves. The technique was complex and every bit as challenging as an intricate piece of weapon play on the tilt ground.

In the warm summer evening, the court was taking its ease in the gardens and dining informally in the open air. A string of attendants ferried salvers of dainties from the kitchens, including these marinated fruits, little balls of almond paste stuffed with dates and crisp hot fritters, oozing with melted cheese. Henry presided over all, seated in an arbour at the centre of the garden on a deeply cushioned high-backed chair, his swollen leg propped on a footstool. The novelty of the evening was keeping him cheerful, as were the ribald jests with which his half-brother Hamelin of Surrey was regaling him.

The wine for once was drinkable and Roger was thoroughly mellow. His expertise with the horses earlier that day had been appreciated and his opinion was in demand.

'You have to breed for what you want,' he said between licking his fingers in as mannerly a fashion as possible. 'And look for beasts that reproduce their qualities well. Mares put to my red destrier all bear foals of his colour and with his heart room and strength of bone.' He bit into an aromatic wine-softened chunk of pear and caught the drip of juice on his chin.

'Grey's the best colour though,' said Thomas de Sandford, the young man Roger had been advising earlier. 'Chestnut and brown don't stand out in a throng.'

'It depends on the looks of the horse and the state

71

of his coat. Quality will always show through. You're fortunate your grey has both.' Roger's tone was diplomatic. Pale-coloured horses were ostentatious and useful to men who wanted to be seen in battle, but it was easy enough to put on a display with the horse's bardings and accoutrements.

A woman walked past with her maids, her train brushing the grass and jewels winking on her gown and belt. A faint waft of musk hung in the air, seductive as lust. One of the maids cast a flirtatious glance over her shoulder at the group of young men, as if bestowing a tourney token. The talk not unnaturally turned from horses to women, although the matter of breeding remained uppermost.

'I wouldn't mind standing stud to some of the fillies out grazing this evening,' Robert le Breton laughed.

De Sandford grinned. 'If you did, you'd likely end up a gelding.'

'Not if he was quick,' someone else quipped.

'That wouldn't be a problem,' de Sandford chuckled, 'from the rumours I've heard anyway.'

'Speak for yourself. I've never had any complaints,' le Breton retorted.

Roger drew back from the banter, which reminded him of the coarse japing at Framlingham when Leicester's Flemings had been billeted there. It was sordid and a little disrespectful.

Having noticed his reticence, de Sandford nudged him. 'So, with whom would you pair me to beget a perfect offspring?' he asked.

Roger half smiled and shook his head. 'Ask me about horses, not men and women.'

'Oh, come now, surely the same rules apply!' De Sandford nudged him again.

'What about Geva de Galle, for example?' suggested le Breton. 'She has the teeth of a horse! What do you think of her, Bigod – would she suit you?'

'I hadn't thought at all since I'm not intending to wed in the near future,' Roger replied awkwardly.

'Come, you must have some notions,' le Breton scoffed. 'That's part of what being at court is about – finding a suitable wife to breed your heirs.'

Inwardly grimacing, Roger contemplated making his escape.

'Forget the lady Geva.' De Sandford slapped Roger's shoulder with alcoholic force. 'You'd need a ladder to kiss her, even if you might feel at home with her teeth. What about all the looks you've been getting from Ida de Tosney. Now there's a filly worth the ride!'

The remark induced guffaws amongst the young men in Roger's group and occasioned several surreptitious glances in the direction of the royal arbour. Roger blinked in outright astonishment. They had to be japing with him. Ida de Tosney wouldn't look in his direction; it was more than her life was worth – or his.

'But then perhaps you're not interested in the King's darling,' de Sandford said slyly. 'Mayhap you're too pure to consider goods that have already been handled?' There was a needling edge to his voice. Roger's reputation for being choosy and avoiding the court whores was notorious and his companions seesawed between ridicule and admiration for his stance, usually the former because it was easier to count him as too finicky or wet behind the ears than it was to acknowledge he had a code of personal honour that made them seem unprincipled and coarse by comparison.

Roger pushed his mouth into a strained smile. 'I doubt she has any interest in me; not with all the privileges that come her way from the King, nor would I do anything to lose Henry's favour while I'm negotiating over my lands.' It was a warning to his friends not to tread any further in that direction and he was relieved that while they were merry, they were not beyond sense. De Sandford changed the subject and the gossip turned to the tourneys across the Narrow Sea where Henry's eldest son and the commander of his household knights, William Marshal, were making a name for themselves. Roger paid attention with half an ear. He was familiar with William Marshal, who was brother to the King's marshal, John. Usually he would have enjoyed talking about the skill of the joust since he was an accomplished performer himself. Now, however, he continued to worry at the bone of whether Ida de Tosney really had been watching him or whether his friends were having fun at his expense. He recalled seeing her that afternoon, but her head had been down over her sewing and no greeting had been exchanged. If it were true, he wondered what he was going to do about it because he couldn't afford to alienate the King.

A contest of throwing the stone had begun on the sward at the far end of the garden, with men seeing how far they could hurl a trencher-sized piece of sea-smoothed mica. Roger strolled with his companions to watch the sport. He had some talent at this himself and, with good technique, could throw far beyond the expectations for his build, but it was the truly tall and powerful knights who excelled. Had William Marshal been present, no one would have stood a chance: he had never been beaten; but since the Marshal was in Normandy, the contest had more of an edge. Roger watched a young household knight of Henry's hitch up his tunic, crouch, turn and release the stone along a roar of effort that saw it sail out, a darker shape against the night sky, before plummeting to earth with a thud fifty yards away. As the competition became more intense, others drifted over to watch, including Geva de Galle of the horse teeth and uncommon height. In making room for her, Roger almost trod on the toes of the person standing behind him, turned to apologise and found himself face to face with Ida de Tosney. She met his startled gaze with one that was soft as a deer's and bright with pleasure.

'I am sorry, demoiselle, I did not realise you were there,' he said woodenly.

'It is my fault for being in the way.' She gave him a quick, dimpled smile. 'And perhaps I am easily overlooked?'

'Not at all, demoiselle.' Roger gestured for her to go in front of him so that she could see the contest. Her veil of rose-coloured silk skimmed her brows and emphasised the dark sparkle of her eyes. 'I do not think anyone could overlook you.'

The dimple deepened and she gave him a warm glance over her shoulder before turning to fix her attention on the competing men. Roger avoided meeting the eyes of de Sandford and le Breton, for he knew they would be smirking at him. Dear God, he thought, what if she truly had taken a fancy to him? Disturbed, he tried to concentrate on watching the contest, but in a lull between throws, he could not resist looking at Ida and felt a frisson as she turned and met his gaze as if he had touched her with more than just his eyes. Her mouth had an upwards curve as if something was secretly pleasing. He wondered what it would feel like to kiss her, and then banished the thought as if slamming a chest lid on something he didn't want others to see. No matter how enchanting she was, Ida de Tosney was fire to burn the fingers of anyone stupid enough to reach out. Only an idiot poached on the King's territory.

'Do you not throw the stone, Messire Bigod?' she asked.

Her voice was clear and sweet and he had to tear his gaze from her lips as she formed the words. 'Well enough, Mistress de Tosney,' he said, fixing his regard determinedly on the game, 'but not sufficiently to compete with these knights.'

'Ah, so you only compete when you think you can win?' she asked with a mischievous gleam.

Roger found a tense, answering smile. 'If that were the case, demoiselle, I would never play chess or merels with the Earl of Surrey, but for the moment I would rather watch men throwing the stone than do it myself.'

'As would I.' Her dimple emerged again and she tilted her head to one side. 'That was a fine horse you were looking at this afternoon.'

He gave a wary nod. 'Thomas wanted a new courser that was showy with good paces. It's a fine beast. I'd have bought it myself if he hadn't.'

'You know horses?'

He gave a self-conscious shrug. 'Somewhat.'

'More than that to judge from the way you put that courser through its paces.'

'My lands have good grazing.' He gave her a diffident smile. 'Perhaps it is foolish of me, but I have a desire to breed the best line of destriers in Christendom.'

'I do not think it foolish at all. Everyone should strive after something.' She turned further towards him. 'What then makes a fine destrier – strength?'

'Well, yes, he has to be strong, but he must also be swift and manoeuvrable in tight corners. Biddable too, and intelligent. Plenty of stamina and able to endure upon poor fodder in times of warfare and hardship.' Once

76

launched upon the subject his enthusiasm overcame his wariness and discomfiture. Here he was on firm ground.

The contest reached its conclusion as the last knight to hurl the stone struck a rose arbour, bringing down a shower of scented petals and breaking one of the stems into the bargain. Flourishing a bow, he was received with a cacophony of whistles and applause. Ida shook her head. 'He will not be the gardener's friend in the morning,' she said, but she was laughing.

'None of us will with all this trampled grass. I—' Roger stopped as an usher bowed before them.

'Mistress, the King summons you to attend him,' the man announced.

Even by torchlight, Ida's flush was plain to see. 'Of course,' she murmured. With downcast eyes she curtseyed to Roger. 'My lord, I have enjoyed talking to you, but you will excuse me.'

'Demoiselle,' he said, and bowed. He did not reciprocate her sentiments nor say perhaps another time, although enormously tempted to do both. For his own good, he mustn't be seen to court or encourage her company, even if he would have liked nothing better. He watched her go to the King. Stooping over him, she listened to what he was saying, her attention solicitously fixed on her lord. Henry reached up, smiled and stroked her face. Exhaling on a hard sigh, Roger rejoined his companions and, somewhat grimly, put all thoughts of dalliance from his mind.

7

Châteauroux, French Border, Autumn 1177

Gasping for breath, Roger cleaned his sword on the sleeve of the footsoldier he had just brought down. At his side Anketil unhooked the mail ventail protecting his face and gulped breath like a toper sinking his first cup of wine after a dry spell.

'God's bones!' he wheezed, swiping his forearm across his mouth and jaw. 'That was too close for comfort!'

Roger bared his teeth in a mirthless grin. He didn't have the breath to retort that seizing a castle from those in occupancy was never likely to be comfortable. Having gained a section of wall walk by scaling ladder, the fighting to secure it had been intense and it wasn't over yet. The battle was still raging elsewhere on the ramparts. Châteauroux was a strategic fortress on the disputed Marches between France and Anjou. Its lord, who had done homage to Henry, had died on crusade, leaving a five-year-old daughter as his heir. The French had laid claim to the castle and occupied it, and Henry was hell-bent on its retrieval and control of the inheritance of little Denise de Châteauroux.

Roger had fought his way into castles before. The battle

for Haughley was burned indelibly in his memory: his father blaming him; his own sense of failure; the loss of his men. In a way, his detested father had done him a service. He had learned some difficult lessons that day, had been tempered in the fire and had emerged as tougher, more resilient steel. It had glittered at Fornham in all its new shine and now, with a patina of experience, it enabled him to organise his men, secure what they had won and move on to the next pocket of resistance with grim and balanced efficiency.

'*A Bigod! A Bigod!*' Anketil recovered enough breath to roar as the gold shields with their red crosses blossomed on the battlements like fire, and the banners of Bigod together with the royal lions of England were unfurled and cracked in the wind, signalling victory.

That night the guardroom was raucous as Henry's soldiers celebrated wresting Châteauroux from the King of France. Seated at a trestle with Anketil, Hamo Lenveise and Oliver Vaux, Roger tipped wine from pitcher to cup, raised his arm and drank. His head was buzzing and he knew if he stood up, his legs would be unsteady. Time to stop even if he was into a rhythm. It was always the same in the aftermath of hard fighting. Get drunk. Forget. Give the raw red wounds of memory time to scab over so that the mind could bear them. But he wasn't a young knight among many now; he had a position of command and drinking himself into a state of oblivion was no longer an option.

He had seen to the prisoners; ensured that they were given a reasonable standard of care and their wounds had been tended. He had told himself it was because they needed to survive in order to be ransomed, but there was more to it than that. Enough was enough and kicking a man when he was down smacked too much of the way his father had behaved.

King Henry had ridden into Châteauroux, triumphant on his white destrier. He had promised riches and reward to all who had fought to retake the castle. Mostly he had spoken in terms of booty, but he had hinted at more wide-ranging prizes for some men, including Roger. Tantalising portents of things to come. Roger hadn't allowed himself more than a brief interlude of optimism. Henry's policy was to feed small but delectable morsels and keep men hungry. Roger suspected that in his case the 'prize' would actually be more work. Henry would see how much he could load on to him – testing his breaking point.

Roger knew, from the gossip around the fires, that he was gaining a reputation for being calm, pragmatic and a good judge of a situation, both on the battlefield and off it. A man who could keep a civil tongue in his head yet use it to flay to the bone if necessary without raising his voice. A man of fairness and judgement. He wondered how long it would be before he was unmasked as a fraud, because some-times the rage and impatience within him were molten.

To a chorus of cheers from the soldiers near the doorway, one of the camp whores who had been flirting with the men began to dance for them, swaying her arms above her head like branches, then lowering them to caress her body in a suggestive manner. She pleated handfuls of her gown at her hips and hitched her skirts, revealing shapely ankles and even a flash of calf. Roger stared, as all the men were staring. She was tall and generously endowed and even if her gown was shapeless, he could still detect the fluid motion of her breasts as she danced, and imagine the rest.

'More!' someone shouted, tossing a coin on to a trestle. 'Let's see your hair!'

Laughing, she pursued the coin on to the table where she reached up to her veil, plucked out the pins and shook down a mass of wiry black curls. Then, using the veil as a kerchief, she stamped and danced on the table, inching her skirt higher with each turn, to show calf and knee, and the red ribbon garters tying her stockings at the level of her lower thighs. With each tantalising exposure, more silver spilled on to the board and the men's encouragement grew increasingly strident and bestial, the bolder ones reaching out to touch her bare legs.

'God's blood,' Anketil wheezed, eyes bulging as she unfastened a garter and a stocking flew off. He delved into his pouch and flipped a coin to join the others. 'Higher, wench, higher! Show us your cleft!'

Oliver and Hamo were slack-jawed and drooling. Roger kept his mouth tightly closed and pretended indifference, but he was not immune and could feel himself growing tumescent.

Teasing her audience, breathless with her power, the woman showed the men a swift gleam of high white thigh, then let her hem fall back around her feet. The initial howls of protest changed to roars of approbation as she laughed, licked her lips and unpinned the neck of her gown. Roger swallowed. His throat was dry and a hot pulse was beating in his groin. He wanted to look away but, like the others, was drawn into the lewdness of the moment.

Her breasts were blowsy white pillows, blue-veined, tipped with long brown nipples, and she obviously had an infant somewhere, for when she cupped a breast and squeezed it, milk squirted out in parody of a male ejaculation.

Hamo Lenveise muttered an obscenity under his breath and Anketil almost choked. Roger clenched his teeth and

81

made himself sit still as the other men bayed around her like dogs unleashed on a deer. Lust coiled in the air as thick as smoke. To men raised to know that fertility and motherhood were two of the most desirable traits in women; to men who worshipped images of the Virgin Mary suckling the Christ child and whose earliest contact with the world outside the womb had been the squashy comfort of a milky breast, the sight was arousing beyond belief.

Her teasing, shocking dance became too much for some of the more worked-up soldiers in her audience, who seized her off the table and bore her to the straw in a corner of the room. One man thrust himself between her spread thighs while his friends made demands on her hands, her mouth, between her milky breasts. Anketil, Hamo and Oliver shouldered their way forwards to watch while they pondered taking their turn. Roger followed on their periphery, but as he gazed on the rutting, bucking mass his lust evaporated on the instant, leaving disgust and a feeling of drained sorrow that was akin to awakening in the aftermath of a sinful dream. What his men did was up to their personal consciences, but Roger had seen enough. Turning on his heel, he left the guardroom, but on his way out he tossed a coin among the spill of silver on the table and reaffirmed his personal vow never to take a woman except in full respect and honour.

8

Winchester, Easter 1179

Having dismounted in the stable yard at Winchester Castle, Roger handed his palfrey to a groom. A brisk April wind flirted with the kingfisher feathers in his scarlet felt hat, and the tilted brim shaded his eyes from the bright spring sunshine. Two doves bowed and pirouetted in courtly dance to each other on the stable's shingled roof. He smiled wryly to see them, reminded of the dances in the King's hall. It was easier for doves to find a mate than for people.

He had been absent from court on his demesne lands near Bayeux for several weeks, but it didn't do to stay away for too long. Out of sight meant out of mind, and he needed to keep himself noticed and positively so. Since Henry's eldest son and heir was visiting his father, putting in an appearance now was a politically prudent move. Apart from his visit to the family estates, Roger had been continuously with the King. He had witnessed charters, administrated, worked on judicial tasks, kept long hours and ensured that Henry saw him keeping those long hours. He had fostered friendships, made contacts, established himself. Wheel-greasing was essential, but that grease had to be applied with diligence rather than slathered on superficially for effect. Deep was what mattered, and deep involved a lot of hard work and thought.

He turned to the horse on the lead rope behind his courser and unclipped the rein. The mare was a gift for Henry from Roger's stud at Montfiquet. Her coat had the sheen of pale honey, dappled over the rump with chains of darker amber. Her mane and tail glittered like silver snow and her gait was so smooth that it would carry a rider all day without leaving him a bone-jarred wreck. At forty-six, Henry was reaching an age when such comforts were more important than they had once been.

He was giving his groom detailed instructions about the palfrey's care when another man arrived with a destrier and a packhorse on a lead rein. Roger's gaze went first to the horses and admired the young red-gold stallion and the knight's handsome iron-grey palfrey, both superb animals. Then he looked at the rider and realised why the quality was so high. William Marshal was the commander of the Young King's military household. He was a renowned champion of the tourneys and unbeaten in foot combat and throwing the stone. The young bloods of the court all aspired to emulate him.

William nodded to Roger, although his gaze too focused on the horseflesh rather than the man holding it. 'A fine beast, my lord,' he said admiringly.

Roger smiled with pleasure and a note of pride entered his voice. 'It's a gift for the King. Bred at Monfiquet.'

'And a kingly gift indeed. I have heard many fine things about the Bigod bloodstock. May I?'

Roger gestured obliging assent. William gave his own horses to a groom and came to inspect the golden ambler. He ran knowing hands over grooved shoulder and rump, examined the teeth, picked up the hooves, then stepped back to scrutinise the whole.

'I do not suppose you have any more like this running on your pastures?' he asked.

'I have a yearling colt born of the same dam and sire,' Roger replied. 'The colt's darker than this one here – amber coat and red dapples.'

'Spoken for?'

'Not as yet,' Roger said. 'If you are interested, I will keep you in mind.'

William said that he was and Roger did not ask if he had the necessary funds for such a purchase. The Marshal might not have landed wealth, but his clothing and equipment spoke for itself. 'Your destrier is magnificent.'

'He is rather fine, isn't he?' William looked smug. 'Lombardy's best.'

In his turn, Roger checked over William's horse, asked questions and the men swiftly established an easy camaraderie. Roger had half expected the younger Henry's marshal to be like his master – charming but superficial. The charm was indeed there by the bushel, but there was strength and depth too. Roger was good at assessing men as well as horses. William Marshal was not the kind to fall by the wayside for lack of stamina, he thought, although given his master, he would probably need every iota of his formidable vigour.

Across the room, Ida watched Roger Bigod talking in a group of men that included William Marshal and Henry's heir, the Young King, so titled because he had been crowned in his own father's lifetime to ensure the succession.

She had missed Roger's presence at court and the time had dragged without that frisson of covert flirtation. Other

85

men would gladly have played a game of dalliance with her, but Ida wasn't attracted in the same way, nor would she have felt safe answering their looks. With Roger, she knew it wouldn't go beyond a glance, a quick smile or a passing word. There was no such boundary with the others. Not that Roger had paid her any attention since his arrival, for he had been deeply engrossed in masculine conversations and interests thus far. She also suspected he was avoiding her on the principle that if you didn't go near the fire in the first place, you couldn't be burned. But it did no harm to warm yourself a little at the periphery if you were careful – surely?

Determined to enjoy herself, Ida joined the ladies of the court to watch a troupe of acrobats performing gymnastic feats on a series of ropes and poles suspended from a beam. The players' costumes were wonderful confections festooned with coloured silks and tassels. One man had showers of blue ribbons at his shoulders that Ida thought were lovely. She admired the supple grace of the performers, their elegant gestures and lithe coordination. The ladies whispered and giggled together about the fine musculature on display.

Chief among the spectators were the Young King's wife, Marguerite, daughter of King Louis of France, and her sister Alais, who was betrothed to Prince Richard, although whether the marriage would actually take place was debatable and a source of much friction. King Louis kept demanding that the couple be married and Henry kept finding excuses, because if something better came along, a betrothal could be broken more easily than a marriage. He already had one son bound in matrimony to France and Ida had heard him hint that a match to secure possessions in Poitou and Aquitaine would be a better long-term policy.

Alais was slim and pretty with straight brown hair, a tilted nose and a wide, laughing mouth. Her sister Marguerite, the Young King's wife, was by contrast plump and serious with eyes that held shadows. She had borne her lord a son who had died soon after birth, and had miscarried of another. Matters were difficult between herself and her superficial young husband, and even though she clapped her hands and laughed at the performance, Ida could see that, like the entertainment, it was an act to please others, and she ached with empathy.

The Young King joined the women to watch the display. Ida's stomach performed acrobatics of its own as Roger Bigod and William Marshal followed in his wake. Roger briefly met her gaze and courteously inclined his head to her and the other women.

'What do you think, my lord Bigod?' Ida asked, using the moment of eye contact. 'Are they not skilled?'

'Indeed so, demoiselle. I wish I was as supple.'

'You are when you are on a horse, my lord.'

He gave a rueful smile. 'That is hardly the same. I would need to be boneless to do some of those things.'

Ida longed to touch his arm and make a playful comment, but she dared not when they were in the midst of such public scrutiny.

William Marshal walked up to the arrangement of poles and ropes and eyed them thoughtfully. He was so tall that he could touch them just by stretching his arm.

'Go on, Marshal!' urged the Young King. 'I dare you! Let's see how good you are!'

William laughed round at his lord. 'Have you ever known me to refuse a dare, sire?' He dusted his hands in the earthenware dish of chalk the acrobats were using to improve their grip before grasping one of the dangling poles and hoisting himself up hand over hand.

The acrobat with the blue ribbons – the leader of the troupe – knew a golden opportunity when it arose and milked William's participation for all it was worth. Watching the Young King's marshal hang upside down from one of the rods, like a bat in a roost, Ida began to laugh until she was holding her sides. Although the knight was tall and powerfully built, he was athletic and muscular too – if not exactly boneless. In fact, she had seldom seen anyone more real and solid. At her side, Roger chuckled and relaxed, leaning towards her a little so that their shoulders almost touched. 'Now you see why he's so successful in the tourneys,' he said. 'And at court.'

'Indeed, but it seems to me hazardous too.'

'He would call it no more than meeting a challenge; he thrives on it.'

'And if someone challenged you?' Ida asked mischievously.

She was briefly caught in the intensity of his sea-wash stare. 'It would depend on the challenge,' he replied, then looked away and with a shout of amusement began to clap as the leader of the acrobats had William grip a flat board in his teeth and began balancing some small blue cups to left and right. 'I would hope myself up to it.'

The last cup was placed on the board and the player flourished to his audience, who applauded, whistled and cheered their appreciation. Cups and board were removed and William, scarlet in the face, somersaulted to the ground. Grinning broadly, showing off the fine white teeth and strong jaw that had served him so well, he accepted the acclaim with deep bows and hand gestures. The Young King clapped William heartily across the back and pressed a cup of wine into his chalk-powdered hand. Several women crowded forward, including Princess Alais, but not Marguerite, who hung back. Ida recognised the look in her eyes as she watched the Marshal, and it gave her pause for thought.

The laughter ceased as the King joined the group and everyone bowed. 'Your talents are many, Messire Marshal,' Henry said. His tone was pleasant, but Ida sensed his tension. He had been on edge ever since his eldest son had arrived at court. The undercurrents were so strong that everyone was working hard just to tread water. 'I can well see the skills for which my son values you.'

William Marshal bowed more deeply and smiled. 'I am accustomed to hanging on by the skin of my teeth, sire.'

Henry grunted with reluctant humour. 'I am sure you are,' he replied. 'And being given enough rope too.' He gestured to the gathering as a whole. 'I desire a word with my son, but pray continue to amuse yourselves.' His glance fell upon Ida where she stood at Roger's side. 'Mistress de Tosney, I would speak with you too, if you will attend on me later.' He signalled to an usher. Ida flushed. She hated it when Henry summoned her to his chamber in public. She knew she should enjoy the power of being the favourite royal mistress, but it made her feel soiled when he did it like this, especially in the presence of his eldest son and with Roger looking on, no longer smiling and relaxed but wearing an expression of polite neutrality. With downcast eyes, she murmured her apologies and left the gathering.

On her way to Henry's chamber, she detoured to fetch her sewing casket and use the vinegar. He had been in a sour mood ever since his heir had arrived from Normandy. He was constantly making dark comments concerning the young man's frivolity and spendthrift ways. There was suspicion in his gaze and a permanent frown set between his eyes. Nothing pleased him. His leg had been plaguing him again, he had a misshapen toenail that was growing inwards and causing him pain and he couldn't see to read without holding a manuscript at arm's length. Pointing up all the petty ailments of Henry's deepening middle age, his son blazed at court like a young and glossy lion.

Ida sat down before the hearth in Henry's chamber, took out the tunic cuff band she was embroidering for him and set to work. She pretended she was making the piece for Roger and imagined a scene where she was his wife, sewing by the fire in their private solar. Roger would be sitting across from her, watching her stitch, a look of fond contentment on his face while he gently stroked the sleek flank of a pet hound. She smiled a little at the image, but it made her throat constrict with sadness too.

After a while, her eyes began to ache and she had to stop. The hour was late even for the unpredictable Henry. The servants were yawning and the candles would soon be stubs. Ida tidied away her sewing, wrapped herself in one of Henry's fur-lined cloaks and, taking a poker, stooped to the fire and stirred the embers. As tentative yellow tongues flickered to life, the door opened and Henry barged into the room, his stride imbued with the vigour of irritation. With a snap of his fingers, he dismissed the servants.

'God's wounds,' he huffed as he threw himself down on the bed and waited for her to kneel and remove his boots. 'My son knows all about display and ostentation and nothing about being a king.' He exhaled on a hard breath and then pressed the heels of his hands into his eye sockets. 'He truly has no idea – thinks that all you need is to smile and scatter largesse like rose petals and everything will rule itself. He says I give him no responsibility, but how can I trust him with greater things when he has proven so fickle with the ordinary?'

Ida set his boots aside and made a maternal soothing

sound. With quiet efficiency, she helped him remove his tunic and chausses.

'He says he doesn't have enough funds. Hah, when I was a child, my mother lived hand to mouth trying to preserve my inheritance – his inheritance, come to that. He has to learn to live within his means; I don't have a bottomless treasury and I won't give my coin to support him and his . . . his foolish hangers-on who would rather squander their time in idiotic sports and looking ridiculous than in the serious occupation of supporting kingship. Tcha!' He scowled at her. 'I suppose you thought he was handsome,' he growled. 'Women usually do.'

Ida gave him a steady look. 'I thought him fair to look upon,' she replied, 'but only in the way I might admire a glossy horse or a fine view at a glance. No more than that.'

Henry grunted, slightly mollified. He got into bed and patted the other side emphatically. Ida modestly turned her back to remove her own clothing as far as her chemise and she heard him chuckle. 'Even now, my lovely girl,' he said, 'even now when you have been warming my bed for more than two years, you are still shy. That's what I like about you – your modesty and sweetness. Come, there's a good lass, rub my shoulders for me.'

Ida obliged, and as she worked, she felt the tension go out of him. Henry closed his eyes and sighed. 'Talking of handsome horses, Roger Bigod presented me with a fine palfrey today.'

'Indeed, sire?' Ida tried to sound mildly interested, although suddenly her heart was in her mouth.

'Colour of mead,' Henry said, 'and a gait like silk. I thought you might like to try its paces next time the court moves on. That mare of yours jars her off hind too much.'

Ida swallowed. 'That is kind of you, sire, but will my lord Bigod not be insulted?'

Henry gave a snort of impatience. 'Why should he be? It is not for him to say what I do with his gifts. Besides,' he added with a sly look, 'I do not think Roger Bigod will mind you riding his horse. He's rather smitten by you.'

Ida almost froze in panic but forced herself to continue kneading Henry's shoulders. 'I hadn't noticed him paying me more attention than anyone else,' she said in what she hoped was a light, natural voice.

'He doesn't want to upset his chances of regaining the earldom and permission to rebuild at Framlingham, but I've seen him glancing your way. At least he has the common sense to know the boundaries of my tolerance – which is more than could be said of his father. But once a Bigod, always a Bigod.'

Ida said nothing but, as she continued to work, realised she would have to be on her guard. She didn't want to incur Henry's wrath or jeopardise Roger's need to remain in favour. Henry obviously saw a great deal and she knew he would be ruthless if he felt his territory was being encroached upon. She felt trapped; yet her cage was gilded and she knew many would envy her position and all she had – it was what she didn't have that impoverished her.

As she finished smoothing the tightness from his muscles, Henry took her in his arms. His lips and tongue tasted of wine as he kissed her and his beard prickled her face. Dutifully she submitted to his demands and even derived a shiver of pleasure from the experience. It was nice to be held. The motion of his body upon and within her own created undulating waves of arousal, although before they could lead anywhere, Henry was gasping as he spilled his seed, and then, satisfied, was kissing the corner of her mouth, her throat, her breast as he withdrew and flopped heavily into the mattress with a contented sigh. Within minutes his breathing had deepened, a snore catching at the top of each inhalation. Ida stealthily started to leave the bed, but his arm shot out, trapping her at the waist. 'No,' he said. 'Stay tonight, my little love.'

Her heart sinking, Ida lay back down. Tender sensation still flickered in her loins like a distant thunderstorm, and gradually faded as she lay awake and gazed at the hangings decorating the walls of her prison.

In the morning he took her again, almost as if proving to himself and the courtiers waiting for him to emerge from his chambers that he was still sufficiently virile to spend all night with a young mistress and have the strength for another bout at dawn – a fact he broadcast to the servants waiting outside the bed curtains by making enthusiastic noises, when usually he was more reticent while taking his pleasure.

Feeling a little sore from Henry's exertions, Ida followed the usher back through the corridors to the chamber she was sharing with several other women whilst the court was in full array. Crossing the yard, she saw that men and dogs were assembling to hunt. The King's groom was holding Henry's courser at the ready and the hound packs milled excitedly underfoot or tugged on their leashes. Men stood with hands on hips, casting impatient glances towards the main building. Ida was greeted with knowing looks, many of them relieved, since with her appearance, the King wouldn't now be far behind. She heard one of the Young King's men jest to a companion that Henry already appeared to have caught himself a coney that morning.

Ida had to pass Roger Bigod and William Marshal at close quarters, where they stood waiting like the others,

93

booted and spurred, keen to be away. Roger's neck reddened and he looked down, pretending he hadn't seen her, while William Marshal inclined his head to her in polite, neutral deference. Both responses made her burn with mortification, for they were each in their own way born of manners and propriety in awkward circumstances. She was never going to become accustomed to being a concubine. Never!

On reaching the sanctuary of the women's hall, she sought her pallet, threw herself down on it and wept.

9

Everswell, Palace of Woodstock, June 1179

Yesterday evening there had been a few small spots of blood on the linen rags Ida used to absorb her monthly bleed. This morning, when she visited the privy, there was nothing even though she felt desperately sick, tired and bloated, as if her flux was about to begin in earnest.

A warm dry breeze was blowing the fluff off the dandelion seed-heads and the woods and meadows were in full green growth as midsummer approached. The window niches cut into the thickness of the walls granted Ida a view of all this largesse as she mastered her nausea and tried to ignore the heavy sensation in the bowl of her pelvis.

Henry loved Woodstock and had built Everswell beside the palace as a private lodging for himself and his former mistress Rosamund de Clifford. She lay entombed at Godstow, but this retreat remained with its perfumed rose gardens, its ornamental pools and fountains: a beautiful, tranquil place that Ida loved, but would have appreciated more had she felt less unwell. Her bones seemed to be made of lead as she returned to the gardens where a group of other women had gathered to chatter – among them Hodierna the former royal wet nurse. The latter was full of herself because Henry's son Richard was visiting his father and had taken time to seek her out and give her a gold ring in memory of her care for him.

Ida joined her on a sun-warmed bench. A peacock paraded slowly before the women and gave his strident call as he spread his tail feathers in a magnificent iridescent fan.

'Just like a courtier,' Hodierna chuckled, rubbing the sapphire-set gold band on her knuckle.

Ida smiled wanly as the bird rattled his ensemble and pirouetted. She admired his colours and thought about putting them in an embroidery. Roger Bigod had a rather fine scarlet hat decorated with peacock feathers.

'Are you feeling any better?'

Ida shook her head. 'If only my flux would start, I know I would.'

Hodierna gave her a shrewd look. 'I thought you said yesterday that it had.'

'It's stopped again.'

'And you are sick, you say?'

Ida nodded. 'I've only had bread and honey this morning and last night I was too ill to dine on more than sops in wine.' She watched a fish leap in the nearest pool, its scales a brief silver dazzle before it splashed back into the dark green water.

'When was your last flux?'

Ida looked perplexed. 'The beginning of May, I think, but it was a few days late and there wasn't much blood then either.'

'I think you should consider whether you may be with child.'

Panic increased Ida's nausea. She refused to contemplate the notion. There had been *some* blood. Surely that meant her body had rid itself of surplus seed? 'No,' she said, vigorously shaking her head. 'No, I can't be.'

'It is the most likely explanation. If you are feeling full, then it is because your womb is growing with a babe. I have known some women continue their monthly bleeds even when they are with child.'

'No.' Ida struck her fists in her lap. 'No! I have been careful. I've used the vinegar every time. I've done what I've been told.'

'My dear, the remedies do not always work if God decides otherwise. Vinegar notwithstanding, it was bound to happen. You are a healthy young woman and the King has sired many children. His seed is potent.'

'I'm not with child,' Ida repeated, clenching her jaw. It was as much to prevent herself from vomiting as from stubborn refusal.

Hodierna sighed and spread her hands. 'Well, we'll know who is right or wrong in a few months' time, won't we?' she said, then put her arms around Ida and gave her a maternal hug. 'Don't you worry, my love. Worse things happen.'

'No they don't!' Ida gasped and, clapping her hand to her mouth, pulled out of Hodierna's embrace and knelt over the flowerbed where she was violently sick. Some of the other women glanced her way and exchanged knowing looks.

The gardens were empty of their daytime occupants and visitors. The peafowl roosted in the trellises and arbours, their scything calls replaced by the soft hooting of owls. Ida sat on the turf seat and listened to the quiet plash of the spring feeding into the garden pools. A thin slice of moon and a scattering of stars cast enough illumination for her to see the dark glint of the water. Fish were still plopping and a cool wind ruffled the grass. She shivered and wished she had remembered to bring her cloak, but she didn't want to go inside to fetch it. She would have to talk to people if she did and she couldn't bear that just now. Hodierna was discreet and wouldn't say anything, but the other women were less caring of her welfare and already the whispers were enriching the veins of the court, where gossip was lifeblood.

She raised her knees on the seat and folded her arms around them, wondering for how much longer she would be able to do that. Her waist was still slender; there was nothing to see, but she knew her body was changing and no matter how much she denied it to herself and others, she was with child and by the late autumn it would be obvious to all. She felt as ashamed and frightened as that first night when Henry had taken her to his bed. Since then, lulled by his reassurances, it had all become unreal – a game demanding the occasional forfeit but rewarding her compliance with fine clothes and jewels and a glimmer of power. Now the game was over. She had been caught and had to pay the forfeit. Hot tears trickled down her face and turned cold in the moonlight. Now and again, she sniffed and wiped her cheeks on the back of her hand. At least Roger Bigod wasn't at court, having returned to Norfolk for the summer months, but he would rejoin the King soon enough and he would see her condition. How could she face him? How could she face anyone?

She became aware of a figure treading along the paler path towards her and prepared to panic, then recognised Henry by the shape of him and the limp in his walk. Someone must have seen her, she thought, and told him where she was, and why.

He paused before the bench and, folding his arms,

looked down at her. 'I hear you have some news for me, my sweet.'

Ida shook her head and began to weep in earnest. 'I wish I did not,' she sobbed. 'What's to become of me now?'

'Oh, sweetheart!' Henry sat down beside her and pulled her into his arms, folding his cloak around both of them. 'Hush now, hush now. It's nothing to weep about. I'll take care of you. How could you think I would not? You are carrying my child in your womb.'

Ida gripped the soft wool of his tunic and beneath it felt the solid strength of his body. 'But born of fornication and out of wedlock. I will be shamed for my sin.'

'No,' Henry soothed, 'never think that, my love. The sin belongs to both of us, but you will bear no stigma for this. I have said before that you are mine, and the King only has the best. No one will dare to look down on you.'

'But I will bear the shame before God . . .'

'That is what confession and repentance are for.' He set his forefinger under her chin and tipped her face towards the light from the stars. 'If God did not mean you to get with child, your womb would have remained barren. Perhaps this is His gift to me – a new child in the cradle to keep me young. Sons and daughters, even if born out of marriage, have their part to play. You must not weep.'

Ida tasted the salt of tears on her lips. She swallowed convulsively and did her best to obey him. Perhaps he was right. Perhaps this was meant to be and not a punishment for sin. Her jaw trembled with cold and distress.

'Come now.' He kissed her forehead. 'Don't fret. I will see that you have the best of care, and when the child is born, he or she will never lack for anything, and neither will you, I promise you that.'

99

Ida rubbed the heels of her hands across her swollen eyes and leaned against him. 'Thank you, sire,' she whispered.

After a moment of holding her, a moment of enforced stillness for him, Henry produced a small loaf of bread from inside his cloak.

Saliva filled Ida's mouth. She was ravenous but felt terribly sick at the same time. 'I'm not sure I'll be able to eat it,' she said.

Henry threw back his head and laughed. 'Girl, it's not for you, although you are indeed welcome to chew on it if you wish. I brought it because I know how fond Rosamund was of feeding the fish at night, in the quiet, before we retired. I thought that you might . . .' His voice caught and trailed off. A pang went through Ida. Although beset by her own troubles, she still heard the undercurrent of longing in his voice.

'Of course,' she said. 'By all means, sire.' Taking the bread, she broke it between them; going to the middle pool where she knew the biggest fish lazed, she tore off small pieces and threw them between the water lilies. He joined her and they watched the surface ripple and twitch as tench, rudd and chub rose to feed.

'Casting our bread upon the waters,' Henry said, but his voice was wistful and Ida didn't smile.

10

Woodstock, August 1179

A thunderstorm growled in the distance and the sky was slowly turning from afternoon blue to a murky twilit purple. In the garden, Ida set her sewing aside and looked towards the white flashes on the horizon. She was well into her fourth month of pregnancy. A fortnight ago she had ceased being sick and had suddenly become possessed of a voracious hunger with a particular craving for wild strawberries. They were becoming hard to find as the season advanced, but Henry was still having them sought for her, together with all manner of other delicacies to tempt her appetite. As he had promised, he was being most solicitous of her welfare. He had ceased commanding her to his bed, although she still went to his chamber of an evening with her sewing and she continued to rub his shoulders because he said no one else had quite the same touch. For his sexual release, he was currently enjoying the favours of a yellow-haired concubine from among the court whores. Ida had seen her on a couple of occasions, rustling along the corridor to the King's chambers as she had so often done herself, hood drawn up around her face.

'Mistress, we should go inside before we get wet.'
Bertrice glanced anxiously towards the imminent storm
and gathered up her sewing. 'Before we get wet' was a
euphemism for 'before the storm gets any closer'. Bertrice,
so forthright and knowing in many ways, was terrified by
thunder, whereas Ida loved the spectacle and had even
pondered stitching such a scene into a wall hanging.

'I suppose we should,' Ida said regretfully. She had
slipped off her shoes while they sat, and now she donned
them, easing her finger round the back of the soft goatskin.
As the women left the garden, a sudden wind blustered
across the grass and the first drops of rain shivered in the
pools. Ida picked up her skirts and, snatching laughter
between breaths, ran towards the buildings. Then she
stopped abruptly as she saw the grooms tending a glossy
chestnut courser. The horse's breast strap bore enamelled
pendants depicting a red cross on a gold background. The
nausea she had thought conquered threatened to over-
whelm her again. Last time she had seen Roger Bigod
they had danced together in the round and spoken as
friendly acquaintances. They had stood side by side at
mass in church and when the court had gone hawking,
Roger had held her falcon while she mounted her mare,
and had given her one of his rare, endearing smiles. Now
everything would be different. She had been going to go
to the hall, but she changed direction and made her way
to her quarters by a more circuitous route.

'He's bound to find out,' Bertrice panted behind her,
for she too had recognised the horse. 'You can't hide. If
you avoid him, people will start wondering.

'Wondering what?'

'Whether or not the child is Henry's.'

Ida gasped in shock. 'They wouldn't!'

Bertrice said nothing, just looked, and Ida realised she

was right. People would misconstrue her actions because they always did. No matter how humiliating it was, she would have to brazen it out.

An usher was waiting for her at her chamber door with instructions to bring her to the King. 'You do not need your maid, my lady,' he said.

Ida's anxiety increased. Henry had abstained from lying with her ever since her pregnancy had been confirmed, but what if he had changed his mind? She gave her sewing to Bertrice, wiped her palms over the dark rain blots on her gown and followed the usher to Henry's private quarters. When she arrived, the thunder was growling fully overhead and Henry was looking out of the open casement at the storm. At his side, watching with him, was a dark-haired young man.

Henry turned as Ida entered the room, and a smile lit his face. 'Ah,' he said, and strode over to take her hand and kiss her cheek. 'I have a fine surprise for you, my love, all the way from Normandy.' He indicated his visitor.

Ida stared blankly for a moment. He was of medium build with wavy black hair and brown spaniel eyes.

'Do you not know me, sister?' he asked with a grin. 'That is no surprise, because in truth I barely recognise you!'

'Goscelin?' She put her hand to her mouth and stared at her brother. He was older than her by three years and she had not seen him since he went for training to knighthood when she was thirteen years old.

'Well, at least you remember my name!' Laughing, he came to take her by the shoulders and kissed her firmly on either cheek. She felt his smile against her face and the rub of soft new beard stubble.

'That's something I couldn't forget!' She didn't know

103

whether to laugh or weep. He had been christened Roger, but their English nurse had called him 'Gosling' as a term of affection and the name had stuck and become altered to the Norman masculine name 'Goscelin'. 'It's been so long. You couldn't have grown a whisker, let alone a beard when last I saw you!'

His glance dropped to her belly. 'You too have changed, my sister.'

Instinctively she laid her hand across her womb in a protective, defensive gesture.

'Your brother and I have discussed your condition,' Henry said smoothly. 'You have nothing to fear; the tale is already told.' He gestured. 'Rest here awhile and talk. I have business elsewhere.' With a brisk nod, he left the room.

Ida rose from the curtsey she had given to Henry's departure and, half turning from her brother, wiped her eyes on the heel of one hand. 'I am overjoyed to see you,' she said, 'but I would not have had you find me like this – with child and unwed.'

The storm growled overhead and the sound of the rain drumming on the roof shingles and pouring through a hole in the guttering came loudly through the open casement. A servant moved to shut it, but Ida told him to leave it. 'I like to hear the rain,' she said.

Her brother looked at the servant, then at her, his gaze widening. 'That may be so,' he replied, 'but you have power and influence.'

Ida looked wry. 'Over whether to tell a servant to open or close a window?'

He touched her arm in a conciliatory gesture. 'But you *can* tell that servant and be obeyed. You have the authority. It is a good thing for our family that you are Henry's leman and carrying his child.'

Ida folded her arms so that the hanging sleeves of her

gown concealed her belly, even though it was still almost flat. 'Do you imagine that our father would be delighted by my state?' she demanded. 'Or our mother?' Her chin wobbled. 'It is not honourable.'

'To be the King's mistress is not dishonourable either,' he said pragmatically. 'The child will be the son or daughter of royalty and have princes for siblings. I am sorry it has happened and I am sorry I was not there to protect you, but it is not a disaster. A disaster would be if you were carrying the child of the pot boy or a scullion. Our family will have the King's favour for years to come, if not Henry's then that of his sons. I will be uncle to royalty!' A delighted grin spread across his face.

Ida struggled not to snap at him. What he said might be true, but he wasn't the one who was to bear the child. He wasn't the one who had had to get into bed with Henry and perform the most intimate of physical acts with him. 'Indeed,' she said a trifle stiffly. Goscelin might be three years older than her, but in terms of experience, she was the more mature. Some days recently, she had felt ancient. And yet he was her only close family and it was so good to see him. She concentrated on this now. They had so much catching up to do of lost years, and not all of those times had been traumatic. She brought him wine and sat down with him on the bench as the thunderstorm rumbled away in the direction of Oxford.

Roger's Bigod's forefathers had all been stewards of the royal household – an office that had been handed down intact. Thus it was his duty to see to the ordering of the dishes at the high table when he was at court. Although a ceremonial post these days and usually delegated to subordinates, Roger was newly returned after an absence attending to his demesne lands, and had opted to perform the task himself. It put him firmly back in Henry's vision, since the King could hardly ignore the man who served his dinner.

From his elevated position on the dais, his dapifer's white towel across one shoulder, Roger sought and found Ida among the courtiers. She was sitting at a trestle down the right-hand side of the room, sharing her trencher with a dark-haired young man. Now and then she smiled and touched his arm and Roger felt a surge of jealousy, which he sought to quash. It was no concern of his if she had used his absence from court to make a new and blatant conquest. Henry seemed uncon-cerned, which was surprising. Roger wondered if he had been over-cautious in his own reticence. Ida had been avoiding his eye throughout the meal and he was irritated because she might at least have the courtesy to acknowledge him.

When dinner was over, folk collected in informal groups to talk as the trestles were cleared and stacked away. Ida's young beau assisted her to rise and saw her from the hall with her ladies. Having parted from her with a familiar kiss on her cheek, he returned to join a dice game that had begun in a corner. Roger was so busy eyeing up the newcomer that he did not see his stepmother until she was standing beside him. Gundreda at least had been giving him looks throughout the meal and making sure he knew of her presence at court. He hoped she would conduct her business, whatever it was, and leave.

'Just because you play the role of steward before the King does not make you the Earl of Norfolk,' she said to him now with venom. 'The King will never bestow the title or lands on you.'

Roger returned her look full measure. 'Nor on your sons either, my lady. The King will not give the earldom anywhere while he can milk the revenues, take the third penny and smile as he accepts the bribes.'

Her nostrils flared. 'Does he know what you think of him?'

'He knows he has me where he wants me and the same goes for you. However you choose to twist, you are still dangling on his rope. The bribes and gratuities you offer won't do anything except diminish your coffers and line his.'

'You give him things too.' She clenched her fists. 'I know about that palfrey you brought to court.'

'It was part of a debt I owed, and I can play the game too if I choose . . . madam.' He gave her a stiff bow and strode away.

Gundreda glared after him, but gradually a more thoughtful expression relaxed the hard lines on her face. He spoke the truth when he said that Henry was playing them off against each other and milking the lands for his own gain. From what she had observed, Roger appeared to have the upper hand, and this despite her marriage to an experienced lawyer of Henry's Curia. Unfortunately her stepson was well trained himself in the letter of the law. But if the father wouldn't listen, then perhaps the Young King would. He was heir to the throne, after all, and Henry wasn't going to live for ever.

Ida's beau had won well at dice. The merrier for drink and almost the worse, he scooped up his winnings, spilling coins like raindrops. Roger stooped, rescued several silver pennies off the floor and handed them to him. The young man slurred a thank you and rose unsteadily to his feet.

'Where are you lodged?' Roger asked. 'I'll escort you.'

'Over near the park.' He waved his arm in the vague direction of the Everswell complex, which was where Ida and the ladies of the court had their dwellings too. The knowledge caused Roger to tighten his jaw.

Once out in the storm-cooled air, his companion staggered a little and clutched the wall for support. Roger studied him by the light of the lantern he had collected on the way out. 'It doesn't do to drink too much in the King's hall,' he said curtly. 'You are not always among friends, even if it seems that way.'

He received a glance that stabbed him with a sense of familiarity. 'You're my friend, aren't you?'

'No, but neither am I your enemy. I am Roger Bigod, lord of Framlingham. I haven't seen you at court before.'

The young man pushed himself away from the wall and began weaving his way in the direction of the Everswell lodgings. 'I've been in Normandy – in wardship – but I'm to be knighted soon.' He stopped again and turned towards Roger, one hand extended. 'I am Roger de Tosney, but everyone calls me Goscelin – long story, to do with my nurse . . . y'don't want to know . . .'

'Ah, you must be related to the lady Ida.' Roger clasped Goscelin's damp, extended hand and began to smile as some of the tension went out of him.

'She's my sister. Do you know her?'

'We are acquainted.' They started walking again, Roger in a straight line, Goscelin weaving all over the place. Roger shook his head and gave a self-deprecating smile. 'I thought when I saw you with her that the King had given her a husband, but I can see the resemblance now.'

Goscelin laughed. 'She's prettier than I am.' He lurched to a halt before a low timber hall – one of the guest lodgings attached to the complex. The door was open, revealing a central hearth and sleeping spaces tucked between the aisles. 'I'll try to do my best for Ida,' he said, stifling a belch. 'At least he is the King. She will not be disparaged and neither will the child.'

'The child?' Roger asked in astonishment.

Goscelin nodded. 'To be expected I suppose. Makes a useful bond for my family, but came as a shock . . . Last I saw Ida she was a child, and now . . .' He shrugged. 'But done is done and at least Henry looks after his bastards.'

Roger said nothing because he was still assimilating the information and feeling dismayed. A child would be visual, indelible evidence of the bond between Henry and Ida. Mentally he shook himself. As Goscelin said, done was done. It was none of his concern. He bade Goscelin good-night, then made his way back to the hall, and thought as he walked that Ida deserved better.

11

Woodstock, January 1180

Ida stifled a cry as the next contraction seized her in its grip. She had never known such relentless, inexorable pain. The bible said it was Eve's punishment to bring forth children in suffering, but the knowledge was no comfort as she struggled and called out to the blessed Saint Margaret to help her.

'Almost there, my love, almost there,' crooned Dame Elena, the senior midwife. 'You've been very brave. Just a little longer. Just a few more pushes. We'll have this baby birthed while there's still daylight to see him by.'

Ida pushed and gasped and pushed and, as the contraction subsided, slumped against the bolsters. Her hair was wet with sweat; she was frightened and beginning to think that she couldn't go on. The women had been saying 'just a few more pushes' for what seemed like a very long time.

She stared through the open shutters at a sky heavy yellow with the threat of snow. She wished herself a hundred miles away and in a different time and season, sitting with her mother in the spring sunshine, an unencumbered child, chattering of inconsequential things as she plaited silk ribbons to make a belt. She wished she had never come to court. How excited she had been, thinking it a great adventure, and now she felt like an animal led to the slaughter pen. The next contraction gathered and surged. The midwife's assistants held her hands and she bore down with gritted teeth and straining tendons and the midwife herself busied herself between Ida's parted thighs, giving rapid instructions.

'Ah, the head, the head,' she said. 'Don't push so hard. That's it, my dear, gently now, gently.' Ida closed her eyes and squeezed the eagle stone in her right hand until her fingers cramped like her womb. Hodierna had given her the token, assuring her that it would help promote an easy birth. The egg-shaped stone with another stone inside it had the ability to ease pain and ensure a smooth passage into the world for the child. If it was working then Ida dreaded to contemplate what giving birth without one was like.

'Here we are, shoulders . . . arms . . . What do we have? . . . Oh, a son, my mistress, a fine boy, just look at him!' The midwife's voice shone with pleasure as she raised up a squalling, pinkish-blue object marbled in blood and mucus and still attached to Ida inside by a pulsating cord.

Ida stared at the infant in numb shock. She couldn't believe that this object had just emerged from her body, and even less that it was a living, breathing being – her son. She was too stunned and exhausted to experience any great outpouring of maternal love. All she felt was relief that the pain had eased and that this part of the ordeal was almost over. The woman cut the cord with a small sharp knife and took the infant over to a shallow basin. Placing him in this surrogate womb, she gently lapped water around his little body, cleaning him of the birthing fluids and murmuring to him. Ida listened to his

111

snuffles and cries and felt her heartstrings resonate, but although there was a vibration, for the moment she was too overwhelmed and exhausted to hear the tune. The woman dipped her index finger in a pot of honey and rubbed the baby's gums. Then she added a tiny dab of salt, making him turn his head and bawl.

'Hush child, hush,' she whispered. 'From this day forth you will only know the sweet things in life.' She dried him in a large linen towel, then wrapped him in a soft blanket and bringing him to Ida, placed him in her arms. 'Your son, mistress,' she said with a warm smile. 'You have worked hard to birth him. Is he not beautiful?'

Ida looked at the little wizened creature resting in the crook of her elbow. His hair was dark and damp and his eyes were of an indeterminate kitten colour. She could see echoes of Henry in the shape of his brows and the curl of his nostrils. His hands were like hers and each one tipped with a minute pink fingernail. Tiny, perfect. Tears gathered at the back of her eyes. She was so tired.

'He's a fine, healthy babe,' Dame Elena said. 'A good strong voice and everything a man should have.' She gave a little chuckle.

Ida smiled, forcing her lips to stretch, even while she wept.

'Ah now, all new mothers cry,' said the good dame. 'It'll pass. You're a little thing, but you're strong. Don't you fret; all's going to be well.'

The women saw to the delivery of the afterbirth, washed Ida, made her comfortable and, removing the baby to a cradle at the bedside, left her to sleep.

When she woke, it was dark. The shutters were closed and candles burned in the sconces. A baby's wail sent a jolt through her aching muscles and cramping womb. This was a new sound in her life and one she had still to assimilate. The cry of her son. She heard a masculine voice, low-pitched and crooning, and, pushing herself up against the bolsters, saw Henry standing at the bedside, the baby in his arms. He had unwrapped the swaddling to look at him, and there was a broad and wondering smile on his face.

Alerted by the rustle of the bedclothes, he turned to her. 'You have given me a great gift, my love,' he said. 'A son, a new son!' He stroked the small, soft curve of the baby's cheek. 'Hah, he has my nose, do you see?'

Ida managed a smile and a nod, although she felt drained and tears were dangerously close. Her chin dimpled and she clenched her teeth. Henry leaned over the bed to brush her cheek too. 'He is a strong, fine baby and he will be a great man. I will make it so, I promise you. I'll take care of you both. You need not worry about anything.'

The baby's wails grew in volume and Henry was clearly glad to hand him back to the midwife now that the acknowledging was done. Dame Elena wrapped the infant in his swaddling. 'See if he will feed now, mistress,' she said and, with Henry looking on, helped Ida put him to the breast. He rooted for a moment, seeking back and forth, then found what instinct sought and latched on to her areola and nipple. Immediately his fretting ceased and he began to suck, a small frown puckering his brows. Ida studied him, still unable to believe he had come from her body, his life created out of the sin of fornication. A pang of emotion cramped her loins as she saw his dependent vulnerability.

'I've arranged for his baptism at first light tomorrow morning,' Henry announced. 'The Countess de Warenne and Eva de Brock will stand as his godmothers, and Geoffrey FitzPeter and the Dean of York will be his godfathers. Your brother will represent your family.' Henry watched the baby suckle. 'I thought to name him William for my great-grandfather.'

'As you wish, sire,' Ida said, thinking it as good a name as any.

Henry smiled. 'It is fitting. My great-grandsire was born out of wedlock too, but by his own endeavours and God's judgement, he became a duke and then a king. Our son might not be a prince, but he is royal-born and he will be raised to know it.'

Ida wanted to weep and she wanted to laugh. Her feelings tilted wildly between elation and despair, yet she knew that for her own sake and that of the snuffling bundle in her arms, somehow she had to find the strength to keep her balance.

Ida rested her son in the crook of her arm and laughed as she watched him reach for the end of her plait and the blue silk ribbon securing it. Here in the domestic quarters she had dispensed with the head covering she wore in the public areas and it gave her a feeling of freedom, and girlhood not quite vanished. The baby had recently nursed at her breast. His napkin had been changed and he was alert and ready to play. Ida smiled at him and was rewarded by a gummy smile in return that melted her being with fierce, tear-stinging love. The adoration had not been immediate. Although she had fed and nursed him in the days following his birth, she had still been stunned and weepy, struggling with a welter of emotion, but on the fifth day, bending over his cradle, his eyes had been open, they had met hers and it was as if the cord that had been severed at birth had been miraculously reattached. She had felt the maternal tug deep inside her body. Her breasts had ached and her womb had cramped.

When she lifted him and settled his little body against her heartbeat, she had felt the resonance. It didn't matter how his conception had come about, he was still hers.

A look of immense concentration on his face, the baby succeeded in grasping her plait and Ida laughed with pride at his dexterity for he was only just three months old.

She was cooing over him, telling him what a clever boy he was, when Henry arrived fresh from a ride out, his cloak snagged with burrs, his hose muddy and his cheeks wind-burned. Ida picked William up and curtseyed. Gesturing her and the other women in the chamber to rise, Henry strode across the room to join her.

'How's my young man?' He poked William gently in the chest. The baby crowed and waved his arms, making Henry laugh.

'He does very well, sire,' Ida said. 'He's reaching for things and looking round all the time. All the women say how quick he is.'

'To be expected, given his parentage.' Henry grinned and cast Ida a speculative glance. 'You look well,' he said. 'Very well indeed, my love.'

She saw his gaze drop to her breasts and was glad she had fastened her brooches after feeding William. 'I am, sire,' she said and felt her cheeks blaze.

He laid his hand to her plait, grasping it, running his thumb over the twists of hair, the man taking greedily what his son had been offered in gentle play. 'I would have you in my chamber again,' he said. 'Now . . .'

Ida's blush deepened. She was aware of the other women studiously looking the other way; pretending they saw nothing. She had been churched forty days after William's birth and since Henry had not summoned her to his bed, she had begun to think he was no longer interested. Indeed, she had allowed herself to become complacent, wrapped up in the baby as she was. 'I . . . I am still feeding our son,' she said. 'It is a sin for a woman to lie with a man when she is giving suck, the Church says so.'

'Give him to a wet nurse,' Henry said brusquely. 'There is no reason why you should continue to feed him yourself. I want you in my bed, or do you no longer answer to me there?'

Ida swallowed. She was a pawn to be moved at Henry's whim. He had said he would care for her and their son, but it was conditional. 'Sire, I do answer to you,' she said, 'but I thought you were no longer interested.'

He gave a short smile. 'No, just biding my time. Your concern for the child is a credit to you, but he will be all right at the pap of a wet nurse.'

Feeling hollow inside, Ida gave her son to Hodierna. The older woman laid her hand over Ida's in a gesture of sympathy and support. 'You're stronger than you think,' she murmured, almost as if bestowing a blessing. 'Remember that, lass. Be as water. Flow around things, find your own path. A boulder will crush and a sword will cut, but the river will wear out stone and rust steel to powder.'

Henry's impatience continued in his chamber, where he scarcely bothered to pull the bed curtains for privacy before he was upon her. Nor did he remove his clothes or hers, but fumbling wool and linen aside with small grunts of effort, took himself in hand and thrust into her. Ida arched at the first hot shock of the intrusion, but then steeled herself to passive compliance. It was almost a year since he had lain with her and when she thought of starting it all again, she felt as if a dark cloud was descending over her life.

Henry was swiftly to business and swiftly finished so

that Ida felt like a hen trodden by a barnyard cockerel. Gasping, he rolled off her and Ida closed her legs and pulled her skirts down, trying to ignore the hot seep between her thighs. She felt used and soiled – like a whore indeed. She wondered why he had wanted her specifically for such a deed when any of the court prostitutes could have serviced him thus. Perhaps it was an act of reclamation.

He sat up and looked at her, his chest still heaving from his exertions. 'You have a woman's body now,' he said, and she thought it sounded almost like an accusation. His right hand followed his words over her breast, waist and hips.

'Did I not have one before, sire?'

He shrugged. 'It was less . . . experienced of life.'

'Because it had not yet carried a life.' It wasn't only her body that had changed, she thought. Her character had altered too as the innocent girl became the more wary and knowing woman. She wondered if Henry's rushed lovemaking had been about chasing after that girl and trying to catch what was already gone.

He asked her to rub his shoulders and as she settled behind him, she noticed there was new grey in his hair. The father of her child was not a young man.

Henry sighed and began to relax under her manipulation. 'No one does this as well as you,' he said. 'Ah, that's good.'

'Not even Christabelle?' she asked with a smile in her voice, referring to the court whore who had been his most frequent partner during her pregnancy and confinement.

He made an amused sound. 'Do I hear jealousy?'

'No, sire, what point would there be? A king will do as he pleases.'

'If only that were true.' He fell silent after that and Ida

117

did not attempt to make conversation as she used the moment to ponder her own thoughts. She did not intend to hand her son over to a wet nurse, and if that was defiance and against God's law and Henry's wishes, then so be it. Hodierna had told her that a woman who was suckling a child very seldom had a flux or became pregnant, so it was another method of preventing conception. The notion of defying Henry had been beyond her before William's birth. Henry might treat her like a pawn, but she was coming to realise that if she was to have any say in her own life, she had to become a player herself, not a piece moved hither and yon at another's behest. But being a player involved some serious thinking. Before one could make a move, one not only needed to know the rules of the game, one had to know strategy and how to play to win.

'Normandy again.' Juliana studied her son. 'When do you sail?'

'A week's time,' Roger replied. He was visiting his mother at her dower retreat at Dovercourt. Doves fluttered around her feet, pecking at the grain she was scattering for them. April sunshine gleamed on new grass stems and the air smelled fresh and green. The manor basked in the first true warmth of the year, the wooden roof shingles making small ticking noises, as if the house was gently stretching and contracting unseen limbs.

'You're not paying the scutage then,' she said, referring to the tax that a baron could pay in lieu of his annual military service.

Roger shook his head. 'Not when I can keep an eye on the men myself and perform my duty at first hand. Besides, it gives me a chance to visit Montfiquet and Corbon and the rest of the Norman estates.'

Her gaze sharpened. 'But you stay close to the King?'

'I keep him aware of my presence. He shows no sign of making a decision on my father's lands, but I serve him to the best of my ability while making alliances and connections at court.'

'Your time will come; I feel it in my bones.'

Roger sighed. 'I hope so, but it doesn't help that Gundreda's brother-in-law has been appointed justiciar. While he holds such power, there is no chance of me gaining my inheritance.'

Juliana raised a thin golden eyebrow. 'Ranulf de Glanville may be the justiciar, but that is not the be all and end all.'

'He will do all he can to further his own family's interests. The most I can hope for is not to slip and lose ground.' He gave a wry grimace. 'I am good at being patient.'

'You are also like a cauldron full of water over a slow fire,' his mother said. 'A measured rise to the simmering point, but it wouldn't take much more fuel to make you boil over.'

Roger gave her a questioning look.

'I am thinking of Fornham.'

He shook his head. 'That's not the same. There was no point in biding my time once I made the decision to leave because there was nothing worth waiting for. This time there will be a reward at the end of it . . . and if there isn't then it truly is my fault.'

Juliana watched the doves peck around her elegantly shod feet. 'Even so, my son, you have that potential. The way you ride your horses shows me you have a fire inside.'

'I am never not in command,' he said defensively.

'And that is all to the good.' Juliana gave him a weighty look.

119

Two maids walked past, returning from the dairy where they had been making cheese. Both curtseyed to Roger and Juliana as they passed. One bore a fleeting resemblance to Ida de Tosney in her bright brown eyes and glossy dark brows and Roger's glance lingered for a moment. His mother, as always, was needle-sharp.

'Perhaps you should marry into wealth while you are waiting Henry's pleasure,' she said.

Roger made a face. 'That too is in the King's gift. As a tenant-in-chief, I cannot wed without his permission and he will only grant me that which is of advantage to himself.'

'But you have had no thoughts of your own on the matter?'

Her tawny glance was too shrewd for comfort. 'Nothing worth taking beyond the thought,' he said diffidently. 'There is plenty of time.'

'So you say,' she cautioned, 'but while you do not wed and until you beget children, Gundreda's sons are your heirs. You should think on that.'

He gave an uneasy twitch of his shoulders. The detail was an irritant, but one to which he was resigned. He had told her the truth in saying that there was no woman he had seriously considered taking to wife for there were none whose dowries and person suited his requirements. Ida was a dream and he was sufficiently pragmatic to know the difference between dreams and reality.

12

Valognes, August 1180

Roger arrived in Valognes on a summer afternoon, having set out from his demesne lands near Bayeux the previous day. The sun, not far past noon, burned on his spine like a molten coin as he dismounted at the water trough in the dusty stable yard and gave his courser to his groom.

Blotting his brow on his forearm, Roger walked across the ward to ease the kinks of hard riding from his thighs and buttocks. The sound of voices and laughter drew him towards the garden area beyond the stables, fenced off and trellised with climbing roses, honeysuckle and other assorted floral delights. The women of the court were within the haven, listening to a trio of musicians while they sat at their needlework and weaving. Striped canvas pavilions had been pegged out to provide shade and there was food on wooden platters to be picked at: small tarts, bread, cheese and jugs of wine, the latter making Roger realise how thirsty he was. And there, among the women he caught sight of Ida with her infant son. Slim and vibrant in a gown of red silk, she was laughing and holding the baby above her head as she sang to him. The baby was crowing back at her and waving his swaddling-free arms. The sight jolted through Roger and he started to retreat, but Ida looked up, saw him and, with the laughter still on her face like sunshine, beckoned him into the garden.

Caught, Roger had little option but to go forward, all travel-stained and sweaty as he was.

'God's greeting, my lord Bigod,' she said, managing a curtsey, even though she now had the baby balanced on one hip. It had a nimbus of soft dark hair and eyes of Ida's bright hazel-brown.

'And to you, mistress,' Roger bowed. 'You are looking well.' Better than well, he thought. Good enough to eat.

'I am indeed well, my lord. And you?' A delicate flush tinted her cheeks. 'It is a while since you've been at court.'

'Yes, I am well.' He beat at his clothes. 'Travel-worn, but nothing that a good wash won't remedy.' He could hear how stilted and awkward his voice was, and he felt that way too. Wooden as a tree. 'I should go,' he said, 'I have matters to attend to.' He was acutely aware of the other women watching them and whispering behind their hands. 'I did not mean to disturb you.'

'Not at all,' Ida smiled and shifted the baby on her hip. It looked at him and sucked its fat little fingers. A plaited blue ribbon encircled its wrist. It was wearing a minute linen shirt with the tiniest embroidery stitches around the neck. 'Please, enjoy the garden if you will. Take some wine; you must be thirsty.'

Roger shook his head. 'Thank you, mistress, but I have to go. Perhaps another time.' He bowed to her and walked away, silently cursing himself for acting like a tongue-tied squire. He knew some men found it easy to engage in idle chit-chat with women, and he envied the likes of William Marshal their way of knowing what to say and being immediately at ease. He had felt an enormous pang

122

at the sight of Ida laughing with the baby, her straight, slender form enhanced by that red dress. She was Henry's; she wasn't for him. He was looking at something he couldn't afford.

Ida watched him leave and felt sharp disappointment. She would have loved him to stay, but knew why he had refused. Even the men who dared to flirt with her were circumspect because no one wanted to incur Henry's wrath, and Roger more than any of them dared not anger the King. Returning to the women, she sat down among them, her son in her lap. Ignoring their nudges, their teasing and giggles, she gave the baby a crust to chew on with his four milk teeth, a distant look in her eyes.

'You wanted to talk to me,' Goscelin said.

Ida looked up from the cradle blanket she was stitching, using up scraps of fabric left over from the cutting-out of gowns. A cold February wind was blasting down the valley of the Eure, but there was an optimism of spring about it too. She hadn't seen her brother since the previous summer for he had been away from court, but he was here now, and she was grabbing the opportunity while she had it. He was of age, had been given seisin of his lands and was thus his own man, albeit a very young one still feeling his way.

'Yes,' she said, and moved on the bench, giving him room to sit and stretch his legs towards the fire. It was one of the top rooms of the castle at Ivry, busy with other women, but they had drawn off a little to give her and Goscelin privacy.

Baby William tottered up to his uncle, a ball of fleece-stuffed leather in one hand.

'Walking?' said Goscelin with a smile.

'Since before the Christmas feast,' Ida replied, her face

123

aglow with pride. 'He's so quick and clever. He's talking too.'

'Ball,' said William, giving credence to Ida's boast. 'Ball, ball, ball!' He laughed on the last exclamation and threw his toy. Goscelin caught it and gently handed it back.

'I expect the King dotes on him?'

'He does,' Ida said pensively. Henry wasn't a frequent visitor to the nursery but neither was his son forgotten. The times he did put in an appearance, he was always fascinated and amused by the infant's doings. Proud too.

'What's wrong?' Goscelin asked.

Ida shook her head. 'Nothing, but I have a boon to ask of you.'

He picked up the ball as the baby dropped it again and made an expansive gesture with his other hand. 'Name it. I will help if I can, you know I will.'

Now she had come to it, the words stuck in Ida's throat. She looked down at her hands, well tended and adorned by the rings Henry had given to her. 'I have been thinking for a long time,' she said hesitantly at last. 'In fact from soon after William was born . . . I do not come to this lightly.' Glancing sidelong, she saw that Goscelin's relaxed posture had stiffened as he realised she wasn't just going to request something simple and domestic of him. She almost lost her courage, but knew that if she did not finish, the moment would pass and it would be her own fault. 'The King has many women,' she continued after a deep breath, 'and I know that one day he will tire of me.'

'But you will still be important to him.' Goscelin patted her hand in awkward reassurance. 'You are the mother of his son.'

'But I want to be more than one of the King's concubines!' she said with vehemence. 'I want a husband and

124

a home and to be cleansed of sin. I want to be an honourable wife, not the King's whore.'

He winced at her last word. 'You are not a whore – never say that. I forbid it!'

'Then what am I?' Ida demanded. 'Cladding my place at court in daintier words does not change what is underneath. If he summons me to his chamber, to his bed, I am bound to his bidding. Is that the life you would have for your sister?'

Goscelin cleared his throat and looked embarrassed. 'No,' he said. 'Of course I would rather see you wed and settled.'

Ida looked at her brother with misgiving and wondered if he were capable of what she wanted from him. But what other choice did she have? 'Then I want you to suggest to him that I should have a husband,' she said. 'You are no longer in wardship. You have the right.'

Goscelin looked pensive. 'That is truly your wish?'

She raised her chin. 'It is. I would not have asked you otherwise because I know it is difficult.'

He rumpled his hair, making it stand up in dark tufts so that he looked like a boy. Ida's confidence in him wavered further. 'Do you have someone in mind?' he asked.

'Yes.' She lifted little William on to her knee and kissed the top of his head. 'I want you to suggest Roger Bigod to him.'

He pursed his lips and said nothing. Ida stifled feelings of panic and waited out the moment, her breathing as soft and shallow as her son's.

At length Goscelin nodded. 'He is an honourable man and I would willingly accept him as my brother by marriage, but I do not know if the King will approve. He might want to keep you to himself.'

'And that is why you must tread a careful path. I do not want him becoming jealous or questioning my loyalty to him. He has been betrayed in the past and it will be all too easy for him to think that way when nothing could be further from the truth.'

'Does Roger Bigod know your thoughts?'

Ida shook her head. 'No, and I do not know his. I would hope him interested enough to agree, but I realise his position with the King is delicate.'

'And this would not tip the balance?'

'Not if Henry were brought to believe it his own notion.'

Goscelin gave her a look filled with surprise and wariness. 'You have been thinking about this, haven't you?'

'Yes,' she said, 'because if I do not do this for myself, I cannot complain when Henry eventually settles a husband of his own choosing upon me.'

Goscelin sighed and rose to his feet. 'I make no promises, sister, but I will see what I can do.'

Ida's stomach swooped with relief and anxiety as she kissed his cheek in farewell. 'Thank you.'

He looked wry. 'Save that for afterwards,' he said. 'I might fail.'

Henry considered the young man whom he had just gestured to rise from his kneeling position. Goscelin de Tosney was fidgety and on edge – he hadn't yet learned the courtier's art of dissembling and control. It was interesting to watch in the same way that it was interesting to watch a puppy learning the perils of chasing after wasps. He had presented Henry with the gift of an ornamental gold flower set with a sapphire. Henry was rather taken with the item and thought that rather than gift it to the Church, which was the usual destination of such objects, he might keep it in his chamber.

'I am deducing you have a favour to ask of me,' he said drily as he ran his forefinger around the tips of one of the stiff, shiny leaves.

The young man glanced around, assessing who else was within earshot. Henry bit down on a smile. The Bishops of Bayeux and Winchester were not going to be interested in what this young lightweight had to say.

'Sire, I would speak with you about my sister.'

Henry raised a curious eyebrow. 'Is that so?'

De Tosney reddened. 'I was wondering what you intend to do about the disposal of her marriage.'

That did take Henry by surprise. He would not have expected such a matter to enter the young man's head, although of course it might be the first flexing of muscle on Goscelin's part. Exerting his authority on a domestic matter was a good testing ground. Intrigued, Henry decided to see where Goscelin would take the issue. 'I have thought upon the matter now and again,' he said with a man-to-man gesture. 'I would be a fool not to realise there are many men keen to take her to wife.'

He had indeed pondered settling her on this courtier or that as a reward. She seldom shared his bed these days. As she grew in confidence as a mother and away from her former dewy, virginal innocence, he had moved on to other conquests, but he still enjoyed her company. Having her sit and sew in his chamber was akin to having a favourite hound at his feet, and no one else could rub his shoulders in quite the same way.

'Certainly, sire, but there is one in my opinion who stands out and to whom I think she will be well suited.'

Henry made a gesture of encouragement.

Goscelin shuffled his feet. 'Sire, I request permission to approach Roger Bigod on the matter.'

Intrigued and mildly surprised, Henry leaned back in

his chair and pressed his forefinger to his lips. The suggestion was sound enough from de Tosney's point of view.
A good match in fact. Bigod wasn't at court, having crossed
the Narrow Sea following the Christmas feast at Le Mans,
so it was doubtful he had put Goscelin up to this.
Interesting. 'Why should Roger Bigod stand out above the
others?' he asked bluntly.

Goscelin flushed. 'He has lands that march with mine
in East Anglia. He is a good soldier and he knows the
law. He will treat my sister with honour.'

'Despite the reputation his sire had with lands and
women?' Henry said cynically. 'Were I in your position,
that would be a concern.'

'Sons are not their fathers, sire.'

Henry gave a snort of bitter amusement. 'If that is
true, then it's to my detriment and Roger Bigod's benefit.
Has your sister said anything to you?'

'She was not averse to the notion should you give
permission.'

Henry narrowed his eyes. 'And Roger Bigod?'

'Knows nothing of this matter, sire. There would be
no point without your yeasay.'

'This is entirely your own notion?'

'Yes, sire.'

Henry eyed Goscelin's red ears with scepticism. He
thought of Ida in his chamber, sitting quietly over her
sewing. He thought of her dimpled smile, her impish
sense of humour, and the soothing motion of her hands
upon his tense muscles. He didn't want to think of her
never performing that service for him again. He
certainly didn't want to imagine her doing it for another,
younger man. Roger Bigod had been remarkably
patient, placid and hard-working despite the fact that
the issue of the inheritance had been dragging on for

four years. He had not quibbled over the third penny of the shire going into the exchequer's coffers rather than his own, or over the loss of income from the disputed lands, which amounted to several hundred pounds a year. The phlegmatic nature went deep, but Henry suspected that fire smouldered beneath with the potential to flare up. If he gave Ida to Roger and Roger rebelled, she would be drawn into it and he didn't want that to happen. Then again, giving Ida to Roger might be a sop to keep him quiet, especially if he conceded a few of the East Anglian manors held in crown custody as a marriage gift. He looked narrowly at Goscelin, who was trying to appear the suave courtier and not succeeding.

'It is an interesting proposal,' he said. 'But a weighty one and it needs more thought before I can give a decision. I am not refusing you, but neither am I prepared to grant you leave on the moment.'

'Sire, I understand.' Goscelin bowed.

Henry glanced beyond him where more supplicants waited to offer him gifts in exchange for his ear. 'We'll talk again,' he said, and consigned the interview to the side of his mind.

Under Hodierna's supervision, Ida crushed the ingredients for a hair fragrance in a mortar. There were dried rose petals and watercress, scrapings of nutmeg and powdered root of galangal. A wonderful aroma rose from the blended elements, fresh and clean, but with an underlying sultry, spicy warmth.

'Now add the rose water,' Hodierna instructed, 'but carefully, no more than a spoonful at a time.'

Ida did so. She loved this kind of work and was good at it, for she was meticulous and had a deft touch with

129

all things practical. Hodierna often taught her lore and recipes – although the one with ingredients involving a dead lizard was not one she intended using very often, even if it was supposed to make dark tresses thick and glossy. This particular recipe was for a fragrance to be combed through clean dry hair.

'Yes, that's it, excellent,' Hodierna said. 'Now you need to—' She looked up. 'You have a visitor, mistress.'

Turning, Ida saw Goscelin advancing on them and her breathing shortened. Hodierna curtseyed and diplomatically moved away to talk to one of the other women.

With great care, Ida decanted her ingredients into another bowl, straining them through a piece of fine linen. She affected an air of calm, even though his expression told her what his words had yet to do.

'He refused, didn't he?' she said woodenly.

Goscelin peered into the cloth and sniffed the aromatic brown sludge. 'No, he said he needed time to think about it.'

Ida prodded the residue. 'Which is as good as saying he refused, or that he will take a very long time to think.' For a moment, her eyes were hot and she had to swallow hard. What else had she expected to hear?

'I think he does mean what he says,' Goscelin said earnestly. 'It took him by surprise, that's all – and he wasn't sure about Roger Bigod. He doesn't trust him.' His expression brightened a little. 'He wasn't averse to the notion of me finding you a husband. Don't worry about that.'

Ida compressed her lips. There were several unwed barons and knights at court who made her feel she would rather remain a concubine than be wife to any of them. 'I am glad he thinks I should be wed,' she said after a moment, 'but I will not go from the frying pan into the fire.'

Goscelin squared his shoulders. 'There are men other

130

than Roger Bigod, sister. He's not the only one who would add lustre to our line.'

'Indeed, but I will not marry a husband because he happens to be conveniently to hand.'

He looked wounded. 'You were the one who said you were dissatisfied with your lot. If the only man you will have is Roger Bigod, then you may be waiting a long time.'

Ida stiffened her spine and lifted the linen to watch the residue slowly drip into the pot. The concentrated scent was powerful and feminine and boosted her resolve. She cast Goscelin a stubborn look. 'Then I will wait.'

He gave an impatient twitch of his shoulders. 'You don't know him beyond moments at court.'

'Would I know any other man better?'

'What if I find someone suitable for you in the mean-time? Would you at least consider?'

Ida shrugged. 'Yes,' she said, to humour his masculine sense of authority, although she did not intend to do any such thing.

He looked at her for a long moment, then shook his head and gave her an exasperated smile. 'Hold out for Bigod then,' he said, 'and pray the King makes him an earl. Then you'll be a countess.'

Ida had considered the notion when daydreaming. Countess of Norfolk. Lady of East Anglia. The idea was like looking at the sea from the safety of the shore. But let Goscelin think that was part of her reasoning. To have an earldom in the family was a thing of great prestige and more secure than the favour a mistress could command.

Her brother sniffed her morning's work. 'What's this, a love philtre?'

She eyed him. 'Drink some and see.'

He laughed and shook his head. 'I wouldn't dare.' Bowing in the direction of the other women, he left the room.

'Well?' asked Hodierna, returning to Ida's side. She had picked up little William and balanced him on one ample hip.

Ida heaved a sigh and took her son into her own arms. 'Now,' she said, 'we wait,' and wondered how much fortitude she was going to need.

13

Chinon, Easter 1181

In recent years, Ida had often had to cope with new and difficult experiences that tested her mettle to breaking point, but never had she felt such terror; never had she felt so helpless. Lying on the bed beside her infant son, she bathed his burning little body with tepid rose water and watched his chest rise and fall as swiftly as a panting dog's as the fever consumed him. A blotchy rash covered his torso and he had been sick several times in the night. The vomiting had now abated but in its place had come a barking cough that racked him so hard it left little room for breath, let alone tears. She had managed to spoon a little honey and water into him and although he was almost weaned, she had begun nursing him again, partly in the hope that he would take in sustenance, partly to give him comfort.

With gentle strokes, she wiped his scalding body and sang him a nonsense song about a bird in a cage. He whimpered and snuffled. His eyes were open, but unseeing and opaque as dull brown pebbles. She had heard there was fever in the town and although the other women had tried to keep it from her, she knew that some children had died, including a shoesmith's infant son who was the same age as her baby. Consumed by guilt and terror, weeping for the pain of the mother who had lost her child, Ida had prayed to Saint Clement and Saint Bueno for their intercession, had lit candles, given alms and begged God to spare William.

She wrung out the cloth again and felt the heat from him within the moist linen as she bathed him. 'Dear Holy Virgin,' she whispered. 'Don't let him suffer for my sins. Don't let him die. Take me instead!'

Goda came to the bedside and gently touched her shoulder. 'My lady, you are sought.'

Looking up through her distraction, Ida met the gaze of Bonhomme, one of Henry's ushers. Sympathy gleamed in his eyes, but his face was expressionless. 'The King commands your company, mistress.'

Ida was appalled. 'For pity's sake! His son is sick and in peril of his life. Would he have me desert a mother's duty?'

Bonhomme shifted his weight. 'Lady, it is for the King to say, not me. I only obey him as must we all. I am sorry for the child's illness, but there are women who can tend him while you are gone.'

'They are not his mother,' she said through clenched teeth.

'Even so, mistress.' He bowed to her, but made it plain she had no choice.

Ida pushed herself to her feet. She knew she must look a draggled mess but had no intention of tidying and perfuming herself for Henry. Let him see her as she was, the haggard, desperate mother of an infant struggling to keep life in his small body. Her only hope was that Henry would see her condition and send her straight back to their son.

'I'll tend him.' Hodierna came to the bedside. 'He'll be all right with me, won't you, little sweetheart?' She knelt stiffly on her arthritic knees, took the cloth from Ida and began wiping the baby. 'Go, do what you must.' She flashed Ida a look filled with warning and compassion.

Somehow, Ida made room in her mind for more than her anxiety and focused on what Henry required of her. The sooner her duty to him was finished, the sooner she could return to her son.

Henry was waiting for her in his chamber, pacing restlessly in front of the fire. There were a few servants about, but their presence was unobtrusive and Henry was obviously having a moment to himself. When she entered, he looked up, smiled and beckoned her to come to him.

'I've missed you, sweeting.' Taking her hands in his, he kissed her on the lips, and then held her away to look at her. 'Tears?' He thumbed her wet cheek. 'What's all this?'

Ida sniffed and wiped her hand with the trailing sleeve of her gown. 'I am sorry, sire. My son . . . our son William . . . he is sick with the spotted fever and I am afraid for him. I thought—' Her voice cracked. 'I thought you knew.'

His voice was placatory. 'Sweetheart, I do, and I also know you need a respite. Let others care for him awhile. The physician says that once the fever passes he will recover.' He drew her to the bed, sat her down upon it and made her drink a cup of spiced wine sweetened with sugar.

'Sire, I know my duty to you,' Ida said as she lowered the cup, 'but I am his mother. I should be with him.' She clutched his sleeve with an imploring hand. The wine lay like molten lead in her stomach and made her feel sick.

'You don't wear my ring any more?' he said sharply.

Ida swallowed. 'It's in my coffer. I took it off while I was tending our son. I didn't want to scratch him and I was too distracted to think to put it on when your summons came.' She heard her own breathless panic and knew she was not handling the situation well.

An impatient frown forked Henry's brow. 'The other women will take care of him for now,' he growled. 'It will be all right I tell you.'

Mutely she nodded.

'Ida, look at me.' He tilted up her chin on his fore-finger to explore her face. 'Ah.' His voice softened. 'You are a beautiful, beautiful girl and I love you dearly.'

Ida's throat was so tight she almost choked. How was she supposed to answer?

'Your brother has spoken to you, I understand?'

'About what, sire?' She looked blank, for her mind was preoccupied with her son and her need to return to him.

'About his notion that I give you in marriage to Roger Bigod.'

His words took Ida's breath. She felt as if she had been slapped in the face with a wet cloth and for a moment could only stare at Henry open-mouthed and stunned. She couldn't cope with this, not now, not on top of every-thing else.

Henry said irritably, 'Do I take it he hasn't?'

She struggled to focus, to bring her mind to the place where it had to be now. 'Sire, he has, but it was a while ago. He told me you were thinking on the matter.'

'I still am, my love. He says you have no objections. Is that true?'

Her stomach boiled. There was acid in her throat. 'No sire,' she whispered. 'I have no objections.'

'Would you find marriage to him agreeable?' He caressed her hair and the side of her neck with the back of his hand and she closed her eyes, willing herself not to be sick.

'He seems an honourable man, sire.'

'And you would give up your life at court for him? All your finery, all the dances and entertainments?'

Ida struggled to control her breathing. 'I would do my best to adapt, sire.'

'You're a brave girl as well as a beautiful one. Sometimes it is the gentle, quiet ones who have the most strength.'

The silence stretched for several heartbeats. Ida heard a candle sputter on an impurity in the wax, saw the flame waver and spark. She tried not to imagine it was her son's life she was seeing, flickering on the border between staying alight and snuffing out.

'I don't want to give you up . . .' he said and, turning her face towards him, kissed her, first softly but with increasing possession and vigour. 'I don't want to lose you to another man.'

As he made love to her, Ida retreated within herself, separating her mind from her body. It would soon be over, she told herself. And then she could return to her vigil over William. The other things she would think about later because she could not face in two directions at once.

When Henry finished, he lay beside her, recovering his breath, one arm flung across his eyes. Ida bit her lip, stared at the top of the bed canopy and wondered how soon he would give her leave to go. The candle was still burning, but for how long? She watched it, dreading to see it gutter again, and closed her legs.

Henry turned his head on the embroidered bolster. 'Perhaps I have lost you already.' He gave a tired sigh. 'Put your clothes on and go back to the child. I will not trouble you more tonight.'

In haste, Ida donned her chemise. 'Thank you, sire!'

With the relief that he was letting her return to William, came gratitude and guilt. She had thought he might make her stay to rub his back or massage his feet.

'I will come and see him in the morning,' Henry said, 'and you.' He kissed her cheek.

Ida ran back to the women's chamber. Mathilde, one of the maids who had recently given birth, was holding William at her exposed breast and he was asleep, his mouth still at her nipple and his cheeks as shiny and red as apples. Hodierna was sitting beside the girl, watching over her and the baby. Ida felt a storm of love for her son, swirled through with jealousy at the sight of the other girl nursing him.

'He has taken one side and sleeps well now, bless him,' Hodierna smiled. 'I think he is a little improved.'

Ida swept her skirts out of the way and sat on the bed, taking him from Mathilde without looking at her. The latter tucked her breast back inside the feeding slit in her gown and exchanged a rueful glance with Hodierna. William whimpered, but as Ida cuddled him and stroked his face, he settled down. Perhaps he was a little cooler, she thought. For the moment at least, the fever had ceased to mount.

Diplomatically, Hodierna and Mathilde moved away to leave Ida alone with him, Hodierna pausing to press Ida's shoulder and give her a maternal kiss on the temple. Ida whispered a 'Thank you' to the women, feeling remorse and guilt for her jealousy now that William was back in her arms.

For the rest of the night, Ida sat propped up on her bed, cradling her baby. By the light from the steady burning candle, she watched him breathe. His hair was damp with sweat and curling at the ends, his eyelashes gummy and the rash on his skin a pottage of deep red blotches. She loved him so hard that she felt as if she herself was being burned up by her emotion. Even if fornication was wrong, even if she had despaired on first discovering she was with child, the love she felt for her son now was immolating her.

In the morning, on his way to hunt, Henry came to see his son. Booted and spurred, keen to be away, he nevertheless stood by the cradle for several moments.

'He is a little improved, sire,' Ida said. She felt desperately tired from her night-long vigil, but William's fever had lessened and his eyes had lost their foggy look. He had recently taken suck again. It was too soon to say he was getting better, but his condition was more settled.

Henry gave an exasperated shrug. 'Women always fuss too much.' After another long look, he turned from the cradle, drawing Ida with him. He tucked a stray tendril of hair behind her ear and said, 'I have been thinking; it is right that you should have a husband and a home before God. I have decided to let your brother moot the idea of a match to Roger Bigod.'

Ida gazed at him, unsure what to say. After the night that had gone before, the words were like straws spinning on the surface of the stream.

'Are you struck dumb by your good fortune, or is it perhaps dismay?' Henry's smile had an edge to it.

Ida strove to pull herself together. 'No, sire,' she said. 'Indeed, I thank you, but I have been at my wits' end over William; I barely know my own name this morning. I am pleased, truly I am.'

'Ah, Ida . . .' Henry's smile softened and grew a little sad. 'One day you'll grow a harder shell and I will be sorry to see it − but for you it will be a good thing, I think.' He removed a ring and taking her hand slid it on to the third finger of her right one. 'I'll have prayers said for the little one.' He patted her cheek and strode out, already calling to his huntsmen, the moment of intimacy behind him as another piece of business accomplished.

Ida knew she should be euphoric, but all that came was a deepening of her exhaustion – as if she had been pulling on a tug rope for a long, long time, and her strength had finally given out. She looked down at the ring he had given her: plaited gold, set with a rare intaglio. Another piece to add to her magpie collection. One to begin, one to end. She swayed where she stood and Hodierna hurried across to her, calling for Goda. Together the women bore Ida back to bed. 'Sleep,' said Hodierna, drawing the hangings around her. 'The child is not in danger now, and you will be of no use to him if you do not rest a little at least. I will wake you if you are needed, I promise.'

Ida was too tired to argue, but remained anxious as she watched them put William in his cradle at the bedside. She was still terrified that she was going to lose him.

'I may be growing old but my hearing is still sharp,' Hodierna murmured as she closed the bed curtains. 'Seems as if the tide is on the turn, hmm?'

'I hope so,' Ida said. She fell into a restless slumber and dreamed of a long, flat seashore with damp sand of dull gold washed by a restless blue-grey sea.

14

Yarmouth, August 1181

Roger paced along the shore, picked up a piece of drift-wood and hurled it as far as the strength in his arm could send it. His two wire-haired gazehounds tore in pursuit, muscles bunching and rippling under their iron-grey coats. The wind buffeted his cloak and streamed through his hair and he absorbed the smell and taste of the sea with pleasure. Further along the shore, fishermen were mending their nets and lines and smoke was rising from the salt-pan fires. Out at sea, he could see several vessels making headway towards the harbour where they would land their catches of sleek silver herring.

'So,' he said to Goscelin de Tosney, who was striding out at his side. 'I assume this is more than a social visit?'

Goscelin had arrived as Roger was setting out with the dogs. Since Roger had needed to feel fresh wind in his hair and firm sand under his boot soles, he had brought him along the beach rather than settling down indoors. With Henry back in England, Roger would be following the court again, and this was his last opportunity for a while to inspect his coastline and please himself. Yesterday he had even been out with his fishermen on one of the herring boats and had enjoyed helping to hoist and reef the sail and haul in the catch.

Goscelin cleared his throat. 'You would think me strange if that were all.'

Roger grinned. 'Perhaps.' The dogs growled and tugged at the driftwood branch, play-fighting each other for it. 'But then there is much in the world that is strange.'

Goscelin stooped and picked up a strand of gnarly green seaweed. 'I came to find out if you have any intentions as regards marriage,' he said.

Roger's gaze swivelled from the dogs to his companion and widened in astonishment. 'Hah, and now I *do* think you strange, my lord. Why would you want to ask me such a thing? Of what importance is it to you or indeed what business is it of yours what my intentions are?' An imperious note entered his voice.

Goscelin flushed. 'It might be of great importance, and it might indeed be my business.' He tossed the seaweed away into the wind. A back-flurry of wet sand smacked him in the face and he had to spit.

Roger had only one notion where this was leading, and the sudden enormity of it was like being struck in the chest by a jousting lance at full gallop. He strove to remain impassive. 'For the moment I have no plans to wed, and if I did, I would need the King's permission. I can do nothing without his consent, as you must know, being a tenant-in-chief yourself.'

Goscelin nodded and a gleam entered his brown eyes. 'Indeed, but suppose he were to offer you my sister and give you his blessing?' He walked backwards, facing Roger. 'What would you say then?'

The words resonated through the centre of Roger's body and suddenly it was hard to breathe. 'Just how far has this supposition gone?'

Goscelin sleeved sand grains off his face. 'I've spoken to the King and he is prepared to release her in marriage.'

'And you suggested me as a candidate?'

'You came first to mind and the King was willing to give his consent. I may be mistaken but I thought you had an affinity for my sister.'

Roger walked towards the sea, leaving footprints that overlaid the sandy ribs created by the motion of the waves. His mind tumbled over and over like a stone rolled into shore by the tide. If this proposal came with the will of the King, it must benefit Henry in some way. Perhaps he was tiring of Ida and wanted to have her off his hands – or else respectably married but still available to him should the whim arise, making of her husband a convenient keeper and bawd. Henry wouldn't make this decision out of unselfishness, for Henry wasn't like that. Yet whatever the baggage accompanying the offer, it was a fine one. Ida had youth, beauty, good dower lands and was proven the fertile mother of a son. While Roger was far from certain he wanted to accept the offer, turning it down here and now would be a mistake. And through his pragmatic thoughts ran a blaze of liquid gold. He could have Ida with the will of the King!

'There is more than affection to be considered in this matter,' he said to Goscelin. 'I am the King's servant in all things and I am cautiously favourable to the match, but the details of the marriage contract will have to be right and I will know everything there is to know before I go further.' He gave Goscelin a hard look, intimating by expression that he was not going to be taken for a dupe.

Goscelin grinned from ear to ear and his feet danced on the sand as if he could not keep them still. 'I would expect no less and I am truly honoured that you agree to consider the match. I was afraid you might refuse out of hand and there is no man I would rather have my sister marry even though many would fulfil the role well.'

Roger raised his brows at the unsubtle flattery, but the words also bolstered his anxiety that many would indeed be capable of keeping the King's darling safe against the King's need. 'Does Ida know of these plans for her future, or is she going to be told at an opportune moment?' His tone of voice was harsher than he had intended.

Goscelin sobered. 'She is aware,' he said, 'and she is content.'

Roger made a conscious effort to relax his tense shoulders. There was more to this than met the eye. If one bought meat, then one also bought bones. 'I would have a meeting with your sister in private conference, rather than depend on matchmakers and go-betweens,' he said, 'and then I will decide.'

Goscelin hesitated.

Roger gave him a hard look. 'Or do you not trust me to be honourable?'

'No, my lord, I do trust you, but Ida . . .' Then he inclined his head. 'I will see what can be done.'

'But Ida' what? Roger wondered. Wasn't to be trusted herself? Wasn't really 'content' and would refuse to meet him alone? Well, like the sea and shore, what he desired to know would wash up in the fullness of time, and whether it was a gemstone or a rotted corpse remained to be seen.

Whistling to his dogs, he turned away from the shore towards the settlement. 'I have no castle for her,' he said, bracing himself against the buffet of the wind. The damp sand, softer away from the sea, yielded and flaked under his boot soles.

Goscelin turned with him, dark curls whipping into his face. 'But you will do, my lord, one day.'

Roger's expression was set and closed. If he did choose

144

to wed her, he had no intention of being compared with Henry and emerging as second-best. 'Oh yes,' he said. 'One day, I will have a fortress to rival anything that an Angevin can raise.' And then he shrugged. 'But first the foundations have to be laid. You cannot build on sand and expect your walls to stand. A fortress needs to be just that: a bastion against all comers.'

Juliana shook her head in dismay over Roger's hands. 'What have you been doing?' she asked. 'Guiding a ploughshare?' She turned them over to examine the palms. 'Look at these calluses.' She ordered one of her women to fetch a pot of salve.

Roger grinned. 'I did plough a furrow a while back,' he said. 'We had a new pair of oxen on the demesne at Framlingham and a new coulter and we had a ceremony to turn the first sod.'

She raised her brows at him. 'Peasant,' she teased.

'If a lord does not take an interest in his land, then who will?' He shook his head. 'No, these are the result of working with the horses, and of sword practice – both knightly pursuits.' His voice held a teasing note of its own, for he knew how fastidious and discerning his mother was. He wasn't going to tell her the worst of the calluses were the result of hauling on nets and seeing to the sail on a Yarmouth herring boat.

Taking the pot of rose-water salve from the woman, Juliana placed a generous dab on his palm and began rubbing it into his skin. A fragrant herbal aroma rose from the unguent. 'I remember your hands when they were as small and soft as petals,' she said, then laughed a little. 'A long time ago . . . I have always regretted that I wasn't there to see you grow up, but I had no choice. My leaving was forced upon me.'

145

'I know that,' he said. 'It is over – in the past.'

For a moment, there was silence between them and the silence itself was a bridge. Juliana continued to rub until the unguent had disappeared. 'So,' she said, 'what have you been doing with your time other than ploughing furrows and attending to your weapon play?'

'Hearing pleas,' he replied. 'Talking to the burghers and shipmasters in Ipswich and the fishermen in Yarmouth. Inspecting the salt pans . . . considering a proposal of marriage.'

Her gaze sharpened. 'Made by whom?'

He told her what Goscelin de Tosney had said. 'I need your advice since it's a family matter – and perhaps a woman's matter too.'

Juliana grew thoughtful. 'Ida de Tosney,' she murmured. 'She has some useful lands and connections. Her kin are married into the royal house of Scotland – even if she is related to that witch Gundreda.'

Roger gestured in negation. 'There is no love between them.'

'I cannot imagine Gundreda inspiring love in anyone,' his mother said tartly, then fixed him with a serious stare. 'If you like Ida de Tosney well – and be very sure that you like her well – then marry her with my blessing.' She raised a forefinger in warning. 'But if you are not certain, then leave her be and find someone else. It is not a good thing to take into your future something that doesn't please you to the soul. Do not reach for something just because it catches your eye. Make sure it goes beyond that. I speak from experience. Will she be a helpmate? Do you think alike?'

'I do like her well,' Roger said, and felt a tingle of warmth in his solar plexus, 'but as to whether we will suit, I have yet to find out. A few conversations and meetings at court are not enough to know.'

'Then find out, because lands and prestige are well and good, but you are building the next generation too, and you need strong foundations. There are many young women with suitable dowries and ancestry.'

Her words were so much like his own thoughts when talking to Goscelin at Yarmouth that Roger almost smiled. He was glad to hear his opinion validated. 'If I do decide to accept this match, I will not go into it blindfolded,' he said. 'I will know the motives behind the King's consent.'

Juliana nodded. 'Indeed. Never take anything for granted.'

'I won't,' he replied. 'I've learned my lessons well.'

She gave him a sidelong smile. 'Even so, I will look to my coffers lest I find myself in need of finery to dance at a wedding.'

Roger rode into Woodstock on a fine morning in late September, with the leaves flickering from the trees in lozenges of orange and gold, here and there marbled with yellow and green. The court was at Marlborough for a few days, but Ida and various others of Henry's domestic household had settled at the palace rather than progress with the rest of the entourage.

As Roger dismounted, a servant directed his groom to the stables with the horses and Roger's other attendants were shown to the retainers' quarters. Roger himself was brought to a chamber in the palace he had not frequented before, it being one of the guest rooms for important royal visitors. Usually when at Woodstock, he had had to make do with the communal lodgings or his own canvas pavilion. This particular chamber boasted a bed with a feather mattress, fine linen sheets and a soft woollen cover. A steaming bathtub had been prepared and Roger eyed it with surprise. Water for washing he had expected, but not the elaborate luxury of a tub. A pitcher of wine stood on a side table and food had been set out: fig pastries, sugar-dusted wafers and small almond paste balls encasing raisins. Roger grimaced. He was being treated like royalty and the comparison was unsettling, because perhaps other comparisons would be made too.

A brightness of red and yellow on the bed caught his eye and he saw that it was a set of tourney barding for a warhorse in his colours, with the red cross of Bigod detailed in the trim around the edges. He stared at it, bemused but admiring the intricate needlework.

'It's a gift,' Goscelin said, stepping over the threshold. 'My sister has a talent with the needle and she wanted to stitch something personal to you.' He advanced into the room. 'Is everything to your satisfaction?'

Roger nodded. 'It is . . . more than I expected,' he said.

Goscelin looked pleased. 'Ida arranged it all. She has a talent for such things. She knows how to make guests welcome and comfortable.'

Roger felt more overwhelmed than comfortable just now. He would have been happier with just a ewer and a towel, but that was because he was on edge and trying to cope in unfamiliar territory. He could, however, see the reasoning behind this display. He was being shown what an asset Ida would be as a wife should he accept the offer.

Servants bustled round him, efficiently divesting him of his garments and encouraging him into the tub. In bemusement, he complied. The water was hot and scented with rose water and herbs he could not immediately identify. A bath maid washed his hair with white Spanish soap and barbered his stubble. In anticipation of this meeting, Roger was already clean and well groomed, but by the time the attendants had finished with him, he felt as if

148

he had been polished until his bones were ready to gleam through his skin.

Goscelin had been hovering throughout the process, drinking wine, sampling the food laid out – more so than Roger who was feeling increasingly ill at ease. At Framlingham, he was accustomed to fending for himself on many levels, and while he demanded quality from his possessions and expected good service, all this twiddling, attention and luxury was unsettling. Would Ida expect this of her daily life if he married her?

'Are you ready?' Goscelin asked as Roger latched his belt buckle. 'I'll take you to Ida. She's looking forward to talking to you.'

Roger's mind was turning like a treadwheel, but going nowhere. What was he going to say to her in these strange and stilted circumstances? He glanced at the horse barding and supposed he could thank her for it, although he was uncertain about the correct level to pitch his gratitude for such a gift. Too effusive and she might think he was ready for immediate betrothal; not enough and it might be construed as an insult.

Goscelin brought him to a large chamber on one of the upper floors – a domestic room with vibrant hangings and painted plasterwork. Benches had been drawn up to the fireplace and women of various ages and stations were sitting there, busy sewing, spinning and gossiping. Several small children played chase, watched over by their nurses. Roger stared at the gathering in dismay because this was not the quiet meeting between himself and Ida he had envisaged. This chamber might be set apart from the masculine hurly-burly of the hall, but it was hardly private. He knew he was being eyed up and assessed by some of the younger women, who were whispering and giggling behind their hands.

Ida emerged from a group of ladies to whom she had been handing over a small child. She looked ravishing in a gown of brocaded blue wool, her lithe waist accentuated by a jewelled belt. She was blushing and the pink in her cheeks enhanced the hazelnut-brown of her eyes. 'My lord.' She curtseyed to Roger.

He half bowed in response, feeling as if his spine would snap from the effort. There was more giggling. Feeling utterly mortified, Roger threw Goscelin a furious look. How could he talk to Ida about a marriage contract with all this foolishness going on? It was neither fit nor fitting. He and Ida were the centre of attention and already he felt as if a layer of skin had been flayed off him by the knowing stares.

Straightening, he drew himself up. 'Demoiselle, this is neither the time nor the place for us to meet and discuss the future.'

Her blush intensified and she cast a warning glare at the women. 'I am sorry for this.' She touched his sleeve in an imploring gesture. 'Please stay.'

'I think not,' he said curtly. 'My affairs are not an entertainment for the gossips of this household. By your leave, mistress.' He bowed to her again, turned on his heel and, feeling utterly humiliated, strode from the chamber.

Once in the cold, fresh air of the courtyard, he leaned against the wall, breathing harshly and flooded with relief at being free of that room full of tittering women. He was in half a mind to order his horse saddled and ride out. As his mother had said, there were plenty of pickings elsewhere. He would rather fight Fornham all over again than repeat the experience of a moment ago.

Goscelin emerged from the doorway and hurried up to him.

'Never do that to me again!' Roger snarled before the

150

young man could speak. 'When I said I wanted to talk to your sister alone, I meant alone. Christ, that room had more eyes in it than a barrel of herrings on Yarmouth quay!'

Goscelin wrapped his hands round his belt and puffed out his chest. 'I thought you would respect propriety and meet in the presence of witnesses and chaperones,' he said defensively.

'Do you think so little of me that you expect me to ravish your sister if granted a moment alone?' Roger retorted, teeth bared. 'I am not the King!' He strove for control because an inner voice reminded him that he was not his father either. 'Perhaps in that case you should look elsewhere to match her!'

'My lord, I do respect your integrity,' Goscelin replied, his own complexion flushed with anger, because by his measure he had done his best. 'But my sister will not have you think her behaviour in any way improper. She is wary of a private meeting because of what has gone before and will give no reasons to have a slur cast on her character.'

Roger swallowed and made an effort. 'I will not consider her behaviour improper in any way if she agrees to a meeting alone with me. I refuse to conduct my affairs amid a bowerful of goggling women and children.' He pointed to the sundial on the wall. 'I will meet her in the orchard in an hour and I swear on my oath as a knight to treat her with respect and honour, or strike me dead. If she chooses not to come, then we both know where we stand.'

'I will do what I can,' Goscelin said, looking prim.

Not trusting himself to speak, Roger gave a stiff nod and strode away. Once in the security of his chamber, the servants dismissed, he leaned against the door and

151

groaned. Why was it so hard? he wondered. Presented with tasks of a military or judicial nature, he was clear-minded and steady as a rock, but give him a room full of giggling women and he dissolved with terror. It would have been utterly beyond him to discuss the future with Ida before such an audience.

As he calmed, he began to see Ida's side of the situation and acknowledged that her concerns were to her credit. Going to the horse barding lying on his bedcover, he unfolded it and gazed at the exquisite needlework. A deal of thought and diligence had gone into this; it must have taken a long time to stitch – perhaps several months. All the answers were here if he had the skill to follow the thread. A thoughtful expression crossed his face. With great care, he refolded the cloth, using the precision to settle his mind. He washed his face and hands in the ewer, straightened his tunic and, taking a deep breath, left the sanctuary of the chamber for the unknown exposure of the orchard.

Although it was almost October, the weather had been mild and there was still a last spurt of growth in the grass around the trees. Apple-picking was under way, but he was relieved to see that no one was at work just now. He came to a bench set under a tree that was still bowed with fruit. Picking a likely-looking candidate with a red blush on its cheek, he sat down on the oak planks, steeled himself, and waited.

Watching from the bower window, Ida saw Roger cross the yard and make his way towards the orchard. She was angry with herself for misjudging the situation. She knew Roger was self-effacing around the opposite sex, but hadn't realised how badly he would be affected.

'I don't want him to think he cannot trust me,' she said anxiously to Goscelin.

Goscelin hissed through his teeth in exasperation. 'Sister, if you do not go down to him, all your plans will come to naught – and my hard work. He's like a shying horse and his head isn't in the halter yet. It's up to you now to find the words and means.'

Ida pressed her lips together. There was no point in being cross with Goscelin. She recognised the feeling for what it was – a bandage for her own fear. She wiped her damp palms on her gown, summoned her courage and left the chamber. Making her way to the orchard, she felt queasy with apprehension. It had been a long time since she and Roger had spoken socially, and the tentative camaraderie they had built up was a slim foundation on which to conduct a discussion of this nature, especially after their recent misunderstanding.

Ida walked along the path then cut across the grass, the hem of her gown brushing the blades and cool dampness stealing up through the thin soles of her shoes. He was sitting on a bench under one of the trees, eating an apple, his legs stretched out and crossed at the ankle. From a distance, he appeared to be at ease and as she looked at him she felt terrified, because so much depended on the next few moments. He was her way out of a situation she was beginning to abhor, and she needed, as Goscelin had crudely put it, to halter her horse . . . and this wasn't just any horse. This was the best one in the stable.

At her approach, he glanced up, met her gaze briefly, then looked away and gestured to the bench. 'Come and sit, demoiselle, I pray you.'

Ida perched on the edge of the seat, folding her hands in her lap and absorbed with trepidation the strained atmosphere. He wasn't at ease in the least. She knew he could fight and administer – that given masculine pressures he possessed level-headed composure. But around women he was shy and Ida found that endearing, especially when set against men who would take what they wanted without a second thought. She had to snare him now and without mistake for there would be no other chances. She had to focus and make it come about. Gathering her courage, she drew a deep breath.

'I am sorry about what happened. I would have asked Goscelin to make a better arrangement if I had known how it would be.'

'Let it pass,' he said. 'The less said the sooner forgotten.'

Silence. Ida pressed on: 'I am glad there is warmth in the day. The nights have been cold of late, but at least the apples have ripened well and they're nearly all harvested.' She put a smile in her voice. 'I know, because I've been supervising their mulching all week.' There, she thought, that would show him that beyond being decorative, she was capable of overseeing necessary domestic tasks.

'Well, here's one you won't need to mulch.'

Ida laughed. 'I am glad to hear it.'

He cleared his throat and looked at the fruit. 'So then,' he said. 'What think you of this match?'

Ida looked down at her hands. 'It is pleasing to me if it is pleasing to you, my lord,' she said demurely.

He held his breath for a moment, then let it out on a long sigh. 'That is no answer. Let us speak honestly and not in the words of the court.'

'What fitting answer am I to give if I do not know your intent?'

There was another silence, then he said, as if dragging each word out of a vat of glue, 'For myself I am of a mind to accept the match.'

Ida's heart began to pound. 'Then I will say I am

honoured to become your wife. I think you are a fine man. Indeed,' she added, 'without false flattery I say you have greatness.'

He swivelled on the bench to stare at her in astonishment. His throat, cheeks and brow were suddenly fire-red, and his eyes as luminous as sea shallows. She wanted to touch him, to feel his skin at her fingertips, to have reassurance, yet she dared not. It was too soon.

He controlled himself and said in a nonchalant voice at odds with his ruddy complexion, 'I am not sure I think that myself, but I will not quibble with you.' A slight smile twitched his mouth corners. 'Indeed, I think we shall do very well together.'

Daring to flirt a little, she tilted her head to one side. 'And what do you think of me, my lord?'

He gave a bemused shake of his head. 'I think that you are beautiful, diligent and kind. You will grace my life and you will be my consolation.'

Ida was torn between humour and compassion, for his speech was very proper, a little stilted, and there was a sadness in it that almost choked her. Consolation for what? Not having his earldom? What he truly desired from life? His words tied her being in knots. 'You jest, my lord. You speak as if your life is over, but you are neither old nor grey.' She glanced at his hair, admiring the tints of bronze, gold and soft brown shining in the autumn sunlight. Recently washed, it gleamed and floated a little. His face was red to the tips of his ears. Ida wondered how she was going to shake him out of this painful bashfulness. Although he had said he wanted to wed her, there were no witnesses and he might change his mind. Her horse wasn't haltered yet.

'Would you care to walk a little?'

He nodded, tossed the apple core into the grass and

rose to his feet. Ida rose too and was glad the women in the bower wouldn't be able to see them even if they craned at the casement.

As they walked side by side, he didn't touch her, even to guide her arm in formal fashion, but clasped his hands tightly behind his back. There was a leaf caught in his hair and Ida reached up and brushed it gently away because she needed that moment of contact. 'The leaves are beginning to fall, my lord,' she said, as it fluttered to the ground. She considered picking it up as a keepsake, but thought it might seem strange or foolish to him and so let it lie in pale gold translucence on the grass.

'Indeed they are.'

For an instant, his gaze met hers and she saw a glint in them. Emboldened, she laid the flat of her hand to his side and, affecting to look dismayed, shook her head.

'What?' His voice was warily puzzled, but there was almost a smile on his lips.

Ah, now this had engaged him, she thought. She gave him a sidelong look through her lashes. 'I thought your side might be injured, sire, for all the woodenness that seems to be there. Perhaps you are in need of physic – in the same way some of these trees have received physic from the gardeners.'

He arched his brows at her, and then suddenly he burst out laughing and it was as if the sun had finally broken through the clouds and she glimpsed the beautiful man behind the awkwardness. 'You are comparing me to a tree,' he said, 'and a sick tree at that?'

'No, my lord, because then you would think me impertinent.'

'Perhaps you are right,' he said. 'Perhaps I am in need of physic, but not I think in the same manner as a tree.' He glanced wryly at the one under which they were

156

walking, where some of the branches had been lopped off. 'And perhaps you *are* impertinent.'

She touched him again for the pleasure of doing so, and then darted away, inviting play. 'And how would you deal with an impertinent wife?'

He frowned and hesitated and she wondered if she had been too forward or read the thaw in him amiss, but suddenly he sprang with the speed of a cat and caught her in a light grip.

'Tickle her,' he said.

Laughing, Ida broke away. 'But first you would have to catch her!' Picking up her skirts, she fled him and they played a game of chase and catch under the trees. Ida knew he must be enjoying himself because, with his coordination and her hampering skirts, he could have caught her easily but he chose to prolong the moment until they were both panting.

Finally, he closed in, grasped her hand and swung her towards his body, but his hold was still light and Ida could have freed herself if she chose – but she didn't. She was breathless, melting. Was he going to kiss her? Should she let him, or would it be too forward? He angled his head as if about to take advantage, but changed tack and, sweeping her up in his arms, carried her back to the seat under the tree and set her down so that her feet were above the ground. 'There,' he said, breathing hard, 'so shall you be served in my household. You will never want for anything, on that I give you my oath.'

Ida gazed up at him and this time he met her look for look. He held out his hand to her again and she placed hers demurely inside it. The hard strength in his fingers as he drew her to her feet sent a shock of warmth through her body and liquefying sweetness followed in its wake.

From the orchard, they strolled into the gardens, which

were losing their summer colour but retained some foliage and greenery and the occasional bloom. The fish moved sluggishly in the pools and a gardener had cast a net across the top to discourage the herons. The peacocks wandered the grounds, the iridescent males trailing their magnificent tails after them like treasure-flecked brooms, although none were displaying.

'I have to thank you for the gift of the barding for my horse,' he said. 'It must have taken you many hours of work.'

'I like to sew, my lord, and I wanted to give you something that was appropriate to your rank and skills – and that would show you mine.'

'As indeed you have. I am moved and most admiring of your industry and ability.' He did not add that her gift had been the deciding factor in the choice he had made. When he thought of the hours that had gone into the making, when he thought of the pride and care, and deliberation, he had realised that there was serious intent on her part. This was no flirtatious whim.

Ida blushed with pleasure.

He gave her a discerning look. 'You must have begun it some time ago, knowing that it might be a wasted effort.'

'Like your toil to regain the earldom that was your father's?'

'That is not the same,' he said, but smiled.

'Only in the way that a grain of sand is not a beach.'

His smile deepened. 'Then mayhap you are right,' he said. 'And one day in the future I will show you beaches stretching as far as the eye can see.'

They walked around the pool and he crouched to dip his fingers in the water. The fish were slow to rise now the weather was cooler. 'So,' he said. 'If we are set upon a match, we must see to the formalising of contracts and agree things in law . . . and choose a day.'

'Let be done whatever is needful,' Ida replied, adding on a rush, 'and let it be soon.' He looked up at her and she blushed again. 'It will be a new life for me – a new start, and such a thing cannot come too quickly.'

He shook the water from his fingers, causing droplet rings to ripple and overlap on the surface of the pond. 'Shall we say early December? Then we have time before the demands of the Christmas court, but also time to arrange a fitting marriage.'

She nodded gravely, although she wanted to laugh and dance and twirl . . . and perhaps pinch herself to prove that this was truly happening. He rose to his feet and now he offered her his arm and she laid her hand along it and shivered a little.

'Are you cold?'

Ida shook her head. 'No,' she said. 'I am happy.'

His smile in response made her dissolve. She had to swallow and blink. He would think her foolish if she cried.

'One day, if God is good, and I scatter enough grains of sand to make a beach, you will be Countess of Norfolk and lady of a great estate,' he said as they completed the circuit of the garden.

Ida was tempted to reply that she did not need these things, but she was sensitive and understood his need to say them. 'And you will be an earl,' she told him, smiling. 'Our sons will follow in your footsteps and our daughters will know how fortunate they are in their father.'

She heard his breath catch in his chest and saw the colour rise in his face again. The look in his eyes made her own breathing quicken. 'I must return,' she said, with a glance towards the main building. 'We have been gone a while and they will be wondering about me.'

Amusement glinted in his eyes. 'I think you are wise,' he said. 'We have broken propriety enough for one day,

159

and those women will be anxious to know how you fared and whether to don mourning or begin stitching a wedding gown . . . unless you already have that in your coffer too.'

'My lord, I would not presume,' she said modestly.

He took her hand and kissed the back of it. His lips were soft and she shivered at this, their first touch on her skin. How would it be to feel them on her mouth – where Henry's had once been. He didn't have a beard like Henry and his lips were fuller and smoother because he was a younger man. Taking his hand, she echoed his gesture, leaving him a similar memento, then disengaged and hurried towards the door. At the threshold, she turned and gave him a dazzling smile over her shoulder. It was a trick learned at court – it was artifice, but she meant it with the full sincerity of her heart too. She swore to herself that she was going to be the best wife in the world. She owed it to the man who was going to remove her from the limbo she currently occupied and with whom she would make her life anew.

15

Woodstock, November 1181

The November evening was dank with fog and darkness had set in early. All the shutters were barred against the bone-gripping chill. Fires blazed in the hearths, supplemented by charcoal braziers and lamps and candles added coronets of light and warmth to the rooms.

The King had been hunting venison for the table and, having returned with corpse-laden pack ponies, was in high good humour despite the inclement weather. A good dinner enhanced by some excellent entertainment in the form of tumblers, fire dancers and a troubadour who had sung a scurrilous ditty about the French had further augmented Henry's good mood.

Roger had joined the hunt and had enjoyed the gallop amongst the misty trees, his courser pounding through the forest mulch. It was good to ride hard, and even in the still air to feel the wind of speed flowing against and through his body.

Replete with food, laughter and the satisfaction of a day enjoyed, he dallied with Ida in a corridor away from the main hall. His fur-lined cloak enfolded both their bodies in the delightful pleasure of courtship. Not that

Roger was taking any serious liberties for he knew the boundaries and had no intention of emulating Henry. Everything would be done properly in its due course and, in the meantime, there was the pleasure of anticipation. Ida was eager to share his warmth under the cloak, to hold his hand, touch his face, breathe his breath, but she refused to let him see her hair unbound because that was a husband's privilege; nor would she open her mouth when they kissed. He was careful to keep his hands at her waist so that touching her was a display of tenderness not lust. While desire rode him hard, there was less than a month to wait and then he could have all he wanted.

'I have to go,' he said with a reluctant sigh, but even so, he lingered. 'The King expects me in his chamber.'

She ran her thumb over his palm. 'Do you know what he wants?'

'To discuss the morrow's business with his counsellors. He hasn't yet spoken to me of our match. I thought he might do so at the hunt but his mind was on the chase.' He raised her hand and set a kiss at the base of her wrist. 'There is no need to look anxious. I've not seen him in so fine a mood for a long time.'

'Bringing down deer does that to him,' she said as she slipped out from the enveloping warmth of his cloak. 'I'll talk to you on the morrow.'

He bowed to her; she flourished him a curtsey, then blew him a kiss. Mutual smiles on their faces, they each went their way.

Henry handed Roger several sheets of vellum, closely written in the elegant dark brown script of one of the court clerics. 'This is pending business,' he said, 'but if you cast your eyes over it now, it will advance matters later on. On the issue of Ida's marriage, I gift you with

162

the return of three of the manors that were your father's. I think you know their worth. I have also instructed that debt of five hundred marks you owe at the exchequer is to be cancelled.'

'Thank you, sire.' Roger studied the list. Acle, Halvergate and Walsham combined were worth well over a hundred pounds. The manors were three over which he was in dispute with his half-brothers. For Henry to bestow them on him was a positive sign as well as a gift. Perhaps this was the first opening of the door and his marriage to Ida was going to prove more fortuitous than he had ever hoped.

'Your future bride is worthy of such a marriage gift,' Henry said. 'I would see her well settled.' He gave Roger a hard stare. 'Take care of her, my lord Bigod. I am giving Ida into your safekeeping, but you should know that she is precious to me.'

A feeling of danger prickled between Roger's shoulder blades. On his own part, he felt indignation and more than a twinge of jealousy, but concealed them behind an impassive façade. The marriage wasn't accomplished yet and these charters had not been sealed and ratified. 'She will be precious to me too, sire . . . she will be my wife.'

Henry gave him a close, assessing look as if sizing up a potential enemy rather than an ally. 'There is one particular detail that is not negotiable.'

Roger's heart sank. He had known there would be a catch somewhere because Henry never gave anything with open generosity. There were always caveats. 'Sire?'

'When you take Ida to wife, you take her alone. My son remains in my custody. He will be raised in a manner fitting to his station.'

The news hit Roger like a fist in the solar plexus. For himself, he was not overly concerned because he didn't know the infant and a baby was a baby. But Ida . . . Dear sweet Jesu, what was this going to do to her? 'Sire, his mother will be grief-stricken . . .'

Henry spread his hands. 'It will sadden her, I know, but that cannot be helped. She has too tender a heart and I have let her affection for him grow too deep. I should have given him to a wet nurse as soon as he was born.' He shrugged as if shaking off an irritant. 'I have no doubt she will bellow for a while like a cow after a calf, my lord Bigod, but I expect her to be distracted by her marriage bed and your heirs in due course. I imagine you'll be swift enough to the pleasure of that duty and you'll find her a sweet and compliant bedmate,' he added with a taunting gleam in his eyes.

Roger was tempted to take hold of Henry by the throat and throttle him into silence.

'Only peasant women rear their own. You and Ida will start afresh. Let everything that has been remain in the past. She will see him at court betimes.'

Which would be like rubbing salt into a raw wound and would only exacerbate the pain, Roger thought.

'Besides,' Henry said, 'I'm fond of the little chap and unlikely to beget many more. I sired him; I'm entitled to dispose of his future as I see fit. He's mine, of my loins. His mother was only the vessel.'

Roger managed to prevent himself from making a reply that would destroy his chances of ever regaining his earldom and rebuilding Framlingham, but the unspoken words created a sour taste in his mouth.

Henry gave him a bright look. 'Do you have any bastards, Bigod?'

'No, sire.'

Henry nodded and ran his tongue around his teeth. 'Well, at least you know your future wife is fertile and a breeder of men children.'

164

The words might have been mere pragmatic comment, or they might be a needling hint that Henry had proved his virility by fathering a son on Ida and that if there was any problem, it would lie with Roger's seed. Roger clung to control, reminding himself that he was being given three manors and pardoned a substantial debt and that everything had its price.

'I will give the order tomorrow when I see to your charters and the cancelling of your debt.'

'What about Ida?'

'I will tell her now,' Henry said, and dismissed him.

Leaving the royal chamber, Roger's heart was heavy and the charters in his hand seemed to weigh like lead. There was nothing he could do about the King's decision to keep the child at court. He had seen the finality in Henry's eyes; battling him would only make things worse for Ida and himself because they could not win. She would be distraught and it was going to cast a shadow over their marriage even before it was begun. Grimacing, Roger began to see his father's belligerence towards the Crown in a more sympathetic light. He wondered how many straws a camel could have piled upon its back before it broke. What was the number of the final one?

Ida watched William at play with his new wooden horse, making it gallop across the sheepskin rug on the floor. Her blood was a frozen river and an icicle had pierced her heart. There was simultaneous numbness and pain, the disbelief of someone mortally injured who had only just begun to die.

One of Henry's chaplains had come to her last night, not even Henry himself, and told her that when she went to her marriage, her son was to remain at court and be raised in the royal household. Henry couldn't do this to

165

her, but he had – given her the world and then crushed it in the same instant with a single command. She was to leave Woodstock early tomorrow for her brother's manor at Flamstead, her custody and person bestowed upon her family until her wedding. And William was to stay here.

'Look, Mama, horse.' He came to show her his new toy and laughed at her with his two rows of perfect milk teeth.

Ida swept him into her arms and held him tightly, as if she would absorb him back into her body and thaw her veins. Oh God, oh God. She couldn't let him go. It would be like tearing a hole in herself too great to heal. Roger might be her future husband; she might feel things for him she had never felt for anyone before – but she had carried William in her womb, had felt him kick and turn against the palm of her hand in joyous quickening. She and Roger would become one flesh upon their marriage, but the binding of words was not the same as the tie of the birth cord. And as she thought this, the pain came, almost like the pangs of labour.

She tightened her grip and William wriggled in her arms, squealing in protest. Ida let him go, watched him toddle away to his other toy animals and stand them all up in a line. His hair gleamed like dark water; his profile of soft curves, his sooty lashes and the tender fold of his mouth made the pangs worse and she doubled over, clutching her midriff, sobs wrenching from deep inside her as the grief cut and severed and tore.

'Oh, there now, there now, my love!' Hodierna, who had been fetching her a tisane, put the steaming cup to one side and hastened to enfold her in a maternal embrace.

A wooden animal in each hand now, William ran to show them to one of the other ladies.

166

'Don't you fret, my love. You'll still see him when you come to court. You'll still be able to visit the nursery.'

'But I can't have him!' Ida gasped between spasms. 'Someone else will kiss and hold him, and soothe his hurts. Someone else will see each change in him as he grows and applaud his achievements. I will be robbed of all that, yet I am the one who should be most attached to those things.'

Hodierna rubbed Ida's back. 'He will have a royal upbringing and the chance to become a great man,' she said. 'He will never lack for anything, you know that.'

William toddled back to Ida and plumped down in her lap with a loud sigh. Ida curled her arms around him again. 'Except for my love,' she choked. 'Except for his mother. You cannot replace such things with worldly goods.'

'He will be well looked after,' Hodierna said firmly. 'He will be with his father and it is good that the King takes responsibility for him. Would you deprive Henry of his son when you can go on and have others with the man of your choosing? I know it is hard, my love, and I may sound cruel, but you must think about it in those terms because you have no alternative.'

'I could have chosen not to wed . . .' Ida whispered.

Hodierna made an exasperated sound. 'Indeed, and eventually the King would have settled someone else on you – someone not to your taste. At least the little one is still too young to realise what this means and that is a blessing for him. That he won't remember you is your curse, but the longer you leave it the worse it will be for all. You must look to the future and your new duties.'

'I can't.' As William ran off again, Ida pushed away from Hodierna and curled herself in a foetal ball of misery and grief. 'I can't, I can't!'

* * *

'Demoiselle, you can go no further, the King is busy and he will not see you.' John Marshal barred Ida's way to Henry's chambers.

'But I have to see him.' Ida's voice cracked. 'It's about my son.'

'That is not possible, demoiselle, but I will give him your message.' The marshal's face was expressionless. She had seen this polite exterior before, bestowed upon supplicants who had no chance of being granted the King's ear.

'Then I will wait for him . . .'

'You would do best to return to your women.'

She raised her chin and stood her ground and wondered if he would order his men to carry her off by force. There was no precedent for what she was doing but she was so far beyond the bounds of propriety, she was in the wild territory where a map-maker would have written Here Be Dragons. Behind the marshal, the door opened and Henry emerged at his usual breezy walk followed by the barons with whom he had been in discussion and several scribes and clerics. Ida darted around the marshal before he could catch her and flung herself on her knees at Henry's feet. 'Sire, I beg you!' she cried. 'If there is mercy in your soul, don't part me from my son. Let me have him!' Under her fingers, she felt the embroidered gold knots on his tunic, the soft edge of his thick woollen cloak, the hardness of his legs. There were hands on her, trying to pull her away from Henry, but she tightened her hold and pressed her head against his legs. They would have to cut her off him.

'Let her be,' Henry commanded, raising his hand. 'All of you leave us.'

The hands relinquished her, although an imprint of bruising pain remained. People departed, and there was silence.

'Take care of your lady, my lord Bigod,' Henry said as Roger emerged from the chamber clutching a handful of freshly sealed charters and absorbed the sight with astonishment.

Documents rustled as he handed them over to someone else and then he was stooping at her side and his own hands were gentle.

'No!' she moaned.

'Ida . . .' Roger's voice was soft at her ear. 'Ida, get up. There's nothing you can do lying on the floor like this. Come . . .'

Because it was Roger, because despite her wounds she was still fighting on, Ida accepted his support and allowed him to lift her to her feet. 'Please,' she implored Henry in a breaking voice. 'Please don't do this. Give him to me.' She tried to make him meet her eyes. At first, he looked away, but when he finally answered her, his gaze was set and stony.

'The decision stands, Ida,' he said. 'My son remains with me and will be raised in my household as befits the son of a king.'

'And how often will he see you? How often will you visit him? Once a year? Twice?' She bared her teeth. 'Whom will he know to call mother?'

Henry's nostrils flared. 'Your fuss is unseemly,' he said curtly. 'You have my answer and it is for the best even if you cannot see it now for the blindness of your womb.' He cut his gaze from hers as if severing a thread and focused on Roger. 'My lord Bigod, I leave Mistress de Tosney in your care.' He strode off. The clerk who had been holding the bundle of charters mumbled an apology and, leaving the documents on the wall bench in the corridor, hastened away.

Ida closed her eyes. She felt drained and sick and utterly

wretched. Roger led her to the bench and sat her down upon the hard oak seat. Despair settled on her like a malignant black cloak, detaching her from everything beyond the pain.

The corridor was dark in the early morning, and chilly with the pervasive musty odour of dank weather. It wasn't just the year that was dying. 'I had to do it,' she said, hunching over. 'It was my last hope. He . . . he sent his chaplain to me after compline last night, as if it were nothing more than a trifling matter – just a bit of ordinary business. I . . . Ah!' She rocked back and forth, cradling her grief where once she had cradled a baby.

Roger held her close, rocking with her. 'I thought he was going to tell you himself. If I had known, I would have come to you.'

'You knew?' Her voice cracked at the notion of another betrayal.

'He spoke of it to me last night and said he was going to tell you. I did not realise he lacked the grace and courage to give you the news himself.'

Ida shivered and he draped his cloak around both of them. They were alone in a silent corridor, embraced in a gesture that to a passer-by would look like courtship, but instead was a rite of grief.

Roger rubbed her spine and said quietly after a long pause, 'Whatever his faults, Henry does care for William.'

'Then why doesn't he give him to me?' she demanded in an anguished whisper. 'That would be the right thing to do by us both.'

'He may trust you, but he doesn't trust other men. He would not consider whomever you married a worthy surrogate father to his son.'

'I would have had you care for him . . . I wanted you . . .'

'Yes, I know. I know. Hush.'

170

Leaning against him, Ida struggled to pick up the pieces. She had to find the strength to bear this thing. What had been done to her wasn't right, but neither was it right to set this upon Roger. It was her burden, not his. She was also aware through her grief that he might be alarmed by her hysteria and back out of the marriage, leaving her with nothing.

Swallowing, she pushed herself upright. 'I would like to return to my chamber,' she said, retrieving the rags of her dignity and raising her chin. 'I still have coffers to pack and matters to attend to. I . . . It will be better if I keep busy.'

She saw relief relax the tension in his features and knew her instinct was right. She couldn't set this upon him beyond what had happened today.

Holding her at his side, he helped her to her feet. 'I know you are grieving and nothing I can say will alter that but I swear I will do everything in my power to make you content as my wife and helpmate.'

It was beyond Ida to smile, but she raised his hands and pressed a kiss to his knuckles. 'And I swear in my turn I will be a good wife,' she said, and gave him a tear-flooded look. 'You will be my consolation.'

Shriven, cleansed, scoured, Ida returned from confession. She was a smooth shore after a high tide – looking little different but with the arrangement of every grain utterly changed. The sin of her fornication had been absolved – washed away as if it had never been, and she had to try and make herself believe that the beach had always been empty and never borne an imprint before. In a way, it was true. The Ida packing coffers in her bed alcove was not the Ida who had come to court brimming with excitement and innocence five years ago.

Standing before her baggage chests, ready to leave for Flamstead, she gazed at the tiny shoes cupped in her hand. They were William's first pair; the ones that had seen him take his first unsteady steps across the nursery floor. Her own exquisite stitches covered the thin, fragile goatskin. He would have many more shoes throughout his childhood, all gorgeously embroidered and embellished. He was, after all, a king's son, but she would not be the one to sew them, and each pair worn out and larger than the previous ones would be a step away from her, a foot, a yard, a mile, until they stood in different countries.

Inside one of the miniature shoes was a lock of William's hair, soft and dark, secured with strands of scarlet embroidery thread. She held it for a moment, consigning the silky feel of the strands to the memory of her fingertips. Hot-eyed, her chin dimpling, she set both the shoes and the hair in the enamelled jewel casket Henry had given her in the first days of their relationship. She closed the lid, turned the small key and heard the soft click of the lock. Such a quiet sound to have such a vastness of finality.

16

Thetford Priory, December 1181

The Cluniac priory of Our Lady at Thetford stood close to the quiet flow of the river Orwell. Roger's grandfather had founded it more than seventy years ago and successive Bigod lords, including Roger's uncle and father, had since enhanced it. Roger had read the foundation charter last night while sorting through a strongbox of documents. *Notum sit omnibus tam futuris quam praesentibus quod ego Rogerus Bigotus, dapifer Regis Henrici* . . . Little had changed even if the number of tomb slabs in the choir had increased. There was still a Roger Bigod and he was a steward to King Henry. And today was his wedding day.

Ironically, Roger's grandfather and namesake mentioned within the charter was buried not here, but in Norwich Cathedral, the victim of a tug of war between the then Bishop of Norwich and the Prior of Thetford.

'It is the first time I have seen your father's tomb,' Juliana murmured, standing beside Roger. She gave the incised slate slab a long look. Her breath puffed in white vapour from between her parted lips and her hands were tucked inside a roll of sable fur.

'Perhaps he would have wanted more,' Roger said, 'but

I was not going to grant him a finer tomb than his brother or my grandfather in Norwich.'

'You have done your filial duty by him, and that is more than can be said of his paternal duty to you.'

Roger shrugged. 'It is in the past.' He went to look at the new round window in the apse that he had had commissioned to mark his marriage. There were many things to be consigned to the past. Let the future write itself in hope.

The window was not quite finished, although the glass-painter had completed the outlines and some of the colours. The depiction was of the Virgin in the stable with the newborn Christ child – appropriate to the season and to the priory's patron saint. The painter had yet to complete Mary's blue robe, but it was still evident what the subject matter was.

Joining him, Juliana remarked upon its beauty.

'I would have liked to see it finished for Ida,' he said, 'but there hasn't been time and I would rather have quality over a hasty job.'

'But it will be finished.' Juliana smiled and set her hand lightly on his sleeve. 'I know you. You will ensure a thorough job is done. Do not let small worries take you away from the joy of your marriage.'

Roger laid his hand over hers. 'You are wise to remind me,' he said with a pensive expression in his eyes.

Anketil arrived, striding up the nave, his new surcoat of parti-coloured red and yellow a bright splash as if he had stepped out of a painted window himself. Against the damp silver of his freshly washed flaxen hair his complexion was scrubbed and ruddy. Roger had not been the only one to bathe within an inch of his life for the purposes of this marriage. 'My lord, the bride's party is sighted. You said I should tell you.'

Roger nodded and his apprehension increased. 'Thank you,' he said. 'Go and greet her and see she is fittingly escorted to her chamber.'

Anketil bowed and strode back out. Juliana kissed Roger's cheek. 'You should go and make final preparations. I will see you shortly.' Her voice suddenly wobbled.

'Mother?' Roger looked at her askance.

'Pay me no heed,' Juliana gave an embarrassed laugh. 'I am happy for you and your bride. I want the best for both of you . . . more than I ever had. Go!' She gave him a gentle push. 'Your men will wonder where you are.'

She watched him leave the church and, when he had gone, wiped her eyes and straightened her spine. She was indeed pleased for him and she had no qualms about accepting Ida as a daughter-in-law. Her tears were born of love, anticipation . . . and concern. Both her son and his bride had had hard experiences of the world. She knew from her own life that one was in danger of either developing an impenetrable shell, or leaving all softness exposed until it was devoured and nothing remained but a husk. There had to be balance, and that was what she wished for them, as much as joy.

Roger entered the courtyard of his house by the river in time to see Ida arrive. Clad in a thick woollen cloak, his face concealed by a deep hood, he stood among the throng and as he saw her trot into the ward on the golden palfrey he had once given to Henry and that Henry had gifted to her, he felt as if someone had kindled a flame at his core. The mare's mane was braided with red ribbons and from each plait hung a small silver bell that rang sweetly each time she moved. Goscelin rode a new horse gifted to him by Roger – a brown courser with an underlying golden sheen to its coat.

As a groom helped her dismount, Roger thought that Ida looked thinner than when he had last seen her a month ago, and a little wan about the face, but she was still beautiful. The loss of weight had put hollows beneath her cheekbones and made her eyes look even bigger. He felt protective towards her and swore to himself that he would bring the smile back to her face that Henry had taken away. He was glad they were not having the wedding at court and that Henry was not attending the nuptials. To have had him present would have been unbearable.

Quietly, unobtrusively, he melted from the throng and went to make himself ready for church and his new role as husband.

Standing in the middle of the bridal chamber, Ida patiently waited while her women removed her headdress and unwound her coiled brown braids. She had combed her hair that morning with the solution of spices and rose water Hodierna had shown her how to make. Released by the warmth of her body, the scent flowed around her in exotic waves like the perfumes in the Song of Solomon. She raised her arms so they could unfasten the laces at the side of her green and gold wedding gown. Although there was no hearth in this upper chamber, braziers had been warming the room all day so that it was comfortable. The dark red bed hangings were drawn back and loosely gathered by ties of amber silk and the women had turned down the matching coverlet to expose fine linen sheets, embroidered red bolsters and fluffy white pillows. The bed textiles were Ida's and she had had her women hang them while the wedding feast was being conducted in the great hall. This was her domain now, sanctioned by the Church and a sealed marriage contract. She felt lightheaded and giddy, from the wine she had consumed,

176

from the joyful dancing in the hall, and from being bathed in the attention of her new husband. Roger had gone out of his way to try and make everything perfect for her, from the blaze of candles and evergreen in the church, to the wonderfully set tables at the wedding feast, to the musicians who had played a composition especially written for her. For all that Henry had surrounded her with luxury, he had never once considered what she might like. That Roger had, and wanted to please her, was worth more than a room full of gold.

Her women removed her gown and then her gartered silk hose, but Ida retained her chemise. Juliana admired the whitework on the latter, which until now had been concealed by the overdress. 'What fine embroidery,' she remarked. 'Did you do this yourself?'

'Yes, my lady Mother, I did.' The title sounded strange on Ida's tongue but she knew she would have to grow accustomed to it.

'You have some skill with a needle,' Juliana smiled. 'I can see that my son will not lack for fine embellishment on his clothes.'

Ida blushed at the praise. 'He will not lack for anything if I can give it,' she answered softly. 'It will be my honour and my duty to fulfil his wishes.'

Juliana continued to smile, but there was caution in her gaze. 'I can tell that is so,' she said. 'I know you will be a good wife, but I will give you a word of counsel. A man needs to believe he is the master, but a woman should rule the hearth in the small things that make up the whole.'

'My lady, thank you. It is good advice,' Ida murmured gracefully but without taking it to heart. She was not quite sure of mother-in-law yet. She liked her, but it was hard to see past the contained serenity. Roger had a degree of that stillness, but in him it was not as dense. Juliana plainly adored her son, although mercifully did not seem possessive. Ida thought all would be well, but she no longer trusted people at face value.

Juliana's gaze was shrewd. 'From what I saw in church and at the feasting, Roger will love you well and you will have a good life with him – better than I had with his father – but then my son is his own man. What there is in him of his sire has been tempered by the experience of seeing what his sire became.'

'I do not know Roger well in the small ways of which you speak,' Ida said, 'but I have seen him in the greater things. He is courtly and steadfast and not the kind who will abuse or trample upon his dependants. He has courage and judgement and honour.' Even though her face was hot from her words, she gave Juliana a deliberate look. 'That was why I chose him.'

Juliana's head came up and suddenly she was alert. Then humour sparkled in her eyes and a glint of respect. 'Ah,' she said. 'That serves me right for not looking under the surface. You are a very sweet girl, but there is more to you than that, I think. My son and the earldom are in safe hands with you.'

Ida gave a small frown. 'But he is not an earl.'

'No, but he will be – and you a countess. That is what you must prepare yourselves to be.' Leaning forward, Juliana kissed Ida's cheek. 'I wish you joy tonight and for the rest of your life.'

Ida thanked her and determinedly banished the image that unbidden had entered her mind – of a red and blue enamelled box holding her son's little shoes. There was no place for such memories tonight.

Her women combed her hair to fall in a perfumed brown skein to her waist. They dabbed rose oil at her wrists and throat, then draped her cloak at her shoulders, fastening it with cords of gold silk. An attendant brought a tray of bread and cheese, fruit pieces rolled in powdered sugar and grains of paradise, and piquant fried nuts. There was a little dish of candied cardamom seeds to sweeten the breath and a jug of spiced wine, should bride and groom require fortifying.

The men arrived in a good-natured jostle of colour and bawdy jesting, bearing Roger to his bride. He had been divested of his dark red wedding tunic and fine blue chausses and now, like Ida, he was clad in a long chemise and full cloak. Bishop John of Norwich, who had conducted the marriage, prepared to bless the couple, although he had imbibed liberally of Rhenish wine and was none too steady on his feet or sure of his words. Goscelin had to support him and one of the Bishop's attendants took care of the ivory-headed crosier. Ida kept her gaze modestly lowered and restrained the urge to giggle. She dared not catch anyone's eye, especially Roger's.

Her women escorted her to the bed and put her in it, on the right side, because that was the one conducive to conceiving male children. The sheets had been warmed with hot stones and even though she was preoccupied, it was still a pleasure to wriggle her feet into blissful heat and inhale the sweet scent of rose water rising from the fresh linen.

Roger was bundled in beside her by the more boisterous men, with ribald quips about mounting and riding and thrusting the lance in the target. The comments made Ida's cheeks burn, but although the jests were near to the mark, none overstepped it. There was respect and affection for Roger, and given her own circumstances, folk were wary of speaking out of turn because of her former relationship with the King.

Once the Bishop had stumbled his way through blessing

179

the bed, Goscelin ushered the guests out of the room to continue the celebrations in the hall.

Juliana lightly touched Roger's shoulder and smiled at the couple. 'I wish you both well.' Humour crinkled her eye corners. 'My blessing may not be holy like the good Bishop's but it comes with my love.' She kissed Roger's cheek, came round the bed to do the same to Ida, and was the last to leave the room, dropping the latch gently behind her. They heard her speak to the Bishop, and the latter's bumbling tones fading down the stairs.

Roger first grimaced, then laughed. 'I had forgotten how weak a head he has for wine,' he said. 'The Archbishop of York can drink everyone under the table and still be sober himself, but not John of Norwich.'

'He will have a sore head in the morning,' she agreed. 'So will many.'

Silence fell again. Roger cleared his throat. 'Do you want another cup yourself? Some food?'

Ida shook her head, then instantly changed her mind because it was something to do and would give them time to settle down with each other now that for the first time today they were alone. 'Just a half-measure,' she said. They had been put to bed with the expectation that they would consummate their marriage some time before the morning, but now that the moment was imminent, there was awkwardness between them, rather than spontaneity.

'I am looking forward to seeing Framlingham,' she said as she took the cup he gave her, and sipped. The wine was warm and the pepper and galangal it contained sent a glow through her veins.

He climbed back between the sheets and pulled up the coverlet. 'It's too far to reach in a day's ride, but we'll visit other manors on the way – then you can see the task in hand. It's been a long time since the Bigod estates have had a proper mistress.'

Ida flashed him a quick smile. 'Then I will be glad to start anew – in all things, my lord.' She handed the cup to him and he drank too. She watched the ripple of his throat and felt warmth flow into her pelvis.

'You will have whatever you need to refurbish. Ask what you will.'

'Thank you, my lord, I am keen to begin.' Which she was indeed. The sooner she embraced her new life, the quicker her old one would fade.

'Indeed.' He grimaced as he returned the cup. 'But we've to be back at Winchester for the Christmas court.'

Ida gazed into the dark, glossy wine. She was torn between wanting to be with Roger, but unsure that she was ready to face the court. If William was there, she would have the pain of parting with him all over again when they left, and if he was at Woodstock, she wouldn't see him at all, and from her current perspective, she couldn't decide which was worse.

'What is it?' Roger asked.

'Nothing.' She forced a smile but did not have to feign a shiver. 'Draw the hangings, my lord, it is cold tonight.' She finished the wine, set the empty cup on the coffer and closed the curtains hanging around her own side of the bed.

'There is something the matter,' he said. 'I would have you tell me.'

Ida gnawed her lower lip, wondering how to answer. She could not burden him with her longing, although he must have an inkling. Besides, she had learned that someone saying they wanted to know was not always the same as meaning it. Sometimes they wanted platitudes. 'You will think me foolish,' she said, telling him most, but not all of the truth, 'but I am torn. I do not want to return to court – or not so soon after our wedding – but neither do I want to be away from your side.' She touched him in emphasis, as she had touched him in the orchard, and felt the hardness of his rib cage beneath the fine linen shirt. Henry had been softer there, more padded with flesh and flaccid with the years.

'Then it is a joint dilemma, because I want you with me, and I do not want to go to court either.'

'We could stay away,' she suggested with more hope than expectation.

He shook his head. 'The King expects my return as soon as I may. I am in his service and I must perform it to the best of my ability. Whatever his reason, he consented to our match and returned three manors to me, for which I am grateful.' A smile curved his lips. 'He does not realise the true value of the gift he has bestowed on me.' Without taking his eyes off her, he closed the hangings on his side of the bed. The only light came from the ceramic lamp above their heads so that they were enshrouded in a soft red almost-darkness, like the centre of a rose.

Having had Henry for a lover for several years, Ida thought she knew what to expect, but was unprepared for how different the act of physical union was with Roger. This time she was with a man she wanted, not one she was forced to bed because she had no choice, and this time she was an honourable wife, a new wedding ring gleaming on her finger, so the deed was not a sin. It wasn't fornication and she could finally yield to all the pent-up tensions of the last few months.

She was dizzy with wine, with the shine of new love, with lust, and she found herself trembling as she had done that first time with Henry, but this time not from shock or fear. Roger was trembling too, but his touch was restrained and a thing of beauty to her for it was a slow,

182

gentle, exploration of new territory. He murmured her name as he kissed her eyebrows, temple and jaw and outlined the shape of her face with little more than his breath. It was a tender, close exploration of Ida herself and because of the unhurried pace, she sighed and relaxed. Responding in kind, she was able to pretend that she knew nothing – that this was the first time; and from that pretence, reality was born because it was indeed a first time and since it felt so different, her belief stayed strong.

She slipped her hands into his hair, longer than Henry's, feathery and thick, and soft ruddy bronze in the tint created by lamp and bed hanging. She touched his face and the column of his throat. With great daring, she set her hand on his skin beneath his shirt and felt the contrasts of hard muscle and bone, smooth skin and springy chest hair. He gasped and, sitting up, dragged the garment over his head, arms crossing over to reveal darker tufts of hair in his armpits. Ida gasped too at the sight of the muscular definition on his arms and wiry, athletic body, the lean stomach, the ferny line of dark gold hair running from navel to groin that drove her to touch him again, the flat of her palms following the line of her eyes over shoulder, rib and side.

He swallowed and said hoarsely, 'Would you . . . would take off your chemise?'

Blushing, feeling shy and wanton at the same time, Ida withdrew her hands from him and unfastened the ties at her throat. She kept her eyes modestly lowered as she shrugged the garment off her shoulders. She heard Roger exhale shakily and, risking a glance at him, saw that his gaze was devouring her. He reached for her and the kissing and stroking began again, but no longer confined to her face. His touch was still reverent, but there was more urgency in it now as he discovered her breasts, her flanks, her hipbones, and the softness between. Ida responded with murmurs of appreciation and sighs of pleasure.

She wrapped her arms around Roger and drew him over her, revelling in the mingling of strength and gentleness within him. She had been holding back, not wanting to seem too experienced, but now, familiar with the moves, she angled her body to help him. And then he was within her and she heard him catch his breath, then let it out through his teeth, and knowing his pleasure heightened her own. She would give this moment to him and she would make it perfect for both of them. She moved beneath him with subtlety and made small, appreciative sounds because the give and take of their bodies felt good. She wriggled down on him, twined her legs around his and gripped him tightly. Sensing his heightened tension, knowing the moment of crisis was close, she ran her fingers through his hair and arched against him. She was close to something herself, could feel it gathering in her pelvis until it was unbearable. 'Give me a child!' she gasped out of her need. 'I want your sons. I want your daughters!' And suddenly she was tumbling over the edge, racked by intense sensations that made her cry aloud. His breath stopped and, pressing hard against and into her, he let go. Ida held him fiercely at the unleashing peak of the storm, and then, as the surges diminished and passed, stroked him tenderly and kissed the thundering pulse in his throat.

A brazier made a soft sound as burning charcoal settled to a new level in the basket. Ida luxuriated in the feel of Roger's relaxed weight upon her. He was not light, but she could still breathe and she didn't want to move, for this blending closeness was something she craved. The warmth of his body was like an extra coverlet, promising she would never be cold again. His head on her breast and the soft movement of his lips filled her with tenderness. She caressed his hair, a little damp with sweat now, and could not stop

184

tears from spilling down her face. Surreptitiously, she wiped them away on the heel of her hand.

He raised his head to look at her. His eyes were smoky with satiation, his features relaxed, although what had been a beatific expression was swiftly becoming tinged with worry. 'Ida? Have I hurt you?' He started to withdraw and immediately she tightened her grip on him, holding him where he was with one hand on the curve of his buttocks.

'No.' She shook her head with vehemence. 'Stay, please stay. You didn't hurt me, truly you didn't. It was . . . I am . . . I am crying because you have restored to me something I thought I had lost.' Her voice wobbled and she had to wipe her eyes again. 'For me, this is the first time, and for love, not for duty or because I have no choice . . . It is because I *do* have choice.'

He raised himself on one forearm, stroked her hair and kissed her with such aching tenderness that it made her cry harder. 'It is the first time for me too,' he replied, 'and I am not disappointed. I do not know what to say – except that you too have given me a gift beyond compare.' He kissed her again, then moved to lie at her side and drew her against him.

Ida wasn't sure what he meant by the remark that it had been his first time too, but she didn't question further. He had not been clumsy with her, nor had he appeared inexperienced, but then she had seen his gentleness and assurance with his horses, and his fine table manners where his enjoyment was more a matter of slow savouring than devouring at speed. She had seen his control and prowess too. The thought that she might indeed be the first made her throat ache with poignant joy. Tonight was a new beginning for both of them and they would go forward from this together.

17

Framlingham, December 1181

Ida and Roger came to Framlingham on a winter's afternoon hard with frost. The sun was already dipping towards the horizon and the air was like a knife in the lungs. Ice frilled the edges of the mere and the branches of the trees on the demesne were a stark black lacework against the pallid sky. The buildings were defenceless other than the stretch of marsh and water protecting the western edge of the complex. There was no castle, only a stone hall standing on a low mound with adjoining kitchens and chapel.

Ida knew Roger had been concerned about bringing her to the Bigod family caput. He seemed to think that because she was accustomed to the court with all of its luxuries, and especially the superbly appointed palace at Woodstock with its gardens, fountains and peacocks, she would judge his home impoverished by comparison – which was far from the truth. If she was uncertain and wary about coming here, it was for entirely different reasons.

She rode at his side, a little preoccupied but still enjoying the smooth pace of her mare and having the right to ride openly at Roger's side. Securing her new cloak of thick blue wool was a beautiful gold and sapphire lozenge brooch that Roger had given her on the morning after their wedding. Incised on the reverse was the motto *Soiez leals en amours* – be loyal in love. She took one hand off the rein to touch the token and bit her lip as they drew near the castle.

'You are disappointed,' he said.

Ida jumped. She had been unaware that he was observing her. 'Oh no, my lord! It is . . . it is perfect.'

'Hardly that. I know its failings, and they must seem even more obvious to you.'

She shook her head. 'I would rather this than any gilded palace.'

'Then why the frown?'

Ida gave him a rueful look. 'I was telling myself that I am mistress of the household and that I must act in a seemly manner and show my authority. At court I learned how to converse with bishops and earls and to move through that world like a minnow through the weeds, but this is new to me.'

He gestured. 'It is not so different. I have seen you supervising the women at Woodstock – apple-mulching.'

Ida laughed and her cheeks grew warm.

'I know you capable of whatever I ask of you; I do not doubt your ability.'

She was touched by his trust, but it made her anxious too. 'Even so I must set my mind in order, or else your people will think that I have a head stuffed with feathers. I have had other things to occupy me these last few days.'

He smiled at her in a lazy, satisfied way that made her loins contract. 'So have I,' he answered, then gently heeled his courser and rode across the bridge spanning the ditch.

Riding into the courtyard, the ground underfoot was

boggy, but a thick layer of straw had been thrown down to soak up the worst of the winter mud. A cluster of knights and retainers waited to greet their returning lord. Ida knew they were all looking at her and wondering about the bride he had brought home. A courtesan, a former royal mistress. They must know the gossip even if East Anglia was far removed from the court. She felt queasy with tension, but held her head high. This was her new home, her domain, and she would begin as she meant to go on.

A groom took the mare's bridle and Roger came to lift her down into his arms. Their breath steamed and mingled in the air. She gripped his hand for a moment, garnering courage, then turned with him and together, formally, they entered the hall. Ida paced with slow dignity as if she were on her way to attend a royal banquet, her palm laid flat along Roger's sleeve, and was welcomed to Framlingham by Roger's steward Clerembald and his wife Roese. Behind Ida and Roger, attendants began unloading the baggage wains and a procession of chests and coffers followed them inside the dwelling.

The interior of the hall had no windows, but the walls had recently been limewashed and shone like new snow. There were neither hangings nor shields and weapons to adorn the bare expanses though, and the effect was cold. A fire blazed in the hearth, but it had been recently lit and had yet to build up strength and heat. A pale layer of oat straw covered the floor and Ida found herself thinking of the swept wooden floors at Woodstock and the decorated tiles in Henry's chamber. Although airy and spacious, the hall reminded her of a well-kept byre. Suddenly her dignified entry seemed a little foolish. There was no one to see it save for the few resident knights and retainers. Although Framlingham was supposedly the core of Roger's domain, there was little to show for it. The hall could be made grand, but for the moment, it was stark and cold. Beside her, she could sense Roger's own dissatisfaction.

'It's not much, is it?' he said. 'If I was seeing this with your eyes, I would be wondering why I had been brought here. We should have stayed at Thetford.'

She moved closer to him and touched his arm. 'I am glad the walls are bare,' she said. 'I have a notion for some hangings and frieze designs. It is like us: waiting to begin, and it has much potential.'

He turned towards her and gripped her hands. Ida found the will to smile at him, telling herself that this place was a challenge and an adventure, not a disappointment. Indeed, she did feel a frisson of anticipation at the thought of bringing it to life with her own flair. She squeezed his hand, then impulsively reached on tiptoe to kiss him. 'I want to see the rest,' she said. 'What about the rooms above this?'

He laughed and swung her in a half-circle, thus completely negating the dignity with which they had entered. 'Come,' he said. 'I will show you. I'm sure that it too "has potential".'

The bedchamber, Ida discovered, was worse than the hall, because the walls had yet to receive their coat of limewash and were yellowish and darkened with soot deposits from candle and cresset lamp. Unlike the hall, however, there were four good arched windows, although shuttered against the December cold. The only light came from the internal-stair doorway, the two thick candles flickering on wrought-iron stands and the glow from the fire in the hearth. A large bed boasted hangings of good, thick wool, but in a murky shade of green that reminded Ida of pond sludge. The bed itself was neatly made up with clean sheets of decent quality, although the coverlet was of the same hue as the hangings. A barrel chair stood near the bed but minus a cushion to negotiate between buttocks and hard wood.

'This was my father's solar,' Roger said in a voice that was heavy and a little sad. 'It is improved in the summer when the windows are open. There's good sunlight then. He sold everything of beauty to pay his debts . . . And I have been too busy on other matters to think about the interior of this place. But it is home, and it deserves better.'

Ida went to the bed and sat on it, testing the mattresses. They were good – thick and well stuffed. She unfastened her cloak and set it to one side. 'It is all on the surface,' she said. 'It can be made beautiful again with a woman's touch.'

'It is not what I would have brought you to though.'

Ida studied him for a moment, then left the bed and, standing before him, unfastened his cloak. 'I would be happier living in a goat shed with you than in a palace with—' She broke off before she brought Henry's name into this, their bedchamber, and instead filled the space of that word with a hungering kiss. 'The bed is comfortable,' she said as their lips parted. 'Do you not want to try it and see for yourself what a woman's touch can do?' There was sudden mischief in the curve of her smile.

Humour broke through his dissatisfaction and evaporated it. He laughed and, catching her round the waist, tumbled her on to the thick mattresses. 'Oh yes,' he said, his fingers suddenly busy with the laces on her gown. 'I would like to do both very much.'

Alerted by a sound, Ida opened her eyes and for a moment lay in a half-waking state, wondering where she was. Her hair was spread on the pillow and her hand rested on

190

Roger's bare arm. Their legs were entwined, almost like a plait. He was breathing deeply. She watched the rise and fall of his chest, and then, as she became fully aware, she sat up and looked around. Their clothes were scattered over the bed in disarray, each item telling its own story of kisses, laughter and lust. Through the open bed curtains, the candles had burned well down and the fire in the hearth was a pile of glowing red embers.

They must have slept for a long time since it hadn't even been dusk when they had come upstairs. Ida felt a surge of guilty embarrassment. She wasn't sure about the sound she had heard, but it was reminiscent of a door latch being stealthily let down. She leaned over and gave Roger a gentle nudge. He grunted and jumped.

'I hope they're not waiting dinner for us to appear,' she said with chagrin.

'What?' Roger looked bewildered, but as the sleep cleared from his wits, he began to chuckle. 'So much for a woman's touch,' he said, playfully tugging a strand of her hair. 'I don't suppose anyone will be scandalised. It's to be expected of a newly-wed couple. Besides, who is to gainsay what we do in the heart of our own home and is not begetting heirs the foremost duty of the lord and his wife?'

Ida blushed. 'Even so, I hope they are not waiting for us.' She moved to put her foot out of bed and then squealed as her bare toes touched something soft and cold. She drew her foot back on to the bed and stared at the white blobs on her sole.

'Curd cheese,' Roger said, looking both mystified and amused.

Ida peered over the side of the bed again and gave a soft gasp. 'They've left us food!' She felt utterly mortified, but there was laughter too. She leaned further over, picked

191

a napkin off the tray that someone had deposited on the floor, and wiped her foot. She was shocked to think that a member of the household had entered the room without their knowing, left a tray of food at the bedside and tiptoed out again. That was what must have woken her, the sound of the bringer quietly leaving. The notion of how vulnerable they had been made her wince. She tried to remember how much flesh had been exposed to view, even though there was little light. Their scattered clothes told an obvious story too. The stories about the licentiousness of the court and its concubines was bound to run riot. They would be saying that the new mistress couldn't wait to try out the bed!

Roger seemed equable enough. His chest was vibrating with laughter as he threw off the bedclothes and reached for his shirt and cloak. 'There's no point going downstairs now,' he said. 'If it's as late as my stomach tells me it is, everyone will have eaten long ago and be preparing for bed. We might as well eat in the chamber and make a new start on the morrow. What have they left for us? I'm ravenous!' He came around to her side of the bed and picked up the tray. As well as the cheese into which Ida had squelched, there was a bowl of pale butter, some fresh bread, small roasted birds and a dish of raisins. His stomach growled. 'Come,' he said to Ida, 'you need feeding up. If you are not ravenous too, you ought to be.'

He took the tray to the hearth and set it down on the bench there. Whistling, he revived the fire with a pair of bellows, cut the bread and set about toasting it on some wrought-iron prongs. Ida donned her own cloak and followed him. Taking her place on the bench by the fire, she felt the warmth of the flames flickering through her body, or perhaps it was the warmth of the moment – Roger's smile, the intimacy of taking their first meal at

Framlingham alone together. Now she had recovered from her embarrassment, she was prepared to enjoy herself. She was indeed hungry and for the first time in several weeks. The combination of fretting over the loss of her son and preparing for her marriage had taken its toll on her appetite, as had the wedding itself and the immediate aftermath: dealing with the guests and not only finding but keeping her feet. Now, when Roger passed her a hunk of toasted bread, dripping in melted butter, she bit into it, relishing the crispness of the crumb, the softer interior and the sweet-saltiness of the liquefying butter. She had never tasted anything so good and said so.

'I learned the art on campaign. Sometimes there is only bread to eat and half stale at that. This makes even the worst horsebread taste decent. Wait . . . you've got . . .' He tilted up her face and thumbed a drip of butter from her cheek. She reciprocated by taking his thumb and licking off the butter whilst giving him a sultry look, and watched his eyes grow smoky. Her body tingled.

Roger gave a husky laugh and gestured. 'Eat,' he said. 'If we continue like this, we're going to starve.'

Ida made a face at him, but turned to pour a cup of wine to share along with the bread. Their meal became a game of feeding each other, both nurturing and suggestive. Ida was curled in his lap, exchanging raisins for kisses when their love play was interrupted.

'Mama?' A child's bewildered voice came from the doorway. 'Mama, where are you?'

Ida sat up and looked round. Roger had been stroking her breasts with teasing delicacy and was half hard against the cleft of her buttocks. She closed her cloak around her unlaced chemise and, leaving him to make himself decent, went to the door. The infant was a little boy not much older than her William and the look of panic in his large

193

eyes sent a pang of longing and sympathy through Ida. She knelt to his level. 'Child, your mother isn't here,' she said. 'But I'm sure she cannot be far away. Is she in the hall?'

The little boy shook his head. 'I can't find her.' He knuckled his eyes.

Ida swallowed. She tried not to think of William saying the same thing about her – wandering a dark corridor lost and alone. What if no one comforted him? 'Come, she can't be far away.' Taking the cold little hand in hers, she went to call out on the stairs.

A flustered Roese Pincerna hurried up to them, and sweeping the child into her arms, kissed his face. 'Robert! I told you not to wander off! I told you not to come up here!'

The infant buried his face against the woman's neck. Ida looked at his leg tucked around her hip, at the scuffed little shoe, so like the one locked away in her decorated box. 'Is he yours?'

'Yes, my lady. I am sorry. I told him to stay with his big sister but she was too busy with her playmates to see him leave his bed and wander off.' She glanced into the room. 'Is everything well?'

Ida nodded. 'Thank you, yes,' she said and knew she was blushing.

'I had food sent up . . . I didn't know what else to do.'

'And I thank you. It was very welcome and thoughtful of you.' She resisted the urge to brush away the crumbs sprinkling the front of her cloak.

'You'd had a long journey,' Roese said with sympathy and a slight twinkle that made Ida warm to her. 'I must return this little one to his bed. My lady, I bid you good-night.'

Ida watched her go down the stairs, carrying the child

194

with all the care of a precious burden. He looked over his mother's shoulder at Ida and peeped her a shy smile that cut through all her defences. Feeling shaky and close to tears, she closed the door and returned to the fireside.

Roger drew her back into his lap and she curled there, absorbing the warmth of his body and the heat from the fire, and although she stopped shivering, there was still a place inside her that remained desolate and cold.

18

Winchester, Christmas 1181

'Marriage suits you well,' Hodierna remarked to Ida with a gleam in her eyes as the women sat with their sewing and gossip in one of the domestic chambers in Winchester Castle. 'There's pink in your cheeks and I swear you are plumper already. Has that husband of yours been feeding you up?'

Ida smiled, thinking of buttered toast, and looked demurely at her needlework. She was embellishing one of Roger's tunics with a design of running stags and intended giving it to him as a gift on the twelfth day of the festivities. The three weeks since her wedding had flown with the speed of a peregrine on the stoop. There had been estates other than Framlingham to visit, although they had not been able to range too far because of returning to Winchester, but Roger had taken her to visit Yarmouth and Ipswich. Watching the bustle on the dockside of the latter town, an icy wind blowing onshore from Flanders, listening to Roger discuss business with his quay master, Alexander, Ida realised that her husband was a greater man than his quiet demeanour at court and the state of Framlingham suggested. Even with substantial parts of his inheritance farmed out to Henry's officers, he was a wealthy man.

'Well?' Hodierna prompted when Ida did not immediately reply. 'Have you nothing to say?'

Ida took another stitch. 'Perhaps I do not know where to begin,' she said. 'But you are right, marriage does suit me well.'

'It certainly suits your husband,' Hodierna smiled. 'I've never seen him so relaxed at court. When he looks at you, the source is plain. He is a very proud and satisfied man, I would say.'

Ida blushed, then laughed and told Hodierna about falling asleep on their first evening at Framlingham.

Hodierna's shoulders shook with mirth. 'It is your honey month, it's to be expected,' she said and patted Ida's knee affectionately. 'You should make the most of each other while all is fresh and new.'

Ida grimaced. 'If I could have my way, we would have stayed at Framlingham or Ipswich or Thetford all winter.' She gave a pensive little sigh. 'There is so much we do not know about each other and I fear we will never have the time to learn.'

Hodierna patted Ida's knee again, more seriously now. 'You had the wherewithal to choose the man,' she said. 'Now use that wherewithal to accomplish the rest.'

There was a sudden flurry at the chamber door and, to a fanfare, an usher cried the arrival of Queen Eleanor. Ida gasped at the announcement. Embarrassment and shame flooded through her and she would have fled the room, save there was no way out but past Eleanor herself. Although Ida had become Henry's mistress long after Eleanor's imprisonment, she still felt dreadfully uncomfortable. She had never thought to come face to face with the Queen. With the rest of the women, she rose to her feet and curtseyed. That Eleanor was here in Winchester rather than being kept under house arrest at Salisbury was a concession to the season, a sign that Henry's rancour towards her was mellowing, and an indication that he needed her presence for political reasons.

Eleanor bade the women be seated and joined them at the fire. She had a separate chair with gold cushions and a footstool on which to rest her feet. At almost sixty years old, she still possessed the charisma that had made her name famous throughout Christendom, first as the young Queen of France who had ridden to Jerusalem with her husband, leaving a trail of allure and scandal, and then as the worldly wife of the nineteen-year-old Duke of Normandy, where, indeed, she had done the same. Ida kept her eyes downcast and tried to remain an anonymous lady by the fire, but soon found herself admiring the rich braid edging the Queen's mantle and pondering the thread sequence needed to work out the pattern. However, she was not the only woman round the fire admiring the sight of fine textile work.

'My lord Bigod is going to be the most handsomely attired man at court,' the Queen said with a smile. 'Is the design of your own making?'

Ida almost jumped out of her skin because it was obvious that Eleanor knew who she was. Then again, it was foolish to think she wouldn't. Even under house arrest, so formidable a woman would not be ignorant of the happenings at court. 'Yes, madam, it is,' Ida managed to say, wishing that she could melt into the wall and disappear.

'Such beautiful colours. Where do you get your silks?'

Ida mentioned the name of a trader in Winchester and the conversation began to flow more easily as other women joined in, wanting to know details, making recommendations of their own. Eleanor had her musicians entertain the women and, under cover of the strains of lute, citole and pipe, lightly touched Ida's arm. 'I know my husband,' she said quietly. 'I do not bear grudges against the innocent, Lady Bigod. Let that be understood.'

'Yes, madam,' Ida said and, although she remained uncomfortable, Eleanor's kindness took the edge off her anxiety.

The lord John arrived to pay his respects to his mother, kneeling to kiss her hand and bowing his head. Eleanor greeted him warmly enough, but there was an underlying friction between them, as if they were two rough-edged stones lying side by side on a swift river bed. But then, Ida thought, they were strangers to each other. Eleanor had been imprisoned when John was a little boy and he had been raised at his father's court under his father's influence. The parallels with her own situation were painful and obvious. How much of a stranger was she going to become to William as the years rolled out? Would she be greeted like this one day by a youth on the edge of manhood, a youth whose experiences of the world had been filtered through Henry's eyes and the life of the court? The missing years to come were a grief she could not begin to contemplate.

More women arrived to pay their respects; among them, Eleanor's sister-in-law Isabelle de Warenne and her children. Her son was a spotty, dark-haired youth about the same age as John. His sister was just beginning to develop womanly curves. Her fair-brown hair fell to her waist in two neat, thick braids and she had a shy smile. John stared at her with predatory eyes and moistened his lips. Beyond the adolescents, a couple of younger children waited their turn to greet Eleanor, and behind them a nurse bore a wriggling toddler in her arms.

A pang seized Ida's heart as she set eyes on her son. He was wearing a tunic she had made for him of warm winter wool and a little blue hood with an edge of coney fur. Seeing her among the women, he shouted, 'Mama!' and struggled to be set down. The woman hesitated for a moment, then let him go, and he ran to Ida. She opened her arms and engulfed him, drawing him into her lap, feeling that terrible surge of love and loss roll through her again like a tidal wave. The anguish was so strong it was a physical pain.

He wanted to play a hand-clapping game with her, but once he had repeated it twice, he grew restless and was off like a buzzy little fly to play with his younger cousins who were dancing in a circle to Eleanor's music and holding hands. Ida sniffed and wiped her eyes on the back of her hand.

'Sons always leave you,' Eleanor said. Her voice was hard and although her gaze held compassion, there was severity too. 'Husbands are no better. Look to them for moments of joy, but do not invest your happiness in them, for they will squander it.'

'Madam, I am sorry . . .'

'Do not be,' Eleanor replied sharply. 'The more time you spend apologising for things that are not your fault, the more you will fade until you become a shadow. Your mother did not bear you to be a shadow, either of yourself, or of a man. Remember that, Ida. You stand in your own light.'

Her comments touched a raw part deep within Ida and made her want to cry even more – in recognition, and at the pain of the illumination. Nor was she certain that she wanted to look at what the light was showing her.

'My lord Bigod . . .' Eleanor said thoughtfully. 'I do not know him well, but men speak highly of him, including those whom I trust to give me straight opinions. I remember him a little when he was much younger – no more than a pup. He was always quiet, a watcher I used to think, not a doer, but he has proven himself since then – if not always to my advantage,' she added wryly.

For a moment Ida wasn't sure what the Queen meant, but then realised Roger had stood against her faction in the rebellion of eight years ago, and brought down her supporters at the battle of Fornham.

'Yes.' Eleanor tilted her head, considering. 'You suit him, I think. You both have great courage and you will give it to your children.'

Ida blinked on the prickling heat behind her lids. Little William, dancing with his cousins, became a sparkling blur. 'I do not feel brave, madam.'

'Those who feel brave are not always the most courageous,' Eleanor said. 'It takes much to stand firm when one is daunted.' She was silent for a moment, then continued, 'Your husband, I understand, is skilled in the finer points of the law, but I suppose he has had to be. I am told that the King restored him three manors and pardoned him a debt as a wedding gift.'

'That is so, madam.' Ida wondered where Eleanor was leading with this.

The Queen arched a thin eyebrow. 'Three manors that were confiscated as part of the inheritance dispute between your husband and the former Countess of Norfolk and her sons. The lady Gundreda has been petitioning me.'

Ida made herself focus fully on Eleanor rather than William. This could be dangerous. 'The lady Gundreda has no right to those manors,' she said. 'If the King chooses to restore them to my husband as a gesture of goodwill, then that is right and good.'

'And my lord Bigod is hardly going to refuse them, is he?' Eleanor said with a dry smile.

'No, madam.' Ida raised her chin. 'They are his inheritance and he has offered neither bribes nor spread rumours abroad in order to have them.'

Eleanor's lips quirked. 'Bribes and rumours,' she said. 'Well, I have been the recipient and the bestower of plenty of those in my lifetime, and look what it has done for me.' She gave Ida an assessing look. 'Sometimes, more than bribes and rumours and even beyond family ties and the obligation of lord and vassal, a bond is a matter of personal preference. I have promoted men in my service because I have wanted to reward valour and loyalty. Sometimes I have rewarded their womenfolk for services too. That is something to think about.'

William dashed back to Ida to sit in her lap but she barely had a moment to put her arms around him before he was off again, brimful of energy. Eleanor had given her so much to think about that her mind was spinning, yet she felt invigorated too.

When Eleanor rose to leave, she gave Ida an exquisite ivory needle case and a dimpled gold thimble. 'No doubt you have had your share of such gauds from my husband, but these carry nothing with them except my good wishes for your marriage,' Eleanor told her. 'Think on what I have said whenever you are at your needlecraft.'

'Indeed, madam, I will!' Ida curtseyed to Eleanor, aware that the relationship between them had been utterly redefined in the space of an afternoon and while Eleanor had done that redefining, Ida had learned a great deal.

It was a wrench for her when William had to leave with his nurse as the court prepared to dine, but after a final cuddle, she pressed her lips together, maintained her composure and watched him depart, even though her heart threatened to shatter all over again. For his sake, she had to let him go.

Roger had rented lodgings not far from the castle, in a complex of houses owned by the monks of Troarn Abbey. It was only a short walk from the castle, but gave him and Ida a little more privacy than sleeping there would have done and in their newly wedded state, being alone was something to look forward to and savour.

Henry had put Roger back in harness. He had witnessed a couple of charters and been consulted on several points of law. He had not had much time to speak to Ida alone, for they had had to socialise with others at the dinner gathering, and this was the first time since this morning they had been alone with each other.

Roger sat down on the bed and waited as Ida dismissed her women to their sleeping chamber beyond the partitioning curtain. He knew she had spent the afternoon with the Queen, but she had said nothing of the meeting. He thought she seemed a little quiet and preoccupied.

Her loose hair gleamed like polished oak. Watching her move towards him, her fine chemise showing her body through the linen, a warmth of love and desire infused Roger's body. Over the past three weeks, it had become a familiar and welcome sensation – like feeling full after the first good meal following Lent. He wanted to take her to bed and love her until they were both flushed and breathless. Indeed, he was not sure how he had lived without such joy in his life before. Having returned to court, his wanting was tinged with jealousy too. With Henry in proximity, Roger was keen to keep Ida to himself and reaffirm his possession every time the opportunity arose.

She came to him willingly when he held out his hand

and her response was as eager as his own, perhaps more so, and in a matter of minutes, she was clutching him and gasping his name in the throes of climax. Roger kissed her soft white throat and felt her pulse thundering against his lips, and he sensed that for both of them the intensity of the release was more than just a thing born of physical attraction, but came from the tensions pent up during the course of the day.

Rolling over, he drew her with him so that she lay over him, her dark hair webbing his chest, her body intimately pressed the length of his. 'Ida,' he said with a tender smile, using her name now in the aftermath as she had used his in the throes.

She lowered her lashes in that lovely shy way she had and then slanted him a melting doe-brown gaze that almost undid him all over again. Then, with a sudden, subtle change of mood, she sat up, straddling him, the move one of comfortable intimacy rather than an invitation to further sexual congress. Roger ran his hands through her hair for the pleasure of feeling its cool silkiness. Henry must have done this too, but he wouldn't think on it. She was his now.

'There is something I want to talk to you about,' she said, and now her mouth was serious.

With the ghost of Henry still in his mind, he was suddenly wary. 'What?'

'You should know that Gundreda has been petitioning the Queen about your inheritance dispute. Eleanor spoke to me about it earlier.'

Relieved that this was not about Henry, or the child, whom he knew she must have seen today, he shrugged. 'Gundreda will have no joy from that quarter. What can Eleanor do? The inheritance is down to the decision of the King's court, and the Queen is under house arrest.'

'I do not think she is concerned either way,' Ida replied. 'I received the impression that she sympathised with Gundreda's position and was unsure about you, but she was kind to me.' She lifted herself off him and went to fetch them wine. Heavy-eyed, Roger watched the gleaming sway of her hair and the way it ended just above the curve of her pert buttocks, each a perfect handful.

Ida poured from flagon to cups. 'I thought the Queen might not take to me because of . . . because of what I had been to the King, but she bore me no ill will.'

Roger grunted. 'She would have been a fool if she did – for something that was none of your fault. And from what I know of Eleanor, she is far from that, even if she has made mistakes of judgement.' He took the cup from her. 'It is a good thing if you can win her approval though – and interesting that she told you about Gundreda when she need not have done.'

Ida sat on the bed, one leg folded and pointed towards him. She tucked her hair behind her ears. 'I think she took to me and felt I should not be at a disadvantage.' She looked down at her cup. 'I also think she was testing me.'

Roger raised an eyebrow. 'In what way?'

'To see if I was clever enough to understand, or if I was no more than a plaything with feathers for brains. I think she likes to try people's mettle. If Gundreda has approached the Queen, might she not have made approaches elsewhere too?'

Roger's gaze sharpened. 'Such as?'

'Your father supported the Young King, and your half-brother fought for him. If Henry has passed the case to London and in the meantime restored you three manors, then perhaps Gundreda and your stepbrothers are considering it more profitable to petition elsewhere.'

Roger almost snorted at the notion of Henry's feckless

heir being of any use to anyone, but checked himself.
When Henry died, that feckless heir would be their King,
and would have his own favourites and preferences to
promote. 'So, was she suggesting that I might consider it
prudent to offer my services to the Young King, or was
she warning me, through you, that the game was afoot
and to cover myself?'

Ida shrugged. 'She spoke in the vaguest of terms. I
think she has cast the dice in the air and left you to decide
how you will deal with them when they land.'

Roger pretended to look studious. 'There is only one
answer to that.'

Ida looked at him.

'Never trust to luck unless the dice belong to you . . .
and they are fixed in your favour.' He smiled at her. 'And
thank God for an astute wife.'

19

Senlis, Normandy, late March 1182

Roger set his foot in the stirrup and swung astride his new young stallion. The horse danced and side-stepped, swishing its tail, and Roger eased in the reins. 'Whoa,' he soothed, 'whoa,' and patted the destrier's sweating neck.

King Henry was at Senlis to discuss matters of policy with the King of France, the Count of Flanders, the Papal Legate and his eldest son, Henry the Young King. Amidst the duties of attending on their lords, the knights were using the assembly to look over each other's equipment, seek out acquaintances from the tourney circuit, catch up on news and test each other's mettle.

Roger had brought several horses to Senlis from the stud at Montfiquet and he intended selling them at a good profit. He had a steward to deal with such things on a daily basis, but Roger regarded working with the horses and choosing their bloodlines as both a craft and a pleasure and involved himself whenever the opportunity came his way.

'I do not suppose that one is for sale?' William Marshal asked wistfully as he watched Roger control the young stallion with heels and hands before dismounting.

Some of the knights had caparisoned their mounts in the latest barding, but Roger had left his stallion unclad save for a magnificent breast-band of polished leather, enhanced by pendants bearing the Bigod cross. The destrier's hide was like black silk shot with tones of ruby and there was no point in concealing the goods. He wanted men to look and remember.

Grinning, Roger shook his head. 'You are right, messire. He is still not fully trained. I intend bringing him on so that he's ready in a couple of years' time to replace the horse I have now.' He rubbed his jaw. 'I do have two colts of the same siring for sale to interested parties though, and when this one is not in the field, he'll be running with my mares and available for siring duties.'

'What's his stamina like?'

'He'll hunt and hack for miles as well as run to the tilt.' Roger turned to slap the stallion's deep, glossy hide. 'Perhaps not enough meat on him yet, but that will come by the time he's ready.'

'I can see that from the set of him.' William Marshal smiled at Roger. 'My father harboured a preference for greys, but that was because they stood out in a crowd and he was always a rallying point for his men. Everyone knew where my father was in the midst of the fray.'

'They say that about you, messire, but you do not need a grey for that.'

William made a gesture of modest negation. 'I have heard stories about you also, my lord.'

Roger shrugged, although he felt pleased. 'A little reputation goes a long way.'

'You would be surprised at how much you have.' William glanced, stepped back and bowed. Turning, Roger saw Ida approaching with her ladies and two male attendants laden with packages.

'Lady Bigod.' William performed a deep bow. 'It would be difficult for anything to gladden a man's eye more than the sight of all these fine horses, but you manage it effortlessly.'

Ida laughed at him as she responded with a curtsey. 'Not effortlessly,' she said, 'but I try.' She turned to Roger. 'I've come to watch you put Vavasour through his paces.' She rubbed the stallion's muzzle and gave her husband a shining look.

William Marshal inclined his head to Roger and prepared to take his leave. 'I envy you, my lord,' he said. 'The best horse on the field and the finest woman to wife.'

Roger acknowledged the salute with a courtly flourish. 'May you be one day similarly blessed, messire, and in the meantime I bow to the greatest knight in the tourney.'

William showed his fine teeth as he laughed, but was clearly pleased by the compliment. 'That has yet to be decided.' He bowed again as the Young King arrived, the latter slapping his gauntlets against his thigh in a gesture of irritation.

'I've been looking for you,' he said querulously.

'I am sorry, sire; I was on my way to your pavilion when I was waylaid by my lord Bigod's stallion. Is this not the best warhorse you have ever seen?'

Roger's eyes briefly met William's and a swift flicker of understanding passed between them. The Young King was being petulant and William was distracting him, as one might distract a child with a sweetmeat.

England's heir swept his gaze over Vavasour and grudgingly admitted that yes, it was a magnificent beast. His gaze fixed upon Ida. 'Does my father know you are abroad?' he asked with a slight sneer in his tone.

There was an awkward silence. Ida reddened and lowered her eyes. Roger realised there was no reason the

Young King should know about his marriage. 'Sire, Ida has been my wife since the beginning of December,' he said.

The young man looked taken aback, and then he laughed and flourished his hand at Roger. 'Then I congratulate you, my lord, for finding my father's favour . . . and you, my lady, for the same.' He dipped his head in Ida's direction.

Roger stiffened. The words in themselves were not an insult but the intent behind them was definitely mischievous.

Young Henry walked around the stallion again. 'A pity he's not a grey,' he said. 'He'd be worth more.' He gave Roger a sly look. 'Your half-brothers are here, did you know?'

Ida stifled a gasp of dismay. 'Yes, I had heard, sire,' Roger said, wishing the Young King to perdition. He had been trying to keep such news from Ida because he knew she would fuss. Huon had recently been following in the Young King's entourage, picking up crumbs where they fell, obviously cultivating what he saw as his future.

'He'll be riding to tourney under my banner. You might encounter him on the field, but of course any combat will be *à plaisance*.' With a slap to Vavasour's glossy rump that made the stallion flinch, Young Henry strolled on his way. William bowed again to Ida and Roger, his expression studiously blank, and followed his lord.

'He tries to rile me because I am of his father's faction and what happened at Fornham still sticks in his craw,' Roger said, his voice calm, although inside he was seething.

'Why didn't you tell me your brothers were here?'

'Because it's not important. Let them petition where they will; it will do them no good.'

'But what if they petition with swords and lances?'

210

Roger gave an irritated shrug. 'As the Young King says, the matches are to prove valour. His father is here to discuss policy with his neighbours. There might be war next month or next year, but not today. These bouts will be all show and no substance. Nothing's going to happen.'

'So you say.'

'I've been defending myself against Huon and Will for too long now to be caught out.' He gave an impatient sigh. 'My love, I know how to look after myself and I am never reckless . . . although, having said that, leaving you to go about the market place with a full purse must be one of the rashest acts I have ever committed.'

'Do not try to cozen me with jests,' she snapped.

'Then trust me.' He raised his thumb to smooth the frown from between her brows, then leaned forward and kissed her. 'I've been forewarned; I'll come to no harm.'

Following more cajoling reassurances, Roger watched her leave in the direction of his pavilion. He could tell that she was still upset and not convinced, but he would make it up to her later. He was not going to skulk on the periphery and abstain from taking part in the day's sport. He was sufficiently skilled to deal with anything his half-brothers might strew across his path.

Once inside the safety of Roger's pavilion, Ida yielded to her distress and had a good cry. The Young King's words were like a shallow cut from a thin-bladed knife. Not deep or mortal, but still hurtful. Men said he was great in chivalry, but he had all of the superficial trappings and none of the substance. Roger was twice the man he was. And the notion of her husband's half-brother being on the field terrified her. What would happen if Roger were wounded – or worse? The thought made her feel sick.

She realised that she was at a crossroads. She could

either lie here in the tent, a cold cloth over her brow, and ignore the world, or she could go out and bear witness. With abrupt decision, wiping her eyes, she rose to her feet and bade Bertrice attend her.

'Mistress, you should stay here,' Bertrice said with concern.

Ida shook her head. 'No, I am well and I will go out and watch my lord at the tourney.'

'But you should not disturb yourself, not when—'

'Whether I stay or go I will be disturbed,' Ida interrupted, lifting her chin. 'I will watch, and my husband will know my pride in him.'

Ida gathered with the rest of the spectators on the edge of the field as the knights limbered up. The sun was warm for March but a cold breeze made her glad of her fur-lined cloak. The chamberlain's boy had carried a wooden bench from the pavilion so the women could sit down and Ida was thankful to do so.

Roger had given Vavasour to one of his younger knights to parade up and down and was preparing to mount his experienced destrier, Marteal, a powerful dark chestnut with white-striped nose, a son and replacement of his sire, Sorel. The stallion wore the barding of red and yellow that Ida and her women had stitched in the weeks before her marriage. Roger himself sported a parti-coloured surcoat of red and yellow silk and a plait of the same colours bound around the brow of his helm. Ida thought she would burst with love and pride as she watched him leap to the saddle as nimbly as the youths who were employed to show off the paces of the coursers and fast horses. His squire handed up his shield and Roger took his striped painted lance from the young man and turned his rein towards the field, Anketil riding at his left shoulder.

212

William Marshal and the Young King were sparring together as they warmed up. Both men were accomplished fighters and Ida could tell they were pulling their blows as they steadily stretched themselves and their mounts. Roger and Anketil began sparring too and Ida was unable to take her eyes from her husband's coordination and nimble grace. He didn't have the bulk of the Marshal, but he was balanced, athletic, and fast.

The field grew busier as more knights arrived with their retinues. The shouts became louder, the smells more pungent, the colours more vivid as the gaps filled in. Men rode to join their companions, and since the King of England and his eldest son were ostensibly at peace, Roger and his entourage joined up with the knights belonging to the Young King to face the French and the Flemish. Ida noticed the Young King welcome Roger with a hand-clasp as their mounts trotted past each other, but she supposed whatever their differences, a good fighting man was a good fighting man.

From small warm-up combats, the groups became larger and the trials of strength more robust and determined. Shields clattered together, scratching colours, feathering rips in the leather coverings, scoring gouges. Men strove to drag each other's mounts out of the fray by the bridle. The yells of the heralds, bellowing commands in the names of their lords, the din of thundering hooves, hard breathing from the toiling destriers and the thud of weaponry on shields made Ida feel as if she were perched on the edge of a thunderstorm.

She watched for Roger among the knights and glimpsed him for a moment, turning Marteal at the gallop and, with precise control, seizing another knight's bridle. The red and yellow barding flowed like coloured water; clods churned from beneath the destrier's hooves. The motion of man and horse combined was like watching a war song come to life and Ida's stomach churned with the queasiness of fear and overwhelming pride.

Two latecomers cantered on to the field, their mounts caparisoned in the same colours as Roger's, although theirs were quartered rather than parti-coloured, and their shields bore not only the red Bigod cross on its yellow background, but crenellations in red across the top section. For a moment Ida thought that some of her husband's knights were late to the meet, but almost immediately realised these must be his half-brothers. As she watched, they spurred their mounts towards the fray, one going left, the other right.

Ida jerked to her feet and stared out across the churn of men and horses, but she couldn't see her husband amid the throng. Dear God. She pressed her hand to her breast, suddenly short of breath.

Her line of sight was blocked as two knights galloped so close to her that foam from a destrier's mouth spattered her dress. The stallion's ears were back and its teeth bared. One knight had hold of his opponent's bridle and was striving to drag him off the field while the captive man battled to win free. His stallion false-footed and pitched; he was thrown and landed heavily. Squires pelted on to the field to help him and his erstwhile opponent grabbed and steadied the sweating, trembling horse. The injured knight groaned and writhed on the ground, his leg twisted to one side at an odd angle. Bile rose in Ida's throat.

Bertrice tugged at her sleeve. 'Madam, you are too close, come away.'

The squires carried the stricken knight off in the direction of one of the pavilions. Ida searched frantically for Roger and Marteal on the tourney ground but couldn't see him. Red and yellow were popular colours and it was difficult to tell who was who at a glance; besides, the mêlée had spread out from the original core and moved to the field beyond and the one behind that too. She dug her nails into her damp palms. Roger's brothers would not dare to attack him at so public an event and wearing identifying blazons, but tourneys were notorious for being venues where men settled their grudges and began new ones. Supposedly, they were fighting on the same side, but that meant nothing. A blow from behind was more dangerous than one to the fore.

Roger enjoyed the warm-up bouts. Although he had kept himself in practice, it had been some time since he had competed on the tourney field. The horses were still a little stale from winter quarters, but like their riders were eager for the exercise. Marteal bucked and frisked at first and Roger let him have his head for a while, before drawing in the rein and steadying him down. It was wonderful to heft a lance and feel the responsive turn of a powerful horse beneath him.

As the competition warmed up, he charged to meet the challenge of a French knight. Marteal was moving faster than his opponent's destrier and Roger's aim was true; but the Frenchman was solid in the saddle and Roger's blow didn't dislodge him. Roger seized the man's bridle and began dragging him towards the back of the English line. The knight used his heels to try and turn his stallion but Roger had too firm a grip. His adversary then thought to unfasten his mount's bridle and escape that way, but Roger covered the move, guiding Marteal round so that he pressed in hard to the other stallion's side. The destriers snapped and plunged as the men exchanged a flurry of blows. For a moment, it seemed

215

that the Frenchman's greater physical strength would win, but Roger held steady and trusted to his skill, and the breeding and courage of his mount. The knight grunted in pain and recoiled as one of Roger's blows landed behind his shield. Again, Roger seized the knight's bridle and spurred for the English lines. The knight made one last desperate bid to escape, but Roger was as determined as his opponent was stubborn, and in the matter of stamina, Roger had the edge. Finally, the knight was forced to admit grudging defeat and pledge his ransom, informing Roger with nasal superiority that the Normans who had settled in England knew how to brawl even if they had no sense of propriety. Roger agreed with him, using the quiet irony of impeccable manners to conclude the exchange. Then, grinning inside his mouth, the first all-important take accomplished, he cantered back into the fray, intent upon enjoying himself.

Ranging further afield, he added two more ransoms to his tally, saved Anketil from being captured in a vigorous bout, and finally decided that it was time to retire to one of the designated rest areas to refresh himself and the horse. It was never wise to ride to exhaustion on the tourney field because there were always carrion crows looking to pick on the vulnerable.

Anketil, who had been rubbing a bruised shoulder, suddenly dropped his hand to his rein and cried a warning. Instinctively, Roger raised his shield and hefted his sword. His own colours flashed at him as Huon, astride a sweating chestnut horse, thundered in from the left. His lance was levelled at Roger and at the angle it was coming, there was nothing to prevent it from striking Roger from the saddle and stoving in his ribs at the same time. Roger had time only to turn his shield to try and guard his body. The impact of the blow was unsustainable and he was flung from the saddle. The remaining air slammed from his lungs as he struck the ground and pain engulfed his diaphragm which had turned into an airless cavern. Through the agony to breathe, Roger knew if he stayed down, he would be trampled to death, his demise explained away as a tragic accident of the day's sport. On little more than instinct, he rolled over and somehow found his feet. Huon had turned his destrier and was pounding back to finish him, his lance levelled. Although the tip was blunted, Roger knew the damage it would do. A punch in the right place was just as effective as a blade.

His younger half-brother had seized Marteal's reins and was leading him off as a spoil of war. Anketil was striving to bring his tired horse to bear on Huon, but his damaged shoulder was hampering his efforts and Roger's other knights were too far away to be of aid in the moment. Roger managed to get his shield up in time, but the blow was punishing and floored him. Huon turned in a tighter circle, fretting his horse. Roger staggered up again, his vision blurring at the edges, each breath excruciating. Summoning his will power and the last of his strength, he took his shield by the long strap and swung it at the chestnut's head. The stallion shied and slipped on its haunches. Huon was thrown and landed hard, half on the curved edge of his own shield. He cried out, pressing his hand to his side. Roger staggered over to him and gave him a kick.

'Get up!' he choked. 'Get up, you worthless turd, damn you!'

The response was a muffled groan from inside Huon's helm. Roger dropped to his knees, his breath sawing in his throat, and having drawn his dagger, slashed the laces attaching Huon's helm to the mail shirt and pulled it off. Huon's face was red with effort and exertion. Blood poured from his mouth and dribbled down his chin. Despite his rage, Roger felt a frisson of shock.

William Marshal arrived at a rapid trot, leading Marteal by the reins. Removing his helm, he dismounted and stooped over the fallen man to examine him. 'Bitten lip,' he told Roger. 'He'll not be chewing bread for a day or two. Cracked ribs too, I hazard . . . Are you all right, my lord?'

Roger strove to draw breath. His chest wasn't big enough to hold the breath he needed, nor to contain the emotion boiling inside him. He was suffocating on rage, shock and the effort of holding back the battle wildness. He was relieved his half-brother was not mortally injured and, at the same time, he was wishing him dead and burning in the pit of hell. He nodded brusquely. 'Just bruised,' he croaked, sheathing his dagger and removing his own helm. He looked at Huon, lying semi-conscious at his feet, and restrained the urge to kick him again.

'I'll escort you and your man to your refuge,' William said. 'That way you won't be set upon by anyone else intent on plundering men in need of respite.' His voice and expression were carefully impassive. 'It is for my lord to say whom he takes into his entourage, but I will not be endorsing your brothers beyond this day.'

Roger nodded stiffly. 'Thank you, Messire Marshal. That will be welcome.'

William gestured over his shoulder to Marteal, whom his knight Harry Norreis was holding by the reins. A spark of wintry humour lit in his eyes. 'I came across a churl with no right to this horse, so I rectified matters. Please, accept his return with my good wishes.'

Roger thanked William again and took Marteal's bridle. Another knight of William Marshal's company held the destriers belonging to Huon and Will. The latter, unhorsed and bereft, was limping disconsolately towards the edge

218

of the field. He shot a glare in Roger's direction, but did not approach.

'I have been expecting something of this ilk to happen for a long time,' Roger said as William escorted him to the refuge. Neither man cast a backwards look at Huon, who was now sitting up, clutching his ribs. 'It was my own fault I was taken by surprise. I knew they were here and I knew that Huon at least was spoiling for a fight.'

'A man can put safeguards in place and have friends to watch his back, but it is not always enough,' William said. 'I am sorry I was not sooner to your aid.'

Roger made a gesture of negation. 'Even so I am grateful. And for the return of my horse.'

William dipped his head. 'You are welcome, my lord. It was my pleasure.'

Roger found a smile. The Marshal was too courteous to state the obvious – that returning the best horse was a sign of knightly largesse and diplomacy, and he was still in profit because he had the other two and their accoutrements to either ransom back to their owners or sell on.

The Marshal left Roger at the refuge, collected a fresh lance and, saluting him in farewell, spurred back on to the field.

Roger dismounted again. Suddenly his legs were shaking and he had to lean against Marteal's solid shoulder and neck for support.

Anketil eased from the saddle with a groan. 'If this is sport, my lord, give me a battle any day.'

Roger eyed the knight sidelong and felt his chest tighten again. Anketil's words were not funny, but they touched a spring inside him and he began to laugh. 'Oh indeed,' he spluttered, 'by all means let us have a battle.' He choked on his mirth and Anketil thumped him on the back, which almost dropped him to the ground again.

'Sire, I can see the lady Ida coming this way with her women,' warned Oliver Vaux.

Roger bent over, hands on knees, and fought for composure. By the time Ida arrived, he was standing up straight and wiping his eyes with his index finger.

'Praise God you are safe!' She grasped his arm as if confirming sight with touch. Her face was white and her eyes full of anxiety. 'What's the matter?'

He shook his head. 'Nothing. Anketil said something funny.' Resisting the urge to start laughing again, he wondered how much she had seen and glanced over his shoulder, judging distance and visibility from where she had been sitting.

'Your half-brothers . . .' Her voice quivered.

'. . . have been taught a lesson. Come, help me unarm.' He gestured in the direction of the pavilions. He badly needed to take a respite away from public scrutiny and Henry would expect his attendance in council later for which he would have to be alert and composed. Besides, he didn't want Ida succumbing to hysterics in front of everyone and, just now, it looked a distinct possibility.

Once within his pavilion, Ida waited while his squires unarmed him, then she dismissed everyone and poured him wine herself. When he gingerly eased off his tunic and shirt to change them for fresher raiment in which to face the King, she was horrified to see the purplish-red marks mottling his arms and torso where he had fallen.

'Bruises,' he said with a rueful shrug. 'I'll be stiff and sore for a few days, but there's no lasting harm. You expect it of the sport. Marshal was telling me he once got his head stuck inside his helm and the only way to get the thing off was to lie down on the blacksmith's anvil.' He gave her a keen look. 'How much did you see?'

220

Ida shuddered. 'Mercifully there were too many others in the way, but I saw William Marshal escorting you to the refuge.' She fixed him with an accusatory stare. 'If you are asking me, it means you have details to hide.'

He feigned nonchalance. 'Not really. I came to blows with Huon but he received the worst of it even though he was first to attack. Marshal dealt with Will, rescued my horse and mopped up.' Carefully and in some pain, he set his arm round her. 'I am all right, my love, I swear, better than my brothers. Huon has broken ribs for certain.'

Her knees gave way. Gasping with the pain of sudden movement, Roger caught her and lowered her on to his camp chair. He had known she was sensitive, but he hadn't thought her squeamish. He wrung out the washcloth in the rose water and wiped her brow with it, wondering if he should shout for her women, but he didn't want them twittering around like a flock of bossy sparrows and making things worse. 'Ida?'

'I have some news for you,' she said as she rallied. 'I was going to leave it until later, but I will tell you now. I am with child.'

Roger heard and understood the words perfectly well, but it took his mind a moment to assimilate them. They had been married for almost four months and she had had her women's courses three times that he remembered. 'You are sure?'

She nodded. 'I have thought so for several days, but what happened just now only makes me more certain.'

She looked so slight sitting there, her soft brown eyes haunted and shadowed. He didn't know whether to grin and caper or enfold her in his arms and treat her like the rarest, fragile glass. Suddenly he was breathless again, emotion replacing the air in his lungs. Could one suffocate on joy and exultation? 'When?' he demanded eagerly.

'Do you know when?' Falling to his knees before her, he grasped her hands and raised them to his lips.

She laughed shakily. 'I am not entirely sure without consulting a midwife, but before the year's end for certain. I have been hoping and praying and God has been merciful and answered.'

He leaned forward and put his arms around her. Her waist was still slender and her belly flat, but new life was growing there and of his making. He knew that when he went into the royal council that afternoon, it would be with equanimity and a satisfied smile in Henry's direction.

20

Framlingham, October 1182

Hands resting on her swollen belly, Ida supervised her women as they finished hanging the new bed curtains. The heavy red wool was lined with good linen to help them drape well and to add an extra layer of warmth and privacy to the bed enclosed within. The edges of the matching coverlet were stitched with the Bigod device of red crosses on a gold background and the canopy was painted with the same blazon. The walls had received their coating of limewash in the summer and had since been bordered with scrollwork of greenery and delicate scarlet pimpernels. Curtained hangings of red and gold enhanced the wall near the window and of a winter's night they could be drawn across the shutters to make the room cosier.

'Excellent,' she said as a maid secured the last ring and hooked the curtain to the canopy so that the bed became a day couch.

'Fit for a king, my lady.' The woman beamed.

Ida winced. 'Fit for my lord Bigod will suffice,' she answered.

'Yes, but if the King visited, we'd not be disgraced.'

The woman, who was new to her duties, obviously had no inkling of Ida's earlier circumstances, although doubtless would learn in due course as gossip had its way.

Avoiding the gaze of Goda and Bertrice, Ida turned away from the bed. Roese's small son Robert was galloping around the chamber on his toy hobby horse, shouting to an imaginary friend. The baby in Ida's womb gave a vigorous kick and the feeling comforted her. Setting her hand to the activity, she was rewarded by the pressure of a little foot against her palm.

Ida paused before a sturdy cherrywood cradle standing at the bedside. She had come across it while clearing out the undercroft. Roger had been amused and a little rueful to see it, telling her that it had been his, and before that his father's and his grandfather's. She had not asked if it had been used to lull his half-brothers to sleep too; in all likelihood, it had. She tapped her foot gently on one of the rockers, her expression wistful and pensive.

'Madam, your lord is here,' the chamberlain's wife said from the doorway.

Ida's spirits immediately lifted. Roger had been absent for several days in Ipswich and then sitting in session at various Hundred Courts. She hurried to one of the windows and unlatched the shutters on the damp, late October morning. Roger had dismounted from his horse and was in the ward instructing a couple of retainers who were busy with a string of laden pack ponies. He glanced up at the window, saw Ida and smiled at her. She waved to him, turned and, having issued brisk instructions to her women, ran down to greet him.

He swung her round in his arms, kissed her with travel-cold lips, then looked down at the bump swelling between them. 'You are well?'

'The better for having you here,' she said with a

breathless little laugh. 'Are you hungry?' Despite the burden of her pregnancy, she suddenly felt as light as a feather.

'Starving.' He went to warm his hands at the fire.

His men followed him in, all in fine good spirits, and Ida saw that bread, cheese and jugs of wine were provided for all.

'What are the roads like?'

He made a face. 'Boggy with all this autumn rain. At least we'd got pack ponies and not baggage carts.' He made a fuss of a dog that came wagging up to him and gestured to several of the men who had entered with bundles and packages to take them to the private living quarters.

'Just bits and pieces,' he said with a casual wave of his hand as Ida glanced curiously towards them. 'I managed to obtain the threads you asked for and two bolts of Flemish cloth . . . Oh, and some more rose water and that cumin you wanted.'

The food arrived and the servants set up a trestle near the fire. Ida noticed Roger had bought a new hat and she admired the long brim, the subtle rich shades of green and the jaunty spray of pheasant feathers. 'You can hide many thoughts under that,' she teased.

He gave her an amused look. 'Why do you think I bought it? A good hat is worth its price in concealment.'

'It has nothing to do with your fondness for hats?'

He reached for a loaf of bread and broke a chunk off the end. 'Not in the least. A hat is the most practical of all clothing items and a necessity – is it not, Oliver?'

'Yes, my lord,' the knight agreed gravely.

As he ate, Roger told Ida about the business of the Hundred Courts over which he had presided, the matter of forest law transgressions at Weston, and the terms of the serjeantry at Tasburgh, where he had come to an agreement with the tenants that they should provide the service of a man with a lance in times of war in exchange for their land. Ida listened and tried to absorb what he said because it concerned the management of their estates and it was useful to know such things, even though he would have deputies and stewards to attend to matters when he was absent.

The first edge of his hunger satisfied, Roger brushed crumbs from his tunic and fed a remaining crust to a lurking hound. 'I heard something in Ipswich that saddened me.' His expression grew sombre. 'I wondered whether to tell you, but it will be a scandal everywhere soon enough and better you should hear it from me than from casual gossip. William Marshal has been banished from court under threat of death – accused of fornicating with the Young King's wife.'

Ida stared at him in shock. 'I don't believe it! He wouldn't! He's like you – an honourable man. Who would say such things?'

Roger looked wry. 'He has enemies among the Young King's followers – men who resent his position and influence and think it should be theirs. He has become too popular and successful for his own good.'

'But to concoct such a story!' Ida pictured William Marshal. He had been unfailingly kind and courteous to her, even in her days as a concubine, and she knew there was respect and camaraderie between him and Roger.

Roger folded his hands in the space between his knees. 'Marshal and the Young Queen are firm friends. It's not difficult to stretch the detail further. The Young King is already jealous of the Marshal's prowess and the way men adulate him; Henry thinks William responsible for the Young King's profligacy, so he'll be delighted to see him fall from favour.'

'Yes, I often heard him complain about the amounts his son was spending on his retinue – he seemed to think William Marshal was responsible.'

Roger unfolded his hands and gestured. 'There is no denying the Marshal enjoys the fine things in life, but he is no wastrel and the Young King needs no encouragement to spend hard and fast.'

'So what's to become of him?'

Roger sighed. 'He's resigned his position as the Young King's marshal and gone on pilgrimage to the tomb of the three kings at Cologne.'

'And when he returns?'

'That I do not know, but he has many friends and the rents of some houses in Flanders. With his skills, he is never going to lack for employment. But even if he is eventually vindicated, the scandal will leave a bitter taste.' Roger's mouth turned down at the corners. 'It is something the King and his sons are particularly good at doing: mixing bitter brews for others to swallow.'

Ida said nothing. His remark was true but she was unsure how to respond. Henry had seduced her, withheld and disparaged Roger's patrimony and parted her from her son. She knew from the hard glint in Roger's eyes that he was thinking of all of those things.

'Thus are the seeds of discontent and rebellion sown,' he added grimly.

'But William Marshal would not turn against his lord,' she said, and between them, unspoken but acknowledged, hung Roger's own name.

He shot her a dark look. 'No, he would not, because of the honour that his lord and his lord's father have slighted. And within me, such seeds will not germinate because I have seen the harvests reaped by allowing such crops to grow. The King took my father's lands from him,

227

razed his castle, levied fines, and from those fines he built Orford to limit our power. If my father had not rebelled, the Earldom of Norfolk would not have been forfeit.'

'You will regain it though.' She set her hand over his. 'It is but a matter of time.'

'So is Judgement Day,' he retorted, then shrugged his shoulders as if physically ridding himself of burdensome thoughts. 'Come,' he said, and rose to his feet, his expression softening. 'If we are speaking of the future, I have something to show you.'

Smiling, mystified, Ida took his hand and followed him to their bedchamber. She giggled when he made her cover her eyes before he opened the door, and then steered her within, an arm at what had once been her waist.

'Now,' he said. 'Look.'

She lowered her hands and gazed around the room. The servants had put the requested bolts of cloth on the bed and there were a few extra bales of sumptuous colours begging to be examined. Then her gaze fell upon the exquisite latten ewer for bathing a newborn and, beside it, a cradle carved from warm golden oak with a delicate design of clover leaves chiselled on the sides and upon the rocker stands. It was lined with the softest bleached linens and an exquisite coverlet of whitework.

Ida raised her hands to her lips, smothering a soft 'Oh!' of astonishment. She went forward to look, to examine by touch. The wood was smooth and glossy under her fingers, no roughness to cause splinters. A row of silver bells twinkled along one side and rang softly as she set the cradle rocking. Suddenly her eyes were sparkling with tears. She was overwhelmed by his consideration. Most men would not have given a thought to such an item, leaving it to their wives to make those kinds of purchases. She hadn't done so, thinking he would want to keep the old one because of tradition. 'It's beautiful!' She turned and flung her arms around his neck. 'Truly, beautiful!'

'This is a fresh start,' he said, gently stroking her rounded womb. 'This is for *our* sons and daughters. They will be raised to respect the bonds and duties of lineage but I swear on my soul that they will never be tied in knots by them.' His eyelids tensed as he spoke and Ida did not miss the emphasis he put on the word 'our'. There was more to this, she realised, than a gift to please her. It was a statement of intent – a symbolic replacing of their past with their future. She nodded with fierce agreement 'No,' she said with brimming eyes. 'They will not be tied.'

Exactly a year from her wedding day, Ida lay in the great bed at Framlingham and laboured to bear the child in her womb. Although she had endured travail before and knew what to expect, it was still hard, painful work. She had been confessed and shriven lest she succumb to the perils of childbirth, although the midwives seemed confident that all was progressing as it should. Supported by one of the women sitting at her back, Ida bore down with all her might. She had spent hours kneeling in prayer, asking God's mercy, filled with fear that she was going to be punished for her fornication with Henry. What if little William was going to be the only living child she ever bore?

'Ah, here's the head,' said the midwife, her hands busy between Ida's thighs. 'Now the shoulders.' Suddenly her voice changed timbre. 'Caution,' she said. 'Caution, my lady, do not push!'

'What's wrong?' Ida demanded, beset by panic.

'Nothing, my lady, nothing is wrong, but do not push. The cord is around the baby's throat and we do not want it to pull tight . . .'

Ida panted and closed her eyes, fighting the almost

overwhelming urge to bear down. *Dear Virgin, dear Saint Margaret, let the baby live. Do not let it be stillborn . . . Oh please, oh please!*

The midwife nodded up to her. 'Ah, that's it free; push again,' she commanded, 'but gently, my lady, soft as a breeze.'

Ida did as she was bidden and a moment later, the woman lifted up a bluish-coloured scrap from between her thighs. 'A fine boy,' she said as she cleaned the baby's mouth and nose and another woman cut the pulsating cord. 'Come, little one, let's have the breath of life in you. By the blessed grace of God's Holy Mother.' Holding him by the heels, she gave him a sharp tap on the buttocks and he whimpered, and then began to cry. The sound, thready and uncertain at first, gathered strength as the midwife righted him and bore him to the large latten bowl which another woman had filled with warm water scented with rose oil.

'Is he all right?' Frantic with anxiety, Ida watched the midwife.

'Yes, my lady,' the woman assured her. 'We just had a bit of a fright for a moment but all's well.' She smiled broadly. 'He's a finely set little man.' The woman at the bowl finished washing the baby and then he was brought to Ida, wrapped in a warm towel.

Ida was almost afraid to look at him as she took him in her arms. The memory of holding her first newborn son was inextricably linked with this moment now. Then she had been frightened, exhausted and bewildered. Now she was beset by a set of feelings that were different but no less difficult. The exhaustion was the same, but this time there was guilt because of what had happened in the past. She was filled with relief and joy that she had birthed an heir for Roger, and a raw, tender love, but it was barbed with terror that she might not be a good-enough mother and God would see through her and punish her by depriving her yet again. It took all of her courage, but she steeled herself to gaze at her new son.

Mercifully, he bore little resemblance to his half-brother. The shape of his features bore Roger's stamp. His eyebrows were delicate threads of pale gold, not defined dark lines as William's had been. A burst of love flowed from her to him. Ida's throat tightened with the exquisite pain of the feeling and her womb cramped. He was to be called Hugh, a name traditionally carried by sons of the Bigod family, and she whispered that name to him now, promising him he would never lack for anything if her love could provide it. 'Tell my lord,' she said with tear-jewelled lashes. 'Tell him he has a son.'

Feeling apprehensive, excited and decidedly awkward in the arena of women's matters, Roger entered the bedchamber. For the last month as the birth approached, he had been sleeping in a partitioned corner of the hall and conducting all of his business from the main room too, so that Ida and the women had the domestic chamber to themselves for the confinement.

He had been on tenterhooks ever since the labour had begun more than half a day since, had never realised until now how time could stretch for ever and be a punishment. He had thought himself skilled in the art of waiting and being still, but ever since Ida's travail had begun, he had been pacing the hall like a caged beast, snapping at men who asked thoroughly innocuous things of him. The news, brought to him by a smiling, tiptoeing woman, that Ida had been safely delivered of a son had filled him with so much relief that it had numbed him.

From the new golden oak cradle, the cat-like mewing of a newborn infant drew him across the room to look down. His son had been unwrapped and placed naked on a soft lambskin so that Roger could inspect him and see for himself that everything was intact and as it should be. The baby wailed and thrashed its tiny arms and legs like a drunken carole dancer. Its face was red and the rest of it a flushed pink. Roger's numbness dissipated like smoke in the wind.

'A fine, healthy boy, my lord,' said the midwife, smiling at him.

Roger nodded, unable to speak. He felt pride, jubilation and virility. He could now look Henry in the eye with composure.

Dame Cecily picked up the baby and, having expertly swathed him in a linen wrap and then a warm blanket, gave him to Roger. For a moment, he was nonplussed. Then, with an instinct he had not known he possessed, he cradled the fragile little skull and small body along his arm. The baby looked into his face with a quizzical expression that bore the wisdom of ages. Ancient and newborn. His father's face; his grandfather's face. His own and Ida's. For an instant it was almost as if he could see a line of generations stretching to the horizons of distant past and a future long after he was gone.

With tender care, he carried the baby to the bedside. Ida was sitting up against the plumped bolsters. Her hair was freshly braided and, although she looked tired, her eyes were sparkling and there was a smile on her lips. He kissed her gently and sat down.

'The women say you are well . . .' he said awkwardly.

She nodded. 'I am, my lord, even if it was hard work.'

'You've done the name of Bigod and de Tosney proud.'

'I hope I have.' She continued to smile but tears filled her eyes.

'Never doubt it. You have given us a son and even more cause to strive for our future.' He set his free hand over hers in sudden concern. 'Ida?'

'It's usual, I'm told,' she said with a shaken laugh. 'Women always weep after a birthing. Their humours are imbalanced. Let me hold him.'

Gingerly Roger handed the baby to her and watched her cradle him. The way she held their son, her downcast tear-dewed lashes, the blue of the loose gown she was wearing, made him think of the Madonna. Perhaps it was blasphemous to do so, but he hoped God would understand and forgive him. This was no virgin birth, but she was a virtuous wife.

'I have sent word to your brother and my mother,' he said. 'I'll have a messenger take the news to my vassals and the Abbot at Edmundsbury. I'll send a courier to the King too.'

There was a sudden air of tension in the chamber. Mention of Henry was like the pain from a shallow, sharp cut that was slow to heal and, even on a joyous occasion such as this, still had the ability to sting. 'Who knows, now we have an heir, he might grant me my patrimony.' He spoke with more hope than conviction on that score. Indeed, he thought, it might even work the other way. Henry might just be petty enough to withhold his favour now that the family line in male tail was secured.

Roger stayed with Ida until she began to droop with exhaustion and the midwife murmured diplomatically but firmly that she needed to rest. He would rather have remained with his wife and newborn child, but he knew his knights were waiting to celebrate with him and broach the tun of good wine saved for the occasion. 'I'll visit again on the morrow,' he said, kissed her and went reluctantly to the door. On the threshold, he turned and saw her plant a kiss on the baby's head before handing him to the midwife, and felt an all-consuming love.

21

Ipswich, May 1183

Ida was singing a nonsense song to Hugh and making him giggle by blowing on his neck when Roger breezed into the private chamber of their Ipswich house. Her heart quickened at the sight of him. He had been campaigning with Henry across the Narrow Sea and was but recently home. The soldiering had made him hard and fit and put vitality in his step. Ida had missed him terribly, and even now could hardly bear to have him out of her sight, although he had absconded just after dawn to talk business with Alexander, his wharf master.

Hugh squealed at the sight of his father and bounced up and down in Ida's lap. An expression of pleasure and pride on his face, Roger picked up his son and held him above his head. Hugh giggled immensely at this treatment and Roger laughed back at him for a moment, before lowering him and supporting him within the crook of his arm and against his chest. Hugh immediately grabbed for the jewelled cross Roger was wearing round his neck and gave it an experimental bite with his new teeth. Then he pulled away, head wobbling slightly, his gaze fixed on the gleaming red stones, a line of dribble connecting him to them.

Roger grinned. 'A taste for gold already, I see.'

'He has my appreciation of colours,' Ida replied sweetly. 'Have you finished your business?'

'Most of it, but there are still a few things left to do.' He kissed Hugh's cheek, swung him around and handed him to Emma, a rosy-cheeked young woman they had employed to help as a nursemaid. 'Look after him awhile,' he told her. 'Ida, fetch your cloak.'

A little mystified but smiling, Ida donned her mantle and, taking his arm, followed him from the dwelling. In the spring sunshine, the river Orwell swirled in changing shades of green, grey and blue and a variety of vessels bobbed at their quayside moorings. The crew of a Baltic galley toiled to unload honey, wax and barrels of pitch brought from the heart of the Rus lands. Furs too of beaver, sable and wolf. There was even the rare and magnificent pelt of a white bear. The latter fascinated Ida. 'My great-great-grandsire had a cloak made of such a beast,' she said, touching the thick, silver-cream pelt. 'I think the King of Scotland has it now. My great-aunt took it with her when she married him.'

Roger smiled to himself. Ida made little of it, but her cousin removed was William the Lion, King of Scotland. 'Would you want such an item for Framlingham?' he asked.

She gave him a secret look through her lashes. 'Perhaps as a bedcover for the coldest nights.'

He squeezed her waist. 'I can think of a better cover than the pelt of a bear.'

'So can I, but sometimes it is not to hand. I think, though, I would rather our bedcover was of my own work,' she said with double entendre and reached up to stroke his cheek for the joy of touching him. 'That is part of the pleasure, after all.'

His colour darkened and he gave a husky laugh. 'Indeed so,' he replied.

'So perhaps some more cloth and embroidery silks are in order, no?'

Roger laughed harder. 'How can I refuse?'

Arm in arm, they strolled along the quay, inspecting the wares for sale. There were markets further into the town, but many of the shipholders had permission to sell straight from their vessels for a fee. One captain had African pepper for sale and Ida had him grind up a sample in a pestle and mortar. She sniffed the aromas and tested the merest dab on her tongue, then promised to send along the household steward to discuss amount and costs. A sample of Burgundian wine from a vintner's galley cleaned the peppery heat from her mouth and Roger ordered three tuns for the household. There was an ivory teething ring for Hugh, dangling on a ribbon of scarlet silk, and a new hat for Roger, understated, but of luxuriously napped wool in a shade somewhere between purple and midnight-blue. Ida took great pleasure in standing close up to her husband, brushing his hair out of the way with her fingers and arranging the hat to suit. It was all about touch, and by the time she was satisfied with the correct angle and the look of it upon him, she was a little breathless and suffused with warmth.

True to his word, Roger bought her some good Flemish wool from a shipmaster with a consignment of cloth and a tumble of silks in rainbow colours from another trader. Ida pounced on the latter with a cry of delight that made Roger grin and want to take her straight to the bed they had earlier been discussing.

Returning from their foray, however, all notion of

dalliance was set aside by the sight of the horses tethered in the yard. 'Visitors,' Roger said with curiosity and the mildest touch of concern as he recognised an aristocratic black courser with a brocade saddle cloth and silver pendants suspended from the breast-band. 'It's Uncle Aubrey. I wonder what he wants.'

Sitting in Roger's barrel chair by the fire, his expression sombre, Aubrey de Vere rubbed his hands over his knees. 'I gather the messenger from Ranulf de Glanville has not yet found you?'

Roger shook his head. 'De Glanville usually leaves messages to me until he is forced to send them.'

His uncle raised his brows.

'Since one of the justiciar's brothers is wed to my step-mother and another is constable of the keep at Orford, shall we say that we do not dwell in each other's bosoms.'

De Vere gave him an astute look, but forbore to comment on the matter. 'You should know that de Glanville has put all of England on the alert and the Earls of Gloucester and Leicester have been arrested.' He bent a severe look upon Roger. 'You, nephew, are on a warning.'

Roger stared at him in astonishment. 'What?'

His uncle grimaced. 'The Young King is in rebellion again across the Narrow Sea. He's sacking churches and shrines to pay his soldiers and the Limousin is burning. He had two of his father's heralds killed under a banner of truce and when the King himself went to negotiate, the boy's soldiers shot an arbalest quarrel through his cloak.' His lips curled as he said 'boy's', and the title spoke of all he felt, since the Young King was almost thirty years old. 'If Henry wasn't struck, it was by God's mercy. He doesn't want the rebellion spreading to England as it did the last time, and de Glanville has a remit to take into custody all those who would rise in arms against him. Given what happened ten years ago, he's being cautious.'

Roger felt sick with anger. 'Surely the King does not believe I would turn rebel?'

His uncle looked grim. 'If he did, you'd already be in a cell with your lands confiscated. This is by way of a warning that you be careful what you do. If you are to benefit from this and not suffer you must keep your eyes open and your senses alert.'

'The King is my lord and I will serve him to the best of my ability as I have always done,' Roger said stiffly, feeling insulted.

'You have heard no word of rebellion? No rumours?' De Vere gestured towards the door. 'None of the ship-masters or sailors have said anything?'

'Not so much as a fart.' Roger gave a sardonic curl of his lip. 'Even if the King and his sons are quarrelling across the Narrow Sea fit to make each other's ears bleed, no one has yet tried to bribe me with an earldom – from either side, more's the pity. Perhaps Justiciar de Glanville should sort through his own mattress for fleas before inspecting mine.'

His uncle gave him an eloquent look. 'De Glanville is loyal to the King. I dare say he will sort very thoroughly through his own mattress, but not in public.'

'No.' Uttering a deep sigh, Roger made a gesture of acceptance and conciliation. 'Yes, my lord. I will look to my lands and warn the reeves of the coastal villages to be on their guard.'

De Vere nodded approval and pushed back his sleeves as if preparing to get down to work now that the telling was done. 'They're a troublesome brood and no mistake. You see baby birds in the nest, mouths agape for as much and more than their parents can stuff down their maws.

Henry's sons are like that. Whatever he gives them it will never be enough.'

Roger stared at his own baby son, nestling in Ida's lap, contentedly chewing on the new ivory teething ring. 'Perhaps it is indeed that way for birds and kings,' he replied, 'but I swear to God that I will raise no child of mine to be the like of Henry's.'

Ida bit her lip and dropping her gaze, nuzzled Hugh's soft blond hair.

'Do you not fight with your own half-brothers over what is yours and what is theirs?' de Vere asked with a mordant smile.

'No, I fight with them over what is mine.' Roger gave a reluctant huff of laughter. 'Hah, you entangle me in my own net, but I still mean it. Henry's heir is a vain, spoiled child who wants the world on a golden plate and thinks his looks and his smile ought to be enough reason to give it to him. Richard sees his life reflected in the blade of a sword, Geoffrey's a conniving snake and John's a brat who thinks it fun to set fire to a cat's tail and watch it yowl. I am not royalty, but I can do ten times better than that.'

Arms pillowed behind his head, Roger lay in the cramped bed box that his chamberlain had set up on the dais of their quayside hall. Curtains screened him and Ida from the other sleepers in the rest of the room. His uncle, being a guest of standing, had the privilege of the main chamber on the floor above and the good big bed.

Ida set her hand on his chest, spreading her fingers across the triangle of skin exposed by the open laces of his shirt. 'You have been very quiet,' she said.

He gave a soft grunt and lowered one hand to touch her hair. 'I'm just digesting the news my uncle brought to me.'

'The King will not move against you . . . against us.'

He heard the note of anxiety out of her voice. 'Who is to say what the King will and will not do?' he asked sourly. 'I am valued, but I am not trusted. That much is obvious.' He made an impatient sound. 'I think we are safe. As my uncle says, had Henry wanted, he could have ordered me arrested with the Earls of Gloucester and Leicester and de Glanville would not have hesitated to do so given the chance.'

Ida pulled gently at his chest hair. 'I am sad for the King, and I am sad for his sons. I . . .' He heard the pain tightening her throat and he tensed too because he knew where this was leading. 'When you said earlier God forbid you raise sons the likes of his, I could not help but think of . . . of all of them.'

He exhaled on a deep sigh. 'Ida, you cannot change that part. It was the King's decision to keep the boy, and whether right or wrong it was final.'

'Yes, I know, I know.' She turned into his arms and pressed her face against his neck. 'But it hurts . . . every day it hurts, even though I have sworn not to think on it.'

'Then concentrate on the beautiful son you do have – that I have given you and who will never be taken away.' His tone was brusque because he had his own raw insecurity. He would never admit to being jealous because it was unmanly, but the feeling rode him hard when he thought of what Ida had been to Henry.

'I do,' she answered in a quavery voice. 'I thank God for him every day. You and he are my world and my consolation.'

He had used that word to her in the orchard on the day they had decided to marry and now wished he had not, for Ida had taken it from him and used it for her own. A consolation might be either an assuagement, or a substitute for something one could not have.

Rolling over, he kissed her with slow, tender thoroughness. He unfastened the tie on her chemise and drew the garment over her head, following it with his shirt, and he made love to her with a blend of fierceness and delicacy that was all consuming. Ida responded eagerly, first whispering, then crying his name and clutching him to her. As Roger moved within her, he swore he would expunge all thoughts of Henry from her mind, all memory that her body had of another's touch. All there would be was him.

22

Greenwich, London, Late June 1183

A warm breeze ruffled the water on the Thames and gently rocked the covered barge bobbing at its mooring rope at the jetty. Further out in the river, galleys, nefs, cogs and barges of varying sizes plied upriver to the London wharves, or made their way down to the mouth of the estuary and the open sea. Fastening the pin on her light summer cloak, Ida watched a sleek white galley with a red top strake making headway towards the city. She and Roger were at Greenwich for the funeral of Juliana's husband, Walkelin, who had died of a seizure. Now they were preparing to return to their London house on Friday Street.

'Fine linen of Cambrai,' Juliana said with a nod at the ship, her grey eyes narrowed the better to focus. 'Probably spices and soap too.'

Ida glanced at her mother-in-law. Juliana's manner was serene. She seemed barely touched by her second husband's demise. She had done her duty by him when he was alive and seen him decently buried now, but the latter event appeared to have created fewer ripples in her life than those on the surface of the river. From brief mentions and atmospheres, Ida had gleaned that her mother-in-law had felt naught but revulsion and contempt for her first husband, Roger's father, and resigned indifference towards the second, with whom she had little in common. Indeed, she was intent on paying a fine of a hundred marks to the exchequer to free herself from having to marry a third time against her will. She intended retiring to her dower estate at Dovercourt, there to dwell as she chose with no one to please but herself.

'How do you know what it's carrying?' Ida asked curiously. The water furrowed away from the white ship's prow in a series of silver frills that gave her a notion for an embroidery.

'It's the *Saint Foy*. Walkelin sometimes did business with her master.' Julianna gave Ida a keen look. 'Such vessels always bear a cargo of news just as valuable as cloth and the means to dye it.'

'Then I hope it is good news.' Ida looked pensively towards Roger who was talking to his knights. They had heard very little during the last month concerning the rebellion of the Young King, other than that he continued to defy his father at every turn and sack shrines and monasteries to pay his mercenaries. They had heard too that he had begged William Marshal to return to his side and take command of his military household – as if the previous scandal and banishment were trifles to be casually flicked away like specks of fluff on a tunic. Ida had been at a loss to understand why William had agreed to return to serve such a lord.

'He does what he must,' Roger had told her when they had discussed the matter one evening by the fire. 'His loyalty is to his sworn lord, and since his lord is the Young King, he is honour bound to answer the summons. We have all been in that position at one time or another. The road you choose defines you. Some might see his integrity as foolhardiness, but all admire the courage it takes to stand firm.'

She had realised anew how fundamental Roger's own sense of honour was to his character because the way he spoke of William Marshal's situation was from the heart. She did not have to ask if he would have done the same; she knew he would, and it was a cause to her of pride and concern.

Juliana recalled Ida's attention to the present by saying, 'I take comfort from the fact there have been no uprisings in England this time. With Gloucester and Leicester under arrest, there is no rallying point and men are less eager to follow the Young King after what happened before.'

'My lord's half-brothers support him.'

Juliana made a disparaging sound. 'I would expect as much from them.'

'Roger says the justiciar will hold them in check, since he has a family interest.'

'Much good it will do him,' Juliana said, her eyes suddenly hard as flints. 'My son will be the Earl of Norfolk. It is his birthright.'

Roger finished his conversation with the men and came to bid farewell to his mother, embracing her tenderly and kissing her cheek. Amid promises to visit soon, he helped Ida into the barge, which was lined with rugs and cushions. As the four oarsmen navigated the vessel out into the current, Ida took Hugh from his nurse and cradled him in her lap, tucking her cloak around him to protect him from the sharp breeze on the river, then sang to him until his lids drooped and he fell asleep in her arms.

Roger felt a lump tighten in his throat as Ida leaned over the baby to kiss his head and stroke his brow. So much of this had been missing from his own childhood. Perhaps there had been such moments with his mother, but if so he had been too young to remember. His memories were mostly of separation and loss. Of becoming an outsider as the safety of the nest was snatched from under him and replaced by thorns.

Ida looked up, caught his hungering stare and returned him a luminous smile that both pointed up the emptiness of those lost years and filled him with determination that his own son would never be thus deprived.

Once home at their London house, Roger absented himself to talk to his steward on a matter of administration, and Ida settled Hugh in his cradle to finish his sleep. Leaving Emma to watch over him, she brought her needlework outside into the good summer light and sat on the bench outside the hall door.

She had barely poked a length of thread through the eye of her needle when a man entered the stable yard, followed by a squire leading a burdened pack mule. Ida set her sewing aside and hastened to greet him. 'Messire Marshal!' She extended her hand to him and managed to sound pleasantly surprised rather than concerned. Surely he should be with the Young King. His presence here could be dangerous to her and Roger.

He blinked at her and it was plain he had not registered her presence until she spoke to him. He immediately rectified his manners and bowed over her hand. 'Lady Bigod.'

His complexion was ruddy brown from a summer spent in the saddle and his brown hair was streaked with lighter tones from the bleaching of the sun. He should have looked the picture of health, but his face was gaunt – haunted, she would have said, with hollows under his cheekbones and dark shadows bruising his eyes.

'It is good to see you,' she said. 'Do come within and quench your thirst. Will you stay to dine?'

He hesitated for a moment, as if unsure of his reply, then nodded. 'Thank you, my lady. That is kind of you.'

'Do you wish a place to sleep too? Forgive me, but you look as if you have been on a long journey.'

His eyelids tightened. 'My lady, I have, and still far to go, but I intend lodging with the Templars tonight. I am here to ask a boon of your husband's goodwill.'

That sounded ominous, but Ida didn't allow her trepidation to show. She told her maids to prepare a bath for their guest and set out clean raiment. Having sent a lad running to fetch Roger, she brought William into the hall, directing him to a seat under the window and fetched him wine with her own hand. 'You must take us as you find us,' she said. 'We have but recently returned from the funeral of my mother-in-law's husband.'

A spasm flickered across his face. 'I am sorry to hear that, Lady Bigod. May God rest his soul. I too have—' He broke off and looked towards the doorway as Roger arrived. Ida saw her husband take in their guest's state as she had done, and pause for a moment before striding forward.

'Be welcome,' Roger said as the men embraced. 'I thought you were deep in the Limousin.'

William said quietly, 'The Young King, my own young lord and son of King Henry, is dead of a bloody flux. Soon the city bells will tell their tale to all. I am on my way to the Queen at Salisbury, and from there to my brother at Hamstead. After that, I leave for Jerusalem.' He gave Roger a bleak look. 'I swore an oath to him when he lay dying that I would lay his cloak at the tomb of the Holy Sepulchre.'

Ida exchanged shocked glances with Roger. William

Marshal's voice had been as steady as always. He had himself under control, but Ida wondered what it was costing him. Her mind filled with the image of the young man she had last seen more than a year ago when she was newly wed. Handsome and arrogant, owning the world. Utterly charming too, towards those whom he wished to court. Henry's son. Henry's eldest living son. She pressed her lips together.

'God rest his soul.' Roger made the sign of the Cross. 'I will have my chaplain say masses for him and have a vigil kept.'

William inclined his head. 'I thank you,' he said with dignity. 'I have penances and reparations of my own to make for the sake of his soul and my own. There is much to repent. I am here to ask if you have horses with which you are willing to part for my journey. The King has custody of my destriers and the mule is hired and must be returned.'

'You are welcome to take the chestnut gelding from the stables.' Roger gestured. 'He's rested up and of sound wind. His gait's smooth and he has as steady temperament. There's a strong sumpter in the stables too – the bay with the white foreleg.'

Ida was familiar by now with Roger's mannerisms and nuances – the small gestures that gave him away. On a superficial level, he was being a courteous host, but at a deeper one, she could see he was assimilating the news and deciding how to react. The chestnut gelding was a favourite riding mount. To offer it to William Marshal, probably never to see it again, was an act of generosity that spoke far more than words of Roger's opinion of the man.

'Thank you,' William said with direct and heartfelt simplicity. 'I won't forget your largesse.'

A servant arrived to murmur that the bath was ready. Ida took William to the chamber and used the moment away from Roger to ask how the King had coped with the news of his eldest son's death.

'Grieving, my lady, but concealing it in public. He has lost a grown son and that is a terrible thing. It eats at him too that when my young lord died, they were estranged and strangers.' His expression grew sad and pensive. 'So much goes wanting for the sake of an embrace, does it not? So many wrong words are spoken in place of the right ones and become obstacles on the road ahead.'

Ida swallowed, unable to answer because what he said had caused a swelling of grief in her own breast. Murmuring an excuse about tending to her son, she left him to his ablutions.

Hugh was awake and crowed with pleasure when he saw her leaning over the cradle. She picked him up and clutched him to her fiercely, even though his clouts were wet. And although she held him for himself, her embrace was also for the vulnerable little boy she had left behind in Henry's keeping. Henry, who let his sons go wanting for embraces and words of love.

'What will you do when you return?' Roger asked William as they dined on roast fowl, frumenty and assorted salad leaves from the kitchen garth with a sharp strawberry dressing. A bath, clean garments and a moment to collect himself had done much to restore their guest. The care-worn expression was less pronounced and his shoulders looked as if their load had been lightened.

William set down his knife. 'If I survive the journey, I am pledged to return to the King and tell him that I have laid my young lord's mantle at Christ's sepulchre. He has promised to find me a position in his household, and from there, we will see. Whatever God wills for me, let it be done.' He reached to his cup, his expression pensive. 'There is much to be atoned for . . . and much to think upon. Deaths that are close to you make you evaluate your own life.'

Roger nodded with sombre agreement. Having come from his stepfather's funeral to this news, he was in a reflective mood himself, and strongly aware of the passage of time. He was of William Marshal's years – not yet into middle age, but no longer filled with the supple optimism of first youth. He had his goals, his ambitions; they were like a strong river carrying him downstream to the sea, but at least he was in a boat and knew his direction. The Marshal's future was less certain.

'So, now the King's heir is Richard,' Roger said thought-fully as the servants produced bowls of late cherries, dark as Vavasour's hide. 'What is that going to mean for the future, do you think? He is certainly a different prospect to the Young King, but I do not know him as well as you do.' Indeed, Richard had been so little in England that Roger didn't know him at all.

William took time to wash his hands in the bowl of rose water and dry them on the towel a servant proffered. 'Richard likes men who speak their mind and whose loyalty is unswerving. Providing you tread a straight path and do not digress from it, you will find favour. He has a fierce temper and he demands good judgement and quick thinking. Do not expect consideration from him. He may or may not reward you, but he will certainly work you until you drop. He is also his mother's son,' he added. 'Think of the Queen in your dealings with him, not Henry, and remember that he was heir to Aquitaine long before he was heir to England.'

William took his leave of Ida and Roger towards sunset,

riding the chestnut gelding and leading the bay packhorse laden with his belongings. Watching him depart their yard and turn towards Ludgate, Roger wondered if he was ever going to see his horses or William again.

Both he and Ida were subdued as they returned to the house. Roger's introspection was caused by what William had told him. He had plans to make and options to mull. Caught up in his own deep thoughts, he didn't notice Ida's silence or the sad and pensive expression in her eyes.

23

Westminster, Christmas 1186

The court settled at Westminster to celebrate the Christmas feast of the thirty-second year of Henry's reign. Roger and Ida were present at the gathering, Roger in his ceremonial office of royal dapifer, which involved seeing to the ordering of the King's table. Not that Henry paid attention to the manner in which a platter was set down before him or what was on it, because for him, food existed to sustain the body and he had little interest in how it was presented or what form it took, providing it was edible.

Roger thought Henry looked older. The years that had sat so lightly on him for a long time were suddenly weighing him down. His limp was permanent now and his hair, which had been rusty-gold when Roger first began the fight for his inheritance, was more grey than red. The pugnacious jaw had blurred. Anyone encountering him in a corridor, who did not know him, would have mistaken him at a distance for a shabby, careworn retainer, not the King of England. Behind the age-worn façade however, the intellect and mental capacity remained – shrewd, strong and sly. The grip on the reins was still as control-ling as ever.

He was still weathering the tragedy of the loss of his son Geoffrey at a tourney in Paris. The young man had fallen from his horse, been badly trampled and had died in agony several hours later. He left a pregnant wife and a small daughter as his heirs. In true Angevin tradition, the reasons for Geoffrey being in Paris in the first place were dubious and, in all likelihood, he had been fomenting rebellion against his father rather than attending for the pleasure of the sport. Now he was dead at the age of twenty-eight, the same attainment as his brother Henry the Young King, and his body laid to rest in the great cathedral of Notre Dame. Everyone was waiting on tenter-hooks to discover if the posthumous child was going to be a boy or a girl.

Henry perused the dish of venison Roger had set before him, hot and fragrant with spices, a little bloody in the middle. Taking up his knife but pausing before he cut the meat, Henry looked at Roger. 'How is your lady? I have seen little of her thus far.'

'She is well, sire,' Roger replied with bland courtesy. The less contact there was between Ida and Henry the better as far as Roger was concerned. She was keeping company in the smaller White Hall with Queen Eleanor who had once more been permitted out of her house arrest at Salisbury to attend the festivities at Westminster.

'You have another daughter, so I hear.' Henry flicked him a look gleaming with provocation. 'Girl children are useful to make marriage alliances, although it's better if sons are vouchsafed first.'

'God has been good, sire,' Roger said, remaining outwardly insouciant, even if inside he could feel his anger popping like small bubbles in simmering water. Hugh had recently turned four and Roger was inordinately proud of his son, who was funny, agile and as bright as a new silver penny. His second child, Marie, at two and a half was just moving from baby smocks into proper dresses, their tiny size giving him an amused pang when he saw them draped over the coffer while she slept. Marguerite had been born in August – on the same day that they received the news about Henry's son Geoffrey. Ida had wept over their new daughter, but Roger had been uncertain as to the source of the tears. Joy and relief at another successful birth, perhaps, but he thought the news had touched on her sore, unhealed grieving for that first infant she had borne.

'So I used to think myself,' Henry said, 'but now I wonder if our sons and daughters are sent to punish us, and then taken away for the same reason.' He cut into the venison and bloody juice ran on to his golden platter. 'You and your father were estranged at his ending, my lord Bigod. Do you regret it?'

'I regret that he died as he did, sire,' Roger answered quietly. 'I regret that we never saw eye to eye, but I do not regret that I defied him.'

Henry speared a slice of meat on the point of his knife and watched it quiver there for a moment before conveying it to his mouth. 'I have been watching you for a while, my lord,' he said. 'You tread a cautious path and you have great patience. Those are fine and useful qualities. I can count the men in whom I have implicit trust on the fingers of one hand . . .' As the King hesitated, Roger's gut swooped. Here it was at last. As a Christmas gift, Henry was going to restore to him the earldom and the third penny of the shire. He was going to be allowed to rebuild at Framlingham.

He could not prevent the hoarse catch in his voice. 'Sire, I have always tried to do what is honourable.'

The King looked half disgusted and half amused. 'My lord Bigod, I had forgotten the company you keep.'

253

When Roger looked puzzled, Henry waved his hand. 'William Marshal,' he said. 'Another "honourable" man.'

Although the King's tone was barbed, Roger took his words as a compliment. Indeed, they fed his optimism. The Marshal had returned from the Holy Land in the spring and Henry had gifted him with an estate in the north of England and the wardship of a young heiress, Heloise of Kendal. William was currently attending to his new lands and overseeing those of his charge. He no longer had Roger's horses, but had visited Roger and tried to pay him their value. Roger had refused, saying they were a gift, and William, a master of the laws of courtesy, had accepted gracefully.

Roger had wondered if the Marshal would attend the Christmas court, but he hadn't. Roger had also wondered if he would marry the Kendal heiress and suspected Henry was waiting for him to do so, but as yet, there had been no word of nuptials. Nevertheless, if Henry had seen fit to reward the Marshal, Roger reasoned that gifts might be forthcoming to other men. 'Indeed he is, sire,' he said.

Henry gave him a look filled with sour humour. Whatever was making him smile plainly related to his own thoughts. 'I have need of "honourable" men of sound judgement.'

Suddenly Roger's palms were cold and moist.

Henry narrowed his eyes like a cat with its paw on a mouse's tail. 'I want you to sit on the Bench at Westminster for the next session of court pleas and hear the cases.'

The disappointment was severe, but Roger somehow managed not to let it show on his face. He would not give Henry that satisfaction. This was privilege, not punishment, he told himself. He was being entrusted with a task that involved responsibility and judgement at a high level and one that would increase his importance. To judge cases on the King's Bench was a mark of high respect and demanded men of wisdom and balance who knew the law. But he had been expecting more. He had been seeing the belt of an earl in his peripheral vision and the soft gleam of ermine. The sardonic light in Henry's eyes told him that Henry knew exactly what he was thinking and was amused. 'Sire, if that is your wish I will do as you ask,' he said with a rigid bow.

'It is indeed my wish,' Henry said. 'And perhaps after that, we might talk about the third penny of the shire.'

In the Queen's hall, a troupe of tumblers was entertaining the women and youngsters of the royal household with sundry feats and tricks. One man wore a chequered costume of red and black and sported a bishop's mitre over a wig of yellow-blond curls. The smaller children were captivated by his little feather-tailed dog that could jump through hoops, beg, roll over and dance on its hind legs.

Ida's gaze fixed hungrily on the dark-haired little boy who was trying to decide under which cup one of the players had hidden a bean. He was long-limbed, dressed like a prince in a tunic of dark red wool and close-fitting blue hose. He had Henry's nose and brows, but his colouring was hers, and there was something of herself in the curve of his cheek and line of jaw. His focus, like his father's, was sharp and he unerringly pointed to the right bean – twice anyway. On the third occasion, the cup he chose was empty. So were the others and the tumbler gleefully plucked the bean from behind the little boy's ear. A look of wonderment crossed her son's face, and then a burst of delighted laughter. Ida laughed too, even though she was in agony. The toddling infant had become a vibrant little boy. She would have known her child anywhere. Even blindfolded, her maternal instinct would have felt him out . . . but it wasn't reciprocated. He no longer knew her and other women had taken her place in his routines and affections. She knew she couldn't connect with him and then leave because the wrench would be too great to bear and unfair to him. If only he could come and live with her and Roger and be raised with his half-brother and -sisters . . . but she knew that would never happen. Henry would never relinquish his youngest son, especially not after the recent losses of his older boys.

A girl, caught in the fleeting space between adolescence and grown womanhood, was smiling as she watched the tumbler's antics with William. She wore a light veil, but her braids showed beneath it, each as thick as a man's wrist, and the colour of ripe barley. Her eyes were a deep blue, made darker by the candlelight. Lord John, the King's son, had been eyeing her greedily for some time and she had been studiously avoiding his gaze with an aplomb that Ida admired. She had not been possessed of such self-assurance at that age. She didn't think John would actually do anything beyond look, though. He was in disgrace for having begotten a child on his cousin Emma, daughter of the Earl de Warenne and thus was on his better behaviour – although that was not saying a great deal.

The tumbler took seven brightly coloured leather balls and juggled them in a circle of whirling colour, finding time in between catches to toss one to William who then had to throw it back into the rotation. The player caught it without dropping any of the others or faltering in his stride and continued in this fashion, throwing one out, receiving it back, his teeth bared in a grin. William's face, in contrast, wore a deep frown of concentration and Ida bit her lip on tenderness and amusement.

The blonde girl clapped her hands. 'I wish I could do that.'

'Doubtless you could if you had to make a living from it,' Ida replied. 'Sometimes I think we women have to juggle our lives like those balls, but the better we manage the less people notice.'

The girl returned her a dutiful smile, and Ida, despite only being five and twenty, suddenly felt ancient in terms of experience. The girl was wearing two gold rings, neither of them a wedding one. 'Forgive me,' Ida said. 'I have not been at court for a while and I can no longer put names to faces and faces to names.'

The girl shook her head. 'I do not know people either.' She hesitated and added demurely, 'I am Isabelle de Clare. My father was Richard de Clare, lord of Striguil and Pembroke.'

'Ah,' Ida said in recognition now. Isabelle de Clare was heiress to one of the greatest estates under Henry's juris-diction. Her lands hugged the border between England and Wales, and she was also heiress to Longueville and Orbec in Normandy and a vast area of Southern Ireland. Her father had been a renowned warrior and her mother was Irish royalty.

Ida reciprocated with her own name and the girl responded politely but with no awareness. But why should she? Ida thought. Isabelle de Clare would still have been a child when Ida was Henry's mistress. As yet the girl was ignorant of the insidious court gossip, unseen but slip-pery as a mass of intestines concealed inside a smooth belly. Innocent too. As I once was, Ida thought sadly.

Henry arrived from the larger hall with a select group of courtiers and joined the women to socialise. Ida and

Isabelle curtseyed. In the periphery of her vision, Ida saw her son execute a perfect bow – elegant, balanced, and so natural she knew he must have practised until it came as second nature. Her eyes misted with pride.

Roger was with the King and Ida sought his glance. He returned it with a quirk of his lips and a swift look that filled her with affection and lust. It was almost like the first time at court when they had exchanged clandestine glances – except now such exchanges were permitted and could be carried to their natural conclusion.

Henry spent a while talking to Eleanor and they were civil with each other, despite her continuing house arrest. Time had gentled the fetters, but even if they were made of silk and wine, literature and song, fetters they remained and would continue to do so as long as Henry lived. Eventually Henry made his way over to Ida, Isabelle and the group watching the entertainers. Ida curtseyed again.

'Lady Bigod.' Henry's voice was filled with warmth that went beyond that of polite greeting. 'What a pleasure to see you at court.'

'Thank you, sire.' Ida stared at the floor, desperately hoping he would not chuck her under the chin or treat her in any way that spoke of former intimacy.

'You have given your lord a truly fine son,' Henry smiled sidelong at Roger. At face value, the statement was inno-cent, but Ida knew how Henry's mind worked and the underlying barb was intended full measure. A swift upward glance showed her that Roger's smile of response was bland, but she could see the tension stiffening his shoulders.

Henry kissed Ida's hand and cheek and gave her an intense look harking back to the past. Had she still been his mistress, it would have been one of those nights when he summoned her to his bed and used her with vigour. In a way, it was like that first time all over again when he had singled her out from the group.

'And Mistress Isabelle,' Henry said, relinquishing his hold on Ida and moving on to the heiress of Striguil. 'You are enjoying the festivities?'

'Very much, sire,' Isabelle answered demurely.

Henry gave her a considering look. 'I must see what can be done for your future.' He pushed his tongue into the corner of his cheek. 'A worthy lord for your lands of Striguil and Leinster perhaps?'

Isabelle dipped her head as gracefully as a swan. 'Indeed I hope he would be worthy, sire.'

Henry looked amused. 'You need not worry. I wouldn't send a spavined old nag or a weak-backed hobby to do the work of a warhorse.'

'Nor an untried colt,' Ida intervened, thinking of John, although she didn't look at him.

Henry gave her a sharp glance, albeit filled with humour. 'Thank you, Lady Bigod. I hope you are not speaking from experience on this matter?' His tone was laden with sarcasm and he looked at Roger again. The latter's expression was a taut mask.

Ida wanted the ground to open up and swallow her. 'No sire; only the experience of what the right man can accomplish if given the chance.'

'The right woman too, if she puts her mind to it,' Henry replied. 'And that can be a dangerous thing on occasion – as many a husband has had cause to rue.' He made to move on, but Ida's inhalation as if to speak made him stop and turn back, one eyebrow raised.

'I wanted to say I was sorry about Geoffrey,' she said. 'I grieve for your loss.'

Henry's expression softened. 'Ida, you have a kind heart and I am glad for it. Pray for me.' He touched her cheek and moved on, and, as he did so, he gently ruffled his youngest son's dark brown hair.

Arriving home at the house on Friday Street, Ida swept Hugh into her arms as he ran to greet her, then kissed him all over his face until he wriggled to be put down. She did the same to Marie, then leaned over the cradle, kissed her fingers and pressed them to the baby's cheek. Hugh looked at her askance out of big blue eyes, shadowed by a tumble of blond curls. He resembled his older brother not in the least – save perhaps in his coordination and precocious dexterity – although in Hugh's case that graceful fluidity of muscle was of Roger's bequeathing.

Roger had been quiet and tight-lipped on the way home, but now he removed his hat and plopped it on Hugh's head. Then he sat down on the bench near the glowing logs in the hearth and took his son on his knee. 'Have you been a good boy?' he asked.

Hugh sucked his underlip, pondering, then nodded vigorously. He bounced on Roger's knee and swung his legs. The brim of the hat came down almost over his short little nose.

'I'm glad to hear it, because I have a present for you. Guess which hand.' Roger held out both fists, tightly clenched. Hugh screwed up his face and tapped the left one. Ida suspected it was because Roger was wearing an ornate gold ring on that hand and Hugh liked the decoration on the bevels.

Roger opened his hand and showed Hugh his empty palm. 'No,' he said. 'Guess again!' Hugh tapped the right and wriggled in anticipation, but that one too was bare. Roger feigned astonishment. 'I know I had it a moment ago.' He looked seriously at Hugh, tilting up the scarlet hat brim to peer into his son's face. 'Are you sure you haven't got it? Is it under there?'

Hugh removed the hat and peered inside. 'No, Papa,' he said solemnly.

Roger cupped his chin. 'What's that behind you then?'

Hugh looked round over his shoulder but there was nothing. When he looked back to say so, Roger was holding the carved image of a knight on a horse. The knight's shield was painted red and yellow, as was his surcoat and striped lance. Hugh's eyes widened with delight, especially when he discovered that the knight and the lance were detachable.

Ida was fascinated. 'Where did you get that?'

'Herluin the groom carves them and I asked him to make one for Hugh.' Roger avoided her gaze as he spoke. Lifting the child off his knee he said, 'Go and fetch your other knights and we'll play at jousts.'

Ida pressed her lips together. It was obvious something was wrong with Roger and equally obvious that he was not going to say anything in front of Hugh and the servants.

As Roger played with Hugh, Marie toddled over and demanded to sit in his lap. He made room for her, his arm slipping around her narrow little body. In the course of the game, he wove the children a story about a king, a lady and a brave knight, and how the knight had to rescue the lady from the king, who wanted to imprison her. As Ida listened, she began to shiver. She had removed her cloak when they arrived home, but now she donned it again and rubbed her hands together, but the cold she felt came from within.

'Did the knight kill the king?' Hugh wanted to know.

'No,' Roger said, 'because it would have been dishonourable, and the knight valued his honour and he had sworn a vow to uphold his sovereign.'

'But he saved the lady?'

'I don't know if he did.' Roger's gaze fixed on Ida but she could not meet it and had to look away. 'That's for another day's telling. Time for supper and bed now.'

'The King has asked me to sit on the Bench at Westminster and judge his cases,' Roger said as he and Ida returned to the fire after overseeing the children's prayers and kissing them goodnight. Hugh had insisted that his new knight and horse be placed on the floor at the bedside facing the door to guard him. 'He also says he will consider restoring to me the third penny of the shire.'

Ida looked at him, trying to gauge his mood. Such news should be cause for celebration, but he still looked grim. 'Is that not a good thing?' she asked.

'I thought so at first, but now I begin to wonder what the price will be.'

'What do you mean?'

Roger's mouth twisted. 'I saw the way Henry looked at you today. He'd still have you in his bed if he thought he could get away with it. And the way you looked back at him . . .'

Ida was appalled. 'That is foolish talk!'

He flicked her a dark look. 'Is it?'

She felt sick. 'You think he gives you this as a bribe to look away while he makes sport with me? Have you so little trust in me? Do you follow a man whom you believe would do this?' Trembling with fury and hurt, she faced him. 'Once in another life I was the King's mistress, yes. Once I bore him a child. If you saw something in his behaviour towards me, it was of that time long ago and for a girl who no longer exists. He is growing old. If I feel anything for him, it is sorrow. Two of his sons are dead. What must that do to a father?'

'Since he barely knew them, I don't know,' Roger said through thinned lips.

Ida seldom quarrelled with her husband, but that was because mostly he was even-handed and good-natured and she adored him. She also knew how different her life might have been without him. He had indeed rescued her from the King. Knowing her good fortune, she had always been the one to back down, in order to avoid confrontation and travel a smooth road. But now all she could see were stones stretching to the horizon, and she thought her back would break. Rising to her feet, she went to the stairs that led up to the sleeping loft. With her foot on the first rung, she paused and turned. 'He knew them well enough to grieve for them,' she said. 'I heard that much at court and I saw it in his face. Since the day I set eyes on you when you came to him to plead your inheritance, I have been yours. May God strike me dead if I ever stray in word, or deed, or thought.' She swallowed and sought for composure. 'And now I am for my bed because in truth I am sick to my core.'

Roger let her go, then uttered a curse to the silence created by her leaving. He raked his hands through his hair. He knew he was not being rational. He had a reputation for being calm and balanced – a force for reason in every situation, a man whom little could faze, but this was different and his judgement was flawed. The sight of Ida and Henry standing side by side had filled him with corrosive jealousy. He was furious at Henry for still daring to look at her in that way. He was angry at Ida for feeling compassionate towards Henry, and it churned him up inside to see the way she stared at the boy Henry had fathered on her with her heart in her eyes. He had no difficulty watching her mother Hugh or the girls. If she bore him another son, he would have no qualms about the affection she bestowed there either, but that was because his children were part of himself. He was their father – had begotten them on her body in love, in pleasure and duty. When he saw her looking at her first child with such longing, he could not help but imagine her and Henry together and envisage those same emotions flowing between them. He dug the heels of his hands into his eye sockets and groaned. He had wanted to talk to her about coming to dwell in London, about what sitting on the Bench and judging cases would entail, but had well and truly made a pig's ear of the situation.

Heaving a sigh, he left his wine and the fire and followed Ida to the bedchamber. She had left the lantern burning on the shelf so he could see to undress. She had removed her gown but still wore her chemise and her braid was a dark rope against the pale linen pillows. Roger sat down on his side of the bed. He hated the feeling of distance. Perhaps he should speak to his chaplain on the matter, but even as the thought crossed his mind, he dismissed it. This was something that he needed to resolve himself and he doubted that a celibate priest was going to be of much use.

He tugged at his boots. He was wearing thick socks inside them because of the cold and they were difficult to remove. Usually Ida would have been swift to help him, but her back remained turned, and he had no intention of summoning a servant to the task. Finally, after much struggling and cursing, he succeeded in pulling them off. Then he had to unfasten the ties on his hose. Ida's fingers were always more dextrous at the task than his, and often her care would lead to other, pleasurable intimacies. Fumbling with the knots, he thought it no wonder that little boys wore smocks for so long and that old men stank of piss.

Behind him, he heard the sound of a suppressed sniffle and felt the mattress shake. Having managed the last knot, Roger folded his hose and set them on the coffer. Staring at the garments, he listened to Ida trying to weep in silence and not succeeding. He had never been able to bear a woman's tears, and the sound of hers was like the pain created by salt in a wound. He lay down, rolled over to her and gathering her in his arms, kissed her neck and her cold, wet cheek. 'Ah, my love, I'm sorry. Don't cry, don't. You will unman me.'

For a moment, she resisted him, then suddenly shuddered and turned into his arms with a sob. 'I won't go to court tomorrow if you wish it,' she said.

Roger grimaced against her temple and inhaled the soft jasmine scent of her hair. He didn't wish it, but playing the ogre would only make matters worse. 'Do you wish it, wife?'

She gave a loud sniff and wiped her face on the back of her hand. 'I am making your shirt damp,' she said with watery apology.

'No matter. It won't need washing so soon.'

'I . . . I do wish it,' she said. 'It is important for me to mingle with the wives and daughters of the other barons there. I have to make friendships and connections as much as you do. It is a woman's duty to grease the wheels that move the cart.' She pressed closer to him and he let his hand drift down to her waist. The scent of her hair, her closeness was making him hard. He made himself concentrate on what she was saying, and knew there was sense in it – but if only sense were all.

'The King has shown you favour,' she continued, 'and now you must build upon it. But if I do not have your trust . . .' Her words trailed off because she did not need to say the rest.

Roger closed his eyes. 'Ida,' he said softly, 'I think you are the most beautiful thing I have ever seen. You restore to me feelings I thought gone for ever and you give me others I did not know I had. Even if I am being a fool, I fear to lose those feelings. I fear to lose you.'

She inhaled to speak and he sensed her denial and reassurance, but he stopped her with a long kiss, and when he drew away said, 'Indeed, perhaps I do trust you, and I don't trust myself.'

'I don't understand.'

'My father was not kind to women,' he said bleakly. 'My mother hated him for his petty cruelties and so did my stepmother. I have no love for Gundreda, but I saw what she endured at his hands, and I swore I would never treat a woman the way my father treated his wives. It came from his own lack and, at the end, I pitied him. He couldn't make them give him affection, he didn't know how, and so he commanded obedience with force.' Roger rubbed his thumb over her face, tracing her delicate bone structure. 'I want to lock you up in a box as I would a precious ring, and at the same time I want to show you off with pride, but I fear you will be stolen from me and I will see you being worn on someone else's finger. I wonder how Henry feels, seeing the bare mark where once he wore you. I know how I would feel.'

Ida took his hand from her face and gently bit down on his thumb. 'Henry is not you,' she said. 'He has a new mistress – several, in fact, and he always did have many women at once. I hold no allure for him any more, except in memory, because I'm no longer the innocent girl who first appealed to him. I'm older, wiser . . . and stronger. And after what he did . . .' Her voice cracked. She leaned over him and kissed him on the mouth. He knew she was seeking comfort in the physical. It was easier than thinking, ten times easier.

'Mama . . . Mama . . .' His voice croaky with sleep, Hugh tottered into their chamber, flushed, disorientated, rubbing his eyes. 'I saw a bear, a big black bear with teeth! I don't like it!' he whimpered. Ida and Roger broke apart and Roger bent his arm across his eyes whilst Ida hastened to put her arms around the child and comfort him.

'Hush now, hush now. It's a bad dream, nothing more. You saw a dancing bear in the market and it's still in your mind. Nothing will hurt you. We won't let it.'

Hugh was hopping from foot to foot, revealing that much of his discomfort was due to a full bladder. Ida found the chamberpot and lifted his smock. Hugh's aim was a trifle erratic, but most of it went where it was intended.

Roger lowered his arm and looked at Ida and his son. In the light from the night candle and from further away, Roger could see how blotchy Ida's face was, how swollen her eyes. She had been crying really hard and it sent a fresh pang of guilt through him.

When Hugh had finished, Ida took him by the hand to take him back to his bed, but he balked and rubbed his eyes, still whimpering about the bear. He was shivering too as the night air chilled his body. Ida picked him up in her arms and brought him into their own bed, placing him between her and Roger within the warm cocoon of sheets and blankets. 'There are no bears,' she said again gently. 'You're safe.' Hugh snuggled down and his shivering stopped. His eyelids drooped, his thumb went into his mouth and soon he was asleep, his hair an angelic golden gleam on the pillow, and his small body barely mounding the bedclothes. Roger thought that Henry would never have allowed such a thing. It might be common for peasants and rustics who only had one bed, but not for a man of rank. He couldn't see Henry having that kind of patience – or tenderness either. 'Go to court tomorrow,' he said quietly. 'Make the connections you need to make. I give you the key to the box. Do not lose or mislay it.'

'Thank you,' she said simply. Her gaze dwelt on Hugh and she stroked his hair with the tips of her fingers.

Roger gave a strained smile. 'Just don't make a marriage for this one with any likely heiresses without consulting me.'

Ida also forced a smile. 'I could have done that today,' she murmured. 'Isabelle de Clare would be a likely catch, do you not think?'

They were moving away from dangerous ground and it was like seeing a thunderstorm rumble off into the distance. With the sleeping child between them, they could not be intense. His presence brought balance and focus to their conversation. 'Indeed, she would,' Roger said, 'and still of child-bearing age when he is old enough to father them.' He sobered. 'Not that he has much chance unless she comes to widowhood. Isabelle de Clare is very wealthy and as beautiful as an April morning. Henry will dangle her as bait in front of every hungry unwed knight and baron and make them all work and wait.'

'You could have held out for her instead of me,' Ida said, a note of challenge in her voice.

Roger shook his head. 'She is handsome and wealthy, I grant you, and she will make some man a fair prize, but why should I want her when I have you?'

'The heart is not usually the first concern in such matters.'

He shrugged. 'I would not have married where I could not be content. I have seen enough of the other side not to want it in my own household. Was your heart not involved? Was all you wanted an escape – a convenient bolt hole?'

Ida gasped and her head came up. 'No, husband! Never think that!'

'Then what should I think when you say such things?'

Her eyes filled again. 'You twist my words. People wed out of duty to their family and their lands. It is good if there is harmony . . . and love, but it is never the first thought – for the man anyway. A woman has no say unless she is a widow and can pay a fine to have her will. I chose you because I thought you strong and good and honourable; I knew I could love you, but you did not immediately seize upon the match. You had other considerations.'

'Even so, I would not have made it without a whole heart.' He rubbed his forehead. 'Ah, Ida,' he sighed, 'tonight I am as bad as my son. I am being chased by bears and all of my own imagining. Let us sleep. The morning will bring a better light for us all.'

Ida nodded and swallowed. 'Yes.' She wiped her eyes, her chin jutting resolutely.

Roger leaned to kiss her, snuffed the candle and lay listening to the soft breathing of his son and the shallowly inhaled silence from himself and his wife.

24

Woodstock, Autumn 1187

Seven-year-old William FitzRoy fixed his nurse with a solemn stare. Her name was Jueta and she had long, dark curly hair. She concealed it under a wimple in the public rooms, but in private she wore it in a simple, unadorned braid, which he liked. She had brought him bread and honey and a cup of milk.

'Why do I have no mother?' he asked.

Jueta laughed and tousled his hair. 'Ah, my young princeling,' she said. 'Of course you have a mother! Indeed, you are greatly privileged because you have many.' She gestured at the other women in the domestic chamber. 'We're all here to look after you and we all love you; after all, you are a king's son.'

William frowned. He knew he was the son of the King and that his brothers were royal. But they were much older than he was and their mother was Queen Eleanor who didn't live at court. He had another brother, also much older, who was trained for the priesthood and was their father's chancellor. He didn't appear to have a mother either, but since he was a grown man, it didn't seem quite so strange. He had heard tales from the older boys in the household about how babies came about. He hadn't been sure about believing them at first, but had come to think they were right. He had seen horses and dogs mating, but had never particularly associated such things with people until prompted by the boys' sniggering discussion.

'Did you . . .' He frowned and used the same term as the boys, even though he knew it was not a polite one. 'Did my father futter you?'

Jueta flushed scarlet to the roots of her hair. 'Oh dear me, no!' she gasped. 'Who put such a thought and such words in your head?' Her voice grew brisk. 'Come, eat your bread, drink your milk.'

'Then where did I come from?'

She wrapped her hand around her braid in the way she did when she was agitated. 'You're the son of the King, that's all you need to know. I told you, we are all your mothers.'

His frown deepened, but knew he wasn't going to get much further. Perhaps he could ask his father, but he wasn't sure he had the courage. His brother John might tell him, but John often told lies for the fun of upsetting people and couldn't be trusted. Although he did as Jueta bade him and attended to his food, he stowed the question at the back of his mind, as if he were putting something he needed on a shelf – out of the way for now, but waiting to be picked up again. He had vague memories of another dark-haired woman who smelled of jasmine; of being sung to and cuddled; but whenever he tried to grasp that memory, it evaporated. Was she his mother? But in that case where was she now? Having all these 'other mothers' was well and good, but didn't compensate for not having the one.

Roger eyed his son's seat in the saddle with an approving eye. Hugh was sitting up as straight as a lance and had

271

such good control of his dappled pony that Roger had unclipped the leading rein. Hugh's posture was natural; he wasn't having to think about it as, straddling his mount, he stared out across the Thames towards the suburbs on the Southwark bank. He was a coordinated child, swift of hand and eye, already capable of fastening the toggles on his shoes and the ties on his braies and hose. Remembering how rough and disparaging his own father had been, Roger was determined that Hugh would not suffer in the same way. He made a deliberate effort to spend time with the boy, to teach him things, and create bonds every bit as strong as the cord that had bound Hugh to Ida in the womb. He would rule Hugh with love, not the rod.

The sound of the rhythmic thud of a pile driver operated from a barge on the water, a little way out from the bank, carried to father and son. Hugh's blue eyes were bright with curiosity. 'What are they doing?'

'Constructing platforms for the masonry bridge piers,' Roger said.

'Why?'

'Because the timber bridge is rotting away and won't last much longer. There's too much traffic coming and going on it and too much weathering. London needs a stone bridge to stand firm for many years. They'll drive stakes into the river bed and infill them with rubble to make a foundation.' Roger and Hugh watched the men haul on the pulley to draw the piling stone up, then release it to smack down on the head of an elm stake and drive it into the river bed. 'The King had declared a tax on wool so that there is money to pay for it to be done.' Roger grimaced. Taxes were the order of the day of late.

'When will it be finished?'

'Oh, not for a long time yet.' Roger shook his head. 'I expect you'll be a grown man with children of your own before it's done. Things like this take a long time and much effort.'

Hugh wrinkled his nose. 'But the old bridge might fall down before then.'

'I expect they'll keep repairing it until it's time to use the new one.'

A barge arrived with a cargo of more elm palings, and another one with barrels of pitch. Father and son watched for a while longer, then Roger gestured to Hugh and they turned for home. A priest approached them from the wharfside, striding with the vigour of an artisan rather than the decorous walk of a cleric, his cloak blustering out behind him. Peter de Colechurch was the overseer of the building work, as he had been for the construction of the earlier timber bridge. Roger drew rein and greeted the priest with courtesy, remarking that the work seemed to be progressing well.

De Colechurch made a face. He had lugubrious features with deep creases in his cheeks and strong weather lines at his eye corners. 'For the moment, my lord Bigod, it is, but that is because the weather is holding and the tides are gentle. Come the storms of true winter, the work will slow down. There'll be repairs needed to the old bridge too and we must pray that a high tide doesn't sweep away the work we have done.'

'Indeed not.' Knowing what was expected, Roger unfastened a small leather pouch from his belt and gave it to the priest. 'To hasten the work.'

'My lord, you are generous,' de Colechurch replied with a gracious dip of his head. 'Your gift will be most useful. Who knows how long the wool taxes will continue to support the building work now that Jerusalem has fallen into the hands of the infidel. Revenues will have to be found for a crusade.'

273

Roger stared. 'Jerusalem has fallen?'

De Colechurch gave him a sombre look. 'You did not know, my lord?'

Roger shook his head. 'No, I did not. I had heard the army of the King of Jerusalem had suffered a serious defeat, but not that the Holy City itself had been taken.' He crossed himself.

'I had the news this morning from a Venetian trader. The city was besieged and could not hold out against the Saracen with half its fighting men dead in the desert. To regain Jerusalem will take a deal of effort and much money.' He opened his hand. 'What is a bridge when set against rescuing the city that holds the tomb of Christ?'

Roger rode home to Friday Street in thoughtful mood. Hugh peppered him with questions, which he answered with half his mind. Two years ago, the Patriarch of Jerusalem had come all the way to England to offer King Henry the throne of Jerusalem. The Patriarch had told them that the young King of Jerusalem was a leper and would not live for much longer. They needed a leader, someone of calibre to succeed. Henry had summoned a great council and asked advice of all his bishops and tenants-in-chief. Should he leave England to his sons and take up the throne of Jerusalem as his own grandfather had once done? His advisers had said he should not. The cynics remarked that Henry had called the meeting in order to obtain a refusal for which he could not be blamed personally. Those less world-weary thought that Henry was showing due care for decision-making and a commendable natural caution.

There would have to be a new crusade now. A vast mustering of effort and resources as de Colechurch had said . . . and that might mean opportunities too. In judging cases on the Bench, Roger had learned one had to look at matters from all angles and find the one that showed the best way forward. He had a deal of thinking to do.

Gundreda watched her eldest son pace the room like a wild boar in a small enclosure. He reminded her uncomfortably of his father when he did that. He had the same belligerence; the same deep scowl between his eyes. 'What good will taking the Cross do?' she asked him.

'It's better than sitting here waiting for nothing,' he snapped. 'If naught else I can get nearer to the King than you and my "kin" seem able to do.' His disparaging glance took in his stepfather, sitting near the fire studying various unrolled parchments, holding them out at arm's length now and again to squint at them.

'It takes time and patience,' said Roger de Glanville. 'Roger Bigod is no closer to obtaining his desires from Henry than we are.'

'And that is supposed to be a comfort?' Huon kicked a stool out of the way, knocking out one of its legs in the process.

'No,' said his stepfather. 'Not at all, but it is the way it is. You taking the Cross will make no difference to the King's decision about your inheritance. He may have shown Roger Bigod favour but he will only go so far. I have it on good authority that your half-brother offered the King a thousand marks of silver to be granted the earldom and have the third penny restored.'

Gundreda turned towards her husband. 'Where did you hear this?'

He waved his hand. 'I forget,' he said airily, thereby informing her that he had his spies out and about. 'The King said he would think about it, but told him to be prepared to triple the amount first.'

Gundreda's lips curled with sour satisfaction.

275

'Serve the bastard right,' Huon growled.

'The King wasn't being vindictive,' said his stepfather, 'just shrewd. He knows how much the man has in his coffers and how much he's worth. He also knows how much revenue the third penny brings in.' He gave Huon an astute look. 'The King has sworn a vow to liberate Jerusalem, but if he fulfils it, I'll burn my parchment and quills. Henry isn't going anywhere.'

'But Richard has sworn, and he will,' Huon said fiercely. 'He is his father's heir. If I bring myself to his attention, he will look upon me with favour.'

Gundreda watched her son and felt his frustration. She too wanted to scream at how slowly everything was progressing, and how, despite what her husband said, Roger was being shown favour, while they were left out in the cold. Their connection to the justiciar through their stepfather gave them some influence but not enough. It had been a clever ploy on Roger's behalf to marry a former, still favoured concubine and the mother of the King's son.

'My son, taking the road to Jerusalem is no guarantee of success, and it is dangerous,' she said.

'It's better than sitting here like a constipated peasant; at least I'll be doing something. You'll still have Will if anything happens to me.' He cast a brief glance towards his younger brother who was sitting by the fire poking the flames with a branch of firewood. 'My life cannot be more wasted than it is now.'

Gundreda shook her head and looked to her husband for support. In his usual methodical way, he arranged the parchments one on top of the other before him until not one edge strayed beyond the boundaries of another. 'There is time to consider this,' he said. 'The crusade has to have money, men and resources. They do not happen overnight. My brother tells me a tithe is to be raised on all revenue and movable goods other than a knight's core equipment. By the time that is done and all matters organised, I do not foresee an expedition to the Holy Land setting out before September of next year at the earliest. A great deal can change between then and now.'

'I don't see why, because it hasn't done so in ten years!' Huon snarled. 'I'm no closer to an inheritance than I was when my father died. And don't tell me to have patience because that particular barrel is scraped to the bottom!' He stormed from the room, calling for his horse.

Gundreda rubbed her forehead, feeling weary to the point of exhaustion. He would ride the beast too fast and too hard and she feared he would take a fall, or his mount would founder and crush him, as had happened to one of her husband's messengers last week. Huon didn't have the mental staying power or temperament to argue from a rational viewpoint or think matters through. Everything in his head was dense, solid and fixed; arguing with him was like putting one's shoulder to the flank of an ox. Her husband said that Huon was like her, but it wasn't true. In the matter of her rights she was an ox, because she had to be, but she had the control her son did not and she was better able to assess a situation and cope with it. Then again, she was a woman, past her flowering, and he was still a relatively young man caught in limbo. The Holy City was bound to dazzle his eyes. At least Will would remain at home, she thought, watching her second son poke the fire. Perhaps being without ambition was a blessing in disguise.

William Marshal grinned at the sight of young Hugh Bigod playing a game of peep with his littlest sister Marguerite, using a blue-and-white embroidered dapifer's towel to hide his face. 'They are fine children,' he said to Roger.

'Indeed,' Roger replied, giving his guest an amused

glance as the family prepared to dine. 'I would not insult you, messire, but you have a look that I have more often seen on the faces of women when they watch infants at play than on men of your reputation and standing.'

William smiled a trifle wistfully. 'You are not so wrong, my lord. Seeing yours and their lovely mother, any man would be envious.'

'From what I heard at Westminster this morning, you may not be envious for long,' Roger said with a twinkle. 'Denise de Châteauroux, so the rumour runs?'

William chuckled and said nothing beyond raising an eyebrow. He took his seat at the place of honour on Roger's right-hand side. The children were led away to a separate table by their nursemaids, there to eat in the vicinity of the adults and learn their manners, but without causing too much disruption to high table conversation.

Lent being over and it not being a fast day or a Friday, Roger's board was well supplied and elegantly presented. The linens were snowy and the sustenance was prepared to a standard well above that in the royal household, particularly the wine, which at court was frequently undrinkable.

William sipped the full Gascon red with appreciation. 'I may be envious of you for a very long time, my lord,' he said wryly. 'Before I can claim the lady de Châteauroux as my bride, I have to help the King take back her castle from the French. And then I have to hold on to it, which is scarcely how a man wants to spend his honeymoon. As the situation stands, Châteauroux might never be retaken and the King of France has knights aplenty who will leap at the chance to comfort its chatelaine in wedlock.'

Roger gave him a shrewd look. 'But you are going there anyway?'

William twitched his shoulders. 'The King has commanded and he has made an offer. Had I stayed in the North, what would I have done beyond count sheep and grow fat?' He opened his hand towards Roger. 'Besides, with a proposal like that on the trestle, there are likely to be other pickings too.'

Roger rubbed a forefinger up and down his cheek and said nothing, although his air was one of thoughtful agreement. The expedition to the Holy Land was still being planned and the taxes to fund it were slowly dribbling into the coffers. Henry had taken the cross in January, but his continuing dispute with the King of France, also under oath to free Jerusalem, had kept both sovereigns preoccupied. Until the matter of Châteauroux was resolved one way or another, there would be no army for Outremer. William Marshal had been summoned away from his business in Kendal to help Henry in France and that call had been baited with hints of rewards for loyal men above and beyond what had already been offered.

'I am going to need more horses,' William said. 'I have my own stud at Cartmel now, but these are early days and I need animals to take on campaign. I was wondering if you had beasts to spare.'

Roger was irritably amused. The Marshal seemed to think he had an endless supply of the creatures. 'The King has me busy at the exchequer, but I still owe him forty days of military service and I need good horses and sumpters myself, but I will give you a writ to take to the master of my stud at Montfiquet. That will save the expense and difficulty of shipping the horses across the Narrow Sea.'

'Thank you, my lord.'

Roger exhaled down his nose. 'If you do become lord of Châteauroux through marriage, I will expect to be remembered.'

William inclined his head. 'If I can ever do you a favour, my lord, I will.'

When the meal was finished, Roger called for ink and parchment and wrote the letter of authorisation himself. Although William was a good friend and Roger would have granted the boon anyway, he was shrewd enough to see that William's star was rising and that being generous now might pay for itself in the future – although naturally, everything in life involved a certain element of risk.

He became aware that William was watching his firm, deft pen strokes with a wistful eye.

'I envy your skill,' William said. 'I have to rely on scribes.'

Roger paused to dip his quill in the ink horn then wrote again, swiftly and neatly. 'It was one of the few things my parents agreed upon: my education. My father said that if a man could write his own hand, he need not be at the mercy of scribes for his private affairs, and they both saw it as another string to the bow when it came to climbing fortune's ladder.'

William looked wry. 'Mine agreed upon it too,' he said, 'but by the time my brother Henry was writing the creed in Latin at six years old, and I at thirteen could barely manage my name, they realised it was never going to be. It could neither be beaten nor reasoned into me. It's a nuisance, I admit. I have to trust to my memory.'

'A sharp wit is just as much use as a sharp pen.' Roger reached for the sealing wax. 'It doesn't seem to have impeded your progress thus far.'

'I haven't allowed it to, but still, it would be useful.'

His meal finished, the writ stored in his travelling satchel, William took his leave, his last act a gentle tousling of Hugh's blond curls.

'Denise de Châteauroux,' Ida said as she and Roger turned to go back inside the house.

'Good fortune to him,' Roger replied, 'although knowing the King, it'll be more word than deed.'

280

'I think he is hoping it is more word,' Ida said thoughtfully.

'Meaning?'

'Meaning he will negotiate for what he really wants. He has his mind set elsewhere, I think.'

Roger gave his wife a quizzical smile. Women had a way of burrowing under the surface as if what they saw on top wasn't as satisfying as the things awaiting discovery beneath. It was sometimes awkward when they made emotional demands based on their delving – uncomfortable too, but such occasions were recompensed by moments of clarity that exposed areas where a man would not have thought to look.

Ida shook her head and laughed at his puzzlement. 'He no more wants Denise de Châteauroux than he wants Heloise of Kendal.'

He looked blank and Ida laughed harder. 'Oh, husband! I will eat my embroidery if he does not ask Henry for Isabelle de Clare.'

Roger blinked at her, momentarily dazzled by the revelation. Then he gave a snort of amusement. 'Then I hope for the sake of your digestion you are right, but I cannot tell from where you glean that idea!'

Ida spread the fingers of her right hand to tick off the points. 'He has had two years in which to wed Heloise of Kendal and he hasn't. He also said there might be other offers on the table, which he wouldn't have done had he been focused only on Denise de Châteauroux. And the de Clare lands are closer to home.'

'Ireland isn't,' Roger pointed out.

'No, but the rest are: the Welsh Marches and Normandy. And he has more chance of holding on to them.'

He pinched his upper lip. 'I suppose you might be right. If Henry has offered him Châteauroux, then it's just as likely he will offer him the de Clare lands. Whichever, it will make of him a great man . . . that is if the King holds to his word. Promises are nothing unless they are kept.'

She dropped her gaze and he sensed some of the brightness leave her. Henry had that effect; his presence was like a small, dark cloud over their lives – all the time.

Roger sighed. 'I suppose I'd better return to my duties. I've work to do.' He cast an involuntary glance in the direction William had taken. It might not be so bad to be on the road to Châteauroux with the spring burgeoning all around and the sap rising in one's veins even as it rose in branch and stem and blade of grass.

'Must you?' Ida gave him a glance both sulky and sultry.

'Yes, I must.'

'Straight away?' She toyed with the brooch at the throat of her gown and then touched her neck. He saw the flush on her cheek, the gleam in her eyes.

Warmth flooded through him at the message in her voice and her look. He did have work to do – a mountain of it – but gazing at Ida, thinking of their bedchamber, imagining the clean scent of the bed linen, the soft spring light on her skin, her dark hair unbound and shining, the delicate responsiveness of her body, then contrasting it with the piles of tallies and parchments awaiting his attention at Westminster, musty and stultifying, he found himself yielding to persuasion. He could as well work tonight as this afternoon, and let Henry pay for the candles.

'No,' he said, kissing her neck and stopping a moment in the porch to pull her close. 'Not straight away.'

As a treat, William FitzRoy had been allowed to spend time in his father's chamber rather than being bundled off to bed with the other boys of the household. On the morrow, he was to return to England in the company of a group of messengers and clerics as his father advanced on Châteauroux.

William loved being at court, especially now that he had the duties of a page. They mostly involved fetching, carrying and running messages, as well as some serving at table. He was absorbing all the rituals involved, all the flourishes and graces. His father didn't seem to set much store by such behaviour, indeed seldom even sat down to eat a meal, but even so, all eyes followed him when he entered a room, because his presence was so invigorating and because he was the King. William would have been content to continue to travel in his retinue, but in this, his first season as a page, it was deemed he had experienced enough and should return to the safety of England to continue his education.

William had been playing merels with one of the older boys, but seeing that his father was momentarily without companions and actually sitting still, he left his game and approached him.

Henry appraised him out of bloodshot grey eyes. He was holding a cup loosely in his right hand and there were several shallow cuts inflicted by the talons of his hawk because he had omitted to wear his gauntlet again. 'Are you ready for your journey tomorrow, lad? All your baggage packed?'

William nodded. 'Yes, sire.'

Henry grunted. 'I'd like to bring you with me, but it wouldn't be wise. You're better off in England at your studies until I return, hmm?'

William nodded again, although he didn't entirely agree. He would have loved to follow the army right up to the walls of Châteauroux.

He gave his father a straight stare. 'Can I ask you a question before I leave?'

Henry smiled indulgently and gestured assent. 'Ask what you wish.'

William took a deep breath. 'Is the lady Jueta my mother?' She had often said she wasn't but she had the same colour hair as him and he had learned that adults told lies and made sins of omission, even while telling children it was wrong to do so.

A look of astonishment crossed his father's face, followed by a bark of rusty laughter. 'What put that notion into your head, child?'

'Because she looked after me.' William jutted his chin. He didn't like being laughed at. 'Because the other children have mothers, or know who their mothers are. I thought she might be, but it was a secret.'

His father's expression held tolerant amusement. Pulling William towards him, he tousled his hair. 'I think we can safely say that Jueta is not your mother, nor ever had a chance of being.' Henry leaned back to study him. 'Your mother's name was Ida,' he said after a moment, 'and she was beautiful.'

William blinked at this sudden revelation, so easily given. The shock was like miscounting steps and falling down on the missing last one. He didn't know any women called Ida at the court – or none of fitting rank. His father had also said 'was'. Did that mean she was dead?

'Of course, you must realise I was not married to her,' his father added, 'but in some ways that was better, because you were born from pleasure, not duty, and you are no less to me because of it.'

William swallowed, feeling panic. He knew all about the women of pleasure. He had seen them at court in their gaudy dresses, their long braids twined with silk ribbons and no decent veil covering their hair. They would allow any man to make the beast with two backs if he had the right price. He could not be born of such a union. It was not what he imagined for himself. 'So she was a whore?' he asked and the word made him feel sick.

His father immediately sat forward, shaking his head, and caught his elbow in a fierce grip. 'No, my son, no,' he said strongly. 'Never think that. She was a good woman and honourable. You must never speak so about her.'

William was a little mollified by the words 'good' and 'honourable' but there was still a horrid feeling inside of him. 'Why is she not here then?' he demanded.

Henry laughed and ruffled his hair again. 'Because you are my son, the son of the King. She had other dreams to follow and other children to make. She had a different path to follow.'

His father's words made William feel shakier still. The mention of 'other children to make' made him feel abandoned and second-best. Why should she leave him to have other children unless there was something wrong with him? Why wasn't he her dream?

His father was looking at him with an indulgent smile, as if the matter was of no consequence. 'You are fortunate,' Henry said. 'There are many women who would have dearly loved to have been your mother, believe me.'

But clearly not the one who bore him. She couldn't be good and honourable if she had gone off and left him. There was a lost angry feeling at his core, and he stood as stiffly as a tree as his father shook his arm. 'We men must bond together eh? You're my son, that's what really matters, and I acknowledge you as such.'

Hubert Walter, Dean of York, arrived to speak with his father, and Henry released him with a kiss on either cheek. 'Go now,' he said. 'Past time you were in bed if you're to be on the road by tomorrow dawn.'

William bowed properly from his father's presence as he

had been taught. He was glad he was too old now for Jueta's care, and that his training was in the hands of clerics and knights. He didn't want to look her in the face – or any of the other women who were her accomplices in the conspiracy of silence. Why couldn't they have told him? He still didn't know who his mother was, only her name, and it was like a foreign language to him. What was she like? Which part of him was hers? She was in him, but how could he be in her if she had abandoned him? He lay face down on his pallet in the chamber allotted to the pages and squires and buried his head inside his folded arms. He had wanted to know, but now he wished he hadn't asked because he was even more miserable and confused.

'What's wrong with you?' Hubert de Burgh, one of the older pages, wanted to know. 'You're not crying, are you?' He was sitting on his own bed mending the toggle on one of his shoes.

'No,' William answered fiercely and compressed his lips. His eyes were stinging and his throat was tight, but he swallowed down his emotion. He was the son of a king who ruled lands from the borders of Scotland to the Pyrenean mountains – places he had not seen but about which his tutor had told him. His father was a sworn crusader too. He would strive to emulate that greatness and make it fill and overrule that other part of him that was hers.

In the morning before he set out, he went to his devotional prayers, but he averted his eyes from the little statuette of the Virgin with the infant Jesus on her lap, when only the day before he had gazed upon it with fervent hunger, desperate for knowledge.

286

25

Framlingham, July 1189

Ida stared at the length of braid she was weaving and swore because she had missed a turn in the pattern cycle and now there was a flaw in the red and white design. The mistake throbbed at her and she had to look away because her head was aching and her eyes kept losing focus. She hadn't felt well all morning.

Pushing the frame aside, leaving her work trestle, she crossed to the window and looked out on the courtyard. Wulfwyn, one of the kitchen women, was feeding the yard hens and, as usual, the big white gander was making a nuisance of itself, lunging its neck and hissing at the other poultry. For some reason Hugh had taken a liking to the thing and had had to be scolded for bringing it into the hall yesterday.

She rubbed her forehead. Unshed rain was making the atmosphere as heavy as a curtain and there was probably going to be a storm. While she wished for a downpour to clear the air, she wanted it to hold off too because it would make the roads boggy and travelling difficult. On the morrow, she was supposed to be taking the family to rejoin Roger who was still at Westminster.

A fractious wail brought her to the cradle. Three-month-old Wilkin was awake and as she leaned over him, a smile broke over his face. His full name was William, so given because it was an important traditional one in Roger's family, but it sent a pang through Ida because of her firstborn. This new son was dark-haired too, and was going to have brown eyes. Every time she looked, she imagined, and felt bereft. It was like having two pieces of a tally stick or chirograph that were close but didn't match. Lifting him in her arms, she carried him to the window and looked out. Hugh was playing chase with Marie and their squeals rang around the courtyard. Marguerite, three next month, tried to run after them and keep up but her legs were too short and she kept tripping over her smock. Finally she sat down in the middle of the yard and threw a full-blown tantrum, her face scarlet against her flaxen curls. Her nurse picked her up, tucked her under her arm, and carried her away into the hall.

'Shall I pack your court gown, my lady?'

Ida looked over her shoulder at Bertrice who was holding up a dress of green silk brocade. The act of turning her head sent pain lancing through her skull and her stomach roiled. 'Yes, bring it.' She forced herself through her lethargy. 'If I leave it behind, I'm sure to need it for some purpose.' Roger might want to entertain guests at their house, or bring her to Westminster.

She hadn't seen him since early May. Throughout her confinement he had been absent with Henry in Normandy. He had been home for her churching, but needed at Westminster, and had deemed it best for her to stay at Framlingham for another month to regain her strength and allow their new son to grow some more before she made the journey to London. She had filled the time with the duties of a chatelaine, with matters of

288

domesticity and demesne, of motherhood and governance, household and lands, and although her days were
full to overflowing, they often felt very empty. It was like
a dance performed alone, or with polite strangers, her
hand holding thin air where a partner's hand should be.
Ida turned back to the window and briefly pressed her
forehead against the cold stone wall and closed her eyes.
She wanted to be on the road tomorrow. She couldn't
afford to be ill.

The sound of a horse galloping into the yard made
her look up. Edwin, one of their messengers, was
dismounting from his blowing courser. The horse was
dripping with sweat and trembling and didn't have the
energy to shy as the white gander advanced on man and
horse, neck stretched out, honking in defence of his territory. Anxiety swept through her. For Edwin to ride his
horse into the ground, the news must be grave. She bade
one of her women go down and fetch him to her straight
away. Sweet Jesu, what if something had happened to
Roger?

Edwin crossed the threshold, came to her and knelt
with head bowed. The stench of hot horse and sweaty
man pervaded the room. When he doffed his cap, beads
of perspiration rolled off his hair and dripped into the
rushes.

Ida braced herself to hear the worst. 'What is it?' she
demanded. 'Tell me.'

'My lady, the King is dead,' Edwin announced. 'He
had been ailing for some while, but he took his final sickness and died at Chinon a week since. My lord sends you
the news from Westminster and bids you hasten to him
as soon as you may.'

'Dead?' she repeated faintly, and then again as a voice-
less breath.

'Yes, my lady.' Edwin's chest was still heaving from the exertion of his ride. 'He is to be buried at Fontevrault.'

Ida stared at him, feeling numb. There was a leaden sensation under her heart and the world around her grew blurred and monochrome.

'My lady . . . Madam . . .' Bertrice's anxious voice was no more to Ida than the irritation of a buzzing fly.

'Thank you,' she said stiffly to Edwin. 'Go and find rest and refreshment.'

'Will you want me to change horses and ride with a reply, my lady?'

She shook her head. 'I will speak to my husband myself soon enough.'

The messenger bowed and departed. Ida felt hollow inside, as if the marrow had been sucked from her bones. Barely aware of what she was doing, she made her way to the chapel to pray. Hugh and Marie were chattering to the groom who was rubbing down Edwin's horse and cooling it off. Hugh was playing with the enamelled red and gold pendants on the gelding's breast-band. The goose had been penned up, but continued to honk threats from behind its withy enclosure. Ida heard and saw all this with a strange sense of detachment, almost as if the scenes before her eyes were pages from one of Henry's books.

Entering the chapel, she approached the altar, knelt and crossed herself, then clasped her fingers around her paternoster beads and prayed for Henry's soul. The fringe on the silk and gold altar cloth wafted gently but there was no air. She fancied she could feel the heat from the candles in their gilt holders, and the flames seemed to burn her skin. Her eyes were dry and sore. As the memories gathered in her mind, and scalded like molten lead, she wanted to cry. But she couldn't.

She could see herself at court, moving the footstool at

Henry's command, lifting his leg, making little adjustments for his comfort. Walking down the corridor to his chamber. That first, painful time when she had wanted to die of misery, fear and embarrassment, and then as she became accustomed, the familiarity that had brought the grace of affection to their exchanges and occasional frissons of pleasure. She thought of the gifts he had given her: the rings, the fabrics and furs. She remembered him smiling at her innocence and being indulgently amused at the wisdom born of that feature. She thought of him leaning over the cradle, giving his forefinger to their newborn son, a smile of delighted pride softening his features. Now that smile was gone, locked up in a tomb. All that vitality, all that blazing life force. Burned down to the stub and guttered out in a dissipating wisp of smoke.

She pressed her scorching forehead upon her clasped hands. What of their son? He was effectively an orphan now, lacking the protection of either parent. What was going to become of him without his father? The new King would be Richard, Henry's eldest, of whom she knew nothing, other than that he was pledged to go on crusade and thus would not be keeping a regular court.

Her belly heaved and she knew she was going to vomit. Frantic not to despoil the church, she staggered to the door, wrenched it open, and fell to her knees against the side wall where she was violently sick. Shouting for help, the priest crouched at Ida's side. A servant went running. Ida shuddered. How could one be hot and frozen at the same time? Her joints ached and her bones felt loose.

Her women arrived and helped her to her chamber where they put her to bed and piled her with blankets while she shivered and burned. They brought her a tisane to settle her stomach and she drank it, but immediately began heaving again.

She was wretchedly ill for most of the night, while flickers of dry lightning turned the sky a strange shade of milky purple and marked in her feverish imagination the passing of a king. Towards dawn, there was a brief interlude of rain. Her throat raw, her stomach aching as if she had been kicked by a mule, Ida fell asleep to the sound of it pattering on the roof and dripping on the eaves. Her dreams were of fire and battle and danger. She heard her firstborn crying for her in a lost, bewildered voice but she couldn't find him because a thick fog enveloped all. Then Roger called her name and came striding through the miasma, his right hand extended towards her in a gesture of rescue. For a moment, she thought that he was holding a purse filled with gold, but when she looked again, there was nothing. She fixed her gaze on him and said in desperation, 'The father of my child is dead.' He returned her stare with the coldness of a judge and replied, 'The father of your children still lives.'

Ida woke with a gasp, tears pouring down her face. Bertrice parted the bed curtains and peered into the gloom with worry-filled eyes. 'My lady, did you call?'

Ida sat up, wiping her face on the heel of her hand. The dream was still with her in colours more vivid than the ones in this chamber. She had a pounding headache and felt wrung out and as weak as a kitten, but the nausea had gone and she was no longer burning. 'Yes,' she said. 'Fetch me a little bread and some boiled water. And rose water for washing.'

'Are you feeling better?'

Ida nodded. 'A little,' she said, 'although I will not ride my horse today. Best if I travel in the wain.'

Bertrice's stare widened. 'You still intend setting out, my lady?'

'I won't get to London by staying here, will I, and my lord has summoned me.' She could feel her tears drying on her face. Her chemise was rumpled and stank of sweat and sickness. Suddenly she wanted to be out of the bed and in clean raiment and away from all this.

'In the circumstances, madam, I am sure he would understand.'

Ida shook her head stubbornly. 'Even so I will go. Make haste.'

As her women washed her and brought clothing from the coffers, the vividness of Ida's dream faded, although it left an indelible residue. She managed to eat a small piece of bread and forced herself to sip the water even though she was parched. The rain had ceased and the air had freshened a little. It was reasonable enough weather for travel.

Before leaving Framlingham, she returned to the chapel to pray, bringing the older children with her to light candles for Henry's soul. Biting his lip in concentration, Hugh held the taper steady as he performed his duty. Ida wondered if her firstborn had done the same, but of course, it would have a different meaning for him. To Hugh, it was a solemn obligation, but also manly and exciting. That the King was dead had little meaning to him beyond the performing of a few rituals, but for her other child it meant the loss of his father and all his security.

Ida slept for much of the first day of the journey, this time dreamlessly, and when she woke, she felt light with hunger and emptiness. An important, defining presence had gone from her life and the space where it had dwelt needed to be filled with other, more positive things in order to heal. Finding those things was going to be hard.

*　　*　　*

Roger watched the baggage cart with its red and gold awning turn into the yard of his Friday Street house, drawn by three strong greys in line. He was surprised not to see Ida on her golden mare, for she was a good rider and seldom took to the interior, leaving that for her women and the infants. Hugh was trotting along with the knights and serjeants, his back straight and his posture displaying the ease of a natural horseman. To judge by the expression on his face, he was pretending to be one of the men protecting the wain and the sight made Roger smile with amused pride.

'Papa!' Hugh drew his leg over the saddle, leaped down from his pony and ran to Roger, then, remembering his manliness and his manners, skidded to a halt and flourished a bow. Roger bowed in return, then laughed and ruffled his heir's blond curls.

'Ah, it's good to see you,' he said. 'I've missed you all. You ride like a true knight already. I see you've been practising hard.'

Hugh puffed out his chest and beamed.

'Where are your mother and sisters?'

'In the wain. Mama hasn't been well, but she's better now. She was sick when she heard the King was dead.'

Roger absorbed the information with a raised eyebrow but said nothing. Henry's death had not come as a surprise to him because news had filtered back to Westminster that he was ailing beyond the usual aches and pains. His own emotions had been of release. Finally, the past could be swept out like old straw into the midden pit and a fresh start made. He went to the wain, arriving as an attendant helped Ida down from it. He took the man's place for the final steps and as he grasped his wife's hand, studied her face. She was pale and wan, but the look she gave him was glad and she responded with alacrity to his kiss.

294

'Hugh says you've been ill,' he said.

She nodded. 'A sick stomach and a fever that lasted a night and a day. Marguerite had it too while we were travelling, but she's better now.'

The rest of his family emerged from the wain followed by Ida's women. He kissed his daughters and was surprised at how much the baby had grown since Ida's churching.

'You received the news?' He turned with her towards the house. Around them, servants bustled, unloading the wain while grooms tended the horses. Hugh had found a branch of kindling and was already engaged in vigorous play with his father's dogs. Marie skipped to join him, while the nurses took the baby and Marguerite within to settle them down.

'Yes,' Ida said. 'I have said prayers for the King's soul and I have ordered vigils to be kept and masses said.'

Roger noted that her words came swiftly and her voice was breathless. It might be a struggle with tears, but could just as easily be the residue of her illness and the general fluster of arriving. 'I have paid for masses too,' he replied. 'All should be done with respect and propriety.' Because then it could be settled and left behind.

She didn't answer, but kept her eyes down and leaned against him as if seeking support.

He brought her to the solar where his chamberlain had set out food and drink. He decided he would not tell her that Henry had died alone and that his servants had stripped the room of its hangings and furnishings, even going so far as to steal the covers from the bed, leaving the King's naked, death-stained body in open, squalorous view. With her soft heart and the history she had with Henry, he knew how vulnerable she would be to such images. He had no love for the King, but they had certainly

295

made him recoil when he learned of what had happened. Instead he told her that Henry had been buried at Fontevrault by the knights of his household with all due ceremony and that Richard had been present to see him interred.

'Richard will not be in England until August at the earliest and he still intends to go on crusade,' he said, sitting down on a bench. 'He's sent orders to have the Queen released from house arrest though, and I have no doubt she'll be taking an active part in helping him rule straight away. I saw a copy of the writs yesterday.'

'Did he . . . did he say anything about what was going to happen to . . . to William?'

Roger had known she would ask and that it would be uppermost in her mind. It didn't matter how much he gave her, including other sons and daughters, she still fretted over the one she could not have. 'I do not think such a matter was his first thought,' he said, 'but they share the same father and Richard knows the value of blood ties that are close but pose no threat. Life will change little for such dependants. When Richard comes to England, I will find out what he intends.'

The gratitude in her eyes irritated him and made him feel guilty too. He had offered. How else did he expect her to respond?

'All I want to know is that he is cared for and cared about.' Her voice trembled at the edges.

'I do not doubt he will be,' he said with a note of finality in his voice and steered the conversation elsewhere. 'I have good news amongst the graver tidings. We are invited to a wedding tomorrow – if you are well.'

Ida lifted her head. 'A wedding?' The brightness in her tone was forced, but she was making an effort.

'It looks as if you have been saved from eating your

embroidery after all,' he said with dry humour. 'William Marshal is to wed Isabelle de Clare in Saint Paul's.'

The warmth of a genuine smile overlaid the sadness in her eyes. 'Even if I have to be borne in a litter I will gladly bear witness to that!' She gave him a triumphant look. 'I told you, did I not?'

'You did indeed, my love.'

'I suppose he is borrowing horses again,' she said mischievously.

Roger grinned at her. 'Naturally. In fact, I bought him a palfrey for the lady Isabelle as a wedding gift. It saved him searching Smithfield for one and took a task off his hands. He's looking for scribes and administrators too, so I've been making enquiries on his behalf at Westminster.'

'It had nothing to do with your own interest in searching Smithfield for a likely beast, or finding him men for his household who will be grateful to you as well as to him.'

Roger acknowledged to himself that his wife was as sharp as a pin, and it made him smile. 'That is an advantage,' he agreed.

Ida looked thoughtful as she sipped a cup of wine and nibbled on a piece of bread. 'So William Marshal is to be lord of Striguil and husband to Isabelle de Clare.'

'Yes, and by Richard's order. Henry had promised him the girl and died still promising, but Richard gave the Marshal his goodwill and sent him straight away to England with royal business and a writ to be wed.'

Ida looked sad. 'Henry often made promises and didn't keep them,' she said. 'He would say he was thinking about them and waiting the right time, but it was never the right time.' She gave Roger a bleak smile. 'I know you think I am grieving when I should not, but I have made my peace with the news and said my prayers. If there are matters that remain to be dealt with, they are for the living, not

297

the dead.' She put her head up resolutely and changed the subject. 'Since you have gifted William Marshal with a horse, I would like to give him and his new bride a present too.'

'You have something in mind?'

'A cradle,' she said. 'I know how much it meant to me when you had that one made for our children. Neither of them will have such a thing in their possession. He will have had no need and he's a younger son. Isabelle de Clare has been kept as the King's ward in the Tower and whatever she has in her family will be far away across the Irish Sea.'

Roger's lips twitched. 'Are you not being forward?'

She shook her head. 'Did you not see his hunger when he set out to serve Henry? He wants a wife and a family. He needs to plant roots. He is the same age as you but has wandered all his life – and that is no longer his desire.'

Roger conceded the point with a mute nod.

She warmed to her theme. 'You have a wife and four children already; you have lands and somewhere to call home. He envies you that. I believe she will be content with him. Like you, he is honourable. Her first duty to him will be to give him heirs, but as lady of Leinster she must give heirs to her own bloodline. A cradle will be a gift appreciated for what it says without words.'

'I believe you,' Roger said, holding up his hands and laughing. 'It is a thing of a woman's perceiving, but in such matters, I admit, women are usually right and men should do as they are bidden.'

The sun had set over London and bats flitted and dived against a sky of turquoise and night-blue spangled with stars. The wedding feast of William Marshal and Isabelle de Clare was being held at the house of wealthy London merchant Robert FitzReinier, who had made shrift to organise a fine celebration at very short notice for the new lord of Striguil and his heiress bride, and provide them with housing and hospitality for the first night of their marriage.

Trestles had been set up in the orchard and covered with white linen cloths. Lanterns twinkled in the apple and pear trees and jewel-eyed moths fluttered pale wings around the beguilement of deadly light. The fresh green scent of crushed grass filled the air and there was laughter, music and singing. FitzReinier had found an Irish bard who played the harp with angelic wildness and sang in the language of his homeland to honour the bride's heritage. And for those who thought the tongue outlandish, the notion that Isabelle de Clare's mother was a princess of that land added a romantic element that entirely complemented the atmosphere in FitzReinier's garth.

Returning from an essential visit to the latrine, feeling light-headed from the effervescent wine, Roger sought Ida among the revellers and smiled when he saw her engrossed in talk with several other women. Her training at court and her own natural warmth made her excellent at social-ising with others and garnering snippets of useful information amidst the general chatter.

The bridegroom quietly joined him and, folding his arms, leaned against a tree. William was smiling and seemed at ease, but then Roger had never known him not to have the measure of any situation, and that plainly included his own wedding. The bride, a vision in rose-coloured silk, had been claimed by some of the guests, although, in mid-conversation, she raised her head to glance at William and they exchanged a look of mutual acknowledgement.

299

'I want to thank you again for your gifts,' William said. 'They were very . . . thoughtful.'

Roger rubbed the back of his neck. 'You can blame Ida for the cradle.'

William chuckled softly. 'Your wife is a woman of great warmth and intuition,' he said. 'Perhaps, if God is good and her gift prophetic, we can someday talk about a closer alliance between Bigod and Marshal.'

'I would welcome that,' Roger replied, 'and not just because of mutual goals.'

William gave him an astute look. 'I know when to hold my silence and when to speak; you know that of me, I think?'

'Indeed, you have a reputation for discretion.' Roger inclined his head.

'As do you. When King Richard comes to England, he will have much business to settle. The matter of your father's earldom has been neglected for too long.'

Roger sucked in his breath. 'You think, or you know?'

'I do know the new King will be making appointments to men he believes will be steadfast in his absence on crusade.' William looked down over his folded arms. 'It goes without saying that the coffers for that crusade are wide open for all donations.'

Roger did not allow himself to feel more than a twinge of excitement. 'Richard does not know me,' he said cautiously, 'or not beyond a few casual meetings at court. His father preferred to keep the third penny and the revenues from my disputed lands in his coffers.'

'That is true, but I know Richard, and he knows me and trusts my judgement. It doesn't hurt matters either that your wife is mother to the King's half-brother. Richard will look after his kin.'

Roger managed to remain equable at the mention of

Ida's first child. With Henry dead, the way was open for more contact and he must come to terms with it. 'I leave it to your discretion, my lord, and I give you my thanks.'

'I make no promises, but I will do all I can. You have helped me many times in the past, and I will be glad to repay the debt.' Bowing to Roger, William excused himself to go to his bride.

The sky was a full, deep indigo by the time the newly-weds were escorted to their chamber amid toasts of goodwill and numerous bawdy but well-intentioned jests, and blessings both secular and episcopal. For those who had not yet drunk or danced their fill, the celebrations continued in the garth by the light of stars and lanterns. Roger sat on a bench in the warm garden sipping a last cup of wine and enjoying the scents of the nocturnal night. Ida joined him and, leaning against his shoulder, rubbed her index finger along his lower forearm where he had pushed back his tunic sleeves and the hair sprang in glinting filaments. Behind them, the shutters were open on William and Isabelle's chamber but there was no sound.

Roger shifted so that he could set his arm around Ida's shoulders. 'The Marshal says there is a good chance Richard will restore the earldom to me – to us. He's going to speak to him and do what he can.'

She ceased her stroking and looked at him.

'There's many a slip,' he said, 'and the whims of kings are not to be trusted, but I do trust William.' He gave her a gentle squeeze. 'Perhaps you will have a gown of cloth of gold after all and the title of countess.'

She laced his fingers through hers. 'More than anything I want my husband to be recognised,' she said. 'I want you to receive what you have worked for for so long. I know William Marshal has toiled for his reward, but so have you, yet only to stand still.'

'That is because nothing could truly change while Henry lived. There was too much old and bad history between him and my father. I was never going to receive the earldom back from him.'

Ida was silent for a time, but continued to play gently with their linked fingers. Then she raised her head and said in a voice hoarse with emotion, 'Orchards have always been good places for us, have they not?'

He touched the side of her face tenderly. 'The best,' he answered, and thought that William was not the only fortunate man in the world tonight.

William FitzRoy sat on his bed feeling numb. His father was dead. Everywhere the church bells had tolled his passing and masses were being said for his soul. William had played his part, spoken the words, observed the customs, doing his best for his father, fulfilling his duty and living up to the high standards expected of the son of a king. But now, in the lull following all the ceremonies and rituals, he had time to think and all the uncertainties were crowding in upon him. He had been assured that his half-brother Richard would take care of him and that his future was secure even though his father had left him nothing in his will. The household would continue to function as before with a few minor adjustments. He would receive his tutoring and training as if there had been no interruption. But even so, there was a gulf beneath his feet. His father was dead and he still did not know who his mother was.

One of the laundry maids was called Ida and he had worried himself sick thinking she had given birth to him because she was bad-tempered and coarse and spoke with a broad Flemish accent. How could his father have lain with her? But if she was his mother, why hadn't she said something? It was a matter he dared not broach to anyone and it preyed on him, eating him alive, the more so now that his father was dead.

'How now, child, what are you doing here alone?'

He looked up to see Hodierna standing over him. She had apparently been wet nurse to the new King Richard when he was a baby. It was hard for him to imagine, because her hair was grey, there were whiskers sprouting on her chin and her skin was as wizened as an over-wintered apple, whereas all the wet nurses he had seen were young and full-bosomed. He had never run to Hodierna out of choice, but she was kindly enough and had a way of knowing things that some of the younger ones didn't, for all that they smelled nicer and were more huggable. 'Thinking,' he told her.

'About your father?'

He nodded and picked at a snagged thread on the knee of his hose. Then he shook his head. 'About my mother,' he said.

'Ah.' Hodierna folded her arms.

He waited for her to go away. That's what the women usually did if the subject matter entered dangerous territory. When she remained where she was, looking down at him, he drew a deep breath. 'No one will tell me who she is.'

'Did you ever speak to your father about this, child?'

William pushed his hair out of his eyes. 'He said her name was Ida and she was a good woman, but that's all. Now he's dead and I can't ask him again.'

Hodierna looked round as if seeking support, and he saw her feet shift as if she was going to walk away after all.

'I need to know,' he said fiercely, willing her with all his being to stay.

303

She pursed her lips and studied him; then, sighing, sat down at his side. 'Your mother is the lady Ida, wife to Roger Bigod, lord of Framlingham. She was your father's mistress a long time ago.'

William's heart was pounding and his hands were slick with cold sweat. He thought he might have seen her on occasion, but he had paid scant notice because back then he had not known. Had she looked at him any differently to the other women? Paid attention? Or had he been nothing to her? A stray pup that should have been drowned in a barrel?

'When your mother contracted to wed my lord Bigod, your father said you were to remain in his household. She had to give you up; she was not permitted to take you with her, although it broke her heart.'

He nodded but continued to look at his hose because he didn't entirely trust her words. Adults often said things they didn't mean in order to get themselves out of tight corners. He felt resentful that no one had told him before – and left him to wonder and worry. 'Why didn't my father tell me?'

Hodierna gently brushed the hair off his brow. 'I believe he would have done in time, but he thought he had some years yet to let you grow up. And as his last son, he didn't want to lose you to another man's household. He never had the opportunity to watch the others grow as he has had with you. He knew your mother would bear other children and have the duties of a wife to keep her occupied, and that since he begot you, you belonged to him. He would not give you to Roger Bigod to raise. I know it is hard for you to understand, but he meant the best for you.'

William compressed his lips and moved away from her smoothing hand. He wasn't a baby to need that kind of comfort. Indeed, although he knew he was a child and people treated him as a child, he had long felt like an adult. His father had not lied – his mother was of good blood – but he still felt angry that she had gone on to make another life and he resented Roger Bigod for taking her away. But he would not have wanted him for a father above his own royal one. For Henry he felt only numbness. It was like a hard slap: that moment of burning between the deed and the sensation. 'I do understand,' he said.

'You think you do,' Hodierna replied compassionately, 'but these things will seem different when you are older. Come with me now and sit by the fire awhile and I'll tell you what I can about your mother.'

Torn between wanting to know everything and remaining in ignorance, William stayed where he was, but finally, under Hodierna's gentle coaxing, he let her lead him to the bench by the fire. He listened to her and heard what she said, but her words seemed to come from a distance and he still couldn't believe that his mother was living, breathing flesh rather than a figment created in the flames like a winter's tale.

26

Westminster, September 1189

Downriver from the city of London, the palace of Westminster blazed with torches, candles and lanterns as dusk descended over the complex of halls, administrative buildings and chapels. The reflection of the lights danced on the surface of the Thames like fallen stars.

Richard had been anointed and crowned King earlier that day in a gilded, glittering ceremony in the great abbey church, involving the earls, magnates and bishops of England.

The feast in the great hall, which had been built a hundred years ago in the reign of the Conqueror's son William Rufus, was a purely masculine affair and the women, who had attended the coronation in the abbey, were gathered for a separate celebration of the event in the smaller White Hall, presided over by Queen Eleanor.

A fringed white towel over his shoulder, Roger attended to his ceremonial duties with the other royal dapifers including Robert, Earl of Leicester, who had recently succeeded his father. Leicester was pledged to go on crusade with Richard to the Holy Land. The Earl was an accomplished soldier and his abilities would prove useful on a prolonged campaign. Roger knew, however, as did everyone else, that no matter how much Leicester strutted his importance at his steward's tasks, Richard's desire to take the new Earl with him on crusade was more about eliminating a threat at home than about having a competent commander on the field. His father had been one of the leaders of a rebellion that had almost destroyed the Crown. Richard wasn't taking any chances.

Roger knew he too was under Richard's scrutiny. Unlike William Marshal, he didn't have an intimate history of royal service, nor Queen Eleanor's long friendship and goodwill to recommend him. Everything still hung in the balance although, to Roger's advantage, Ranulf de Glanville had been removed from the justiciarship and Richard had made it clear he expected de Glanville's presence on the crusade. He was not to be left in control of England. Rumours of massive fiscal abuse were circulating that Roger could well believe, although proving that Ranulf had embezzled the money was more difficult. Ranulf wasn't the only de Glanville taking the Cross. Gundreda's husband was expected to go in support of his brother, and Huon was already pledged to the crusade. The only disadvantage Roger could see was that it would give them an opportunity to put themselves in good odour with Richard.

Roger's gaze lit on a page of the royal household who was serving at the high table and performing his tasks with swift, meticulous precision. His dark hair gleamed against the rich red and gold of his tunic, and Roger recognised the deft movement of his hands because when at home he saw it every day as Ida plied her needle and wove braid on her loom. Roger had been too busy to notice the boy before, but now he paid attention, and his body tightened with instinctive resistance. As if Roger's recognition was a magnet, the boy looked up and stared at him, and it gave Roger a shock, for his eyes were so like Ida's – and yet unalike too, because Ida's had always been fixed on him with the softness of love, and the boy's were hard and hostile. Why should the child look at him like that unless he knew his background?

A fanfare sounded and Roger had to give his attention to his duties as another course was borne up the great hammer-beamed hall to the dais. By the time Roger had ensured that the roasted peacock, its tail feathers decorating the dish in a sweep of iridescent colour, had been presented in fine order, the boy had gone.

Roger discovered him again a short while later as he was checking the salvers being sent into the women's hall. Young William FitzRoy was peering round the open door into the chamber, gazing intently at the assembled ladies. Something in his posture spoke of biting hunger and a stab of compassion caught Roger by surprise. This could have so easily been himself once, hungering for something that had long been missing from his life.

As if sensing his presence, the boy turned, a flush creeping over his face. The look he cast at Roger was guilty, defensive and angry.

Roger hesitated, uncertain what to say. He was never at a loss with his own son, but this wasn't his son. He felt resentment and knew he shouldn't, because the child was innocent. Henry's was the sin. 'That is a fine tunic you are wearing,' he said.

The boy jutted his chin. 'It was given to me by my brother the King.'

Roger raised one eyebrow at the emphasis on the last two words. The child's attitude might either be caused by touchy pride or just mean he was a pretentious brat. 'I am glad to see he cares for you,' he said. 'You must have an important position at court, hmm?'

The boy nodded. 'I am going to be a squire soon,' he said, then looked beyond Roger as the King's brother, John, Count of Mortain, arrived, sauntering and hitching his braies as if he had recently visited the latrine.

'My lord.' Roger bowed to him.

'Don't you love family gatherings?' John asked lightly and put his hand on the boy's shoulder. 'What are you doing, little brother? Shirking your job to go peering at women through keyholes? Tsk, tsk. You should leave that to older men like my lord Bigod who have the where-withal to do something about their desires.'

William's complexion turned the same colour as his tunic. 'I wasn't. I was just . . .'

'. . . catching your breath for a moment,' Roger supplied helpfully, with a sidelong look of reproach for John. 'It is always useful to know what is happening around you. As to looking through keyholes . . . I leave that to others who find such subterfuge appealing.'

John narrowed his eyes for a moment, then chose to be amused and gave his half-brother a playful cuff. 'Go on, rascal,' he said. 'Be gone.'

William ducked under John's arm and darted away in the direction of the Rufus Hall. Hands on hips, John grinned in his wake. 'I'm almost fond of the little runt. My father was always good to the bastards he begot on his whores. You can tell your lovely wife not to worry. Richard will see him advanced as was my father's inten-tion for him and should the responsibility fall to me, I will do the same . . . in memory.'

'Thank you, sire,' Roger said stiffly and, although he desired nothing more than to flatten his tormentor and stamp on his windpipe, controlled himself. John's reput-ation for verbal cruelty and sly, underhand behaviour was notorious. He would never walk straight ahead if there was the delightful possibility of digging a tunnel, and whenever he spoke, his words made someone bleed.

However, as John went on his way, it occurred to Roger that perhaps John too had paused at the women's hall, lured to gaze upon a mother he barely knew. You couldn't go back and recover those missing years, but going forward without them in your baggage made it difficult to balance the weight of your life in adulthood. His own mother was not attending the coronation, but he knew how easily it could have been himself looking through that door.

William leaned against the wall of one of the outbuildings feeling utterly mortified. He had only wanted a swift look at the woman who bore him so he could fix her image in his mind. Ever since Hodierna had told him who she was, he had come to imagine her as a beautiful, ethereal lady like the Queen of Heaven, whom his father had tragically been unable to marry because he could not secure a divorce from Eleanor. It had been a true love match and her marriage to Roger Bigod was only one of convenience. The children she had borne of that marriage were products of duty, not love as he had been, and were of lesser blood. He had heard that the Bigod line stemmed from a common, impoverished hearth knight in the pay of the Bishop of Bayeux, whereas his own line was true royalty. His father had been a King; his half-brother was one. If his father had divorced Queen Eleanor and remarried, he himself would have been in line to the throne.

All he had wanted to do was look at his mother for a moment and find out if the sight of her evoked any memories. But he had been unsure who she was amongst all the shimmering silk-clad ladies. His blood had not cried out to any one of them in particular and it was frustratingly like the times when he had wondered which of the women in the domestic household had borne him, when the truth was none of them had. He could have asked, but it would have exposed his vulnerability and been embarrassing. Just now he had been utterly humiliated at being caught out by his half-brother and his mother's husband – the man she had been made to marry. He thought of the hard, blue-grey stare and the set lips. How could she be happy with him? William told himself that his father had made the best decision. He wouldn't have wanted to go and live in a poky tumbled-down manor in the middle of nowhere with a litter of snot-nosed half-siblings. Roger Bigod spoke French with a thick Norfolk accent. He probably let pigs wander about in his hall too. If William had been raised by him, he'd be halfway to a peasant by now. He pressed his head against the wall and clenched his fists and told himself that he was in the better place and had been given the meaty end of the bone, but it didn't stop him from feeling as miserable as a starving, homeless cur.

He squeezed his eyes shut until the urge to cry had passed, brushed down his tunic, and returned to his duties in the Rufus Hall. His chin was up and his eyes were down. He made himself focus on what he had to do, as if the collecting of pitchers and aquamaniles to take them for refreshing was the most important part of his life. And in a way, it was, because it anchored him to stability and gave him a fixed point in the whirlwind.

Ida's women curtseyed and left the chamber, drawing the door curtain across on the way to their own pallets in the small cubicle beyond. Seated on the bed, Roger set about undressing. Clad in her chemise, her hair loose, Ida washed her hands and face at the ewer and dried them on a fine linen towel.

311

'I saw your son,' he said. 'Serving as a page at the high table. He worked hard and did well.'

Ida stiffened, her posture suddenly wary. 'I saw him too, from a distance in the cathedral.' She slowly turned round, still drying her hands. 'But not again after that.'

'He was busy, although I caught him looking through into the women's hall.' He told her about his encounter with William and she hung on to his every word, her eyes brimming with hope and anxiety.

'Now that Henry is dead, perhaps it is time to rebuild bridges that are broken down,' he said quietly, 'but it must be done with care for all concerned lest more harm be done than good.'

'He knows who I am?' Ida said hoarsely.

He clasped his hands between his knees. 'From what I gather, yes, but I do not think it is ancient information.' He sighed. 'Henry wanted him raised at court in the manner of a prince, and that will not change with the new King, nor should it. The court is the boy's home and he has embarked on his training towards knighthood . . . but the bonds should be acknowledged.' He unclasped his hands and came to embrace her. 'It won't be easy, for anyone, but given the fullness of time, it can be achieved – like the new bridge spanning the river.'

Ida reached on tiptoe to touch his face. 'You give me hope to balance my fear.' Her voice quivered. 'And you are generous.'

He made a face. 'No,' he said, 'I am selfish, more than you know.' He didn't want to speak of his boyhood, the loss of his mother and the struggles since then to adjust. He had not come to understanding until he was a grown man. He could also see now why his mother's second husband had not wanted him intruding on the new marriage and claiming her attention. 'He is a tie with the King,' he said instead, because it was a practical consideration and advantage and did not involve delving into emotional murk. 'And such ties must be strengthened and fostered.'

Her face fell a little. 'Yes, of course,' she said. 'You are right.'

Unspoken between them lay the detail that before Henry's death, she had been the glue that bound the arrangement together. Henry had had an interest in her wellbeing because of their son. But Richard was a step removed, and while he might acknowledge his bastard-born half-brother, he was going to set little store by his father's former concubine.

Roger took her face in his hands and kissed her. 'I do not say it for that reason alone. I know how much he means to you. He cannot mean the same to me because he is not my flesh and blood and the man who begot him has sometimes seemed very close to being my enemy, but I am willing to lay the foundations now that . . .' He broke off with a shrug. He did not have to say the rest.

Ida set her arms around his neck and kissed him in return, and he knew that now was not the time for talking. Besides, he didn't know what to say because for the time being he had run out of wisdom. Her skin bore the faint scent of rose water and there was a lingering muskier fragrance upon her throat of perfumed unguent. He nuzzled beneath her earlobe and felt her shiver.

As always when the subject of Henry arose, he was riven by jealousy – by the need for reassurance that she belonged to him alone. Drawing her to their bed, he laid her down upon it and made love to her with teasing, merciless delicacy. Tonight he needed to be the pleasure-giver and kindle her body until she writhed and cried in the grip of sensations he knew with exultant certainty Henry had never once roused in her.

313

Westminster, November 1189

William Marshal strode past the ushers and into the King's chamber. Clad in a robe of thick red wool powdered with gold stars, Richard sat at a trestle covered with sheets of parchment and strung tallies. A magnificent rock-crystal flagon held down one pile of parchments and a platter of bread and venison the other. Nearby two musicians played a lute and a rebec and Richard was humming a tune half under his breath as he considered the lists before him. Although he was alone at the trestle, his chancellor and treasurer, William Longchamp, recently appointed Bishop of Ely, was lurking in the background instructing some scribes.

Richard's expression lightened as he looked up and saw William. 'Ah,' he said, and beckoned him to the chair at his side.

William sat down, concealing a grimace because the cushion was still warm from Longchamp's backside, which was closer than he wanted to get to the King's chancellor.

Richard gestured to the flagon and William poured wine into Richard's cup and the empty silver-gilt goblet standing beside it, fortunately unused by the chair's former occupant. The King speared a slice of venison on the tip of his penknife and conveyed it to his mouth, indicating between rotations of his jaw that William was free to avail himself if he wanted. William didn't need a second bidding, for he had been busy for most of the day, balancing matters concerning his vast new lands with his duties to Richard, who had nominated him one of the co-justiciars to rule the realm during the royal absence on crusade. There weren't enough hours in the day and finding time to eat was often annoyingly difficult.

Richard swallowed, drank to rinse his mouth and then said, 'So, Marshal. What do you think about this business of the Earl of Norfolk?'

William raised his eyebrows at the King. 'What Earl of Norfolk, sire?' he asked playfully. 'I did not realise there was one.'

Richard smiled a little and shook his head. 'There isn't, but there soon will be. He indicated one of the piles of parchment spread out in front of him. 'Which man would you like it to be?'

'Well, a Marshal would be your ideal man,' William said with a completely straight face, reaching for another piece of bread.

Richard snorted. 'I was not thinking that far from Framlingham, my lord, as well you know.' He tapped the parchments under his fingers. 'Roger Bigod has offered me a thousand marks for the position and sundry items for my goodwill. Packhorses and palfreys, two hunting dogs and a length of purple silk.'

'Purple silk holds more value than gold, and Roger Bigod's horses are the best you will find anywhere in your realms.'

'That is as may be, but how certain can I be of the man's loyalty? His father's name was a byword for

315

treachery. My own father had to strip him of his castles and build Orford to keep the whoreson in check. East Anglia is rich and its ports face Flanders.'

'But that was his father,' William pointed out, 'and Roger Bigod is no more Earl Hugh than you are your sire or I am mine. I have a long acquaintance with Roger. He's honourable and he's a workhorse.'

'Trustworthy?'

William chewed and swallowed. 'If he was going to rebel, he'd have done it long ago. He carried the day at the battle of Fornham. If he hadn't, then who knows what might have happened to England. He's also married to your half-brother's mother, so that makes him your kin.'

Richard gave a caustic laugh at that remark. 'But not by blood, Marshal, not by blood.'

'Sometimes that is no bad thing.'

'But would you trust him with your life? Would he take the sword that was meant for you? I have seen "loyal" men turn their backs at the last moment. I will not give the Earldom of Norfolk to someone who is not steadfast.'

William met Richard's stare directly. 'He is steadfast,' he said. 'Yes, he would take the sword.'

'You are certain of it?'

'Sire, I would swear it on my life.'

Richard looked thoughtful. 'His half-brother has joined the crusade and has offered his own modest sums for me to find in his favour. He claims all of the Bigod lands that were acquired after his father came into the earldom and that accounts for more than seventy estates.' He tapped the parchments again. 'A father may bestow his lands where he chooses at his death and although it is traditional for a younger son to receive the acquired lands, it is not written in law.'

'So Roger Bigod's brother has no right?'

'The father's will is disputed, as you would expect. Roger is the more likely candidate. I doubt his half-brother would stand hard if asked – although I may be proven wrong. I'll find out on the way to Jerusalem.'

'Sire, you should settle this matter before you leave for Outremer,' William urged. 'Roger could be of great use to you. You have raised me to the lordship of Striguil in order to help govern, but I must have the support of men of affinity and Roger Bigod is one. You can bind him to you in loyalty with the title.'

Richard turned his cup in his hand and pondered the gemstones set in its base. 'A thousand marks to have the earldom, the third penny of the shire and permission to rebuild at Framlingham,' he said. 'It's a decent sum, but he has calculated his offer to a nicety.'

'Roger Bigod is no man's fool when it comes to accounting,' William agreed.

Richard glanced over his shoulder at his chancellor. 'Not as good as the Bishop of Ely though, I'll warrant,' he said with amusement.

William looked a little wry. Longchamp's loyalty to Richard could not be faulted; indeed, he was as jealous as a favourite hound, and like a hound, you had better hope that it was not your flesh between his teeth when he locked his jaws. Longchamp existed to extort money from folk and keep them firmly under the fiscal and regnal thumb. He had spies in almost every baronial household, and knew to the last piece of silver how much each lord was worth.

Richard finished his drink. 'So be it. Let Roger Bigod have what he desires for what he has offered – for the moment, at least, and I will review the sum at leisure. For now, I would hate to deprive you of the stalwart support

317

you seem to think he will give you, and him of the coin for a fine hat to celebrate his elevation.'

William grinned at Richard's remark, because Roger was indeed somewhat vain about his headwear. He didn't say that Roger would see the bestowing of the earldom as restoration rather than elevation. Such subtleties wouldn't concern Roger and the King. The important thing was the granting of the title.

It didn't matter that the late November sky was grey from horizon to horizon and that the heavy rain falling upon London and Westminster was threaded with silver needles of sleet. It didn't matter that the braziers were giving off more smoke than heat, or that the abbey was as cold as a tomb. All that mattered was the belt of an earl glittering with gems and thread of gold at Roger's waist, the coronet binding his brow, and the charter in his hand. *Sciatis nos fecisse Rogerum Bigot, comitem de Norfolc* . . . Know that we make Roger Bigod, Earl of Norfolk. Finally. Twelve years from the death of his father, Roger had his earldom. He had the third penny of the shire; he had his lands, including those in dispute, and all the rights pertaining. And he had permission to begin rebuilding the castle at Framlingham, and rebuild it he would to stand against adversity as a mark of achievement.

His chest was tight, swollen with emotion, and he knew that he dare not breathe hard lest he lose control and begin to weep. Receiving the kiss of peace from Richard, he was exultant. At his side, Ida curtseyed deeply to the King. Her gown shimmered with thread of gold too and her veil was woven with strands of the same, now adorned with the delicate circlet of her new rank. Countess of Norfolk. Roger thought he would burst with the pride and triumph of the moment. It had its price, and the thousand marks was only the edge of it. He knew he was being fitted for a position in government during Richard's absence, but he was eager to don the harness. It was all immensely satisfying.

His kin, his friends and the most important churchmen and magnates were present to witness the event; his mother, surreptitiously wiping her eyes on the long sleeve of her jewelled gown; his uncle Aubrey; Ida's brother, Goscelin, the Bishops of Durham, Salisbury and Ely; and William Marshal, his expression dignified as marked the occasion, but his eyes bright with pleasure.

This was a new beginning for all, Roger thought. There was much to be accomplished and the road ahead was still strewn with boulders, but he was confident they could be moved or worked around. The greatest obstacle was gone. The thought he spared for his stepmother and half-brothers was that they too knew where they stood. The de Glanville family had been torn down from power and they had nothing else to strew in his path. Even if his half-brother and his kin did go on crusade, what could they do? The Earldom of Norfolk was his.

Ida gazed with ambivalence at the gown of gold silk damask her women had recently helped her to remove. She had had her share of fine dresses when she was Henry's concubine, but this one outshone them all as a frippery of confection, like the subtlety at the end of a feast. Although it had been made to fit her figure, she was not sure that she was going to be its match.

Roger sauntered into the room and put his arms around her. He too had stripped off his rich tunic and removed the golden belt that King Richard had girt around his hips. 'Countess,' he said, kissing her ear.

319

Ida gave a little shiver and leaned against him. 'It feels strange answering to that title.'

She felt him smile against her neck. 'You'll grow accustomed.'

'So will you, my lord, to yours.'

'I suspect it will wear its shine for some time to come,' he admitted, 'although I know payment will be exacted in toil.'

His words said one thing, but she heard the proprietorial satisfaction in his tone. How far they had both come. When she looked over her shoulder, the innocent girl with her hopes and dreams intact was a distant speck on the horizon, and the woman she was now had a different set of ambitions, whereas Roger, she supposed, must have held the same goal all the way down the years of his youth and young manhood.

She had hoped her firstborn son might be present at the ceremony, but he had been absent from court, receiving training and tutoring at Dover Castle. Ida had pushed her disappointment aside to concentrate on Roger's triumph, which was what this day was all about, but even so, a glint of sadness remained.

Roger released her and went to lie on their bed, pillowing his hands behind his head. 'While we're in London, I'll enquire after a mason and carpenters to begin work in the spring, and find an engineer to design the structures.'

She joined him and he drew her into his arms. His voice shone with pleasure as he said, 'Framlingham is going to be the greatest castle in East Anglia – better than Orford or Castle Acre. This time it will stand for generations to come. We are no longer marching on the spot and pacing ourselves into a rut. We are building our future for our sons and their sons and their sons after them.'

*   *   *

320

In the priory church of Saint Mary at Thetford, Gundreda rose from her knees. Her joints were stiff; indeed all of her ached, and not just with the burden of encroaching years. She felt bruised, beaten, battered by life. She was losing everything and there was nothing she could do.

Her eldest son rose from his position beside his father's tomb, crossing himself. His lower lip was thrust out and turned down and the frown lines between his eyes were carved like chisel marks in stone. 'My father never meant Roger to have the earldom.' The force of his breath as he spoke stirred the squirrel fur edging his cloak. 'It wasn't his true belief.'

'I know,' Gundreda said, 'I know.'

Huon's mouth compressed until it resembled a down-turned bow. His father's mouth; his father's ghost. 'He never liked him. I was the one who stayed by him. I won't be denied my inheritance by some bastard runt.' He glared at his father's tomb. 'If my father got rid of his wife to please God, why didn't he get rid of Roger too?'

'Because he was foolish,' Gundreda said. 'Because he made a mistake.' Her own gaze on the tomb was filled with loathing. 'And now we pay for it.'

'It isn't finished yet,' Huon growled. 'I will be with the King, and my half-brother won't.'

Gundreda curled her lip. 'No, he'll be building his great castle at Framlingham to crow his triumph.' She had heard it was going to have massive walls with fighting towers built at intervals all the way around. The rumours of what he intended made her feel sick to the soul with bitterness. She had even seen some of the cartloads of timber and stone on the road, transferred from barges at Ipswich, and had cursed them as they rumbled past.

'Let him,' Huon snapped. 'I'll have the King's ear, and that's worth ten times more than a pile of stones.

321

Framlingham has been razed once, it can be razed again.'
He strode towards the door, pushing brusquely past the
monk who had come to tend the shrine lamp. Gundreda
followed her son outside and walked towards the guest
hall where the rest of their party was preparing to bed
down for the night. Tomorrow Huon and her husband
would leave with their men for a south coast port and
she might never see them again. Her only comfort in their
absence was her youngest son, her do-nothing, wastrel
hearth-gazer, and that was no comfort at all.

28

Windsor Castle, October 1191

Frowning, Roger contemplated his new helm. His old one with the straight nasal bar that had served him since before Fornham had been relegated to his spare kit. This one had a face guard, perforated with breathing holes and rectangular eye slits. The range of vision wasn't as good, but the level of protection was better. As an earl of the realm, it behoved him to have the newest equipment of the highest quality. He had had the helm made by an armourer recommended to him by William Marshal, who insisted on the best. He was hoping the helm was only for show and that he wasn't going to need it. There was always hope. He returned it to its leather sack and told his squire to take it down to the courtyard and load it on the packhorse.

Anketil arrived, one hand on his sword hilt, the other pushing his flaxen hair off his forehead. 'The men are ready, my lord,' he said. 'The Earl of Surrey's just come down to the yard, and the Bishop of London.'

'And the Bishop of Ely?' Roger's tone was expressionless.

Anketil grimaced. 'Still in his chamber. If it was up to him I think we'd be staying here this morning.'

Roger checked the fastenings on his sword belt. 'But it's not up to him, is it – even if he wishes it were. He has questions to answer to the satisfaction of all.'

Anketil eyed him sidelong. 'He doesn't think so.'

Roger donned his arming cap, which doubled as a hat. 'Give him a few moments more, and then I'll drag him out by his crosier if I must.'

Anketil said dourly, 'King Richard should never have appointed him justiciar in the first place. It's like putting a wolf amid sheep and expecting it not to attack them.'

Roger grimaced in agreement. Richard had been gone a year on the crusade and in that time matters in England had deteriorated alarmingly. Chancellor Longchamp was a tyrant, claiming he had the King's permission to do as he saw fit for the benefit of England. However, the 'benefit of England' was closely tied into the benefit of Longchamp and his relatives who had seized castles and lands as they saw fit and imprisoned dissenters in the name of the King. The King's brother, John, was exploiting the ensuing resentment for his own gain and had taken up the cause of the oppressed with enthusiasm. A power struggle had begun in earnest and Roger was not pleased to be trapped in the middle of it. While not a justiciar like William Marshal or Geoffrey FitzPeter, he was still embroiled up to his hat in matters of government and being forced to spend time in the company of a man he heartily disliked, in a situation that was becoming dangerous. 'Well,' he said, as he strode to the door, 'the wolf is now facing the shepherd and his dogs, isn't he?'

Anketil looked askance. 'I wouldn't call the lord John a shepherd.'

'Neither would I. I was speaking of the Archbishop of Rouen and the other justiciars who at least have the good of the country at heart. John's just another wolf in search of a meal.'

'In search of a kingdom,' Anketil qualified.

Roger lifted an eloquent eyebrow. John was manoeuvring himself into the best position to claim the crown if Richard didn't return from this crusade. The other contender was Arthur, Richard's nephew, born seven months after his father's death at a tourney in Paris. There had already been several skirmishes. Roger had been partially responsible for brokering a peace between Longchamp and John during the last serious outbreak of hostilities, but it had been inevitable that the accord would break down. Longchamp had overreached himself by arresting and mistreating Geoffrey, Archbishop of York, who was another of Henry's bastard sons. Supported by a goodly proportion of the baronage, John had responded with vigour to the news of his half-brother's mistreatment. Now the rival factions were supposed to meet at the Loddon Bridge at noon to discuss their differences, and since discussions were not always verbal in such cases, Roger was being cautious and bringing his armour.

The courtyard thronged with squires, knights, serjeants and soldiers. Hamelin de Warenne, Earl of Surrey, had already mounted his destrier. A knight was boosting the Bishop of London on to his white mule, and William de Braose, lord of Bramber, was standing by the mounting block waiting for his stallion to be brought. Longchamp's horse, conspicuous by its sumptuous gold-embroidered livery, was tethered to a ring in the wall. Roger gazed further and saw his own men standing near the watering trough. Alard, his groom, held Vavasour in readiness. The stallion was restless, pawing the ground and vigorously swishing his tail. Probably sensing all the pent-up tension, Roger thought grimly as he went to the horse and took the reins. The only other time he behaved like that was around mares. Perhaps that was a response to Longchamp's proximity.

De Braose came over, his walk as solid and belligerent as his character. 'The way Longchamp keeps us waiting,' he growled, 'anyone would think he is the King.'

Roger set his foot in the stirrup. 'He represents the King until we hear otherwise,' he said. 'Although you are wrong. Most folk can tell the difference between the King and the Bishop of Ely.'

De Braose gave a huff of humourless laughter. 'Except the Bishop of Ely himself.' He gestured to the leather helm sack hanging from the packhorse's saddle. 'You are prepared for difficulties, my lord.'

'It is always better to be prepared,' Roger replied. 'And often a show of force is better than force itself.'

De Braose eyed him thoughtfully. 'Providing you are ready to follow it through.'

Roger returned his look. 'No one should doubt that, but rather a man of reason slow to draw his sword than one who lives by it.'

'Wise words, my lord, but then I would expect no less from you,' de Braose said in a needling tone. He was a marcher baron with a reputation for violence and a swift hand to his hilt.

Roger remained unfazed. His own reputation at Fornham and as a battle commander since then stood him in good stead with such men. They knew he could fight if he had to, and perhaps they feared him the more because he was versed in the law as well as the blade.

'Ah,' de Braose said with a glance upwards. 'The Bishop graces us.'

Roger turned to gaze at the man entering the court-yard and had to suppress a shudder. Longchamp's robes

326

coruscated with embroidery and he was encircled by an entourage of knights and clerics, their numbers and ostentatious mode of attire designed to bolster his importance. His crosier shone with gold leaf; his knuckles were barely visible for rings, and his shoes were embroidered with purple silk scrollwork. Roger thought it was rather like looking at a beautiful shell and then being repulsed by the slimy creature inhabiting it.

Longchamp glanced around the waiting, mounted men and hesitated. His dark eyes rested on Roger and de Braose, who both bowed deeply.

'He's afraid,' de Braose muttered out of the side of his mouth. 'You can see it in his face. The matter of the Archbishop of York will be his downfall.' There was relish in his voice.

Roger said nothing. Longchamp was going to have a difficult field to hoe this morning and did indeed look as pale as an old tablecloth – but then he was facing the unpalatable. Apology was not in his nature, and arrogance had always stood in the way of diplomacy while he held the whip hand. Collecting his reins, Roger heeled his stallion over to the Bishop.

'My lord, if you are ready, we should be on our road if we are to meet the other party by noon,' he said.

Longchamp glowered at him from beneath heavy black brows. 'I well know the facts, my lord Bigod, I do not need to be reminded of them like an erring child. If they are so keen to have this meeting, then let them wait. I am the bearer of the King's seal and I will not be at the beck and call of treacherous men who oppose our anointed sovereign's will. Do you understand me?'

Roger stiffened. 'Perfectly, my lord,' he said with frozen civility and reined about to gesture his men into line.

The party set out towards Loddon Bridge, Longchamp

riding at the centre, protected by a palisade of spears borne by his knights and serjeants, who were armed to the eyeballs. Longchamp sent scouts ahead to report on any signs of ambush and Roger had to clamp his jaw on his irritation. He wouldn't put ambush beyond the Count of Mortain acting alone, but not when he was in the company of the Archbishops of Rouen and York, and the sub-justiciars, including William Marshal.

They had ridden four miles when one of the scouts returned to make his report, bearing the news that the other party had already arrived, had control of the bridge, and outnumbered their own men by a quarter as many again. There was also a mob of Londoners, who were not with the others as such, but had come as hangers-on to see justice done.

Longchamp had stopped to hear the scout's report and, having done so, abruptly turned his horse around. 'There is treachery afoot,' he declared. 'The Archbishop of York and the Count of Mortain have poisoned men's minds against me. I will go no further.'

'My lord, we have to meet them,' pleaded the Earl of Arundel. 'We have to settle this dispute before it deepens further into war.'

'I have to meet no one!' Longchamp snapped. 'My allegiance is first to God, and then King Richard, not a mob of traitors intent on bringing down the appointed justiciar.'

Roger folded his hands on his pommel and said icily, 'My lord chancellor, it behoves me to direct you to accompany this party to the meeting on behalf of the King whom you say you serve.'

Longchamp threw a hostile glare in Roger's direction. 'I will do what I consider is best, my lord Bigod. Do you go against my word?'

'If you do not attend this meeting you will bring a siege

down on Windsor itself,' Roger replied. 'The justiciars and Lord John will not retire. There has to be a meeting to discuss differences.' He watched Longchamp's throat move as he swallowed and saw the pallid sheen of fear on his face. He was like a cornered rat, eyes darting, seeking a way out between the dogs.

'I am not well.' Leaning over the side of his horse, Longchamp retched then vomited. 'My belly and bowels afflict me,' he gagged. 'I cannot meet them today.'

Roger was not impressed. 'You mean you have no stomach for it.'

'I mean I am sick.' Longchamp straightened and fixed Roger with a glittering stare. 'No one shall oversay me save God and my King. None of you will tell me what to do – none of you!' He gestured around the gathering, his lips drawn back in a snarl. 'You will all return to Windsor with me now, I command it!'

'My lord, I cannot do that,' Roger said curtly. 'The justiciars and the Lord John require an answer. If this meeting does not take place, the situation will only worsen. It is my duty to attend, whether you are present or not.'

'Do you defy me, my lord Earl?' Longchamp hissed.

Roger used the voice that served him on the judicial bench, and fixed the chancellor with a frozen stare. 'I am not your servant,' he said, 'and someone needs to speak, even if it is to say that you are unwell and will meet them as soon as you are recovered.'

Longchamp glowered, but obviously realised that he had little room for manoeuvre. 'Very well,' he snapped. 'Do as you will, but on your head be the consequences. Nor will I have you speaking for me. Let Arundel be my spokesman. He at least does not deal in weasel words.'

Inwardly Roger choked on Longchamp's remark. He prided himself on his balanced plain speaking; and if anyone was a weasel, it was the man accusing him. Self-control held him silent. At least, he told himself, he was going to be free of Longchamp's odious company. Arundel's own expression was as stiff as a sheet on a tenterhook, but Roger suspected that he too would be glad to be free of the chancellor.

Eventually, Longchamp turned back for Windsor under the escort of de Braose, de Warenne and a strong contingent of Flemings for his protection, while Roger, Arundel and the Bishop of London continued to the meeting.

A spread of tents and pavilions awaited them on the far side of the bridge and as Roger rode into the camp, he saw the ecclesiastical banners of the Bishops of Lincoln, Winchester, Bath and Coventry, as well as the colours of Marshal, Salisbury and the various justiciars.

Arundel grimaced. 'I would as lief not do this,' he said.

Roger nodded agreement. 'But we are burdened with it. Treat it as no more and no less than your duty and do not be drawn into argument. We are serving Richard, not Longchamp – and not John, no matter that he will make a fine meal out of this.'

Removing his hat, Roger sat down on his bed in one of the guest chambers at Reading Abbey with a heavy sigh. The smell of fresh hay rose from the mattress. There was a sheepskin underblanket and good linen sheets topped by a cover of plaid wool. Several ceramic hanging lamps illuminated the room and Roger was glad of the homely comfort. Following some tense, fraught discussions, Roger had opted to remain with the justiciars rather than return to Windsor for the night. Another meeting had been arranged for the morrow, closer to Windsor, and either Longchamp would come out to answer the charges against him, or it would indeed be all-out war.

Roger raked his hands through his hair. Arundel had done his best, but there had been no counter answers to the accusations of laying violent hands on the Archbishop of York, the King's own half-brother, and hindering the legitimate work of the under-justiciars. Walter de Coutances, Archbishop of Rouen, had produced the killing stroke with a letter from the King, authorising him to depose Longchamp and assume the post of senior justiciar himself should Longchamp fail to govern in cooperation with his advisers.

Roger glanced up as William Marshal ducked under the door arch. Earlier they had sat side by side at the council table in Coutances's pavilion by the Loddon Bridge, seeking to find balance on a slippery slope that led down to mayhem.

'Longchamp isn't going to comply, is he?' William said without preamble as he walked further into the room, his movements graceful for a man so tall and broad.

'I doubt it,' Roger said glumly. 'He truly is convinced that he is seeing to the King's will and anyone who thinks differently is obstructing him.'

'De Coutances's letter should put him in his place.'

Roger opened his hands, palm outwards. 'He will say Richard has been given false advice and that he only has Richard's good at heart.'

'What heart?' William said with an eloquent look. 'I know the King well. He is neither naive nor trusting, but he has his weaknesses like all of us, and Longchamp is one.'

'The Chancellor is good at putting over schemes and plans for making money,' Roger replied. 'He promises the King wealth and power, but it's an illusion – like the tricks I play with my son, making a penny appear and disappear between my fingers. Richard needs money, so

Longchamp fills his mind with visions of overflowing treasure chests and promises he will make them come true. If Longchamp had not let ownership of the royal seal go to his head, he might yet be in office. I suspect the King wrote that letter for de Coutances with the utmost reluctance.'

William considered the matter, then nodded. 'Mayhap you are right, but now we have to decide what to do.'

Roger sighed. 'It's difficult, isn't it? Even if you do have a letter from the King granting you authority to depose the Bishop of Ely, it has to be done in the open and in such a manner that others do not see it as a mandate to snatch power for their own ends.' He did not have to mention Count John.

William gave him a bleak smile. 'Indeed it is difficult, but I hope that with men of balance pulling on both sides of the rope, we can hold the ship steady at its moorings.'

Raising a doubtful eyebrow, Roger went to the flagon standing on a chest. 'Wine?'

'Why not?' William hooked up the stool near the bedside and sat down on it. 'I see you have a new helm.' He nodded at Roger's acquisition gleaming near the flagon.

Roger handed him a filled cup. 'I hope not to wear it often. Let it decorate my chamber, not the battlefield.'

A grin broke across William's face. 'I am afraid to say that last time I left my helm in my chamber, my heir used it as a piss-pot.'

There hadn't been much opportunity for mirth of late, and William's comment lightened the moment. 'I suppose it is a better use than warfare,' Roger chuckled. 'How is your lady wife?'

'Well but looking forward to the end of her confinement. The child is due any day.' A brief moment of irritation showed on William's face. 'If not for Longchamp, I'd be with her at Caversham now. What of your own family my lord?'

Roger turned his cup in his hand. 'They are well from what I see of them. 'My eldest son is nigh on nine years old.' He grimaced and thought that given half of that span again, Hugh would be almost a man. Time passed at an alarming pace.

'And Framlingham?' William enquired. 'How goes that?'

Roger's smile was wry. 'It will be a while in the building. Ida sees more of it than I do and complains of the dust and the noise, but it will be worth it when it is done. Each turret will give covering shots to its neighbour and have the capacity to be isolated, so if one should fall, the rest will still remain intact – and of course their positioning will make a killing ground of the bailey should it become necessary.'

A gleam of enthusiasm entered William's eyes and the talk turned to military defences. William spoke of the castles he had seen in the Holy Land and how he had masons constructing two new round towers at Striguil and had commissioned new doors for the main gate. That topic of conversation pleasantly explored, the men drank in silence before William returned to business.

'We both know the chancellor is going to be deposed, but, as you say, there is a balance to keep. Even if Longchamp's power is curtailed, he will still be entitled to the castles the King gave him before he left, and they are strategic.' He paused then said slowly, 'Dover, Cambridge and Hereford. All will require castellans who are impartial and not open to bribes.' He looked at Roger. 'Would you consider being one of those castellans – or at least be responsible for the custody? You have acted in the Lord Chancellor's service against your will, but with fairness and you have a reputation for balance.'

Roger felt a spark of excitement but kept an impassive profile. 'Is this your own thought, or in consultation with the others?'

'In consultation, naturally. The Archbishop of Rouen feels you would be ideal for one of the posts and everyone agrees. Hereford was mooted if you desire to take on its administration.'

Roger pinched his upper lip and took his time to ponder. The Marshal was a trusted friend and they had much in common. Roger had had to work hard for advancement at court in the wake of his father's treachery. William too had climbed fortune's ladder in royal service and whatever he was now had been earned through his own endeavour. Nevertheless, there were politics to consider here too. Friendship and mutual interest might unite him and William, but there was Richard's attachment to Longchamp to be taken into account. Even if Richard had been forced to write a letter deposing his chancellor of power and appointing the Archbishop of Rouen in his place, that did not mean Longchamp was finished for ever. 'I am willing,' he said eventually, 'but only within the course of the law. If Longchamp does not comply with the terms of the letter, I will gladly fulfil the duty, but in the name of King Richard.'

'Naturally,' William said, his tone grave but pleased. 'It would relieve us of a burden, knowing you had such a command.' He set down his cup and rose to his feet. 'I would not ask you to compromise your honour, but if we have your willingness, it will make for a smoother path – and, God knows, we have need of that.'

Bidding Roger goodnight, William left for his own bed. Roger poured himself another half-cup of wine and, leaning against the bolsters, considered the day's happenings and what had been said. He glanced at his new helmet and smiled, remembering the Marshal's comment about the piss-pot, but after that, his mouth straightened and his eyes grew sombre as he thought of the offer of Hereford. He had meant what he said. He intended to hold it for Richard alone and not be swayed by pressure from either side – and there would be pressure, he knew, both the benign and the not so benign. However, he was accustomed to standing his ground. He had been a long time in the training – and what else for if not this? There would be advantages to holding Hereford, both of prestige and revenue. Responsibility too, and new challenges to broaden his scope.

Unbidden, as he prepared to sleep, the image of his children came to his mind. Hugh at his lessons, making artistic capitals with his quill, Marie with her apricot hair and necklace of blue glass beads, Marguerite with a bonnet tied under her chin. But the littlest ones, William and Ralph, were anonymous babies in his vision. Asked to pick them out in a room, he wouldn't have known them. There was a price to pay. There was always a price to pay. No road was ever free of a toll for passage.

His bladder woke him in the middle of the night and Roger blearily lit the candle and fumbled out the piss-pot. He was thirsty again but he and the Marshal had emptied the wine jug. Throwing on his cloak, he stirred awake his chamber attendant Godfrey, and bade him fetch watered wine. As the young man blearily opened the door, he came face to face with a startled William de Braose who was in the act of walking past.

Standing behind his servant, Roger stared. So did the lord of Bramber, before a sardonic smile parted his lips. 'Well met, my lord Earl,' he said and drew himself up so that his stance was imposing and dominant. Roger refused to be intimidated. An ox was bigger than a ploughman, but he knew who held the whip.

'I am not so certain about that,' Roger replied. 'What are you doing here when you should be at Windsor with the chancellor?'

De Braose ran his tongue over his front teeth, lips closed. 'I am here at the chancellor's behest.'

Roger's spine prickled. 'What's he plotting now?'

De Braose gave Roger a long, assessing look. 'My message is for the Count of Mortain alone.'

'In the stealth of the night?'

De Braose smiled again. 'You know John. Such things please him and make him amenable. If the negotiations bear fruit, you will learn of them soon enough. I bid you good even.' Bowing, he swept on his way.

Roger frowned after him. Why would de Braose be bringing messages to John from Longchamp in the middle of the night? What was being muttered in the darkness that could not be openly said in daylight?

'When you've fetched the wine,' he said to Godfrey, 'go and rouse the Archbishop of Rouen and the justiciars and request a meeting. Tell them I would speak with them on a matter of importance.'

John entered the chamber belonging to Walter of Coutances, Archbishop of Rouen, the senior justiciar. Roger, who had been regaling a somewhat bleary gathering of clerics and nobles with the news about de Braose's clandestine visit, glanced towards John and immediately felt uneasy. The Count of Mortain had the look of a very well-fed cat and Roger could almost imagine him cleaning cream from his whiskers on the edge of a satisfied paw.

'What's all this, my lords?' John purred. 'A conspiracy?' He turned a look of gleaming amusement on Roger.

'You tell me, sire,' replied Walter of Coutances, pushing back the loose sleeves of his robe. 'I understand you have received a visit from my lord de Braose tonight.'

John continued to smile and approached the trestle around which the men were gathered. 'Indeed yes,' he said. 'In secret and of a personal nature – as the Earl of Norfolk will doubtless have told you.' He flashed Roger a triumphant smirk.

'Where is de Braose now?' asked Hugh Nonant, Bishop of Coventry.

'On his way back to Windsor with my reply,' John said pleasantly. 'There was no point in him staying.'

'Would you care to enlighten us as to the nature of the visit?' De Coutances extended his hand in invitation.

'By all means.' John leaned against the trestle, and then stared around the gathering, fixing each man with a strong look before moving on to the next. 'Chancellor Longchamp wondered if I was interested in joining forces with him and making a stand against the justiciars and their allies. He was prepared to offer me Hereford Castle as surety, five hundred marks and a chest of gold plate.'

There was a shocked silence. Roger flushed at the mention of Hereford Castle and deliberately avoided the gaze of the Marshal and de Coutances. This was indeed murky water and he felt soiled to be dabbling in it.

'Of course,' John said nonchalantly, 'I had to refuse. I may be ambitious, but I am no fool. Show me anyone who would want to climb into a bed with the Bishop of Ely from choice – other than my absent brother. It is disgraceful that the chancellor should try to subvert the course of justice in this way.'

Roger raised an eyebrow, knowing full well John didn't consider it disgraceful at all. He just had the good sense

337

to know this particular ploy was hotter than an iron bar freshly drawn from the coals of a blacksmith's forge. By claiming the moral high ground, John had gained a fine advantage over his rival. It did show, however, that Longchamp was desperate.

'Indeed my lord, it is,' de Coutances said smoothly, 'and you were wise to resist the bribes of the chancellor. Be assured we will deal with the matter at our meeting on the morrow.'

John inclined his head. 'I am sure you will,' he said, 'remembering of course that I could have been halfway to Windsor by now with my troops.'

De Coutances returned John a benign smile. 'But you said yourself, my lord: you are not a fool.'

In the morning, the party from Reading set out to the rearranged meeting point near Windsor while their baggage train turned for Staines, where they intended to spend the night.

John rode up to join Roger as they jogged along. 'My lord Bigod, I have not spoken to you alone about the bribe Longchamp offered me last night.'

Roger had pulled his hat brim low so that there was no chance of it blowing off in the stiff autumn wind. He was glad of that camouflage now. 'Why should you need to speak to me alone, sire? Let the will of the justiciars be the will of all.'

John flashed his teeth in a lupine smile. 'I don't know about you, but I am never offended when propositions are put to me, even if, regretfully, I cannot accept them. The chancellor must be desperate, don't you think?'

'He has made some errors of judgement,' Roger said. 'And he has gone against the law.' He looked straight ahead between his mount's pricked ears. 'But yes, to offer money to a man he has been intent on dominating, he must indeed be feeling the wall against his spine.'

John's smile deepened. 'They say every man has his price, my lord. I wonder what yours is.'

Roger heard the teasing note in John's voice, but there was speculation behind it and a genuine, ruthless curiosity. 'My lord, I suspect both you and the chancellor would beggar yourselves finding out.' He chose not to think about Hereford Castle.

John gave a dark chuckle. 'Is that so? Well, perhaps the price you have paid to my brother has already beggared you – and may break you yet.'

'Then by all means let us be ragged together,' Roger retorted, then suddenly drew rein for a scout was pounding up the road towards them on a sweating courser.

'Ah,' John said silkily. 'News of the illustrious chancellor I suspect. His bowels obviously continue weak at the notion of confronting those he has wronged.'

The scout made obeisance to the gathering and announced that Chancellor Longchamp had indeed set out again to the meeting, 'but then he turned round as if chased by the devil's breath, and now he's taken the same road as the baggage carts at a pace that's going to founder his horse.'

The men stared at each other in bewilderment. There were rumblings to the effect that Longchamp's wits had finally deserted him.

'Why is he chasing our baggage carts?' John demanded on a rising note of incredulity. 'I know he is avaricious, but surely he is not planning to seize our pots and pans and bed coverings?'

'Perhaps he mistook the baggage train for us and thinks we are riding to seize control of London,' Roger suggested because it seemed to him the only rational explanation for such lunatic behaviour. Whoever controlled London controlled the most vital city in England.

'What do we do now?' grumbled Bishop Reginald of Bath. 'Retire to Reading again? I swear I am beginning to feel seasick with all this parading hither and yon.'

Hugh Nonant, Bishop of Coventry, gave a sardonic smile. 'With respect, my lord, I think going back to Reading would be pointless. I believe we should follow the chancellor's example and go to London to buy ourselves some winter clothes.' His comment drew snorts of laughter from those close enough to hear. 'And then we might even catch up with the chancellor again and have this discussion he seems so keen to avoid.'

'He takes us all for fools,' John said with just the right note of aggrievement, 'and leaves us standing here while he persuades the Londoners to shut their gates against us.'

'Have you ever tried to persuade a Londoner to do anything?' Roger said. 'It's easier to put a saddle on a wild boar. The Londoners will do what they think is best for them.'

'Then it behoves us to make sure that what they think is best is what we think is best too,' John replied with a sardonic grin, and reined his horse towards the city.

29

Friday Street, London, October 1191

Ida watched Hugh and some companions kick an inflated pig's bladder round the yard of the Friday Street house, their excited yells ringing on the air. At almost nine years old, Hugh was lithe and wiry with a mop of golden curls and eyes the deep blue of a summer sea. His features still bore the softness of childhood, but he was reaching towards independence at a rate that frightened her. She knew she shouldn't cling, and she took great pride in watching him run and catch, shout and throw, bursting with confident joy, but still, her heart ached because of the small ways in which she was having to let him go, and each hair-thin strand that was severed was another on the way to cutting the cord.

Roger was busy with affairs of government and although they were living under the same roof, she barely saw him, and the times she did, he was distant and preoccupied. The city had been filled with unrest ever since the chancellor had arrived at a tearing gallop and shut himself in the Tower with the justiciars hard on his tail. Some citizens wanted to uphold the chancellor's rule, but others preferred to support John. Following several days of hard negotiation and frayed tempers, Longchamp had finally agreed to give in to the justiciars, but not to John. That was where Roger was today, overseeing the handing over of the Tower of London to de Coutances.

One of the other boys tackled Hugh for the pig's bladder, but Hugh threw it hard and high and it landed in the gutter of the poultry shed roof. Hugh ran to fetch the thatch gaff to knock it down.

'Me, me!' cried Marie, her apricot braid snaking. 'Let me do it, Hugh!' Laughing, he handed her the gaff and picked her up in his arms. Ida felt a flood of warmth for her son. Not many boys of his age would pander to their younger sisters − or not when playing with other boys − but Hugh had no such qualms. He was so at ease with himself and others.

She heard voices at the entrance to the yard and the clop of hooves as Roger returned from his mission. Hastening to greet him, Ida noticed that his hat was sitting low over his eyes − not a good sign. As he dismounted, Marie succeeded in dislodging the pig bladder from the roof ridge with a swipe that sent it flying. It struck Roger on the side of his head, knocking off his hat and breaking the peacock feather in the band.

There was a momentary silence. 'I'm sorry, Papa,' Marie said, biting her lip.

Roger stooped, picked up his hat and studied it for a moment. A muscle moved in his jaw. He turned the brim through his fingers and eyed the bent feather. 'It doesn't matter,' he said in a tight, quiet voice, and strode into the house.

Ida kissed Marie in reassurance, gestured that the children should continue their game and hurried after her husband.

He was standing in the main room by the fire and he

342

had put the hat down on a trestle. The broken feather was singeing in the flames.

'Is it bad news?'

'It depends what you mean by bad,' he replied as he watched the feather burn. 'Longchamp has yielded the keys of the Tower to the justiciars, so that particular matter is dealt with. I am to take custody of Hereford Castle for the time being – which suits me well enough – and Longchamp is to be banished from England once his castles have been handed over.'

Ida had known and expected both these things. Indeed, she had been quietly packing in the background, aware that a move was probably imminent. 'Then why so downcast?'

He gave a heavy sigh and set his hand at her waist. 'I am sick of wading in the mire. Longchamp didn't yield gracefully and laid threats on us all even while putting the keys in the hands of de Coutances. He may have had his authority removed and his castles are to be handed over as soon as can be arranged, but it does not mean he is finished – far from it. Whatever he has done to others, his loyalty to the King is absolute, and Richard prizes that trait in men above most other things.' He rubbed his free hand over his face. 'There will be repercussions from today and on both sides. John has seen his chief rival in power defeated and is strutting like a cockerel on a dunghill. I'm stuck in the middle . . . and that means still in the mire.'

From outside came the noise of the resumed ball game and Marie's imperious voice shouting, 'Me, me!'

Roger said, 'Richard raised me to the earldom for a reason. It wasn't done out of love or to finish business and right wrongs. Whatever other men do, I have to ride straight down the line. That's my part in it.'

343

Pride in her man tightened Ida's throat, but there was fear and resentment too. They had so little time to spend together and there was always so much to do. 'Would that all others did the same,' she said.

'Amen to that, but unlikely.' He gave a hard sigh. 'My duty now is to ride to Hereford and secure it on the orders of the justiciars – although officially I'll be holding it by proxy for Longchamp.'

'I've started the packing,' Ida said. 'When do we leave?'

'Well, not that anyone is suspicious of Longchamp, but I have said I will set out as soon as I've eaten. It's four days' ride to Hereford – three if we push the horses, but obviously that's without the baggage carts. They will have to follow. I want you and the children to go to Framlingham and I'll join you there when I can.'

Her heart sank. 'Not to Hereford?'

He shook his head. 'I don't know what I'm going to find when I get there. If Longchamp's castellan refuses to open the gates or hand over to me, I'll have to besiege it. I don't want you in the thick of it. At Framlingham you and the children will be well away from trouble and safe.'

Ida felt a surge of disappointment at the thought of being parted from him again. The masons and carpenters would be busy with the new towers and buildings. There would be no peace anywhere with the ringing of their hammers and chisels, the banging, the dust and noise. And while he was saved worrying about her and the children, she still had to worry about him, and from a distance.

Something must have shown in her face, for he cupped her cheek on the side of his hand and kissed her swiftly. 'It won't be for long, I promise. As soon as I can, I'll appoint a trustworthy deputy, but first I need to see for myself.'

344

Ida managed a nod of understanding, but she felt bereft. At least, she thought, she would have time to stock up on fabrics and thread before she left for Norfolk, and while there, she could continue refurbishing the hall and bedchamber to her taste, but it was small recompense when there would only be her and the children to see it. Knowing that Roger was right about Hereford, she made a determined effort to shrug off the self-pity, but the disappointment remained.

30

Ipswich, March 1193

Roger stood with Alexander, the master of his quay, and watched the sailors taking down the mast of the ship tied at the wharf. The tide was in and the brackish water of the estuary chopped against the mooring posts. Rain spattered in the wind and the damp air carried the tang of the sea. It was almost sunset but the western horizon showed naught but bruised deep grey. In his hand Roger held a creased piece of parchment, and on his middle finger, placed there for safekeeping, was the heavy gold ring that had accompanied the letter.

'Bring the man,' he said.

Alexander turned and snapped his fingers to a serjeant, who strode off on his errand.

Roger pinched the bridge of his nose and suppressed a sigh. He was very tired, having arrived from Hereford late in the afternoon. Alexander's news had brought him straight to the quay, his buttocks still numb from his saddle and the smell of hard-ridden horse clinging to his hose. There was no peace, no rest. If the information in this letter was any indication, the country stood on the verge of turmoil.

Returning from the crusade, Richard had taken the over-land route and been captured in Austria by its Duke with whom he had quarrelled during the crusade. Duke Leopold had handed Richard's custody to Emperor Henry of Germany, who also had political reasons for keeping Richard prisoner. With his brother incarcerated, John was making his bid to become King and the justiciars, Queen Eleanor and those who remained loyal to Richard were striving to prevent him. He looked at the ring, which was set with two rubies and a sapphire, and which he had seen the Count of Mortain wearing at Richard's coronation. Ironic then that it was being used to try and topple Richard, and just the sort of jest that John would enjoy.

The serjeant returned with two companions, dragging between them a bruised and bloody fourth man, his hands tied before him with competent sailor's knots.

'Captain says the fellow bought a passage in Saint-Omer,' Alexander said. 'Searched his baggage when he was asleep and found the letter and the ring and thought you should see them.'

'That was well done.' Roger handed a pouch of silver to Alexander. 'See that the captain is rewarded for his diligence.'

'Yes, my lord.'

Roger focused on the captive. A livid plum occupied his left eye socket and there was a spectacular split bisecting his lower lip.

'I don't know anything!' he pre-empted Roger, speaking in a broad Flemish accent.

'Then explain how you came into possession of these?' Roger held up the letter and spread his hand to display the ring.

The man shook his head. 'It is true I work as a messenger for the Count of Mortain, but I do not know

347

what I carry. I was told to bring them with all haste to Windsor and take my orders from there . . .'

'You were expecting to travel further?'

The man swallowed and nodded. 'But I wasn't told where.'

'It seems you weren't told a great deal,' Roger said coldly, wondering how much of the messenger's fear and ignorance was a screen. They could always swing him to find out, or stake him in the harbour and let him think about it as the next full tide rolled in. Then again, the letter and the ring were proof enough that John was commanding his castellans to stuff their keeps with men and supplies and informing them that he was gathering an army of mercenaries across the North Sea at Wissant ready for invasion. Would he himself have told a messenger such things if the scheme were his? He pondered, his gaze fixed on the man like stone, his mind busy on the implications of what he had just read, not least that some of the dissidents mentioned in the letter were kin to men that he himself counted as allies.

Where there was one messenger, there were bound to be more. John wouldn't entrust it all to the one, lest he be intercepted. The Queen and the justiciars would have to know immediately so that the coastline could be defended, and John's castellans dealt with. They could contain and prevent this, but they would have to move fast.

'Take him and put him in gaol for now,' he said. 'I may yet have more to ask him.' He turned towards his house as the last of the light faded to dark, and bade his chamberlain fetch his scribe, and two messengers of his own.

Feeling queasy with anticipation, Ida gazed around the bedchamber, reassuring herself that everything was ready.

A bathtub full of steaming water stood before the fire with fine white soap to hand. She had laid out fresh clothes for Roger, including a tunic on which she had been working for several weeks. A new embroidery of a picnic scene brightened the wall behind the bed and she had employed an artist to paint a matching scrollwork frieze above it. There was light and air, but balanced with colour and richness to make the atmosphere tranquil rather than cold. Intimacy was provided by the cheerful fire, Ida's sewing basket and the gaming board placed on a trestle close to a candle sconce, affording good light to anyone desiring to play. Ida was pleased with her efforts. Who would not want to spend time in this room? Who would want to leave it for the vagaries of the open road?

'Mama, they're here!' Hugh dashed into the room, his face bright with excitement and flushed from standing on the blustery battlements while he watched for his father's entourage.

Ida took charge of four-year-old William and had the nurse bring two-year-old Ralph. The girls went before her, hand in hand, and Hugh led the way, very much the man. Outside the hall, the towers continued to rise in a protective curtain wall that would eventually enclose the site. The dwellings of the masons clustered in the ward, making a little village of timber huts with thatch and shingle roofs, and the scale on which Roger was rebuilding meant that it was likely to be there for years to come. The dust got everywhere, and although Ida had become accustomed to the presence of the masons, she often longed for them not to be there and to have respite from the constant clamour of their industry. The children loved it. Hugh was fascinated both by the business of the construction and by the masons themselves. He would often abscond to their hearths at night to listen to their stories and songs.

Sometimes Marie would abscond with him and Ida would have to send an attendant to fetch them when it grew late and they had not returned.

A cavalcade of knights and squires, clerics, servants and laden pack ponies began disgorging into the bailey. Ida's gaze fixed on Roger astride his chestnut palfrey and her heart turned over. It had been so long since he had been home. Between administering Hereford, conducting affairs of state and now taking the field against the King's rebellious younger brother and organising the coastal defences, she had barely seen him since last autumn.

Roger dismounted and Ida curtseyed to him in formal greeting while the boys bowed and their daughters followed her example, giving each other little glances and giggling. Roger raised Ida to her feet and kissed her with equal formality on both cheeks. 'You look well,' he said.

'I am, my lord, and the better for seeing you.' Her tone was heartfelt.

His forced smile in response was not the greeting Ida longed for and needed and her face fell.

Roger tousled Hugh's fair hair. 'I swear you've grown again, lad,' he said over-heartily.

'I've grown too,' Marie declared.

'So have I!' Marguerite was determined not to be left out.

'You're all going to be giants then.' Roger raised his eyes to the battlements. 'Coming along,' he said with a nod. 'They'll have that tower finished by midsummer.'

'You are going to be here at midsummer then?' Ida heard the querulous note in her own voice and hated it.

He twitched his shoulders. 'I hope so, but it all depends on what happens.' He entered the hall and climbed the stairs to the bedchamber. Then he stopped and stared at the steaming bathtub, the beautiful décor, the food, and palmed one hand over his face.

'What's wrong?' Ida asked with concern.

He shook his head. 'We've been hard pressed and the sight of home comforts is almost too much.'

Ida's nurturing instincts overrode her disappointment. 'Come, bathe and eat,' she urged. 'You'll feel better then.' She reached to his belt buckle and unlatched it and, for a moment, they stood intimately close. Her breathing quickened and her loins grew warm and sensitive. Dear God, six months was a drought.

Continuing to disrobe her husband, she checked his body and was relieved to see no marks of war upon it. His hands and wrists were clean, his face too, but his body was layered with the grime of long days in the saddle and the constant wearing of armour. He stepped into the tub and heaved a deep sigh. Ida placed a cushion at his back and had a stool brought to the bath side to use as a table for a cup of wine and a chicken pasty. In times past, they would have shared the tub and made a private time of the meal and the bathing, but with the bustle of servants and children in the room and the other demands of the moment such intimacy was impossible. Still, Ida took the opportunity to perform the task of bath maid and renew her acquaintance with his body. Beneath the ministrations of the soaped cloth, she felt him relax.

'Is it over?' she asked.

Roger screwed up his face. 'I don't know about that. A truce has been arranged to last until All Saints' Day, but that's in John's favour because he was losing anyway. His fleet hasn't sailed and the only mercenaries he's been able to hire have been a few sweepings from Wales. Since we intercepted his messages in time, we've nipped that particular invasion scheme in the bud. He's still insisting

351

to everyone that Richard will never return from Germany and he should take the crown.'

Ida dipped the cloth and lathered more soap on to it and Roger bit into the pasty. Crumbs flaked into the bathwater, joining the scattering of herbs and dried petals. 'Fortunately for us, we know now that even if a prisoner, Richard is in good health and spirits. John's posturing and schemes will get him nowhere.'

'So what happens now?'

He chewed and swallowed. 'We have to ransom the King. Everyone must pay a fourth of their income. Every knight's fee is to be assessed at twenty shillings. All the treasure in the country – gold, silver, whatever can be found – is to be paid towards his release.'

'And how much is the ransom?' Ida refilled his cup then smoothed away the water droplets on his shoulders for the pleasure of touching him again.

'A hundred thousand marks is the sum that's been mooted.'

Ida stared at him in shocked astonishment. 'How is that going to be found? Richard almost beggared us to raise the money to go on crusade. What's left?'

He finished the pasty and swilled his hands in the cooling water. 'There are still some reserves and renewable resources such as the wool clip. While Richard lives, even in captivity, John can never be King. I am the custodian of these lands for my son. I will not see them wasted and ruined by war after all my efforts to regain and rebuild.'

'But twenty shillings on the knight's fee . . .'

'A little short of a hundred and ninety marks to us. I have no doubt it will be rounded up to two hundred – and more will be expected in the way of plate and jewels and the like.' Heaving a sigh, he rose from the bath. 'The Emperor of Germany is not a fool. He will have calculated how much England can afford to the last penny, but not beyond it.'

Once dressed, Roger went out to inspect the building work and talk to the masons. Leaving the children with her women, Ida accompanied him as he discussed his requirements with the master and how the timing would have to be revised owing to the need to raise the King's ransom. Then they climbed to the top of the timber palisade wall overlooking the mere and the fields of new spring grass. Lambs gambolled beside their mothers, the latter clad in fine fleeces. Ida felt a twinge of resentment that they were already pledged to buy the King out of imprisonment.

Leaning against the timbers, Roger said, 'I was here when they demolished all the defences at Framlingham and left naught but that old hall. It was my duty to witness it all being torn down, and I swore then that I would have the earldom restored to me, and everything not only rebuilt, but made magnificent.' He gave her a grim smile. 'When you have nothing to lose it does not matter if you lose it. But when you have more, it does.'

Ida bit her lip, not wanting to think about it. Not now. It wasn't fair. He was home and even though she knew he had duties and heavy responsibilities, there had to be moments of respite. There just *had* to be, or she would go mad. 'Do you remember that first meeting of our courtship?' she asked. 'The one in the orchard at Woodstock?'

He had been focusing on some point on the horizon, but now returned his attention to her. His frown remained but a half-smile curved his lips. 'What of it?'

Ida touched his side. 'I said you were neither old nor grey, but that you were in need of physic.'

353

'Like a sick tree,' he said wryly. 'I remember it well.'

'I think perhaps you are in need of such again.' She reached up to stroke his hair. Freshly washed, it felt like soft feathers under her fingers. 'I know that I am.' Lightly she touched the side of his face and, as he turned into her caress to kiss her palm, she whispered, 'I have missed you.' Her throat suddenly aching, she clung to him. 'Every day has seemed like a year.'

'Every day *has* been a year,' he said and gathered her in his arms.

Astride his destrier, Roger watched Hugh canter his mount across the paddock. A small, light spear couched under his arm, the boy rode towards the first of three stands from which was suspended a circlet fashioned from plaited osiers. Hugh had his horse well collected, his seat in the saddle was good and his aim straight. He lanced the first circlet and continued down the run to collect the second and third, to the applause of the onlookers.

'He's going to be as fine a jouster as his father,' commented Oliver Vaux with a grin as Hugh turned his mount at the end of the run and trotted back towards them.

Roger smiled with pride and didn't contradict the knight, although he thought privately that Hugh was unlikely to spend time on the tourney circuits. The lad had aptitude if he cared to develop it, but Roger knew that, given the chance, Hugh would rather have his nose in a book, a treatise, or be busy with the masons. He was greatly interested in how the stones were cut and assembled, and fascinated by the production of the ornate and embellished ones. He had his mother's eyes for symmetry, colour and pattern. The warrior skills were necessary to his education, but to Hugh they were incidental, whereas

354

his youngest brothers were already charging around with their toy swords, intent on sweeping all before them.

'Well done, son!' Roger said as Hugh rejoined them. The boy flushed with pleasure. With a pang, Roger realised how much he had grown during his absence. He was still a child, but looking towards adolescence rather than further years of boyhood. Roger had a squire set up the rings again, took a lance from an attendant and rode to perform the same manoeuvres as Hugh. Partly it was to keep his own skills honed, but there was more to it than that. The act of coordinating hand, eye and horse gave him pleasure and reminded him that somewhere among the burdens and responsibilities that had devolved upon his shoulders a young man's blood still burned in his veins and there was joy to be taken in the small pleasures of life.

He had been home a week, and although he had been kept busy with the estate, overseeing the building of the keep and working on the matter of the ransom, there were brief moments like this when he was able to relax. It was a luxury to wake up in a bed with a feather mattress and Ida at his side. To have her company at mealtimes and in the evening, curled against him with her sewing, or singing with him for pleasure and entertainment. There was the luxury too of physical contact. He was no slave to lust and fornication the way some men were, but bedding his wife – and being bedded – was a delight he had sorely missed. His children were a pleasure too. Their antics amused him and their liveliness had the same effect as this ride down the tilt. They made the blood sing in his veins. It gave him a protective pang to have his smallest daughter curl in his lap, enfolded in his fur-lined cloak, and fall asleep there. Such unconditional trust and love. His own father had never experienced such a privilege; indeed would have recoiled at the very notion of taking a child on to his knee, and it mingled Roger's pleasure with a sharpening of sadness.

He caught the three rings on the tip of the lance and returned to the group at a bouncing canter, basking a little in the adulation in his son's eyes.

As he was dismounting the enormous white gander from the poultry yard flapped across the sward, pursuing several squawking, agitated hens. Neck outstretched, honking and hissing, he attacked with full aggression to protect his territory.

'Watch out, sir,' warned the groom who had come to take Roger's horse. 'He went for the master mason last week because he thought he was threatening his females.' The groom jerked his head in the direction of the four drab brown geese plucking at clumps of grass against the wall of a storage hut.

Roger gave a snort of amusement and watched the gander bustle the hens across the yard. Several of the stupid creatures flustered themselves into the water trough, where they flapped and clucked in panic while the gander continued to threaten. Roger began to splutter. The rest of his men were holding their midriffs and laughing as a florid woman emerged from the kitchens, sleeves rolled up and a large ladle in her hand.

'Trouble now,' choked Anketil. 'Here comes Wulfwyn.'

She marched towards the chaos, her face a furious shade of red. 'You'll not be laughing, my fine lords, when there are no chickens for the pot or eggs for the table!' she cried, not in the least set down by any consideration of rank. 'This will put them off laying for a month!' She glared at Roger as if the situation was his fault, which only brought tears to his eyes.

Reaching the trough, Wulfwyn plucked the bedraggled chickens out of the water, seized the gander round the neck in a grapple hold, pinned its wings, tucked it under her arm and stumped off in high dudgeon, muttering about the stupidity of all males. The hens tottered about round the base of the trough, flouncing their feathers and complaining while the men wiped their eyes and tried to recover.

'She won't wring its neck,' Hugh piped up. 'It's her pet. She loves it and talks to it all of the time, even if it's mostly scolding.'

'Like having a man around then,' Anketil remarked.

Hugh shook his head. 'She says it's better than a man. It protects her and it doesn't want to futter her every time she gets into bed.'

Everyone burst out laughing again, staggering and holding on to each other. Hugh reddened and grinned. Roger gave him a good-natured cuff. 'What have you been learning in my absence?' he demanded.

Hugh shrugged, his complexion brighter than ever. 'It's what she said, and in front of everyone.'

'Sounds like wishful thinking to me,' Anketil chuckled. 'No man in his right mind would want to bed with that harridan. Even if he did, who'd want to risk being pecked in his stones?'

'It might be worth it for a good breakfast,' opined Thomas of Heacham, who was a renowned trencherman.

'Come off it, man, you'd be the breakfast!'

The jests and banter, the camaraderie gave Roger a warm feeling. He was amused to see Hugh lapping it up like a hungry adolescent pup. It was good for the boy to learn the lessons of interaction with the kinds of men on whom he would have to depend when his time came to rule. There were boundaries, of course, as was right and proper, but a good leader of men, a good lord, knew where to set them and when to be fluid.

As the men were recovering from their mirth, a

messenger arrived at a hard gallop, dismounting even as he drew rein. Seeing Roger, he strode over to him, knelt and handed him a packet. Roger knew the messenger for one belonging to Chancellor Longchamp. 'Geoffrey, isn't it?' He gestured to him to stand up.

'Yes, my lord.' The man removed his cap in deference revealing a head of grizzled curls. He looked anxious. Roger glanced at the packet, which bore Longchamp's seal, the King's and that of Queen Eleanor. Taking his knife, he broke open the document and studied the contents. As he read, he began to frown and at one particular line, his glance flickered to his son.

'Trouble?' asked Anketil. The men were no longer smiling. Longchamp's messenger wiped a hand over his sweating face. Roger glanced at him too and gave him leave to stable his horse and claim a drink in the kitchen. It wasn't his fault he was the bearer of the tidings, but Roger almost hoped that the gander was still on guard duty around Wulfwyn.

'Whenever is the Bishop of Ely not trouble?' Roger said grimly. 'I am summoned to a council at Saint Albans to discuss the King's ransom.' He looked again at his son and his face felt stiff. 'Oliver, gather everyone together. I need to read this again and speak to the Countess, and then I have to decide what to do.'

Ida sat in the upper room of the solar by the open window with the spring sun spilling across her lap and the shirt she was stitching for Roger. She could have had one of the seamstresses do it, but she preferred to sew it herself because then he would be wearing her work against his skin wherever he went. The first intimation she had of trouble was when Roger thrust open the chamber door and strode into the room. A slight waft of horse and hard exercise accompanied him, but his mood was not the one of vibrant wellbeing she expected to see after such sport. And then she saw the parchment in his hand and a hole opened up inside her.

'What is it?' she asked. A week, they had had a week. Was that all they were going to be granted?

He came and sat opposite her in the window seat where they had fed each other morsels of toasted bread dripping with butter on their first night here in intimate, firelit darkness. 'William Longchamp has returned,' he growled. 'Landed at Ipswich of all places – my own port. He's called a meeting at Saint Albans a week hence.'

Dismay coursed through her. Despite his banishment, Longchamp had tried last year to set foot in England and been warned off. She could not believe that he would make another attempt – and apparently succeed. 'A meeting about what?'

'This comes with the sanction of the King. Richard has put him in charge of raising the ransom and having it brought to Emperor Henry in Germany.' Roger looked at the document in his hand as if it were a piece of rotting flesh. 'Once the first seventy thousand has been paid Richard can go free, but the Emperor demands hostages as a guarantee of good faith.'

Suddenly alarmed, Ida sat up straight. 'What are you saying?'

He was silent for several heartbeats, then he said, 'Longchamp has ordered me to stand as one of the hostages as well as Richard de Clare and the Bishops of Rochester and Chichester. He's also demanded that men give their sons as hostages too – including Hugh.'

Ida's hands flew to her mouth in shock. 'He can't do that!'

'He's asked for one of Eleanor's grandsons too.'

359

'You can't give him up, not Hugh!' She felt sick.

'I don't intend to,' Roger said with grim determination. 'It's all part of the negotiation. They ask for more and seem reasonable when they accept less. By all means, let Longchamp have me. I am not ten years old and I can look after myself. But I will not yield our son.'

His words barely reduced Ida's anxiety. Standing in defiance had its own perils, and even if he protected Hugh, he was putting himself forward as a shield and a sacrifice. 'But you will still have to go to Germany?'

'In all likelihood.' Roger turned his gaze to the window, avoiding hers.

Ida thrust her hands under the sewing so he wouldn't see them shaking. Germany! It might as well be Jerusalem. 'When do you leave?' she asked in a thready voice.

He folded the parchment and stuffed it through his belt. 'It'll have to be the morrow. I don't have much time.'

She felt as if she had been punched. 'I had better pack your baggage,' she heard herself say. 'You'll be needing your court clothes and several changes of linens . . . I . . .' She swallowed. 'I thought I would have longer to finish your shirt . . .' She looked down at the soft bleached linen under her hands and blinked. A tear splashed on to the fabric and made a transparent blot. Another summer gone. Another season from the prime of life.

'Ida . . .' He stretched across the embrasure space and took her hands in his. 'It is my duty . . .'

'Yes,' she said stiffly. 'I would not have you go away at all, but I know my own duty.' She disengaged from him and taking up the shirt began to stitch again, erratically. The seam wobbled and she pricked herself, staining the clean white fabric with her blood.

'Leave it,' Roger said. 'It does not matter. I have shirts aplenty.'

'But it does matter,' she cried, feeling fierce and angry and raw with pain. 'Perhaps not to you; to a man a shirt is a shirt. But to the wife who has sewn it and cried over it and bled upon it, it is so much greater than – than a duty.' She jerked to her feet. When he put out his hand to her, she held out her own to stop him. 'No,' she said. 'I need to compose myself . . . Let me be.'

She removed to the bedchamber and drew the curtain across. There was a gathering pressure of tears behind her eyes and she knew she had to give vent to the storm in order to come through to the other side, cried-out to numbness and seemingly calm.

Roger followed her, clashing the curtain aside and then back into place. 'If I could stay, I would,' he said and hearing the irritation in his voice, she flinched. 'But when I swore fealty to Richard, I promised my body to serve him in tasks such as this and what would I be if I did not uphold my oath to him? All the weeping in the world will not make a difference.'

'I know,' Ida said wretchedly. 'But at least I can choose whether to weep or not.'

He reached her, turned her round and pulled her roughly into his arms. 'And you think that when I leave on the morrow I want to carry the memory of your tears with me?'

'Perhaps I need you to carry that memory,' she said, striking out through her pain.

They stood in each other's space, their breathing suspended. Ida thought he was going to turn from her and stride out. A part of her wished he would and make her misery complete, but instead his grip tightened and he kissed her hard and she responded, so that they exhaled into each other. 'I will tell you the kind of memory I want

361

to carry,' he said. 'Indeed, I will show you.' And lifting her in his arms he carried her to their bed.

In the early morning, the dawn still at the stage of grey twilight, Ida watched Roger ride away from Framlingham with his entourage of knights, squires and clerics, the sumpter horses piled with baggage. He wasn't taking a cart because he said it would slow him down. Hugh stood proudly beside her, his head up and his hands gripped in manly fashion around his belt, although she knew that within the hour he would be a boy again, playing camp ball, or racing his pony against his friends.

Ida was unable to smile, but she raised her hand to answer Roger's salute of farewell. She couldn't see the expression on his face as he rode away, but she could feel its intensity, holding her to the memory of the hour they had spent in the bedchamber yesterday afternoon and all the things that had gone unspoken but not unsaid in the intimate language of touch. He wasn't smiling either. What they both had for the moment was the kind of grim balance needed for walking along a narrow rope with sharp knives either side, some of their own making.

As the last horse trotted out of Framlingham's gates, Wulfwyn's gander flurried across the yard in its wake, hissing and honking, as if chasing out intruders. Normally such a comical sight would have caused great amusement among the onlookers, but today no one laughed.

31

Sandwich, August 1193

A heavy squall had turned the waves to grey and marbled them with white striations of foam. Water slapped against the strakes and exploded in small starbursts of salty spray. It wasn't stormy weather in the true sense of the word but Roger knew it was going to be a cold, wet crossing and those who suffered from the seasickness would be puking in a couple of hours. He was not particularly afflicted that way unless the swell was really heavy.

A youth arrived and stood near Roger, staring at the newly equipped and provisioned ship. His shoulders rose and fell with his rapid breathing and he had the alert look of a highly strung gazehound. At almost fourteen years old, William FitzRoy was a squire in the household of the justiciar Geoffrey FitzPeter – or he had been until called upon to fulfil the role of hostage for the payment of his half-brother's ransom.

The youth was wearing a tunic of gorgeous brazil-dyed red wool dotted with silver jetons. A silver disc brooch secured his fur-lined cloak at his shoulder and his feet were shod in shoes of soft red leather that Roger admired but thought impractical. His own garments were serviceable, robust items that would withstand the vagaries of travel, and his boots were tough cowhide, heavily waxed to repel rain and sea.

Roger was extremely glad that Ida was ignorant of the youth's presence as one of the hostages because he knew that awareness would have undone her. His own leave-taking had been difficult enough for her, and the way she had reacted to Longchamp's demand that Hugh be surrendered had led him not to tell her that William was on the hostage list. What she did not know could not harm her.

'We should board,' Roger said.

With a stiff nod, the youth advanced to the gangplank. He walked with his head high, an imperious expression on his face, and ignored those around him. Roger realised the lad was trying to conceal his apprehension, but knew his own sons and daughters would never behave thus. They had been raised to have manners to all, no matter their rank, because that was the true sign of nobility. The youth acted as if his own nobility would be soiled by interacting with those of lesser degree.

Roger had been intending to invite William to meet his mother and half-siblings, but there were always more important matters to claim his attention concerned with government and the judiciary. There had been neither time nor opportunity to arrange the visit, especially when he was so ambivalent about the matter. It was easier to say 'some day' rather than committing himself.

Glancing beyond the harbour mouth as he stepped on to the decking, Roger saw that out to sea the rain was a thick grey veil. 'We're in for a wet crossing,' he told the youth as he joined him inside the deck shelter. 'Do you have any stouter footwear in your baggage?'

William frowned. 'I have my riding boots,' he said, but

364

there was a curl to his lip, revealing what he thought about exchanging his fine red shoes for such mundane footwear.

'Then I suggest you put them on if you want to save what you're wearing for the Emperor's court. Sea water will do to your boots what salt will do to a slug.' Roger shrugged. 'Not that it matters to me. I'm dry shod and intend to remain so. Depends if you value being a fop above being a good soldier.'

William flushed. He thrust out his foot and Roger could see him deliberating between retaining his sartorial appearance or swallowing his pride and opting for practicality. Roger pretended to turn away, but continued to observe him, because the youth's decision would be a reflection on his character and give an indication of how he might be handled.

Finally, the lad heaved a sigh and, calling for his man-servant, set about changing the soft red goatskin for plain cowhide boots. Roger said nothing, allowing him pride of space, but vowed he would have William FitzRoy drinking ale out of a wooden cup yet.

As the tide turned from its zenith, the sailors cast off the mooring ropes and set sail for the open sea. The youth left the shelter to watch the activity, returning only as the rain grew heavier and the wind began to gust. His waxed riding boots were saturated but, by unspoken mutual agreement, nothing was said on the matter.

The ship toiled through the swell like a powerful horse plodding against the wind. Roger settled down on the floor of the deck shelter, which had been covered by oiled canvas and a thick layer of sheepskins. The knights passed around the wine costrels and Roger's cook provided bread, cheese and portions of cold roast fowl. William ate and drank with them, but continued to look finicky, as if the rustic food was not really good enough, but would have to do. Roger bit his tongue and bore with the behaviour. It was like training a young horse that someone else with different ways had started to break in. He included the youth in the conversation, neither deferring to him nor setting him down.

Anketil produced a leather merels board from his pack and a set of bone counters. Roger partnered him and the men played the best of three games while the ship creaked around them and her keel knifed the cold channel waters. Roger lost the first one and won the second two. 'Do you play?' he asked William, who had been watching the game intently.

He received a wary shrug. 'Sometimes.'

Roger gestured him to take Anketil's place. 'Come then, let's test your mettle.'

The youth sat down, folded his legs and placed his pile of counters in the dip of tunic over his lap. A look of concentration crossed his face as they began to play. He was quick and intelligent and understood the strategy very well. As the game progressed and he became absorbed, his posture relaxed and his guard dropped. Engrossed in studying the youth rather than the game, Roger went down to defeat the first time. A gleam filled the youngster's eyes, which reminded Roger so much of Ida that it sent a jolt through him. He made himself concentrate on the second game and this time he won. The third game was closely contested but, despite William's sharp wits, Roger had a far-seeing ability and the experience to anticipate several moves ahead, so that eventually he triumphed. The lad accepted his defeat without rancour and Roger thought it a good sign, because such behaviour revealed that William had absorbed the less pompous side of courtliness too. The boy had a strong competitive streak, but there was no acrimony.

As the rain eased to a soft drizzle, William left the deck shelter to go and watch the sailors at their work.

'Good sea-legs on him,' Anketil said with judicious approval as Roger handed the merels board across to two others who desired to play.

Roger smiled inside his mouth. Anketil came from a seafaring family and the remark was a compliment of the highest order. 'He'll do,' he said, folding his arms. 'I've been intending to have him stay with us – reunite him with his mother and introduce him to his brothers and sisters, but the opportunity has never been right.' He glanced out through the gap in the canvas flap to the grey sky and sea and the rise and fall of the ship breasting the waves. William was watching a sailor adjusting one of the yards and his focus was direct and absolute. Roger could almost see him sucking in the detail and making it a part of his knowledge. That particular intensity was all Henry's. 'I suppose the opportunity will never be right.'

'You mean you won't?' Surprise filled Anketil's blue stare.

Roger shook his head. 'No,' he said. 'I'll do it as soon as I may when we return. I've put it off for far too long already.'

In the heat of the August afternoon, Ida was glad to accept a cup of stream-cooled buttermilk from Alditha, one of the village spinsters. Ida's escort had tethered their mounts to the willow trees by the stream at the foot of the woman's garth and had settled in the shade to wait on the Countess's pleasure.

Ida sat on a bench inside the woman's house. A small fire burned in the central hearth and an earthenware pot of mutton and vegetable stew simmered gently on the stones. One of the main reasons for Ida's visit, Alditha's week-old daughter, slumbered in a willow basket on the table, her little limbs bound in swaddling.

'You are generous, my lady,' said Alditha, who was plainly touched and delighted by Ida's gift of a dress length of sage-green wool.

'I am glad you like it.' Ida smiled. 'I thought I would bring it now so you have time to make it up for your churching. A woman should always have a new dress for the occasion.' She had brought an ivory teething ring for the infant too, tied on a fine piece of blue silk ribbon. Alditha was a skilled spinster who could turn combed fleece and flax into strong, even yarn with efficient speed. The birth of her daughter had curtailed her output, although she did have her mother on hand to help with the baby and her other two children. By visiting and bringing gifts, Ida was keeping an eye on the part of the earldom's economy she could influence, and doing what she could to maintain the goodwill and hard work. With Roger a hostage, she was determined to help raise the King's ransom payment as swiftly as she could.

On hearing that the first levy had not raised sufficient funds and thus a second was in progress, she had emptied her jewel casket of every ring, brooch, jewel and buckle. She had stripped her sideboard of the silver cups and platters, had taken the hangings from the walls and the fine silk coverlet from the bed. She had replaced the gold strap ends on her best belt with carved bone plaques, and had made do and mended wherever possible. Her mother-in-law had done the same at Dovercourt. Everywhere that the Bigod patronage ran, demands had been made.

'I do not suppose my Goldwin will be home for the churching,' Alditha said wistfully.

Ida hesitated, then shook her head. 'I think it will be

a little longer than that. The Earl wrote to me from Antwerp to say they had had a wet but calm sea crossing.'

Alditha nodded and looked knowledgeable, although Antwerp was no more than a name to her, as it was to Ida.

The baby woke and began to grizzle. Alditha lifted her from her basket and put her to her breast. A regretful note entered her voice. 'I only wish that Goldwin could see her now. Men don't set the same store by new babies as women do, especially when it's not their first, but I would have liked him to be here all the same.'

Ida knew too well how Alditha felt. She and Roger had been wed for almost twelve years, but she could not bring herself to weigh the time they had spent together against the time apart because she knew what the scales would show. Watching the baby suckle, she could almost feel the tug in her own breasts and loins. She suspected that the poignant, anguished farewell she and Roger had made in their bedchamber would show its own result come the spring. She had been queasy for several mornings and her breasts were tender and full. Time enough to sow seed, she thought, and then, task accomplished, move on to other pastures.

She thanked Alditha for the buttermilk and took her leave, saying she would have some fleeces sent for spinning from those she had kept back from the wool clip to be worked on the demesne.

At the castle, the masons were toiling in the sun, many of them shirtless, although still wearing their bonnets and hats. She wondered if it was hot where Roger was. What was he doing now? How was he faring? She tried to picture him, but all she could see was one of his hats, broad-brimmed, pulled low, concealing his face. It was not the image she desired, but no other would come to her.

Entering the hall, she heard squeals of glee coming from the corner, and saw the children clustered around someone sitting on a bench. Closer inspection revealed Alexander of Ipswich, Roger's harbour master. He had rolled up his shirtsleeve and was showing the children a spectacular whirlwind-shaped scar on his forearm.

Noticing her mother, Marguerite ran to her and tugged her over to Master Alexander. 'Look, Mama! Look where a dragon's breathed on him!'

'A dragon?' Ida laughed and shook her head.

'Aye, my mother-in-law,' Alexander said with a wink, although he directed the latter at the children so as not to be disrespectful to Ida. 'Go on, touch it, I dare you!' He extended his arm to Marguerite, who shied away with a squeal. 'If you do, you're allowed to make a wish.'

'You said last time it was a burn from a lantern in a storm at sea,' Hugh challenged him.

'Ah.' Alexander touched the side of his nose with his forefinger. 'You know that the seas change with the weather and the tides with the moon?'

Hugh nodded.

'So do stories. Never the same twice.'

Hugh folded his arms. 'Then how do you know what's true and what isn't?'

Alexander continued to rub his nose. 'Well, that's the thing. Sometimes the truth changes too. You have to decide what you believe when others tell you things and come to your own truth.' He gave Hugh a narrow white grin. 'So you have to decide whether this was caused by a lantern, or a dragon's breath, and whether my wife's mother is one of those creatures. Then again, perhaps it happened in a fight with pirates off the coast of Barbary when I went to the Holy Land . . . but that's another story for another day when the tides have turned, hmm?'

With great daring, Marguerite set her forefinger to the scar, then with a little shriek leaped away.

'Did you make your wish?' Alexander asked.

Marguerite gave a solemn nod.

'Don't say what it is, or it won't work,' he warned, wagging his forefinger, then pressing it to his lips.

'What if it doesn't come true?' Marguerite wanted to know.

'Then the tide turned while you weren't looking.' With a smile, he clapped his hands and shooed the children off to their nurses. They went with dragging reluctance. Hugh, very much the man, remained behind, but sat down quietly on the bench beside the quay master.

Ida suppressed the urge to ask how he had really come by the fearsome scar, knowing she was as susceptible to tales as the children. Alexander rolled down his shirt-sleeve, tugged his emerald-green tunic straight and rose in a belated bow. 'Countess.'

'What brings you to Framlingham?'

'Barrels of herring, goods from the Norman estates and timbers for the castle,' he said. 'They were bound here so I thought I would escort them myself and see how matters stood with the building work. It is useful now and again to escape from one world into another, do you not think?'

'Yes,' Ida said, thinking that chance would be a fine thing. 'You will stay to dine?'

He bowed acknowledgement. He was of knightly birth, but as the youngest of six sons had few prospects of inheritance and had pursued a career, first on the seas as a mariner in the Bigod employ, and now as the master of their quay at Ipswich. He was a man of good manners with few pretensions, and not only a trusted employee but a friend.

'I heard from a shipmaster that the earl had made safe landfall in Antwerp,' Alexander continued as a servant brought him a mug of cider.

Ida nodded. 'Indeed yes. I pray he has a swift, safe journey the rest of the way.'

Alexander pinched a moist line of the drink from his upper lip. 'Amen to that, my lady. I have added him and your son to my prayers.'

Ida blinked at him. The hall door was open and sunlight streamed across the rushes towards the bench where she was sitting. Hugh gave Alexander a puzzled look. 'The Bishop of Ely said I had to go, but my father refused,' he said.

Ida swallowed. 'My son,' she repeated. 'Which son would that be, Master Alexander?'

Consternation flickered across his features. 'I am sorry,' he said. 'I thought you knew.'

Ida put her hand to her mouth. 'Tell me,' she said through her fingers. 'Tell me now so there is no mistake.'

'Messire William FitzRoy is with your husband, Countess. I understand he was chosen as one of the hostages to go to the King in Germany at the meeting in Saint Albans. I am sorry you did not know.'

Ida shook her head. 'No,' she said, feeling sick. 'No, I wasn't told.'

'Countess, shall I summon your ladies?'

His voice came as if from a distance. Hugh was staring at her with big eyes. 'No,' she said. 'But you will excuse me.'

She was trembling as she made her way up to the solar. She waved away her women when they came to her in consternation. Entering the bedchamber, she sat on the bed and cupped her face in her hands, feeling dreadfully ill. Distracted by her fight to prevent Hugh being taken, she had been attacked from another side and been blind to the danger. How long had Roger known about this, and why hadn't he told her? Did he think she wouldn't find out? Was she of so little consequence? She felt betrayed and isolated . . . and angry.

What was she to do? Ida asked herself the question repeatedly as if telling her prayer beads. Eventually, she left the bed and fetched a small enamelled jewel box from her coffer – one that Henry had given to her in another life. As she unlocked and opened it, the scent of cedar rose from the interior of the box in a vapour of memory. She picked up the tiny pair of goatskin shoes and removed from the right one the soft strands of dark hair tied with red silk. She stroked it gently across her cheek and in her mind's eye saw her eldest son as he had been on the day she had cut this lock from him. She had tried to sever the ties even as she severed the hair from its roots, but the untimely cut had opened a wound in her heart that had bled ever since. With great gentleness, she replaced the shoes and the hair in the casket. There was a ring in there too; the one Henry had given to her on the taking of her virginity. Another memory. Another tie that had left its mark like the sting of a shore-washed jellyfish.

Cupped in her palm, the ruby gleamed like pitch. She put it on and for a moment looked at it shining on her finger. Her hands were smooth and well tended because she did not want rough skin snagging her embroidery. She rubbed unguents and rose oil into them on rising and each night on retiring, but she had never seen their first purpose as carriers for ornate rings. She removed the ruby one now. She would ask Alexander to sell it in Ipswich and she would contribute the sum fetched to the ransom. The jewel coffers were empty following the latest collection, but she still had a bolt of silk she had been saving

373

and a belt woven with gold and pearls. Who, after all was going to see it here, and she could easily weave herself another one and pattern it cunningly so that it looked more than it was. She would sell her amber prayer beads too and have others made from plain wood. She would go out and she would chivvy, plead and beg so that the hostages might come home safely. But while they might be ransomed, she wondered if she would ever escape from her own prison.

Hugh gave a surreptitious glance around and entered the dark, musty-smelling undercroft. He was almost sure no one had seen him come in, and he had Tib the terrier with him and the excuse that they were hunting for rats.

A row of wine casks stood along one wall and one of them had a faulty spigot that leaked the barrel's contents in a slow drip. It would take a man several hours to get drunk from the spillage, but Hugh found it entertaining to lie under the tap and let the good red wine trickle into his mouth. It was more the novelty and a frisson of excitement at the notion of being caught that drove him to the deed rather than actual need for a drink of wine, which he could have purloined much more easily from the hall or the buttery chamber. Here, if he was lucky, there was no one to disturb him and he could have privacy for his thoughts.

As Tib snuffled in the corners, nosing between the barrels of supplies, and as the wine plopped on to Hugh's tongue, he pondered the matter of his older brother. It was always the same when he was mentioned. A haunted look would enter his mother's eyes and she would withdraw into herself. Sometimes it was a fleeting thing, no more than a cloud across the sun, but on other occasions, it was like a rainy day – or even a week – with grey from one horizon to another.

One of his earliest memories was of standing at his mother's knee as she stroked his hair and told him that he was going to be a big, strong, beautiful boy just like his brother William. He remembered thinking that being big and strong was a splendid thing, but wondering who his brother William was, because he knew of no such person. She had said too that his older brother was the son of the King, and couldn't live with them because he had to be raised at the court. Hugh had still been young enough to think it strange and marvellous that he had a royal brother and through him a connection to the King himself. He had been too young to wonder why he never saw him, too accepting to ask the difficult questions. That was just the way it was. His mother seldom spoke of this magical being, but when she did, it was as if he had the ability to light up her world.

Recently though, Hugh's perception had begun to change. There had been vague talk of his 'royal' brother coming to visit them. His father had mentioned in passing that a meeting was going to be arranged, but then the fighting between Longchamp and Count John, followed by the King's imprisonment, had interrupted things and nothing had happened. The apprehension, excitement and curiosity engendered by the notion that he was finally going to meet this princely being had faded into the background, while other awarenesses had come to the fore as he entered adolescence.

Before a woman could bear a child, she had to lie with a man. Thus, his mother must have lain with the King in the same way that she lay with his father and in the same way that Alfreda the dairy maid lay with Mark the groom and now had a belly the size of a swollen harvest moon. The notion made him shudder. Had his mother really done the mating deed with the King? He didn't want to believe it, but she must have done, because otherwise he would not have this brother, supposedly made of such fine stuff – and now it seemed a hostage with his father. Disturbing emotions rose from that knowledge too. Hugh's bond with his father was deep and strong, but what if this absence diluted it? What if his half-brother usurped his position?

There was a sudden scuffle round the back of the casks and a growling Tib lunged, seized and tossed an enormous rat from his jaws. The dying rodent landed on Hugh, who shot up with a yell and hurled the thing off his chest. Tib sprang again, repeated the move on his victim, then stood back to look at Hugh, his tail wagging vigorously and a laughing grin on his brown and white patched face.

'Good dog,' Hugh praised him despite his shock. He wiped a drip of wine off his chest. 'Good dog.' It was a pregnant female and worth well more than a single rat. Hugh picked it up by its scaly tail. It was still twitching, but without life. He took it from the undercroft and as he slung the rodent on the midden heap, thought to himself that his half-brother had probably never done such a thing. He'd probably never gone into the undercroft to drink wine from a leaky spigot either.

He walked the dog around the precincts and paused to watch the masons at their work, although today he wasn't particularly interested in joining them. Alexander was watching them too, his sleeves pushed up again in the heat of the day and his scar showing. 'Your mother was looking for you,' he said. 'She's gone to church to pray for your father's safety, and your brother's too.'

Hugh looked at the ground. Alexander placed his hand on Hugh's shoulder and gave it an encouraging squeeze. 'You're shouldering the burdens of manhood right well, lad,' he said.

Hugh flicked him a glance to see if he was being patronised, but Alexander's gaze, although it held its usual amusement, was steady and sincere. 'Your father would be proud of you . . . I know your mother is.'

Hugh set his jaw.

'You have courage by the barrel-load, because you take after both of your parents. I don't think I know many people as brave as they are – and for reasons you'll understand when you're older.'

'Whom does my half-brother take after?' Hugh demanded.

Alexander gave him an assessing look, then shook his head. 'That I do not know, never having met him. I'll have to wait and see, and so will you.' He showed his scarred arm to Hugh again. 'Do you want to know the truth? My brother spilled a cauldron of boiling porridge over me when I was a lad. We were fighting at the time, I don't recall the reason, but he caught the porridge pot and over my arm it went. I forgave him long ago, but I don't know if he ever forgave himself.'

Hugh wasn't sure what Alexander was trying to tell him – if anything. The harbour master tousled Hugh's hair. 'Go on, go to your mother, although if I were you, I'd chew some mint from yonder herb garden before you do, or else she'll wonder how you've been spending your time.'

Hugh flushed, but as Alexander grinned, he gave him an answering one.

32

Speyer, Germany, January 1194

Roger ducked over his saddle to avoid a low hoary branch and reined to the right with a yell of encouragement to his bay mare. She responded with a twitch of her ears and broke into a gathered canter. Frost silvered the lacework of bare branches and glittered like fine sugar crystals on crouching holly bushes and mossed-over fallen trees. His breath was white smoke as he followed the hunt, chasing hard after boar through the majestic forests beyond the walls of Speyer. He knew King Richard was somewhere ahead, for he had seen the rump of his white stallion through the trees only moments since and the brazil-wood red of his ermine-lined cloak bannering around him. 'Hah!' Roger shouted again to his mount and once more felt her surge beneath him.

Hound-keepers and beaters ran either side, the brach dogs four to a leash. The belling of the slot hounds filled the forest. The thunder of hooves set up a vibration that trembled small avalanches of frost from the trees, and being alive was a thing of cutting clarity, sharp as a new knife. Roger's mare splashed across a stream with icicle daggers fringing a stone overhang on the banks. The dogs were louder now and Roger felt the hot blood flowing in his veins.

King Richard was under house arrest but had leave to hunt and hawk, indeed to conduct court business from his chambers at Speyer. All he was not permitted to do was return home until his ransom had been paid into the Emperor's coffers. Escape was impossible. For all that he had leeway to chase boar, wolf and deer through the dark forests beyond the city walls, Richard was still closely guarded.

Roger had been attending on him for five months and in that time had grown accustomed to the life of the German court with its protocol and rituals, its ceremonies and almost Byzantine richness of clothing and surroundings. The days might be dark, short and bitterly cold, but the flash of silk and gold lit the chambers and the wines were rich and strong. Sometimes it became difficult to recall what home and family looked like. Sometimes when he tried to remember Ida's face, all he saw was a blank oval and he would have to remind himself by looking into the face of her son. Occasionally it helped, but other times he would see Henry and he would have to turn aside.

The lad joined him now, his smaller chestnut gelding blowing hard, steam curling from his nostrils. 'I need a faster horse,' William gasped with frustration. His voice grated in the space between boy and man as he put pressure on it to be heard above the noise of the hunt.

'Doubtless you'll have one when we return to England,' Roger answered. The boy made no reply of his own, too busy coaxing speed out of his mount and trying to keep up as they turned hard right then left. Both horses jumped a fallen log, Roger marginally in the lead. There were others to either side of them, German lords, yelling in their native tongue, driving in their spurs. Ahead of them, the sound of vigorous shouting accompanied by deafening squeals gave notice of a kill.

'We're too late!' William's voice was rife with disappointment.

Roger didn't reply that such was the nature of the chase, especially when following the King, and there would be other opportunities for valour. Young FitzRoy seemed to have inherited his father's appetite for the hunt and loved to be in the thick of the fray, hence his disappointment with his horse. But no one was going to give one of the best mounts to an adolescent hostage, even if he was the King of England's half-brother.

The huntsmen were busy eviscerating and dealing with an enormous boar. Hounds milled in excitement and the horses swished and stamped, eyes rolling at the raw scent of blood. Richard, wearing an ear-to-ear grin, was talking to some of the German lords, slapping their backs, sharing the exhilaration of the moment. His hat was jammed over his ears, concealing all but tendrils of his copper-gold hair, and his cheeks and lips were bright red from the cold. Against the latter, his teeth looked very white as he laughed. Roger watched him work his alchemy on his companions and admired the way he charmed and cajoled them. The Emperor might have his plans and agendas, but there was nothing to stop Richard from working to undermine them, or at least build himself a buffer by winning friends and sympathisers at the German court.

Richard turned round towards his horse, and met Roger's gaze. A knowing look passed between them before Richard's focus switched to William. 'Here, Brother "Longespée",' he cried. 'A gift for you. Make yourself a knife hilt!' He tossed a white object across the air towards them. The youth instinctively thrust out his hand to catch the blood-smeared boar's tusk.

Roger looked at the sharp curl of stained ivory that William held. The lad had taken to calling himself Longespée of late, after a royal ancestor who had been so titled because he had wielded a particularly long sword. To that end, the youth had begun training with a longer blade and a great deal of determination. There had been some amusement at his expense, not least from Richard, but when William had persevered despite the mockery and even shown some aptitude, Richard had taken to sparring with him and promised that when he was free, he would buy him a weapon to reward his newfound skill. William had also spent time designing a shield on scrap pieces of parchment and said that when he was knighted he would adopt the device of his paternal grandfather, Geoffrey le Bel, Count of Anjou: a bright blue background powdered with golden lioncels. Roger had raised his eyebrows but said nothing. Lapis-blue was an expensive colour with which to cover a shield, but quite in keeping with the youth's tastes. No doubt he would want a valuable horse too – nothing under fifty marks.

As they returned to the city, the dusk marbled the sky with striations of indigo and bruised pink and the atmosphere was jocular. It wasn't only the prospect of good food and drink and the exchange of tales around a blazing fire that was raising spirits; it was the knowledge that the bulk of the King's ransom was on its way down the Rhine from Cologne, accompanied by Queen Eleanor, the Archbishop of Rouen and an entourage of earls and prelates. Richard's release had been set for 17 January and they were all only a week from freedom and a month away from home.

On reaching the castle, Roger dismounted, gave his

courser to a groom and went to his chamber to wash and replace his hunting hose with something suitable for dining in courtly company: chausses of red twill, tight to the leg, shoes decorated with gilding and his court robe of midnight-blue wool, intricately embroidered by Ida with small golden knots. His cloak was lined with the fur of Norwegian squirrels. At the time Roger had thought it all a little ostentatious, but against the opulence of the German court and Richard himself, his garments were understated. He combed his hair, and then his beard. The latter still felt strange to him but it had been easier to let it grow whilst travelling. It also gave him a certain elder statesman dignity that a clean jaw did not – something that was particularly useful just now.

Since joining Richard, Roger had been fully occupied in poring over documents, sitting in council, listening to arguments, advising, balancing, assessing as he had done on the Bench at home. The work was not dissimilar and sometimes he could almost imagine himself back at Westminster. The language surrounding him was German, not French, but everyone with an education could understand each other in Latin.

He was on the point of leaving his chamber when William FitzRoy arrived, flush-faced and heaving from his run. 'My lord, the King summons you to the council chamber now,' he panted. 'He sent me to fetch you!'

'Why, what is it?' Roger grabbed and fastened his cloak.

William pressed his hand to his side. His eyes were enormous. 'The Emperor says he's not going to release him!'

Roger stared at the youth, appalled.

'He . . . he says the stakes have changed. He's been offered more silver to keep Richard hostage until the autumn!'

'By whom?'

'The King of France and . . . and the Count of Mortain.'

There was a tight feeling in Roger's chest. He was occasionally angry in the mundane course of life, but it was a long time since he had felt absolute rage. After Fornham he had tried to avoid it. 'That will not happen,' he snarled and strode from the room. The youth trotted at his heels, saying he was Richard's duty squire, but Roger barely heard him because his mind was churning with other thoughts. There had been excuses and delays throughout the negotiations. At first the ransom had been set at a hundred thousand marks of silver, but that had been increased by half as much again. Although Richard's prison was that of a gilded cage, it had already lasted more than a year and it was both illegal and immoral to prevent a crusader from returning to his home. The messenger must have arrived during the boar hunt and quite likely Emperor Henry had been reading the parchment at the same time that Richard was making his kill.

Roger paused before the door to Richard's chamber and took several deep, calming breaths. He had no doubt there was already rage enough within. He needed a clear head for this if they were to find a way through.

Richard was pacing the room with savage energy as if he had not spent the entire day at the hunt. Resembling a pecky bird, Longchamp followed in his wake, the sleeves of his robes fluttering like wings. Roger noticed a large splash of wine on the wall as if someone had thrown the contents of a cup at it.

'I have heard the news, sire,' Roger said as he bowed. 'It is a disgrace and a dishonour.'

Richard pivoted to face him. There was no laughter in his expression now. Even masked by candlelight, his complexion wore the choler of fury. 'The King of France is a perfidious liar, but I did not believe he would stoop this low!' he spat. 'John, yes, because digging tunnels has ever been his way. I will not be bound; I will not suffer more of this captivity!'

'Nor will you, sire,' Longchamp said. 'We will find a way round this.'

'How much have they pledged?' Roger asked.

'Two hundred thousand marks,' Longchamp replied with a sneer. 'In instalments.'

'A pledge is only as good as its fulfilling,' Roger said. He went to stand by the fire and held out his hands to the fierce red heat. 'Where will the money come from? King Philip will have to levy his people and I suspect they will object to paying a tax to keep the King of England in prison. England is drained dry. John would be fortunate to extract the squeak from a butchered pig, let alone that kind of sum.'

Richard had stopped pacing, although the anger still emanated from him in waves as hot as the fire. 'We know they cannot raise the money and the Emperor knows it too, so this is bluff on his part. He has no love for Philip of France either, so why should he make him an ally in this?'

'He knows he must soon let you go,' said Longchamp. 'And when he does, he will lose his leverage. This is an effort to wring the final drops from us.'

'The notion of taking money from Philip of France pleases him, I think,' Roger said, 'but he knows the silver from England is secure and almost within his grasp. He needs it for his war with Sicily; he won't let it go.'

Richard threw himself down on the bench before the fire and plucked at his beard. 'I cannot stay longer in this place. I need to be home by the spring when the campaigning season begins.'

'Indeed, sire, there are many traitors to be dealt with there,' Longchamp said darkly. 'Not all whom you have trusted have kept faith. You should beware your marshal. His brother is deep in the Count of Mortain's counsel and the Marshal himself has ever favoured your brother.'

Richard raised his brows at his chancellor. 'I would need more evidence than hearsay before I called the Marshal traitor.'

Roger gave Longchamp a narrow look. The Bishop of Ely was the kind to bear his grudges like a honed dagger that he would stick in his perceived enemies the moment they turned their backs on him. 'You missay the Marshal, my lord chancellor. He has had his differences of opinion with you, but so have all the justiciars – and myself for that matter. That does not make us disloyal to our sovereign lord. Nor is this the matter of the moment, surely? What we must decide is how to respond to this new development. All else can be dealt with at the proper time.'

'Norfolk's right,' Richard said. 'I have no reason to doubt my marshal.'

Longchamp inclined his head. 'It is my duty to advise on matters as I see them, sire.'

'Well, apply yourself to visualising the matter of springing me from my cage,' Richard growled.

Roger bowed low as Queen Eleanor swept past him, but he knew that he and all the others making their obeisance to her went unnoticed for she only had eyes for Richard. She was incandescent for him.

'My son, my light, my son!' Eleanor touched his face with trembling hands and tears rolled down her cheeks. 'I knew this moment would come. I never gave up hope – never!'

Richard's eyes were wet too as he smiled and kissed

385

her fingers. 'My lady mother, I never doubted, nor do I doubt that I will soon be free to go as I please.'

The court had moved from Speyer to Mainz, there to greet the Queen and discuss the continuing matter of the ransom. Roger wondered if Eleanor knew about the attempts of her youngest son and Philip of France to hinder Richard's release and decided she must. Eleanor had never been without her network of intelligence-gatherers even when held prisoner by her husband, and although she was beyond seventy years old, she had the vigour and determination of a woman half her years.

Roger watched her draw herself together. Even though she continued to show her joy at being reunited with Richard, she was now bearing herself as a queen and a diplomat. Her maternal concern was genuine, but it did not harm her cause that everyone saw it shining from her. There was still a hard battle to fight; coupled with a deal of delicate political fine-stepping if they were going to gain their freedom.

Emperor Henry was superficially affable and concerned, but there was a hard glint in his eye and he too was prepared for the coming fray. No one was in any doubt about his determination to gain what he could from the dice he had been thrown. Following a formal banquet, discussions commenced, and he showed Eleanor and Richard the letters he had received from John and Philip, the latter still with its seal dangling from the edge of the parchment in proof.

'What am I to do?' he asked with an apologetic widening of his hands. 'It is a tempting offer and I must act as I think best for myself and my rule.'

'Would you sup with the Devil, my lord?' Eleanor asked.

Henry shrugged. 'It would depend on the length of my spoon,' he replied, and shook his head. 'These are not devils, but men intent on their own ambition, as we are on ours. I am no man's dupe.'

'Neither am I, my lord,' Eleanor replied tartly. 'I have fulfilled your requirements and it grieves me to think you would renege and continue to hold prisoner a King who has fought for Christ.'

'It grieves me too,' the Emperor replied. 'Nothing would please me more than to come to an agreement . . . if one can be arranged.'

'You have the ransom here in your hand,' Eleanor said. 'Will you take the chance that any will be forthcoming at all from your other source? Will you court disruption among your followers because of the lure of a few more pennies in your coffers? In truth, you do not have a spoon that is long enough.'

'My mother is right,' Richard said, folding his arms. 'Better to deal with us than with my brother and the King of France. If John ever kept his word, there would be a fanfare in heaven.'

The Emperor stroked a large sapphire ring on his middle finger. 'You are right to say that the amount of silver is merely "a few more pennies".' A sly glint kindled in his eyes. 'But there is something you can give to me that your brother and Philip cannot.'

Richard lifted an eyebrow. Roger, who had been sitting to one side, quietly listening, felt his hair stand upright at his nape.

'A kingdom,' said the Emperor. 'Give me England.'

The mist enveloped everything in a white haze and although it was possible to see from one end of the royal galley to the other, the place beyond might as well have been off the edge of the world. Roger remembered tales he had been told as a child of his ancestors: Vikings who had come to Normandy in sleek ships down the Seine, muscles and tendons tightening and relaxing on their oars as the blades scooped and released the water, making it flash like the bitter steel edging their weapons.

The damp February air wove like Candlemas smoke between the bones, insinuating its way into joints and marrow. Swathed in fleeces and furs to keep warm, Roger leaned his shoulder against the *Trenchemer*'s side and listened to the plash of the oars and the surge of the brackish estuary water against the ship's keel. Other than that, there was little sound on the ship – no sailor's voices rose in song, and each action was performed without undue noise. Emperor Henry had finally released Richard. Richard had knelt to him, put his hands between his and sworn to be his vassal in respect of England. It was more by way of a courtly gesture than having a practical element, but it soothed the Emperor's notions of pride and domination and made progress possible. It did not mean, however, that they were free and clear yet. Arriving in Antwerp yesterday evening, they had heard disquieting rumours that Philip of France had increased his offer and exhorted the Emperor to pursue Richard and recapture him. They had heard too that French ships were patrolling the waters of the Narrow Sea so that if the Emperor declined the proposal, Philip himself would act. Rumours were sometimes truth, sometimes lies, but were always a fog that one had to penetrate in order to find clarity.

Roger shifted his position and strained his ears. Through the drifting swathes, another craft was approaching. He reached for the sword lying at his side. His breathing wanted to quicken and yet he stifled his lungs until they burned and he thought he would burst. The other vessel sounded a horn and passed close on the steerboard – a merchant galley, Antwerp-bound with a Flemish crew.

Exchanges were shouted, and expletives too, because the *Trenchemer* was bearing neither lantern nor sounding horn, but moving in stealth like a pirate ship.

Roger exhaled his tension and sucked air into his starving lungs. At his left side, Anketil muttered that it probably wasn't going to matter about the Emperor or the French catching them, because they'd be rammed and sunk of their own volition, or else they'd run aground on one of the many islands populating the mouth of the Scheldt.

'All right, lad?' Roger glanced at William Fitzroy, now reborn as 'Longespée'. Richard had gifted him with a long-bladed sword when the royal party had paused in Cologne on its journey to Antwerp and the weapon had not left his side since. He slept with it more closely than some men slept with their wives and it received cherished treatment above and beyond that which the latter could ever expect. His boar tusk had been incorporated into the grip, and then bound over with strips of plaited red leather. Currently he was clenching the hilt in his fist, his own breathing shallow.

The youth nodded. His throat worked in a tense swallow.

'It's the waiting,' Anketil said. 'All soldiers will tell you that.' He rubbed his palm across his face. 'With good fortune, waiting's the only thing that'll trouble us.'

'Ever fought at sea?' Roger asked the knight.

Anketil shook his head. 'Had pirates chase our ship once when crossing from Southampton to Barfleur, but we outran them and I'm glad. It's enough trouble fighting on firm ground without a deck rolling under your feet.'

Roger gave a grunt of amused agreement.

'I think it would be interesting,' said William Fitzroy.

Roger raised his brows. 'You do, do you?'

The youth nodded. 'If you fight on horseback you have

389

to learn to manage your horse as well as your weapons, so deck fighting is just another skill – and if it is one that other men do not have, then it gives you an advantage.'

Roger eyed him with approval, for the comment was mature, born of observation and reflection.

The *Trenchemer* sailed on through the murk and as what little light there was began to fade the smell of the open sea grew stronger and the water became brine.

'England,' Anketil said, 'I can smell England.'

Roger gave a sour smile. 'Wishful thinking, man. We've still an ocean to cross and the French to avoid. We'll be a few days yet.'

'Better than a few months,' Anketil said. 'What I could just demolish now is a hot eel pie and a horn of honest Norfolk ale brewed by Gythe at the Tub in Yarmouth.'

'And Gythe herself.' Roger chuckled.

Anketil spluttered. 'There's by far too much of her to demolish,' he said, 'but a bite or two wouldn't come amiss. I've missed Norfolk dumplings too.'

The song of a ship's horn surging strongly through the misty dusk arrested their soft-voiced jesting. Three times it blasted. Then three again, sounding close, although distances could be deceptive. Roger scrambled to his feet, his hand at his sword grip. Richard emerged from the canvas deck shelter on the prow where he and his mother had been closeted and came to stand at Roger's side.

'Rest easy, my lord Bigod,' he said. 'These are friends and unless I am badly mistaken, you won't need your sword.'

Once more the three blasts shivered across the misty water and Richard turned to the *Trenchemer*'s master, Stephen de Turnham. 'Answer her,' he commanded. 'Put a lantern on the prow and let us all have good food and dry beds tonight.'

'Sire.' De Turnham signalled to one of his crew and soon a lantern shone at their bows and the hornsman sounded the *Trenchemer*'s reply. The notes rode across the water, parting the swatches of mist, and were answered but it still seemed an age before the other ship hove into sight, emerging like a wraith but gradually gaining solid, dripping form. The *Grace Dieu* was a large galley, a supply ship out of Rye, armed with new fighting castles and bristling with knights, serjeants and archers. A collective sigh of relief rippled through those aboard the *Trenchemer*.

They were not yet home and certainly not dry, but they were closer than they had been.

Aboard the *Grace Dieu*, Roger sat within the larger deck shelter at a trestle table with Richard, Longchamp and the various barons and churchmen who had come to escort Richard home. Eleanor had retired with her women to the ladies' deck shelter at the other end of the vessel and the men too were thinking about bedding down for the night.

Longchamp was in his element because the Archbishop of Rouen, whom he detested, had remained behind as surety for the remainder of the ransom thus giving Longchamp leeway to preen and make much of himself. No one was left in any doubt who had worked the hardest to secure the King's release and that Longchamp was returning to England in a state of favour that would cause much detriment to certain lords and prelates. Longchamp had an additional gleam of malice in his eyes. The news brought from England by the master of the *Grace Dieu* appeared to bear out the warning he had given in Speyer.

'Did I not say William Marshal shouldn't be trusted?' he said. 'Blood will out. His father was a renowned rebel.'

Roger leaned back from the table. He was wearing a

391

favourite hat: a felted green affair with a long brim that put his eyes in shadow. Added to the concealment of a beard, he felt reasonably shielded. 'So was mine, my lord Bishop,' he said, 'but that doesn't make us the same. Even if the Marshal's brother has declared for the lord John and made Marlborough Castle ready for war, it doesn't make the Marshal himself a traitor.'

Longchamp's eyes glittered. 'No, my lord, it does not, but when the Marshal is seen going to Marlborough, then it becomes more suspicious. Perhaps his liaisons with traitors are more than the actions of a concerned justiciar. I for one question his motives.'

'Not having been there myself, I can only guess, but I expect he went to negotiate. One cannot judge a case until one is in possession of all the facts – or as many as one can garner.'

'Bigod's right.' Richard cast a sharp look at his chancellor. 'We don't know everything and I am willing to give the Marshal the benefit of the doubt. He could have killed me on the road from Le Mans as simply as altering the angle of his lance, but he didn't. He protected my father when all hope was lost and he would seemingly have gained more by deserting.'

'You will find he has become your brother's man in your absence,' Longchamp persisted.

'My lord chancellor, I would counsel against such a statement without knowing more,' Roger answered with quiet assertion. 'We simply do not know.' He was aware of Richard measuring him and the chancellor and knew that the latter had the edge because his spies must have seen the Marshal at Marlborough.

'We'll find out when we arrive in England, won't we?' Richard said. 'I will send for the Marshal and deal with him according to his merits, as I will deal with all men.'

'If he comes to you,' Longchamp replied with scepticism.

Roger clenched his teeth. Longchamp always had to have the last word and the conversation would go round in circles all night to no avail.

Richard eyed his chancellor with tolerant humour. 'You're an old crow and doomsayer, Longchamp. I expect him to come to me and to have an explanation. If he does not, then you can tell me I was wrong and have the satisfaction of knowing I should have heeded you.'

Longchamp looked mournful. 'I would not do that, sire. Indeed, I would be grieved.'

Roger turned his snort of disbelief into a cough.

Longchamp glared at him. 'I have ever had the King's good at heart.'

'I do not dispute that, my lord Bishop,' Roger said evenly. 'But I doubt you would grieve to see certain men brought low. I speak as I see.'

Longchamp held his tongue, but the look he cast at Roger was answer enough. Roger knew well that what he had just said was on the nail and that he would do well to watch his own back.

33

Framlingham, March 1194

Roger spurred his tired, muddy horse the final yards across the ditch and clopped into Framlingham's bailey at a trot. He had outridden his escort and the baggage wain and intentionally arrived ahead of his entourage. Gazing at the two new completed towers, he marvelled at how much the building work had advanced during his absence. There was still much to do, but Framlingham's stone coronet was actually beginning to gather proud substance. Against the background of the great towers, the hall and chapel seemed diminished, yet they were cared for and gleamed with a recent coat of limewash. The porch hoarding had been repainted recently too and stood out in bold red and gold against the white of the paint. Assorted poultry pecked the ground outside the door but, fortuitously, Wulfwyn's gander was absent.

Roger dismounted and tied his horse at the bridle ring in the wall. A groom who had been forking dung stopped and stared, then dropped to his knees. 'My lord, I did not realise it was you, forgive me!'

Roger gestured him to his feet. 'No reason you should.

I've ridden ahead of the men. Best rout out the others though. There'll be horses to attend within the hour.'

'Yes, my lord, I . . .'

He paused and both men looked round as four children tumbled around the corner of the stable building, playing a wild game of chase. There were two boys and two girls, mingled in a blur of running limbs, flying hair, bright dresses and tunics. They jostled to a halt as they saw the groom and the black courser. And then Marguerite detached herself from their number. 'Papa, Papa!' she shrieked and threw herself at him.

He picked her up and swung her round. 'Sweetheart!' It was a relief to be remembered because he was not sure they would have carried his memory. She gave him a smacking kiss on his recently shaved cheek, then squeezed him round the neck, and he didn't know if it was the force of her arms or the tightness in his own throat that made it suddenly hard to breathe. Marie hung back, although her face was alight with a smile, and it gave Roger a pang to see how much the young woman she was even in the midst of a children's game. Three-year-old Ralph demanded to be picked up too, although Roger could see that his clamour was born of bravado rather than wild affection, and he felt the child's braced stiffness as he lifted him. William, two years older, waited, planted as solidly as a young oak tree, but he smiled at the same time, revealing a gap where a front milk tooth had recently fallen out and the adult replacement had yet to grow in.

And then Roger looked beyond the children and saw Ida emerging to greet him, a tiny swaddled baby cradled against her left side. The look she gave him was guarded and even a little hostile. There was no smile of welcome and his stomach dropped. He set Marguerite and Ralph down and went to her.

'This is your new son,' she said stiffly. 'I named him for his father, to remind myself that he has one.' She placed the baby in his arms before Roger could embrace her.

It was still very small, no more than a fortnight old at most, and had yet to plump out. Its eyes were dark and were going to be brown like Ida's.

'You should have written,' he said. 'You should have told me.'

She gave him a hard look. 'Where would I have sent the messenger? I did not know where to find you, and I did not think you would be bothered with such concerns.'

'I would have been bothered to know you were with child again, and to know how you were faring.'

'Would you?' She gave him another long look. They had not yet embraced.

'Of course I would!' He put his arm around her and made to kiss her, but she turned her head and he received her cheek, soft but cold in the spring afternoon.

'You will want to bathe and eat,' she said. 'And I suppose you have ridden ahead of your men and they will be here soon.' She took the baby back into her arms and started towards the hall.

'Not for an hour at least.' He looked round. 'Where's Hugh?'

'Out riding with a groom and the dogs,' she said. 'I do not know when they will return. He takes after you.' She gave the baby to one of her women and ordered a bathtub prepared and food brought.

Roger felt the emotion within him coil tighter, the exasperation developing into anger. 'It was not of my choosing to spend so many months at a foreign court, but it was my duty.'

They climbed the stairs to the solar. The women had

already dragged out the large oval bathtub and were filling it with pails of hot and cold water. He noticed that all of them kept their heads down and averted their eyes, and knew it was more than just deference. The atmosphere could have frozen the flames of hell.

Ida opened a coffer lid and fetched out a neatly folded, clean shirt, braies and chausses. The smell of lavender and spices hung in the garments. 'I made these for you,' she said. 'In the autumn. I thought you might be home before Christmastide. I thought . . .' Her chin wobbled. 'Well, you weren't, and I put them away together with my hope of seeing you before the year was out.'

Roger removed his hat and set it carefully on another chest.

'I sold every last jewel in my coffer,' Ida said. 'I stripped the wall hangings. I harried and chivvied our tenants and vassals. Every silver penny I gleaned, I counted as one moment less on the time you had to stay in Germany.' She put her palm to her mouth and he saw her struggle. But as he made to speak, she took away her hand and looked at him with drowning eyes. 'And one moment less for my son too. Why should I tell you that I was with child when you did not tell me about William? I had to learn the detail from Alexander of Ipswich. Do you know how painful that was? Why didn't you tell me? Why?'

Roger opened his hand towards her. 'Because I knew you would only worry, and to no purpose.'

'You thought I would not find out?'

He grimaced. 'I hoped you would not.'

Ida gasped.

'I had seen how distraught you became at the notion of Hugh being taken, and I knew you would be the same over your other son – possibly more so because you have never been able to call him yours. Perhaps I was wrong, but to have put it in a message when it was something that couldn't be changed . . .' He sighed. 'I made a decision and if it was a wrong one, then I am sorry, but it is done.' He removed his belt and tunic. 'I intended to tell you now and set things straight, but I am too late and for that I am sorry too. Be angry with me if you will, but a judge can make wrong judgements, especially when he has no guidance beyond what he feels he should do.'

He saw her bite her lip and look away and wondered if he was indeed too late.

'For what it is worth, I thought of you every day I was away,' he said. 'And the children. I did not forget you.'

'But I felt forgotten, even so,' Ida said, and her voice cracked. 'And overlooked.'

'Never that . . . You do now know how much I missed you.' He pulled her into his arms and held her fast. He could feel the pulse pounding in her throat. He inhaled a faded perfume of honeysuckle from the unguent she liked to use.

'No, I do not know,' she said, and suddenly she dug her fingers into the hair at the back of his neck and tilted her head back so she could look into his eyes. Hers were angry and bright with tears. 'Sometimes I feel as if this place is the end of the world and I might as well be a widow.'

'That is foolish talk,' Roger growled. 'You are my wife. You are a great lady. You are the Countess of Norfolk.'

'Yes,' she said. 'So I have often told myself in the dark watches of the night when I have spent the day trying to conjure ransom money out of empty or reluctant coffers, or entertain great men on their way to the shrine at Edmundsbury, or deal with matters of estate, but sometimes the words lose their meaning and then I no longer know who I am, or I begin to wonder if I am an imposter

– a ragged girl with a begging bowl who will be found out.'

He held her tight and close again because he didn't know what to say. Words of wisdom came better to him on the judicial bench where the boundaries were defined in ancient custom, and having been so long absent, away, living in a masculine environment, his skills of a domestic nature had become rustier still. Nor did it help that she was so recently out of childbirth and weepy and fragile. 'You have never been ragged to me,' he said awkwardly. 'I have always thought you full of grace and honesty.'

She muffled a sound against his tunic. The word 'honesty' was like a wound between them and he realised it had not been the most prudent one to use. But valid nevertheless.

They stood together for a long time and she grew calm under his hands. He felt her soften, and relax. At last, she pulled away and he dropped his arms.

'The bath will be cold.' Her voice was breathless, but she had herself under control and he sensed that the first storm had been weathered, although he knew there were probably more to come.

He gave a wave of negation. 'The water hasn't been standing that long.' He finished undressing and stepped into the tub. The bath was indeed on the lukewarm side, but he decided diplomacy was the better part of valour.

'I see you have a new hat.' She pointed to the coffer.

He gave her a sheepish smile. 'They had a good hat-maker in Speyer and I liked what he made. I've brought you some embroidery silks and a new belt.'

She fetched soap and a washcloth. 'I sold the one of gold and pearls that . . . that Henry gave me and a ring from my days at court.'

There was a moment's awkward silence. Roger

wondered how to pace the rest of what he had to tell her and decided that easing it into the general conversation was the best way. He told her about the sojourn in Germany, picking out the brighter strands along the way, trying to tell her things that he thought a woman might want to hear. He also told her about her son and how well he comported himself. Seeing the glow on her face, he had to suppress a twist of jealousy. This moment was for her, and a gift with probably more value than either her silks or her new belt. He mentioned the boy's new nickname and how he was doing his best to live up to it.

'I watched him train every day,' Roger said. 'He looks at tasks in the world the way that you look at your needlework: so focused that he could make a hole in the fabric with his eyes alone. He is going to be a fine man. He has honour, pride and courage. Granted he stands too much on ceremony and makes overmuch of his kinship to the King, but there is no malice in him.' He swilled his face, blotted the water from his eyes then looked at her. 'There's to be a crown-wearing in Winchester to take away the blemish of the King's imprisonment – and all are summoned to attend. The King wants young Longespée to bear one of the poles of his palanquin as we enter the cathedral and I am to carry Richard's sword. You and your son can meet while we are there.'

She leaned away from the edge of the tub. He saw the swiftness of her breathing and her mingled expression of hope and fear. 'When?'

'Easter,' he said. 'You will be fit to travel?'

She nodded, her eyes very bright. 'I will be churched by then.'

'Good, that's settled.' He stood up and the women rinsed him down with more clean, scented water.

Once dressed in fresh garments, he sat in the window-seat with Ida to drink a cup of wine and eat some small savoury tarts. The baby woke and started to fret. Ida unwrapped his swaddling and settled him to feed at her breast. Despite the fashion for wet nurses, she had always nourished the children herself – at least until her churching ceremony. The unthinking ease with which she cradled the baby, the tender expression on her face, made it difficult for Roger to continue with what he had to tell her next.

'You know there are still rebellions against King Richard in parts of the country,' he said.

Ida nodded. 'Yes, but I have heard that the lord John has fled to the French court, so surely the worst is over.'

He shook his head. 'With Nottingham still holding out, and Tickhill and Marlborough, it's dangerous. The King cannot allow them to remain in rebel hands. Hubert Walter has gone to besiege John Marshal at Marlborough and I am summoned to Nottingham with as many troops as I can muster.'

Ida looked down at the feeding baby and adjusted his position. 'When?' Her voice was devoid of expression.

'As soon as I may.'

She fussed with the infant's wrappings. 'And Framlingham I warrant is a necessary detour to collect men and supplies and replenish yourself for battle.'

'Is that what you think?'

She said nothing, but he could see her pain in the tightness of her lips and the way she wouldn't look at him. One of the younger children had left a toy hobby horse in the embrasure. Ida had woven it a set of reins out of bright scraps of wool and it even had a little stitched pendant on the brow-band showing the Bigod cross. He picked it up and looked at it. The head was made of stuffed fabric rather than wood, so that it would be soft to a child's touch, and there was a blaze marking of bleached linen on the front so that it resembled Vavasour. So much love. So much care. So much need.

The baby finished suckling and gave a milky belch. Ida gently prised him off her nipple and covered herself, her movements careful and precise. When she spoke, her voice was tight but controlled. 'What point is there in a great castle and finely appointed chambers when I do not have the father of my children to share it, save for the occasional moment when he returns to beget yet another fatherless child? When we were first wed, we were always together. I woke up in the morning and you were there. I remember looking up from needlework and seeing you smiling at Hugh in his cradle and my heart was so full I thought it would burst. I loved you beyond measure.'

He heard the past tense and wondered if he was sitting at a wake. 'And now you don't?'

'No, I do, but what was full seems perilously close to being empty.' She beckoned one of the women, who took the baby away to change his swaddling, then she turned back to Roger. 'I found myself wishing I was a man while you were gone. I wished that we could change places. That I could mount a horse and ride where I pleased. That I could walk into an alehouse unlooked-at, that I could converse in the market place without a maid. That my horizon held things other than stone dust and mire and a pregnant belly and the fear of being the one who waits.'

Roger frowned at her. 'You have a roof over your head; all of our children, by God's goodness, are strong and whole. Even if we have had to draw in our horns to find funds for the King's ransom, you lack for nothing.'

'No,' she agreed stiffly. 'You are generous, my lord. My desert is caged with filigree.'

'Then what would make you happy?' He began to feel exasperated. The ways of women were impossible. 'What do you want?'

'Not to be lonely,' she said. 'That was the one thing I had at court that I don't have now.'

'You have your women, you have the children, and enough ado about the estate to keep you occupied!'

'You don't see, do you? You have always been content to live within yourself. You don't—'

The sound of a fanfare cut her off short. Looking towards the window, Roger saw that his men were riding in, and that Hugh had joined them somewhere along the road and was trotting along, straight-backed on his black pony. The lad was talking to Hamo and Oliver and gesturing now and again. A feeling of pride glowed in Roger's solar plexus and radiated outwards.

Leaning forward he grasped Ida's hands in his. 'We'll talk later about this,' he said. 'The men will be on us at any moment, and you should be resting. He touched her cheek. 'There are shadows under your eyes. I'll come back later and we'll eat alone, the two of us, I promise.' He kissed her cheek and, feeling both guilty and relieved, left the room and went out into the bailey.

Ida closed her eyes after he had gone and hugged her midriff. This was not what she wanted, not the way she wanted it to be. Roger was right, she did need to rest. The birth had taken its toll on her resources and she knew she was weepy and out of sorts. Had he sent word ahead she could have prepared herself better. As it was, everything had gone spinning awry like a straw on the flood. She had said things to him that she felt, but the words frightened her with their saying, for it gave them form beyond thought, and once they had substance, who knew

403

what they might become? She should be overjoyed that he was safely returned from Germany and had a moment, however fleeting, to come home, and all she could think of was that he was leaving her again in the morning to go to war.

Amidst this turmoil, the notion of being reunited with her firstborn son gleamed like a jewel. To be able to speak to him and touch him – if only in a limited way. But what if he didn't want to know her, and how was that first approach going to be managed? It was like reaching for a wonderful dish on a banquet table, knowing full well it might be poisoned, but being prepared to take that risk because without ingesting it, she could not be cured. Therefore she had to have the courage, and if it killed her, then so be it.

She forced herself to straighten up and, rising to her feet, looked out of the window. Roger had emerged from the hall and had his arm around Hugh's shoulder. He was obviously speaking to him man to man and, even from the distance of this upper storey, she could see Hugh responding to him with a smile and open gestures. Hugh had weathered the absence better than her, but then he had his father's ability to go inside himself and be content whereas she did not thrive without tactile personal contact.

She watched Roger say something that made them both laugh before they turned together towards the hall, and the sight pointed up to her even more strongly what had been missing in Roger's absence. There was a fire in the hearth and it was adequate, but it didn't blaze with full heat and light without him. How could it?

34

Nottingham Castle, April 1194

Richard's senior barons and commanders had seized several houses not far from the gatehouse of Nottingham Castle. Roger stood by the hearth, appreciating the warmth of the fire in one of the dwellings and drinking a cup of ale. Outside, the roosters were crowing to announce an insipid spring dawn to a population already awake and on tenterhooks at the arrival of the substantial royalist force within its enclave.

Thus far the castle gates had remained barred and the constable of the fortress, William de Wenneval, was refusing to open them. Instead, he had sent a message of defiance in the form of arrows, quarrels and slingshot when the royal army drew up before the walls and had refused to believe that Richard was present in person to conduct the siege. It was a trick, he said, and he would not be duped.

Richard had erected a set of gallows before the walls and had hanged several of the garrison serjeants whom he had caught outside the keep as the army arrived. Their corpses twisted in the strengthening light, heads lolling, hands lashed behind their backs. Richard's brutal act of warning had called forth a fresh barrage of missiles and invective, but no surrender.

Roger glanced up as the door opened and William Marshal entered. Like Roger, he was clad in his mail shirt and chausses, sword at his right hip, dagger at his left. He was wearing his arming cap, the strings untied, and his face wore its customary expression of relaxed impassivity.

William accepted a cup of ale from Roger's squire, and, having greeted Roger himself, said, 'I have to thank you for speaking up for me, my lord. There are some who were convinced I had turned traitor.'

Roger gestured. 'I did what I could, although your own arrival at the King's side was the best way of silencing those whose tongues were set against you.' He didn't have to speak Longchamp's name. The Bishop of Ely had been pushing and pushing for William Marshal to be named amongst those in rebellion against the King. 'I knew you were not a traitor.' He gave William a steady look. 'I was sorry to hear about the death of your brother. I had known him a long time, God rest his soul.'

'He had been ailing for some while,' William said sombrely. 'I tried to dissuade him from his path, but he wouldn't listen to me.' His mouth curled in an expression that was half-grimace, half-reminiscent smile. 'My father held Marlborough for many years and I lived there as a child. I believe my brother had some notion that if he could hold on to it for John, it might be restored to our family, but he misjudged the situation and paid for it, God rest his soul.' He crossed himself and heaved his shoulders as if shifting the weight of a burden. Then he changed the subject. 'I heard you had been blessed with another son.'

Roger nodded. 'A fine healthy lad, praise God.'

'The Countess is well?'

'Thank you, yes.' Roger forced a smile. 'And your own lady?'

'In confinement with our third. Isabelle says it will be a girl this time and I take her word for it. She seems to know. I have an heir for England and an heir for Normandy. It will be useful to have a daughter in the cradle and I can play the doting father.' He cocked his head at Roger. 'Useful for marriage alliances too. Have you betrothed either of your girls yet?'

Roger shook his head. 'I'm considering suitable candidates. They still have much growing to do, and skills to learn.'

'They will be well taught, I think, and grace any household they join as wives. Your lady is the kindest, most hospitable woman I have ever met.' A smile crinkled William's eye corners. 'Were I to carve her a niche it would be as a provider of warmth and welcome for the weary in need of respite. She is like a lantern at the end of a tiring road.'

Roger looked rueful. The lamp had not been shining brightly on his return from Germany and had dimmed further as he set out to Nottingham. He said wryly, 'Perhaps my wife would be better married to an innkeeper. She would see more of me then. Germany was hard on her, and now this siege.' He sighed heavily. 'Once we have peace again, I am likely to be on Eyre hearing pleas.'

'Bring her with you,' William suggested. 'When you go on your circuits do you not have manors where she can stay and that you can visit for at least two nights in seven and bring guests?'

'Depending on where I am sent, but yes,' Roger said dubiously, thinking of the logistics of transporting his household.

'I make arrangements for Isabelle when I can. Women

407

need such contact and it is good for political purposes too. Men talk more openly when they are lodged in sociable comfort. Besides, I want to spend time with my wife and watch my children grow while I still have the wherewithal to enjoy such pleasures. I find the reward is worth more than double the effort it takes to move one's household.'

The conversation ended there as the Marshal's close friend Baldwin de Béthune arrived, lacing up his mail coif even as he put his head round the door. 'The King's armed up and asking for both of you,' he said.

William and Roger drank up in haste and hurried outside. Richard had emerged from his own commandeered dwelling and was gazing at the stout palisade surrounding Nottingham's outer bailey with a predatory glint in his eyes. A hauberk of light mail covered his body like a silver snakeskin and he was wearing an iron cap that exposed his face. The golden leopards of England rippled against the red silk on his banner which flaunted in full view of the walls.

Roger studied the castle. It occupied a narrow sandstone ridge a little to the west of the town. The keep itself stood in an upper bailey on the southern end of the ridge, surrounded by a strong curtain wall of stone. Below was another bailey, also enclosed by a curtain wall, and then to the north and east came the outer ward, which followed the line of the rock southwards, protected by a palisade of earth and timber with a single massive wooden gate. Defenders stood ready on the ramparts. The demand to surrender had been refused, and the sight of the hanged men had only led, thus far, to increased defiance.

Turning from his scrutiny, Richard gave the order to have the targes brought forwards – great straw shields behind which the archers and troops could take shelter and approach close enough to the footings of the palisade to put up siege ladders. A battering ram stood ready to assault the great wooden gates.

Roger gestured his squire to bring his helm – not the fancy one with a perforated face guard, but his foot-fighting one with a straight nasal bar, the kind that the household knights wore. He donned it over his arming cap and checked his sword to see that it was free in the scabbard.

'How soon can we expect the Bishop of Durham to arrive from Tickhill, sire?' Roger asked.

'In time to eat an early dinner tomorrow, I hope,' Richard replied. 'Tickhill will be an easy nut to crack for a man of Durham's experience.' The lines at his eye corners creased and deepened. 'This one may take slightly more, but I have an appointment in Winchester three weeks hence, so the sooner the better.' One corner of his mouth tilted in the direction of a smile. 'If we can break them before the week is out, there might be time for a few days hunting in Sherwood and I'm partial to venison.' He nodded brusquely to his commanders. 'My lords, you know what to do. Push forward the targes; get the ladders up, take the first bailey and advance to the barbican. The arbalesters will pin down their archers and slingers.' Richard fixed them with a hard blue stare. 'No quarter,' he said. 'If there are survivors from this, I will hang them. I want this place taken with an iron fist.'

Roger's heart began to pound and his hand was damp at his sword hilt. He sensed the tension around him, the fear, the aggression, the determination, and even the edge of a wild and wonderful exhilaration. They were gamblers caught in the moment between the tossing and landing of the dice.

Richard drew his sword and raised it on high. 'Ten marks to the first man over the palisade!' he roared. As he brought his arm down, the serjeants charged forward with the targes and the archers began shooting over the palisade, aiming to pin down their counterparts on the walk boards there. Under cover of their shields, other soldiers plunged into the ditch and up the other side bearing the scaling ladders. Some men were dropped by arrows or slingshot, but the rest pressed on.

Roger detached his mind from the hiss of arrows, the vicious clatter of slingstones, the shouts of effort and howls of abuse. He was a leader and a commander and that meant fighting to show an example while keeping his wits about him and directing operations. 'Saint Edmund!' he bellowed to his own men. 'Ten marks from me as well!'

He hefted his red and gold shield, muttered a prayer under his breath and ran from behind the safety of the targes towards ditch and palisade. A chunk of stone bounced off the shield surface. A piece of slingshot pinged against his helm. There was a flurry close to him as the defenders succeeded in dislodging one of the ladders with its burden of men and toppling it into the ditch. A second ladder crashed down after it. Elsewhere other attackers were receiving arrow-shot, scalding water and powdered lime.

Roger heard William Marshal urging the men on and he bellowed his own encouragement. With the targes protecting them, other soldiers had run the ram up to the gate and the boom of the iron head reverberated against the timbers.

Roger directed his troops to heave more ladders up: a cluster of three at once and distanced from those crowded near the gates, forcing the defenders to split their resources. The men started climbing at the run. Anketil set his foot to the left ladder and Roger to the centre one. It was dangerous but there was nothing else for it if they were

410

going to take the outer bailey. Above him, one of his soldiers shuddered and dropped off the ladder, his throat quilled by an arrow. Roger kept his shield high, his head down and kept going. His breath roared in his ears. It had been a while since he had taken vigorous exercise or trained, even if he had been generally active. Nor, although he had performed military service, had he been asked to fight in the thick of it and fight to kill. It was more than twenty years since he had ridden into heavy battle at Fornham, a young man carving an independent path for himself. Now he had paths of another kind to carve.

The serjeant above him on the ladder gained the parapet and forced his way on to the wall walk. The clash of weapons resounded. Anketil leaped forward from the top of his ladder. Then Roger himself was on the final rung and heaving himself over. A soldier charged him, brandishing an axe. Roger planted his feet, ducked the blow and for a moment they grappled. His sword was no use for this close-in work and in the wrong place to draw, but he managed to pull his dagger from its sheath and thrust it into his adversary's unprotected armpit. The man sagged and Roger threw him off the wall walk. He didn't bother to watch how he landed, knowing that a fall from such a height would finish him anyway, but exchanged his dagger for his sword and fought on towards the ladders near the gate.

The latter was shuddering under the impact from the ram. As more of the King's men gained the palisade, the defenders retreated, yielding the rampart to the besiegers. The battle continued to rage around the gatehouse and Roger found himself fighting beside William Marshal as they strove to break the desperate efforts of the garrison soldiers. It was fraught, bloody work, but as Roger's muscles remembered the pattern of training, his movements

411

grew more fluid. The Marshal's skill was so formidable that few dared tackle him, and Roger was supremely glad they were not enemies.

A horn sounded from the castle and Roger recognised the call to retreat. Fighting all the way, the garrison soldiers pulled back to the barbican guarding the first curtain wall. Once the last man was safely within, the arrows and sling-shots started again. The noise of the ram ceased as Richard's troops opened the gate from inside and the rest of their men poured in. The ram itself was run into the compound to loud cheers.

Panting hard, Roger gestured Anketil to regroup the men around the Bigod banner, carried by Hamo Lenveise. The gold silk was blood-spattered and the banner stave was damaged where a sword had chopped into it. Clutching the stitch in his side, Roger approached a dead soldier and took the spear lying beside his body. 'Use this,' he said.

Lenveise carefully untied the banner and transferred it. On the curtain wall behind the barbican, the opposition continued to hurl threats and invective. William Marshal joined Roger, who was relieved to see that his shoulders were heaving – proof that he was mortal after all.

'That's the first obstacle down,' William panted triumphantly. 'Now only a barbican and two curtain walls until we reach the keep.'

'Simple, then,' Roger said, wondering how stiff he was going to be in the morning. He summoned his squire and told him to find out how many wounded there were.

William shrugged. 'It might be,' he said. 'It all depends on how defiant they are now.'

Roger eyed the barbican and the second curtain wall. A clod of manure showered into the bailey. 'I'm not opti-mistic of their common sense.'

William smiled. 'Even among fools there is hope for reason. Sooner or later their dung will run out, and then we'll see.'

Roger paused beside the sentry and watched flames consume the timber barbican and the great gates they had won that morning. The continued fighting had been hard and bitter, and although they had reached the barbican, nightfall had put a stop to endeavours on both sides. Richard had ordered the burning of the gate and the barbican because otherwise he would have had to deploy men to hold them against a night assault. This way they were removed from the reckoning.

'Keep your eyes peeled, Thomas,' Roger said, not because the soldier needed to be told such a thing, but because it was a sign that Roger himself was alert and taking notice. 'You're from Tasburgh, aren't you? You hold the serjeantry?' Roger always made a point of knowing his soldiers. A man given pride and confidence – and pay – was twice as likely to stand his ground as one ignored and left to fend for himself. 'You fought well today.'

'Sir.' The man's eyes gleamed with surprised gratification. He shifted his feet and added with a hint of awe, 'Sir . . . I saw you fighting at the gate with my lord Marshal.'

Roger's lips curved. 'He's taller than I am,' he said with self-deprecation. 'He has a longer reach, for which I am glad. It was a hard fight and every man played his part.'

'What will happen tomorrow?'

'That's still to be decided in council. The Archbishop of Canterbury and the Bishop of Durham are due to arrive, and they'll bring siege machines.' He slapped the man's shoulder and continued on his round. A woman approached him, hands to her hips, her walk sinuous with suggestion. Roger quickened his pace before he was propositioned. The whores were ever present in the army's tail, plying their trade among soldiers waiting to fight. One last night of pleasure, one final chance to leave something of oneself behind in the world lest death should swoop in the next day's battle.

Some household knights were playing dice at a trestle in one of the houses adjoining the King's. Roger noticed young Longespée among them. The youth was a little loud with drink and he was losing. He had paused between throws to boast to a woman that he was the King's brother and she was refusing to take him seriously.

'You're too young,' she laughed, hands on hips. 'A shaveling like you, brother of the King – who are you trying to fool! You look nothing like him!'

Longespée flushed. 'I am the King's brother!' he reiterated and gestured around the gathering. 'Ask any of them and they'll tell you!'

'Aye,' slurred one of the knights, 'he is that; I'll vouch for him. He's one of the old King's bastards begotten on a court whore!'

Longespée started towards the man with a snarl, but Roger was there before him. Seizing the knight by the tunic, he propelled him towards the door in a move so swift the man had no time to react and defend himself. 'My lord Longespée's mother is an honourable lady and it behoves you to remember it,' Roger snarled. 'If we didn't need you for tomorrow's battle, I'd flay your skin from your hide for that remark.' He slung the man into the street and gestured two sentries to take custody of him.

The knight crawled to his hands and knees and vomited. Roger was tempted to have him whipped and put in the stocks, but decided against it because it would only make

414

a bigger issue of the matter and, as he'd said, they needed every fighting man they had. Turning back into the house, he glared at Longespée.

'If you must boast, don't do it when drunk and to drunks.' He took the youth by the arm. 'Come. You can attend on the King's council meeting as my squire. I assume you're sober enough to pour wine?'

'Yes, sire.' The youth jutted his jaw. 'Thank you . . .' He made a vague gesture that encompassed the situation. A belch marred his stiff and formal response.

'I didn't do it for you,' Roger said curtly, 'I did it for your mother.'

Richard stared round at his assembled battle commanders. 'I expect the Bishop of Durham and the Archbishop of Canterbury tomorrow, and the stone-thrower will be up and ready by mid-morning.'

'Those curtain walls are still going to be time-consuming to take,' William Marshal said, and bit at a strip of skin at the side of a bloody thumbnail. 'And costly in terms of men. There were many wounded today.'

Richard rubbed his jaw. 'They may yet surrender when they see our reinforcements arriving and they've had a taste of the siege machines.'

Roger said, 'Send someone to parley, sire, and convince them that you are truly conducting the assault. Perhaps they still believe they are only under attack by the justiciars.'

Richard's mouth curved up at one side while he considered this. 'Perhaps,' he said. 'But whom would I send?'

Longchamp, who had been leaning back, toying with the jewels edging his mantle, said with narrowed eyes, 'Send my lord Bigod, sire. The constable will know he has been absent in Germany and they will have seen him fighting today. He has a lawyer's glib tongue. Let him persuade them.'

Roger raised his brows at that, and heard Richard's grunt of amusement. Glib was not a word he would ever have applied to himself, but then Longchamp was good at inventing characteristics for people and then trying to make them stick. 'I will certainly go if you wish it, sire,' he said. 'It is true I would rather speak my way out of a situation than fight.' He inclined his head to Longchamp. 'I have known some men who manage to talk their way into fights and then expect others to do their swordplay for them, and I know which I consider the more prudent.'

This time Richard guffawed. Roger saw the Marshal's lips twitch and humour crinkle his eye corners.

'My lord Bigod yields the proof of what I suggest,' Longchamp said with silky venom.

Roger inclined his head to Richard and ignored the chancellor. 'I will do what I can to bring them to parley,' he said.

Richard returned the nod. 'It is worth trying first before we expend men and weapons,' he agreed.

A guard ushered Roger into the presence of the joint constables of Nottingham, William de Wenneval and Ralph Murdac. Both men looked haggard, and had likely been awake all night, hatching plans to keep the besiegers out of the second ring of defences.

'My lord Bigod,' de Wenneval, the senior of the two, greeted him. 'Be welcome.' He gestured to a bench. Roger returned de Wenneval's bow and took the proffered seat. Roger's attitude was relaxed. There was much at stake in the discussions, but he was accustomed to negotiating and he did not fear an assault from either of these men who were honourable – if deluded.

'I only wish we were sharing company as allies in less difficult circumstances,' de Wenneval said.

'Amen to that.' Roger accepted the wine that a servant brought to him and allowed the moment to settle into its natural rhythm before saying, 'You do know it is madness to defend this place against the King of England when he is in personal command of the campaign? The lord John has fled to France and left you and his other castellans and vassals to face the consequences of his treachery.'

Murdac rubbed a forefinger up and down his bristly cheek. 'With respect, my lord Bigod, and I mean that, because I do respect you indeed, we know that King Richard is still a prisoner of the Emperor.'

'Because the lord John has told you so?' Roger asked. 'You know well that I went to join the King in Germany. Do you think I would return and leave him still there? I can tell you all about the letters that the Count of Mortain has sent to the Emperor offering him bribes to keep the King prisoner, and how they have failed. We sailed from Antwerp on the *Grace Dieu* and arrived in England two weeks ago.' He looked at the men, but their expressions were impassive – as his own would have been in their circumstances. 'The Archbishop of Canterbury and the Bishop of Durham are expected before midday and will bring strong reinforcements and siege machines. From where do you expect your aid to come, my lords – France?' Roger crossed his legs at the ankle. 'I can assure you, there will be no succour from that direction.'

De Wenneval folded his arms in a gesture of negation. 'It will take you weeks of siege to reduce this place,' he growled.

'The King will doubtless leave a contingent here if he must,' Roger replied. 'He is to wear his crown in Winchester three weeks hence. Obviously, he would prefer to have Nottingham returned to the fold by then. He offers good terms for surrender.'

417

De Wenneval raised his brows.

'Fines, naturally,' Roger said smoothly. 'The King's coffers are empty, but pardons and lives intact seems to me a good exchange. Once your honour is restored by a kiss of peace, you can work your way back into favour.'

There was a long silence. Roger sensed their doubt and their reluctance to contemplate that they were indeed facing Richard himself.

De Wenneval bit his thumbnail. 'I need time to consider this, my lord Earl.'

Roger inclined his head, rose to his feet and moved to the window. The air was heavy with the smell of woodsmoke from the barbican and gates and he knew the ashes were still hot, for he had recently walked past them and felt the burning air on his skin. The gallows couldn't be seen from here, but this morning Richard had hanged three more soldiers caught during yesterday's fight, and the men on the perimeter wall would have had a full view. When Roger had left to parley, a perrier team had been erecting a stone-thrower and making ready to assault the outer curtain wall.

De Wenneval finally said, 'My lord, I must be cautious if I go forward in this matter. If I send out two of my men who know the King, I require a guarantee of their safe return to report back afterwards.'

Roger opened his hands. 'Naturally, my lord. I will guarantee that on my word and on behalf of the King from whom I have authority – as they will see for themselves and tell you.'

De Wenneval nodded. 'So be it.' He sent a squire to summon Henry Russell and Fulcher of Crendon from the wall. Both had served at court and knew Richard by sight. Returning with the men across the outer bailey, Roger saw Russell and Crendon eyeing the corpses on

418

the gibbets, both those from the previous day and the new ones from this morning. He led them past the hanging men without comment, except to cross himself, but also made a point of taking them close to the perrier team who had almost finished assembling the stone-thrower. He ensured too that they felt the heat from the smouldering remnants of what yesterday had been two solid castle gates.

In Roger's absence, both Bishops had arrived and the outer bailey and the area immediately outside the gateway was crammed with knights and soldiers, pack beasts and baggage wains, the latter bearing yet more siege machines of considerably larger size than the perrier. Roger's two companions said nothing, but he sensed their disquiet. Hand on sword hilt, he led them to the King, who was standing beside one of the trebuchet carts, talking to Hubert Walter, Archbishop of Canterbury.

Richard glanced up as Roger approached and exchanged looks with him before focusing his attention on the two knights. Roger knelt and was aware of the dismayed shock rippling through his charges. He knew they had still been half hoping it was all a ruse, but it was impossible now.

'Sire, these men are here to see for themselves that you are present in the flesh and no impostor,' Roger said.

Richard looked amused. 'Is that so?' He beckoned Russell and Crendon to stand up, and spread his arms wide, palms outspread. 'Messires, what do you think? Am I an impostor dreamed up by the justiciars to dupe your lords into surrender? Or am I England's rightful king?' He turned slowly round and faced them again, a half-smile on his lips, his eyes deadly.

'Sire.' Russell fell to his knees again with Crendon an instant behind.

419

'Get up,' Richard said with an imperious gesture. 'Now you have seen that I am here in person and it is no ruse – and that my army has doubled in size – it behoves you to return to your lords and persuade them to surrender. They have until noon before my mercy runs dry. Go back and do your best, because if you do not, I will do my worst.'

Visibly shaken, Crendon and Russell returned to the keep under escort and Richard turned to Roger. 'You spoke with de Wenneval and Murdac. Will they yield?'

'They do not like the notion, sire, Murdac in particular, but like medicine, they will swallow it. Perhaps a couple of shots from the perrier might be the final touch to convince them.'

Richard nodded. 'Thank you, my lord Bigod; you have done well.'

Roger bowed and turned to rejoin his men, then stopped short as he saw his half-brother standing among the knights in Hubert Walter's contingent. Huon's garments were shabby. His hair was like wispy yellow grass combed over his skull, and the Outremer sun had pleated deep creases into his cheeks and eye corners. Filled with a world of bitter anger, his eyes locked with Roger's and did battle.

'You think you've won,' he snarled. 'You think you're the great Earl of Norfolk and nothing can touch you, but I will have justice and the lands to which I am entitled. You're not the only one with influence.'

'Your entitlement is to your opinions,' Roger replied coldly, 'not my lands. I grant you that going on crusade might store you up credit in heaven, but you are deluded if you think it will further your cause on earth.'

Roger de Glanville had been standing nearby and now he joined Huon. 'He is right,' he said. 'It behoves you to

420

make a settlement with us, because, Earl or not, you will not be safe until you do.' The whites of his eyes were yellow and filmy.

Behind them came the whump of the perrier launching its first stone at the curtain wall, and then the sharp crack of the missile striking the sandstone. Immediately another rock was set in the sling, the range adjusted and a second missile followed the first, this time sailing over the wall and landing with a dull crash.

'Do you threaten me, my lord?' Roger demanded.

De Glanville shook his head. 'I have no need to threaten. All I do is state the truth. The King needs money, and everything will be up for sale when matters settle down to government again – everything.'

'I doubt you have the wherewithal to buy an earldom,' Roger said tightly.

De Glanville gave him a knowing look. 'No, but do you have the wherewithal to keep one?'

On the curtain wall, a stave appeared bearing a makeshift banner of a strip of bleached table linen. The flag swept back and forth, attracting the attention of those in the first ward. The trebuchet crew locked the securing pegs on their machine.

A cold sensation prickled between Roger's shoulder blades. 'What does that mean, my lord? Let us be clear on this matter.'

De Glanville shrugged. 'What it says. My stepson has naught to lose since he has nothing – but other men have more at stake.' With a half-smile that was perilously close to a smirk, he walked away. Roger had no time to dwell on the words, disturbing though they were, because the banner of truce demanded his full attention, and a squire was already on his way to him from the King.

* * *

421

At her mother-in-law's dower dwelling at Dovercourt, Ida returned from hearing the children's prayers and kissing them goodnight and, with a sigh, sat down by the fire to resume her sewing. Juliana had entertained the children earlier with a story about a fox and a crow. It had apparently been one of their father's favourites as a child and had been written in the time of the Greeks by a man named Aesop. The girls had practised their needlecraft while they listened, and Ida had given the boys some small pieces of armour and harness to polish to keep them out of mischief. While her mother-in-law was deeply proud of her grandchildren, she preferred them to be quiet and seemly in her presence and reserve boisterous activities for elsewhere. As an infant, the jewels and embroidery on her dresses had always fascinated Hugh, and Ida had forever to be watching him and keeping his sticky fingers away from Juliana's gowns.

'You are always industrious, my dear,' Juliana said with a smile. 'I seldom see you without some piece of stitchery in your hands, and if I do, it is because you are making cheese, or directing the spinsters, or overseeing the apple-pressing.'

Ida gave a rueful shrug. 'There is always work to be done.'

'There are always servants too,' Juliana replied. 'You do not have to do everything yourself.'

Ida avoided Juliana's gaze. 'I enjoy being busy.'

'Do you?' Juliana raised one thin tawny eyebrow. 'That is most laudable, but there is a difference between being busy doing what a woman of your standing must do, and being rushed off your feet.'

Ida said nothing and hoped Juliana would let the matter drop. She was fond of her mother-in-law, but acknowledged she could be autocratic and forthright when the mood was upon her.

A maid moved unobtrusively in the background, replacing candles, bringing the light closer at Juliana's instruction. The older woman left her place by the fire and went to look at the baby in his cradle.

'I remember his father swaddled up like that,' she mused with a half-smile. 'I was a young wife then – a reluctant one. I was told it was my duty to serve the interests of my family and marry Hugh of Norfolk and I had no choice. I remember being astonished that his brutish demands could have resulted in my son.' She leaned over the cradle. 'You have seen that I am not the kind to fuss over infants, but I loved Roger from the moment of his birth and I was desperate to protect him. I knew there were two sides to what he had it in him to become. All the time he was growing from infancy to childhood I did what I could – tried to instil honour in him and duty and a sense of fairness and courtesy to all, because I knew all he would receive from his father was ruthless self-interest and the desire to scramble over everyone else to be top of the dung heap and let decency go hang. I was determined that my son was not going to turn into his father.'

Ida ceased sewing and looked at Juliana. Her mother-in-law's usually smooth face wore an intense expression that made the hair rise on Ida's nape. She didn't want Juliana to say anything else, but didn't know how to stop her.

Juliana adjusted the sleeping baby's coverlet with a gentle touch and returned to her seat. The red light from the fire, the yellow glow of candle flame made the jewels on her gown sparkle as if wet. Juliana rubbed her hands together. 'Roger wasn't my only one, you know,' she said. 'I bore a daughter, stillborn, eleven months to the day from Roger's birth, and seven months after that I miscarried another boy after my husband beat me for looking at him in a certain way.'

Ida stared at Juliana, appalled.

'At least I had recourse to kin,' Juliana added. 'I complained to my brother and he had words with Hugh – threatened to turn the violence back upon him if he ever touched me again. It was an insult to the family honour, you see – the sister of the Earl of Oxford beaten black and blue by her husband. I was sent to the priest for a lecture on the virtues of being a good wife and made to do penance. Hugh didn't want to quarrel with my brother so he left me alone after that – except to procreate, but I didn't conceive again, and he couldn't make me fear him. All I felt for him was contempt. In the end he had the marriage annulled and threw me out.' She gave Ida a sad, knowing look. 'My dear, I lost my own firstborn son too – but at seven years old, and I did not see him again until he was a man.'

Ida made a sound to keep her throat open. She was strangling on grief.

'Roger hides it well, but he is like me. Much goes unsaid and lies deep, but it is not dead. It is buried alive. Ida, I have seen that you make my son happy, and that is beyond price.'

Ida couldn't see her sewing for tears. She wiped them away on her sleeve, but fresh ones immediately took their place. 'No I don't,' she choked. 'What you have seen is in the past.'

'It is only in the past if you make it so,' Juliana said gently.

Ida sniffed. 'Yes, but also if he makes it so, madam.'

Juliana gave a thoughtful nod, her judicious manner showing whence Roger had obtained his ability to detach. 'Both my marriages were made for duty and I had no say in their arrangement. Walkelin and I rubbed along tolerably at best, but it was not what I would have wished

424

for myself. I paid a fine to the King not to be married again and gladly so. You had a say in your choice – and so did my son. It would be a pity to see such sweetness turn sour. You have so much, my dear, more than I had. You mustn't let it slip through your fingers.'

Ida couldn't contain her grief and began to sob. Juliana was not the kind to whom displays of affection came naturally, but she rose and sat beside Ida and set her arm around her shoulders. 'Weep all you want,' she said. 'The world would be parched without rain and this storm needed to come. Let it go.' She signalled to the woman who had been trimming the candles and told her to have the other maids turn down the bed and to bring hot milk sweetened with honey.

Ida shook her head. 'You must think me weak and foolish,' she said in a cracked voice.

Juliana gave a faint smile. 'Weak no, foolish yes. You and my son have positions to maintain. It would be easier if you were both pulling in the same direction instead of one going north and one going south, but that is for daylight to decide. Leave your sewing. It will wait another day.' Gently, Juliana tugged at the fabric in Ida's hands until she relinquished it, secured the needle and, helping her to her feet, drew Ida into the bedchamber.

Ida found it a relief to be told what to do. Usually she was the one making the decisions, ensuring the bed was aired, the drinks fetched, the candles lit, and usually she enjoyed that nurturing side of her duties, but she sorely needed the respite. As she slipped between the lavender-scented sheets, her eyes were almost closing, although she managed to drink the hot milk and honey that one of Juliana's women brought to her. Juliana herself tucked Ida's shoes at the bedside and unfastened the hangings to draw them across.

425

'Sleep well, daughter,' she said.

Ida almost gave way to a fresh burst of weeping when she heard Juliana say that word because it carried a parcel of love and acceptance. Allied to what Juliana had said about her stillborn baby girl, it was an immensely powerful statement, even if Juliana had now re-established the distance and did not lean to kiss her.

Feeling hot-eyed and exhausted, but immeasurably more at peace than she had done before, Ida slept.

It was late in the night when Ida stirred and turned over, making a small sound that mingled pleasure with a hint of anxiety. She was aware enough to know she was having an erotic dream and that such manifestations were sinful and dangerous. Soft lips brushed her shoulder, whispered over her collar bone and nuzzled her throat. A weight other than her own bowed the mattress and strong arms gathered her in and drew her against a hard, warm, masculine body. Ida lifted one arm to explore and touched skin, hair, the soft burr of stubble. She breathed in a familiar scent and felt its effect unwind through her body, loosening her limbs, making them gelatinous. She opened her eyes. The room was in darkness, but she knew she was awake, and the presence was still there, powerful and undeniably male.

'Roger?'

'Ssshhh.' One arm supported her, the other swept down over her body. He kissed her eyelids, her cheeks, the corners of her mouth and then her mouth itself, with subtlety and pressure. She moaned and arched against him, ready and desperate almost on the instant. He entered her in one thrust and she wrapped her legs around him and arched her spine, wanting to take more of him into herself. His rhythm was slow and measured, and although

426

he was as hard as bone, he moved gently, like a low summer tide. She could feel the effort of his holding back shuddering through him and thought about saying he didn't have to, but a part of her wanted it to go on for ever, this slow, tender surge and subside. She gave back to him, barely moving herself, but still the tension built and her body locked and strained, and suddenly, like a strand caught in the curl of the tide as it rolled to shore, she was tumbling over and over until deposited above the main strength of the swell, lapped by the smaller waves following behind. Above her, Roger breathed her name, and she felt him pulse within her again and again until he was spent, and then let himself down, gasping like a half-drowned man cast on to the shore.

Ida stroked his hair and the side of his face, welcoming his weight for the moment before he lifted off and withdrew from her. His breathing calmed and he softly kissed her shoulder. The pitch darkness enclosed them within the bed curtains like a cavern.

'We arrived very late,' he murmured. 'It's a long time since I've ridden by moonlight. My mother said you were sleeping and not to disturb you, but I'm afraid I didn't heed her advice.'

'I am glad you did not,' Ida said shyly, 'although I have been very thankful for her other wisdom. What are you doing here?'

'Fetching you and the children for the journey to Winchester.'

'I thought you would still be with the King.'

He was silent for several heartbeats and the atmosphere changed. 'I sought leave from the court to come and escort you,' he said, and she heard a flat note in his voice. Concerned, she groped for the tinder and flint on the bedside coffer, found the lantern and struck a light. She needed to read his expression because something was badly wrong.

As the lantern bloomed the chamber with grainy light, she looked at him. There was a chaff mark at his throat that she guessed came from his mail and a bruise on his arm, but otherwise his skin was unblemished. His eyes, however, held shadows beyond natural tiredness. 'Was that the only reason you sought leave?' She found another candle to light and thought about what Juliana had said about not letting things slip through her fingers.

He gave her a wary look. 'It was the main one,' he said cautiously. Then he sighed and shook his head. 'I left the court because I needed a respite from my fellows, if only for a few days. There are men with whom I have to associate, but would rather not.'

Ida fetched the wine jug from the coffer. There was food under a cloth – bread and cheese – and she brought that too. 'What's happened?'

He grimaced. 'We took Nottingham – you received my letter?'

She nodded. It had been to the point, written in haste before he set out on the road to the King's hunting lodge at Clipstone. On receiving it, she had felt irritated that there was time to chase deer when there was no time to spend at Framlingham.

'It was a hard fight, but a short one.' He flapped back the bed covers, inviting her to rejoin him. 'When they realised it was indeed the King besieging them, they saw sense and surrendered. From there, we moved to the hunting lodge at Clipstone, and then to Northampton for a council.'

He fell silent again and she sensed he was settling calm upon himself because it was not his way to stamp and rage.

428

'The King is short of funds, as you would expect,' he said. 'He stripped England to pay for his crusade, and any rags of meat remaining on the bones went to secure his ransom – on which the balance is still owing. Until it's paid, the Archbishop of Rouen can't come home. There's also the matter of dealing with the rebels in France and Normandy.' His jaw tightened with anger. 'Richard has removed sheriffs from office and constables from castles. If men want their offices, they will have to buy them back.'

Ida frowned. 'But you are not a sheriff and I did not think you were bothered about Hereford.'

'I'm not, and Hereford is back in Longchamp's custody anyway. It's not that.'

'Then what?'

He sighed and rubbed his eyes. 'Richard has put Longchamp in charge of raising the money, and he's a leech. He says that there are estates of my earldom that are in doubt and I must pay a fine if I want to keep them.' He curled his upper lip. 'A thousand marks, if you please.'

Ida gasped. 'That's outrageous!'

'I agree, but the alternative is to lose the lands.'

'But surely, with what Richard owes you . . . what you have done for him . . .'

'He sees what I have done for him as no more than his due. It is the duty of a vassal to support his lord.'

'And of a lord to support his vassal!'

Roger drank. 'Indeed, and he would say he has done so and been fair and generous to restore my earldom, give me the third penny of the shire and permission to rebuild Framlingham. I am not alone. Others have had similar demands made on them.'

'So what lands are in dispute for such a sum?'

'Five manors. Dunningworth, Staverton, Hollesley, Framingham, and Claxthorpe. I had to pay a hundred marks there and then, and the rest is due in increments at the exchequer.'

'And when that is done he will charge you another thousand, and another?'

Roger said nothing and she knew it was because such a state was an appalling possibility.

'What if you do not pay?'

'I suffer more forfeiture. While my stepbrother continues to dispute with me, Richard – or Longchamp – can make these demands and I must either pay or lose the lands to Huon. Ranulf de Glanville may have died on crusade, but his brother remains at court and their nephew is the Archbishop of Canterbury. Hugh and Gundreda still have influence among those who make policy and Richard will take whatever revenue comes his way and make few bones about its source.' He looked at her. 'There is more.'

Ida wondered if it would not have been better for Richard to have stayed a hostage and let John take the crown. 'What more can there be?'

He reached for her hands. 'I am to sit on the Westminster Bench for the autumn term, so we'll be remaining at Friday Street.'

Ida frowned because that seemed like a good thing. It meant they would be together; the house was not much smaller than the hall at Framlingham.

'But after that, the King will want me to go on another Eyre and enquire into the state of widows and orphans in wardship, among other things, because it's another source of revenue. I've to complete four counties by the end of the year, and there will be another nine next year.'

Ida swallowed. Enough time then to beget another child, she thought, and then leave. She tried to pull her hand out of his, but he gripped it tightly. 'I thought you could come with me,' he said. 'We have manors in several of the counties. I cannot promise to be with you every day or even every week, but it will mean the absences will not be as long. I know it is not what you want, but it is a compromise.'

She looked down at their linked hands and bit her lip.

'You may have to entertain guests too,' he added. 'The other justices will be seeking hospitality on occasion.'

She searched his face. 'Is it what you want?'

He stroked her cheek and tucked a tendril of her hair behind her ears. 'I have missed you, Ida . . . for a long time, and part of that is my own doing.'

The tight knot at her core begin to unravel and she suddenly felt almost shy. She had a tenuous feeling of new growth – of delicate shoots turning towards the spring, but still in danger of being withered. 'Yes,' she said. 'I want that with all my heart.'

35

Winchester, April 1194

Ida gazed anxiously round the solar chamber of the house they had rented in Winchester. The furniture gleamed with beeswax polish; the rushes on the floor were fresh and scattered with herbs. The wine in the flagon was Rhenish, and the glass cups, pale green with twists of blue, stood ready. Her hands trembled as for the tenth time she plumped the cushions on the bench before the hearth. As she nudged a footstool straight, she thought about the first time she had had to move a similar stool for King Henry and position it where it was most comfortable for his injured leg, while all the time he watched her with the gaze of a predator.

She smoothed her green gown with damp hands. The neckline, hem and cuffs were stiff with embroidery and she felt stiff too, as if her limbs were made of jointed wood. Her centre was a hollow cavern. Going to the window, she looked out on the garth. Hugh was playing a boisterous game of camp ball with his father's squires and their shouts rang up through the open shutters. She had thought about summoning him inside to wash and change his clothes, but had decided she would rather deal with matters one thing at a time. She didn't want Hugh in the room when she greeted his older brother. She didn't want Roger with her until the first moment was over either and, although patently anxious about her, he had yielded to her wishes and absented himself to some judicial work in the scribe's corner off the hall.

Geoffrey, her chamberlain, who had been on the lookout, poked his head around the door. 'Countess, he is here.'

Ida swallowed. Her stomach felt as if it was joined to the base of her throat. She had been sick several times that morning. It was almost like being with child, she thought, and wondered if the pains would come when she saw him. And yet, like giving birth, it had to happen. She couldn't walk away from this and she needed to be free of the burden.

She summoned her women and taking a deep breath went down to the courtyard. Her son was dismounting from a fine black palfrey that she knew Roger had gifted to him. The saddle cloth was gilded and silver pendants hung from the horse's chest strap and brow-band. The young man had thick, gleaming dark hair. He was tall and straight, limber and handsome. He wore a long sword at his hip and the manner he kept it from fouling his movements showed the ease of long practice. Ida's heart filled her chest and suddenly it was difficult to breathe.

'Madam.' One of her women moved to catch her, but Ida locked her knees and forced her will through her anxiety.

'I am all right,' she replied, even though she wasn't. Gathering her reserves, she walked forward to greet him and curtseyed as she would to any noble guest on his arrival. 'Welcome,' she said. 'Be welcome . . . my son.' The words were out although they almost closed her throat in their passing. A brief upward glance showed her

433

that his expression was pale and tight – and imperious. He had Henry's brow and nose, but his eyes were brown like hers and he had a masculine version of her jaw. She wanted to follow the outline of his features with her fingertips, but knew it was too intimate a gesture. There was no trace of the baby whose swaddling she had changed or over whom she had sat and prayed while he fought his fever. No sign either of the spindle-legged little boy dancing with other children in Westminster's hall. All she had to carry through the years that might have been and never were were a lock of hair and a tiny pair of shoes.

She saw the prickle of stubble on his throat as he swallowed. Already he was old enough to grow an embryo beard. He raised her to her feet. 'My lady mother,' he said, 'or so I am told.' His voice had a slight catch in its timbre that might have been the result of strong emotion but could equally be no more than an inheritance from his father.

'I . . . I do not know what you have been told, but indeed you are my son. Will you come within?' She gestured towards the open door. 'Please.'

He gave a stiff, uncertain nod. 'I have attendants. They'll be arriving shortly.'

'The grooms will see to their mounts and there are refreshments in the hall.'

She led him up the outer stairs to the solar, very aware of his tread behind her and of the atmosphere as heavy as the air before a thunderstorm.

He stepped over the threshold and she saw him stare around the room like a suspicious dog in a stranger's territory. His gaze slid over polished furniture, the hangings and embroideries, the sheepskin rugs before the benches, then fixed on the youngest children who were playing with their nurses in a corner of the hall.

434

Ida dug her fingernails into her palms. 'These are your brothers and sisters,' she said, and again it was difficult to speak because she felt embarrassed. The admission was almost sordid.

He looked away from them, but not at her, preferring to gaze at the wall instead. 'My father the King said that you had other dreams to follow and other children to make, but he never told me who you were. I only found out after he had died.'

Ida so much wanted to touch him, to place her hand upon his sleeve and take away the years, but that was impossible. 'I had no choice. Believe me when I say this to you. The King desired to raise you in his household. He would not let me bring you to my marriage and it is my greatest regret. Please – sit.' She gestured to a bench.

'Thank you, madam.' He addressed her with polite distance. What else had she expected? Her dreams – not the ones he spoke of – were of closeness, her nightmares of rejection. This middle path was painful, but at least it was civil and inching forwards.

She sat down beside him on the bench and clenched her hands in her lap. 'I was very young,' she said. 'And I was new to the court. Your father . . .' She trapped her underlip in her teeth. This was so difficult: what to say to set matters to rights without accusation and blame. 'Your father was the King and I had been raised to loyalty and obedience. He desired me for companionship and comfort and I could not refuse his will. After I bore you, we lived at Woodstock, but sometimes we travelled with the court. I do not suppose you remember those times, but I do – every moment . . . and sometimes I think that has been my curse.'

His eyelids were down and his expression was sealed like a good drawbridge.

435

'I wanted to bring you with me, truly. I did not willingly leave you behind, but your father insisted. He would not give you up.'

'But you . . .' His lip curled slightly. 'You chose to leave the court.'

'Yes,' she said. 'Because had I stayed, I would eventually have lost all honour and respect for myself. Your father would have given me in marriage at some point to a man of his choosing and I would still have lost you. While I had a choice, I made it – and I have lived with the guilt ever since.' Her voice cracked. 'For whatever harm has been caused to you, I ask your forgiveness.'

His mouth twisted further. 'Let it be what it will be,' he said. 'I was raised at court with privilege, and I am the son of a king, which very few can claim. I have no quarrel.'

They both looked up at the sound of Roger clearing his throat in the doorway. Ida was glad of his interruption, because she did not know where she would have gone from that moment. He had not said he forgave her, just that she should let it be.

'My lord "Longespée".' Roger came forward with a taut smile, his hand extended. 'You are welcome.'

Ida watched her son rise and bow to Roger.

'The sword practice is going well?' Roger gestured to the young man's scabbard.

'Yes, my lord, well indeed.' He set his hand to the grip and jutted his chin with pride. 'The King, my brother, is to give me land and privileges. I am to have a manor and to have charge of collecting the licence fees for the tourneys.'

'Tourneys?' Ida queried in surprise. Henry had often spoken about the sport with disdain and had outlawed them in England. He said they fomented rebellion and

436

unrest and were foolish arenas for young men to flex their muscles and show off their gauds.

Her son nodded. 'The King is licensing five places in the country where tourneys may be held and there are to be fees for entering them. Two marks for a knight and ten for a baron.' The pride was augmented by enthusiasm. 'I'm to be responsible for collecting the fees. So is Theobald Walter.'

'Ah,' Roger said knowingly. 'That's a fine way of raising revenues, and it will be popular with the young bloods. Theobald Walter is brother to the Archbishop of Canterbury and an experienced courtier and statesman. You are kin to the King and of a younger age, so it is a good combination. Men will be eager to train too, and that can only be good for the battlefield.'

Ida winced at the word 'battlefield' but otherwise was proud and delighted by the news. It was a good sign of advancement for her firstborn and proof that his royal brother was taking care of him. Now that the ground had shifted to a subject less fraught, they could move forward in their current situation too. She sent Roger a look filled with gratitude, and he returned it with a swift gesture of encouragement. The conversation about tourneys continued to carry the moment and create a steady flow of talk. There was even room for smiles and humour and, despite both being tenuous, they were positive signs. Ida began to think that it might just be possible to weave the past into the present and thereby craft a balanced future for all concerned.

William Longespée had been steeling himself for this meeting ever since it had been arranged following the siege at Nottingham. He had dreamed of it on many occasions but facing the reality had taken every ounce of courage he possessed. During his sojourn in Germany, he had come to a measured understanding with Earl Roger. The man's air of calm, his balance in trying circumstances had given William a glimpse of what true manhood was. Even if his French did bear a strong East Anglian twang, even if he did wear some outrageous hats and extravagant jewels and furs, even if his ancestors had indeed been common serjeants, he had a steadfast and noble character. But Longespée did not know what to expect of his mother. There were too many conflicting thoughts and emotions. What if she turned out to be an unfeeling concubine who had abandoned him when a good marriage had presented itself? People told him she was sweet and good, but sweet, good women did not become royal mistresses. That led him to wonder whether his father had coerced her. But if he were born from such a union, he didn't want to see his reflection out of that particular mirror.

The woman who had greeted his arrival did indeed seem shy and gentle. She had brown doe-eyes, delicate features and dimples that appeared when she smiled, although she was pale and her expression full of strain.

Notions of a scheming concubine had fled, but he was still not sure he believed her about having no choice when she left him behind. His father's words about 'other dreams and other babies' still gave him cause for doubt. She obviously adored the Earl and the proof was there at the other end of the room, all five of them. Roger had occasionally mentioned his children in Germany, but never in detail. To see them as a single brood was a shock because it meant he had to imagine his mother making the beast with two backs again and again and again. Yet he was pleased at how he had coped with the situation. That he was the son of a king had helped. His half-siblings were several of many and bore lesser blood in their veins. It behoved him to be magnanimous because of his royalty.

'You have seen your brothers and sisters?' the Earl asked him, smiling.

William looked across the room to the playing children. 'Yes, sire,' he said courteously.

The Earl glanced in that direction too. 'And have you met my oldest son? Have you met Hugh?'

A jolt shot through William. *Oldest son?* He narrowed his gaze. The most senior children among the brood in the corner were both girls. The three boys were no more than small children and infants. The notion of a son closer to him in age tumbled his equilibrium. He shot a suspicious, almost angry look at his mother. She hadn't told him that. Was she ashamed? Did she not want him to know? 'No,' he said, managing to remain polite although there was a bitter taste in his mouth. 'I have not met him.' He saw the mutual exchange of glances between the Earl and his wife, and felt excluded. It was a conspiracy after all.

'Come.' Roger rose to his feet. 'I'll show you.'

Clutching the grip of his sword for reassurance and support, Longespée followed Roger to the window that looked out on to an area of sward where some older boys and youths were engaged in a vigorous game of camp ball.

'There.' Roger pointed. 'In the green hose; that's Hugh.'

Longespée stared at the boy the Earl had pointed out. He was as swift and straight as an arrow, lithe, graceful and lightly muscular with hair the colour of ripe wheat in the field. The sport was hard and his hose were mud-stained. He looked as if he had been rolling with pigs, William thought disdainfully. The boy's voice soared up to them, filled with joy. 'Here, Thomas, here, to me!' William almost winced when he heard the thick country accent.

'I'm sure you'll grow to be friends,' Roger said.

Longespée wrenched his gaze from his half-brother and looked at the Earl. The latter's expression was bland, but still there was an eloquence about the arch of his brow. 'Yes, sire,' he said, thinking that the flames of hell would turn to icicles before that happened.

Roger beckoned Hugh to finish his game and come within. In the meantime, the younger children were formally introduced to Longespée and somehow he found the wherewithal to respond in the correct manner. His mother he barely looked at, although he sensed she was struggling – and he was glad because he was angry.

Hugh entered the room still panting from his game. His face was aglow with exertion and a streak of mud daubed his cheek. From outside and below, William could hear the boisterous noise of the others still at their game and it filled him with both jealousy and contempt.

'Hugh, this is your brother William Longespée,' the Earl said. The boy turned towards Longespée, the smile on his lips enhancing his sea-blue eyes. 'Welcome, brother,' he said, and held out a dirt-smeared palm.

Taking the whelp's hand was the last thing Longespée wanted to do, but courtesy forced him.

'Hugh, go and wash and put on a clean tunic,' Ida said quickly. 'You're in no fit state to greet anyone looking like that.'

The youth glanced round and gave their mother that same unalloyed smile. 'Yes, Mama,' he said. The ease with which he bestowed that title increased William's antipathy.

'Do you play camp ball?' Hugh asked as he moved towards the door.

'On occasion,' Longespée replied down his nose. 'When I was in Germany with my brother the King and your lord father, I played it sometimes.' It was a small dig, saying that he had had Roger's attention when Hugh had not, but it was wasted on Hugh, who continued to look cheerful.

'Good, perhaps we can play sometimes then. I like your sword—'

'Hugh,' Ida said on a warning note, and with a roll of his eyes but still grinning, Hugh left.

William surreptitiously wiped his palm down his tunic. That same blood was in him. Suddenly he was glad he had been raised at court.

'You will find with Hugh that what you see is what he is,' the Earl said. 'There is no guile or subterfuge in him.'

A muddy grinning idiot then, William thought, and forced himself to return Roger's smile, although his mouth was so tense, it made it ache to do so. He was the first and the best because he was the son of a king.

Having seen the way that his half-brother had looked at him as they clasped hands, Hugh was meticulous about washing the mud away. He cleaned his fingernails, scrubbed his teeth with a hazel twig and chewed a cardamom seed to sweeten his breath. He donned a fresh shirt, his blue tunic with the gold embroidery, his best red chausses and the shoes with the blue silk vamp strips. He would show the newcomer that he could dress to the occasion if called for.

Although he had smiled and done his best to make his half-brother welcome, his presence had unsettled Hugh's equilibrium. His mother's firstborn son . . . the one he had heard stories about throughout his childhood, the one she had cried about when she thought no one was looking. The one who had gone to Germany with his father. Hugh was generous and giving by nature, but this was a hurdle higher than he had jumped before. His half-brother had the advantage of being older – almost a man. In a way it was good because it created detachment, but in a way it wasn't, because men had more power. There was a glamour about Longespée, especially around that sword he carried.

Hugh combed his hair and squared his shoulders. For his mother's sake and by the tenets of his upbringing, he would do his best to accept the newcomer, but it wasn't going to be easy.

When he returned to the solar, Ralph and William were both standing around Longespée admiring the sword. His sisters were doing the same with his clothes and his person. His mother was looking on and smiling, but Hugh could tell from the way her hands were clenched in front of her that she was anxious. Joining the group, he showed a friendly interest in the sword too, but the older youth barely spoke to him, although he was more open with the little ones. Noticing that Longespée had finished his wine, Hugh took up the empty cup. 'Would you like some more?' he asked, preparing to fetch it himself.

Longespée gave him a level, superior stare. 'Do you not have servants for that task?'

Hugh shrugged. 'It is no bother,' he said. 'Besides, I meant it as a mark of honour.'

Longespée returned the shrug, although his was a contrived lift and fall that emphasised the gold clasp on his shoulder. 'If you will, then thank you,' he said. 'I suppose your sire is a cup-bearer to my brother the King at court.'

Hugh glanced towards his father, but he was out of earshot, talking to one of the knights about an arrangement for the crown-wearing. Hugh replenished the wine and returned. 'What do you think of the shrine of Saint

Edmund?' he asked, knowing that the King had stayed there on his way to Winchester. 'Isn't it fine?' Hugh loved the abbey shrine himself. The panels of beaten silver, the wonderful workmanship never failed to sing to him.

'Indeed, very fine,' Longespée agreed, 'but not as fine as the shrine of the Three Magi in Cologne. That is richer by far.'

Hugh set his jaw, uncertain whether he was being challenged or snubbed. 'My father bore the banner of Saint Edmund into battle for the King,' he said with pride.

His half-brother quirked a superior smile. 'My father was the King.'

Hugh frowned. He knew his mother was willing this meeting to be a success, but how could it be when his half-brother was such a prig? He had thought about showing him the new litter of pups born to his father's favourite gazehound, but he decided they would probably not be grand enough for Longespée, who would only smirk and say he had seen better in Germany or at his brother's court. And anyway, Hugh suddenly didn't want to share.

'I am going to be one of the King's canopy-bearers at the crown-wearing,' Longespée said loftily.

'My father is going to carry the King's sword into the cathedral,' Hugh replied. It was like making wagers, piling on higher and higher bets until you had nothing left.

'What are you going to do?' Longespée asked.

Hugh returned him a direct stare. 'Stand beside my mother,' he said, and felt a guilty but satisfying spurt of triumph as he saw the flush rise in the older youth's face.

The visitor had to leave soon after that, for there was much to be done before the crown-wearing, and everyone concerned with it was frantically busy.

Ida curtseyed to him again and he formally kissed her hand. 'You *must* come to us at Framlingham,' she said.

'Madam, I would like to do that.' There was genuine desire in Longespée's voice rather than courteous platitude. Other than his instinctive dislike of Hugh, it had been pleasant to be viewed with admiration and seen as an adult by the little ones. He was not about to live in the pockets of his Bigod relatives when his royal ones were so much more illustrious, but a question had been answered. In many ways he was glad he had not been raised among this brood. Heaven help him, he might have found himself doing things that were below his dignity, but at the same time, he had felt a pang at seeing how well his siblings were loved. It was with a sense of accomplishment and deep relief that he swung into the saddle and turned his mount in the direction of the palace. He would come to Framlingham, and he would come proudly, to see his mother, but always as the son of the King, not as a half-brother to the heirs of Norfolk.

After William Longespée had gone, there was a hiatus while the day's events settled their layers over what had gone before and each person found his or her new level. Hugh went off alone to visit the hound pups, and after a while, Ralph and William followed him, the former yelling and whirling an imaginary longsword around his head.

Roger took Ida's hand. 'It will grow easier,' he said. 'Today was awkward because everything had to start afresh.'

She looked pensive. 'I hope so.'

He drew her to his side. 'He has many fine qualities,' he said fairly. 'He's courageous, honourable, a good horseman, and doesn't complain about hardship on the road. He has stamina and determination.'

'You say those things as compliments, but I sense they are sweeteners to the bitter.'

444

He shook his head. 'Not at all, but a lot of water has flowed beneath the bridge for everyone and carried us all far downstream from where we started. You cannot trap the past in a net and remake it.'

'That is not my intent.'

'Is it not?'

'No.' Her voice caught. 'I want to mend the holes so that the future will not slip through it.'

'I am not certain that such a thing is possible.' Roger kissed her temple to soften his words. 'He is focused on his royal kin. Yes, I think we have mended the great rents that existed, but do not expect fond and frequent visitations because you will be disappointed.'

'I won't,' she said with brave resolution, even though tears were close. 'An occasional glimpse is all I need. I hope he will come to Framlingham though, and grow to know his brothers and sisters, but I will understand if he does not.'

Roger wondered if she would understand, but he said nothing. That was something for time to tell. He suspected other members of the family had their adjustments to make, particularly Hugh. He had not missed the frisson between the half-brothers, and he knew all too well how keenly sibling rivalry could cut, and how long it could last.

36

Yorkshire, February 1196

Roger rode into the courtyard of his manor at Settrington. He had been sitting in session all day and his mind was both numb and filled with the details of the cases he had been hearing – mostly land disputes and pleas of dower and maritagium. It would have been so easy to let them all blend into one, yet he had to judge each case on its merits and therefore had to make the effort to keep each plea separate, bearing in mind that the King needed money and the plaintives had come before him for justice. Balancing the two was not easy and he had a thrashing headache.

It was raining again, a steady drizzle of the kind that entered the bones and gradually numbed the marrow. A wet early February day that could only belong to this part of the world, the grey of the dry stone walls blending with the sky; the land one of wind-whipped grass in bleak shades of dun, taupe and grey, with pockets of half-melted snow lacing the nooks and hollows.

Riding beside him, Hugh was pale with exhaustion. He had been attending the Eyres with Roger, serving as his squire and learning the business of the law because one day it would be his business too, and Yorkshire was a county where the family had a strong presence and vested interest. Roger saw nothing but advantage in educating his son on the matter of legal rights. A man thus armed was seldom duped. He not only enjoyed teaching Hugh, he took pleasure in his company, but today had been hard and long, and both were silent as they approached the manor, reserving their concentration for the ride.

The troop dismounted in the courtyard and, with much easing of spines and buttocks and many groans of relief, turned towards the torchlit warmth of the manor. Roger wearily climbed the outer stairs and entered the solar above the hall. There was no sign of his wife, but the room glowed with the light of beeswax candles and a good red fire blazed in the hearth. A rich aroma of beef and cumin made his mouth water and, as he removed his hat and put it on a coffer, he saw that a trestle had been prepared with white napery and cups of green glass. A new embroidery depicting a scene of pilgrims and travellers decorated the wall above the table. She had finished it then, he thought. On his last visit four nights ago, it had been nearing completion. His younger sons were running around, playing some boisterous military game with their hobby horses and toy weapons.

'Papa!' Five-year-old Ralph dashed up to him, grabbed the hat from the coffer and pulled it on over his dark curls, then laughed at Roger from under the brim, showing two neat rows of milk teeth.

'Do you want to take my place on the morrow?' Roger asked. 'I swear I'd let you.'

Ralph shook his head. 'I'm riding in a tourney tomorrow – I'm a knight!' Still wearing his father's hat, he straddled his hobby horse and galloped off round the chamber.

Roger's smile became a chuckle. 'I hope he's paid the

fee, otherwise Longespée will be down upon him like a sack of lead.'

Hugh removed his own cloak and cap. 'He'd have to catch him first without tripping over that sword of his,' he replied tautly.

Roger arched an amused brow but said nothing, looking instead to the door as Ida bustled in and came to kiss him.

'No guests tonight?' She cast a swift glance around.

Roger shook his head. 'The other judges stayed to sup at the Bishop's lodging, but I said I would ride on here and meet them on the road tomorrow.' He made a face. 'It's going to be a foul night and bad roads in the morning. The ford will be flooded.' He handed his cloak to a servant and went to wash his hands and face at the ewer on the sideboard. 'I've to add two more Eyres to the list. When I've finished these, the King wants me to progress through Warwick and Leicester. I received the letters today.'

'He is working you to the bone,' Ida said with disapproval.

Roger gave her a tired look. 'An earldom and its privileges come at a price, as we both have cause to know. He keeps William Marshal constantly in the field in France. On balance, at my age, I'd rather be sitting on a court bench hearing pleas from dawn until dusk than climbing a siege ladder in full mail.'

Ida shuddered at the notion, and poured him a cup of hot wine. She didn't know how his wife, the lady Isabelle bore it, especially with a growing family of vulnerable small children. The Marshal boys were rising six and five, and the daughter Isabelle had borne at the time of Richard's crown-wearing was an infant barely walking. To have their father engaged in warfare for more than half the year as one of Richard's senior captains must be

448

a source of constant worry. Although Roger had to perform military service too, at least it was for six weeks, not six months.

Ida handed a cup of wine to Hugh also and kissed his cheek. He was taller than she was now and bid fair to outstrip his father. His voice had started to deepen, he was developing an apple in his throat and soft golden down fuzzed his upper lip. Ida didn't know whether to weep at the loss of her little boy or burst with pride at the fine adult emerging from the chrysalis.

'A messenger arrived with a satchel of letters not long since,' she said, and gestured an attendant to fetch the bundle.

Eating a hot fried pastry from the dish that had been brought fresh from the kitchen, Roger studied the seals on the various documents. 'Archbishop Hubert,' he told her, 'and the King.' He slit the tags and read swiftly. 'More instructions about widows and wards,' he said. 'The King is like a starving gleaner in a field of stubble. Every grain has to be picked up and ground in the mill. Ah, what's this?' He swiftly scanned the lines.

Ida looked at him. 'Is it trouble?' She had come to be extremely wary of the satchels of letters and the messengers that were a constant part of Roger's daily life because usually they carried demands and instructions that involved yet more toil for him, or dilemmas to be sorted out.

'Far from it.' He gave her a keen look. 'Roger de Glanville has died of a congestion.'

Ida's lips formed the words as she absorbed what he was saying. 'What does that mean for us?'

'Gundreda is a widow again. She will lose influence at court – although the chancellor will still give her and my brother the benefit of his ear because it is to his advantage.'

His lip curled with distaste. Longchamp continued to demand money from him concerning various manors that Gundreda and Huon were disputing. Roger's charter granting him the earldom and all the hereditary lands was worthless while the King and his chancellor continued their extortion. They would extort from Gundreda too, of course. Silver was silver and the treasury was threadbare, and one of the reasons why he was trekking from county to county, hearing pleas and fining miscreants. Ten marks here, three shillings and eight pence there, two palfreys, a hawk, a saddle. 'It's a weakening of the grip,' he said, 'albeit a small one. Time will tell.'

He picked up another packet, this time with a seal impressed in dark green wax. Ida recognised the sigil of a mounted knight on one side and a shield bearing small lioncels on the other and felt the familiar jolt through her womb.

Roger opened the letter, scanned the lines and then with raised brows, passed it to her. Ida read the salutation, which was in a scribe's neat, professional hand, but it was her son's words she heard in her mind, and what he said caused her to give a soft gasp.

'So, the King gives him an earldom,' Roger said. 'All he has to do for it is marry a nine-year-old girl.' He looked at Hugh who had been eating a fried pastry and who had stopped in mid-mastication. 'The King has given Ela of Salisbury to your half-brother in marriage,' he told him. 'I admit I had hopes of matching her with one of you, but I suppose from Richard's point of view it's perfect for Longespée. It's enough to raise his dignity, but not sufficient to make him a threat. Salisbury is hardly a great earldom as far as matters go – only sixty-five knights' fees, but the girl is kin to William Marshal.'

Galloping past on his hobby horse, Ralph had overheard

the conversation. 'I don't want to get married.' He screwed up his face. 'Girls are boring.'

Roger's lips twitched. 'They improve as you get older,' he said, 'but don't let it worry you for now.'

Ida wasn't sure how she felt. It was troubling to think of her eldest son being married when he was barely out of boyhood. Sixteen years old, and being joined to a girl of nine. But then at sixteen, Ida had been his father's mistress. There was the jealousy of realising that this girl child would have the right to share his life as she never had. She pushed the feeling down. 'It is a fine step forward,' she replied, 'and proof that the King intends to do right by him.'

'Of course, it will be in name only for the time being,' Roger said, 'but it will give him revenues and income and accustom him to the notion of handling power . . . She has the right to repudiate him when she turns twelve should she not be content – although I doubt she will be encouraged to do so.'

'Have you got anyone in mind for me?' Hugh asked mischievously.

Roger grinned. 'Your mother will want a say in such matters.' He cupped his jaw. 'Do you have anyone suitable in mind yourself? I saw you eyeing up Thomas de Bohun's daughter in York the other week – and I don't think your opinion was the same as Ralph's.'

Hugh's complexion reddened, but he was smiling. 'I thought she was pretty,' he replied with a shrug.

'Good dowry,' Roger said thoughtfully.

'He is still too young,' Ida snapped. She knew they were teasing both her and each other, but she was still goaded to speak up. 'He's your heir. I can see the sense in my oldest son taking the opportunity, because such chances are few and far between, but we have time to consider.'

451

She saw father and son exchange wry glances, filled with masculine amusement that excluded her. 'Indeed so, my love,' Roger said. 'We will search long and hard to find a suitable bride for Hugh – and a daughter-in-law you can welcome. And in the meantime we have a wedding to prepare for.'

Roger sat before the fire, legs stretched out and ankles crossed as he enjoyed a final cup of wine before retiring. 'The carts and pack ponies will be ready at first light,' he said to Ida and glanced at the assembled leather sacks, travelling chests and laden baskets. 'Travelling light, I see.'

Ida sat down beside him and, tilting her head to one side, began to braid her hair. She had combed the rose-water lotion through it and now the tresses gave off a floral spicy scent as she worked. The dimples showed in her cheeks. 'I would have more room if I left that one behind.' She nodded to the chest containing his hats.

Roger gave her a look of mock affront. 'That is perhaps the only one you should bring.' He turned a little towards her and changed the subject. 'He will be Earl of Salisbury.'

'It is great news for him, although I could wish them both older.' She managed to keep her voice steady. In fact, she was equable about him marrying so young a bride, because it gave her time to adjust to the notion. One could not be jealous of a little girl. One could only feel compassion for her – and so soon after losing her father too.

'He is already mature beyond his years in certain ways,' Roger said, 'and she will have time to come to know him.' He reached out to run his hand down the weaving of her plait. 'I was teasing about Hugh earlier. His is a different situation to Longespée's. He has no need of an heiress to give him standing in life, although plainly we must seek one who will bring lustre to the earldom. He has brothers to follow him too, so there is no haste.'

Ida recognised his attempt to reassure her. 'I know.' She covered his hand with her own for a moment. 'I also know that the time will come, and while I may be fond and foolish, I am not stupid.'

'Never that. Only in some matters of the heart you bear more scars than I do.'

'I want all of my children to be happy and safe and protected – even if they themselves are the protectors in times to come.'

He wrapped his hand around her plait and, setting aside his wine, drew her to him. 'We'll do our best for them, but beyond our care, their road is of their own making.'

Her throat tightened. She and Roger had weathered their difficulties. Likely, more would come, and she prayed for the wisdom and grace to see them through. There had been times in her life when she had been neither happy, nor safe, nor protected. She had been Hugh's age when all three had been taken from her and she had had to live in daily uncertainty. To smile and pretend everything was well with her when it wasn't. She had been beyond parental care then and her brother in wardship. No one had done their best for her. As Roger had said, she had had to make her own road. At times, the path she had chosen had been stony and narrow. She had bled to walk it, not knowing what was around the corner; but at least her feet were still upon it, and the man with whom she had chosen to make the journey was here at her side, his hand in hers. All she could do was pray that her children had gentler roads to travel.

37

Salisbury Cathedral, January 1197

William Longespée's bride was a small thin child who looked much younger than her years. She had pale blonde hair, a pointed face and serious light grey eyes. Her bosom was flat and her hips narrow. Bathed in the light of the painted glass from the great window of Salisbury Cathedral, she knelt, stood, and knelt again beside her young bridegroom.

Watching at the front of the congregation, Ida's throat ached with pride for her eldest son, and compassion and admiration for the child whom he was marrying. Ela of Salisbury was only ten years old and clearly afraid, but she had tremendous courage and had forced it to conquer her fear, answering the priest's questions in a clear voice that spoke of a steadfast character concealed within the waif-like body. Ida was certain she would grow to become a fine mate for her son in the fullness of time. The age gap wasn't too great. William would only be in his mid twenties by the time Ela was old enough to assume all the duties and responsibilities of being a wife and countess.

The mass completed, the couple processed solemnly down Salisbury's great arcaded nave to the doors. Ida sought her son's eyes and he met her gaze briefly. His lips curved at the edges and she could feel his pleasure and triumph. She was so proud of him and the way he was treating his young bride – with deference and courtesy as if she were a great lady, and not a child still bound to the nursery.

The newly-wed couple and the throng of witnesses and guests repaired to the palace crowning the wind-blown hilltop. Ida was glad she had used extra pins to secure her veil to the cap beneath as the strong breeze buffeted her. Roger was clinging grimly to his new hat and the sight made her want to laugh, although she managed to restrain herself. Hugh had a new hat too, with a jewelled band, but having removed it in church, had not put it back on. The wind ruffled through his golden hair and he was the object of more than one admiring feminine stare. Clinging to his arm, Marie cast devastating blue glances hither and yon in search of other gazes. Ida made a mental note to be on her guard, even while she recognised that her eldest daughter was practising a new art from the safety of the family bosom.

Ida had seldom visited Salisbury. It had originally been built as a palace for one of the previous bishops of the diocese, who had ruled like a prince. Later, it had housed Queen Eleanor during her long years of imprisonment and even though it was a defensive site, it was more domicile than fortress. The rooms and apartments were luxurious. Ida admired the rich hangings on the walls, the embroidered cushions and the glass cups through which the wine shone a pure, clear ruby.

Her son settled his girl-wife on a cushioned chair at his side and, full of decorum and courtesy, saw that she was served and treated like a queen.

The marriage feast was conducted with dignity. No one

was allowed to get drunk and it was made clear that bawdy talk, the usual province of such celebrations, would not be tolerated. Yet there was no want of entertainment and mirth. A troupe of jugglers had been engaged and the best musicians. The food was delectable and the wines were either dry and clear, or sweet and effervescent, with none of the sludge that had been the stamp of the court wines served by Longespée's illustrious father. There was dancing and games in the hall and courtyard for both children and adults. Everything had its place and the organisation was meticulous.

Sharing a slice of rose-water tart with Ida, Roger's expression was amused and rueful. 'I wish I had planned our own wedding half as well,' he said. 'Do you remember, the Bishop was drunk?'

Ida smiled. 'It was still a great occasion.' She rested her leg against his. 'And we had a wedding night afterwards.'

'Yes.' He returned the pressure, and then shook his head as Longespée gravely toasted the guests at the high table with the marriage cup before taking a fastidious sip. 'You know,' Roger murmured to Ida as he raised his own cup in salute, 'he reminds me not so much of a courtier, as of a king holding court.'

Ida nudged him in protest. 'He is proud to have his earldom and a place and a title to call his own; that is all. Look how courteous he is being to Ela. Look how much thought he has put into the celebrations.'

'Indeed he is to be credited, but I suspect it is for his sake as much as hers. He enjoys the flourishes and the grand gestures – it is a part of his nature, or perhaps his upbringing.'

'There is nothing wrong with good manners and consideration,' Ida said sharply.

'Indeed not, and his manners are exquisite and precise,' Roger replied. 'But a man must know when to hold to the boundaries and when to loosen them. He has organised and controlled this well, which is all to the good, just as long as he remembers he is not a prince, even if born to a king.' He gave her a long look and softened his tone. 'I speak as I find. You are rightly proud of him, and this is an auspicious day.'

'I want him to have recognition of his own,' Ida said. 'To stand in his own light, that is all.'

'He will do that; he has that kind of presence.' Roger did not add that it would always be in the shadow of his royal kin, because it would have been cruel. The looks exchanged between Longespée and Hugh had not gone beneath his notice and he knew there was the potential for trouble in that area. With the girls and the other boys, it was different. There was no challenge from the younger ones; Longespée could play the prince and they would not question it. The girls, in the way of women, were sympathetic to him because he was their brother, and they were bedazzled by his glitter, his manners and the fact that he was of royal blood. But Hugh was older and less taken in, and that made for rivalry.

His ruminations were curtailed by Hamelin de Warenne, Earl of Surrey, who was Longespée's uncle and lord of Castle Acre, which lay to the north-west of Framlingham. Between courses, the Earl had gone to use one of the urinals set in the corridor walls and now, on his return, he paused to speak to Roger, leaning one hip against the table and folding his arms. 'One of my messengers has just brought some interesting news,' he murmured, giving Roger a shrewd look. He had once possessed the same rusty colouring as his half-brother, King Henry, and although his hair was more grey than

457

red these days, his brows and eyelashes had remained the colour of wheat stubble.

Roger looked interested but held his peace and waited.

'The good Bishop of Ely has breathed his last, God rest his soul. We have no chancellor.' Hamelin crossed himself in a gesture that was superficially pious and negated by the sardonic gleam in his eyes.

Roger signed his own breast. 'Indeed, God assoil him,' he said and resisted the urge to grin because it would not have been seemly and one ought to have compassion because it was the Christian thing to do. Besides, Longchamp being dead did not automatically mean that matters would improve. Richard needed money and whomever he appointed in Longchamp's place would be a man skilled in filleting men to the bone. 'Who's to succeed him?'

'As Bishop of Ely?' Hamelin's lips pursed in a speculative gesture. 'I had heard Eustace of Salisbury.' He glanced at the silver-haired prelate sitting further along the board, resplendent in embroidered robes of blue and gold.

Roger was momentarily surprised. Eustace was a quiet, efficient and unprepossessing churchman; the kind in whose hands matters could be safely put, but somewhat less forceful of character than William Longchamp. Traditionally the bishopric of Ely had always been linked to the chancellorship, but Eustace of Salisbury had never struck him as having the sort of mettle and aptitude to take on such a task. 'To be chancellor too?'

'For the moment.' Hamelin glanced round as the heralds announced the next course with a series of fanfares. 'Here comes the subtlety.' He bowed to Roger, inclined his head to Ida and returned to his seat.

Roger gave a snort of reluctant humour at Hamelin's parting remark.

Ida was eyeing him in a puzzled manner, plainly wondering what there was to smile about.

He put her out of her misery. 'Who was until recently the Bishop of Salisbury and Eustace's immediate superior?'

Realisation dawned in her eyes. 'Hubert Walter.'

'Yes indeed. The Archbishop of Canterbury still commands every piece on the chessboard. He's more refined than Longchamp but just as wily and probably more dangerous.'

'So why did you laugh at the Earl de Warenne's remark?'

Roger smiled wryly. 'I was amused by his wordplay. Like a marchpane subtlety, the success of future projects is going to depend on the creative talents of the craftsmen involved.'

The moment came for what would traditionally have been the bedding ceremony, where bride and groom were taken to their chamber, undressed before witnesses, put into bed and, after a blessing from the priest, would be expected to consummate their union. Since the bride was still a child, the wedding guests escorted her instead to the former chambers of Queen Eleanor, and there handed her over to her attendants.

Longespée could see that his young bride was beginning to wilt. It had been an exhausting day for her, filled with duty and ceremony, but he was pleased at how well she had coped. Her manners and bearing were impeccable. He could not fault her, and even now, with shadows under her eyes, she still bore herself with presence, knew her part, and was able to give him a smile as they came to her chamber door. Taking her small, pale hand in his, he kissed the back of it, and then her wedding ring. He had had it especially made to fit her delicate heart finger. Later, when she was a woman, she would have others, set with jewels and finely wrought. He was going to treasure her for she was his means to greatness.

'My lady wife,' he said with courteous formality, 'I bid you good rest, and I will attend you in the morning.'

The curtsey with which she responded delighted him, before she withdrew into her chamber, her eyes modestly downcast. The latch fell with a gentle click, and Longespée and the witnesses returned to the hall to continue their feasting and socialising.

Resuming his chair on the dais, Longespée watched his guests dancing a carole in the well of the hall. He intended joining them, but his mind was brimming and he needed a moment to digest his thoughts before he moved on.

He was well pleased with the match because it made him a man of standing and an earl, exactly like his uncle Hamelin or William Marshal, to whom he was now kin by law. Although he had not officially been belted yet, he intended to address himself by that title. His appetite for security and recognition was stronger than the need to wait on a formality.

His gaze fell upon his eldest Bigod half-brother who was prominent among the dancers. Hugh moved with lithe co-ordination, his hair catching the light in twists of shining gold. He had pulled a serving girl into the dance and she was blushing and laughing as she followed the steps. William's top lip began to curl. No good would come of associating with stable boys and servants as if they were equals.

It galled Longespée a little to think that although he had gained an earldom by this marriage, although his father had been a king and his brother was one, renowned throughout Christendom, this foolish, leaping youth was, by dint of his legitimate birth, heir to the Earldom of Norfolk, the territory that had once been the kingdom of the East Angles. His father was building a great castle at Framlingham and they answered for 163 knights' fees compared to his own 65. It wasn't right that this capering dolt should be heir to so much. His gut twisted as Hugh detached himself from the dance and, in a spontaneous flourish of joy, seized Ida's hand and made her join in. She laughed and tried to bat him away, but he wouldn't take no for an answer, and eventually she yielded, flushed and rosy as a girl. The adoring way she looked at Hugh sickened Longespée. He told himself he could have been like that if she had raised him and he had had a narrow escape, but still the resentment festered. He had been going to partner her in the dance himself, but in a formal, dignified measure that would have graced the proceedings, unlike the silly abandon of this common carole. Now he would not dance at all.

Compressing his lips, he resolved to wipe Hugh from his mind the way one might wipe a stain of mud from one's cloak. Anyone with an iota of discernment could see who had the better breeding.

38

Framlingham, April 1199

Ida folded her arms at her waist and stared round the new great hall. Built on the western side of the compound, it was ready for occupation as soon as she could organise to transfer from the old block, which was to remain as a guest house.

She was delighted with the new hall. It would bask in sunlight for much of the day, there were plenty of windows and these were to be filled with glass. There was going to be a pleasure garden opening directly from the hall, and a postern entrance so folk could stroll down to the mere and watch the swans and water fowl on the lake. Ida had the task of choosing all the hangings and furnishings for the new hall and having recovered from the birth of a third daughter in early February, she was ready to expend her creativity in other areas.

'The hall will have to be in your father's colours,' she told Marie who stood beside her, watching men apply a layer of whitewash with brooms. The red and yellow was bold and bright for men to latch on to in battle and to fly in bold proclamation from the castle walls, but it wasn't restful, although perhaps she could mute it by using rich colours and fabrics. 'Blue and green for the bedchamber.'

Marie tilted her head to ponder. The sun streaming through the windows shone on her braided hair, enhancing the colour to golden fire. 'We could order some new glass cups in Ipswich,' she said, 'like the ones my brother had at his wedding.'

Ida's heart jumped as it always did at the mention of her eldest son. She had seldom seen him since his marriage; he had had other fish to fry, but occasionally he would visit Framlingham or their Yorkshire estates – usually when he wanted to hunt or needed a new horse. At Christmas, though, he had brought his child-wife and the entire family had sat around the red winter fire singing songs together. Pure happiness had flowed through Ida like honey. Goscelin had been there with his wife Constance and their offspring. Even the edginess between Hugh and William had been mellowed by the warmth of the gathering and the brothers had sung in harmony. A perfect moment, fleeting but remembered for ever. 'Yes,' she said. 'Some cups and a flagon to match.'

'And a water carrier,' Marie said. 'I saw one in Norwich shaped like a lion, with a big smile on its face.'

Ida laughed. 'Lions don't smile!'

'This one did!' Marie wrinkled her nose and laughed in return. Her eyes, grey-blue like her father's, sparkled. 'Or perhaps we could have one that looks like one of Papa's hats.'

Ida nudged her daughter, but began to giggle nevertheless.

'The one with the long pointed brim – it would make a good pouring spout.'

Marie was incorrigible. Ida glanced round to make sure her husband hadn't returned to be in earshot. He had earlier gone to the stables to look at a brood mare that was due to foal. Instead her gaze fixed on Martin, the usher, escorting a woman and two men into the new hall. Ida narrowed her eyes the better to focus and then stiffened as she recognised Gundreda and her second son. Another younger man accompanied them, but Ida didn't know him. He wore his thick brown hair in a side-slanted fringe and had eyes the hazel-green of moss agates. Ida's first instinct was to snap at them to leave, but in the same instant logic told her they must be here for a reason – and what harm could they do?

Marie was eyeing the newcomers with enquiring surprise but no hostility. To her these people were strangers she had never seen before.

'Welcome, cousin,' Ida said politely. 'Will you come to the other hall and take wine?' She gestured towards the door.

Gundreda's nostrils flared. 'This is not a social visit. It is your husband I am here to see.'

'And so you shall.' Ida looked to the usher. 'I assume you have had him summoned?'

'Yes, Countess.'

As Ida led their guests to the door, Gundreda paused and swept a long look around the hall. 'You have a fine home here,' she said, managing to heap scorn with praise. 'I see what the fruits of justice have built for you.' She spat the word 'justice' as if it were a fish bone.

Ida smiled through gritted teeth. 'Indeed it is justice,' she said, putting a different slant on the word, 'and my husband was long without it.'

Gundreda's eyes narrowed. Marie was looking bewildered but, despite her obvious bafflement at the boorish behaviour of these strangers, her glance kept darting to the other, unknown man of the party, who was standing a little aloof.

Hoping that Roger would make haste, Ida crossed the ward and saw her 'guests' settled on benches before the hearth in the old hall.

Gundreda continued casting barbs. 'What of justice for those without bottomless coffers and the ear of the King?'

Ida was having none of that. She directed Marie to plump the cushions and serve wine and said assertively, 'I have lived at court, my lady, and I have a good memory. I know all about people who seek the ear of the King by whatever means they can. Plainly your own memory is not as strong on that score.'

Gundreda sniffed. 'My memory tells me that it was not the King's "ear" that gave you your own exalted position at court – cousin.'

Ida gasped. 'You know nothing about my position and what I endured!'

'"What you endured"?' Gundreda exhaled with mockery. 'Would that we could all live in the lap of luxury for no more price than the "endurance" of opening our legs.'

Ida recoiled as if Gundreda had slapped her. 'How dare you!'

Gundreda gave a world-weary shake of her head. 'I dare because I have nothing left to lose. I dare because if you think a few years of attention from a king is endurance, you should have tried twenty with Hugh Bigod and then another twenty striving for what is yours by right. It is you who knows nothing . . . Countess.'

A part of Ida wanted to curl up and die from the onslaught, but she summoned her strength, calling upon the woman beyond the frightened girl, calling upon the wife, the mother – the Countess, indeed. Imagining Juliana, she cloaked herself in dignified composure. 'Those are harsh words,' she replied with icy calm. 'There are parts of my path you would be unable to tread, but I am sorry for your own plight. I do not think you came here to trade insults – cousin.'

Gundreda drew back like a fighter disengaging from the fray and Ida saw a flicker of self-irritation cross the older woman's features. 'No,' she said, 'I did not, but even so I will not apologise for what I have already said.'

'Then we are equals in that at least,' Ida inclined her head. Marie was staring at her with round eyes and an open mouth. It boosted Ida's conviction that she was right to respond as she had. Let her daughter learn by watching how to deal with a vile situation.

Roger and Hugh arrived from the stables then, Hugh plucking burrs of straw from his cloak, Roger rolling down his tunic sleeves which had been pushed back exposing his freckle-dusted forearms. He cast his gaze over the visitors and greeted them with cold courtesy. 'To what do we owe this pleasure?' he asked.

'Come now, my lord, surely you must know,' Gundreda said in a hard voice.

'Well, I know it isn't a social visit, although you are welcome to dine and rest your mounts. We never turn visitors away from Framlingham.' Roger eyed Gundreda's second escort. 'I do not think I have made your acquaintance before, messire.'

The young man bowed. 'I am Ranulf FitzRobert. The lady Gundreda's husband was my great-uncle.'

Roger's gaze grew thoughtful. This then was the former justiciar's grandson. The Archbishop of Canterbury was his mother's cousin. The young man, although still in wardship, had recently become heir to some rather useful lands in Yorkshire following the demise of his two older brothers. Roger had been meaning to investigate the situation and find out the precise details of the inheritance.

466

Gundreda gave an impatient shake of her head. 'I have no intention of eating your bread or drinking your wine,' she snapped. 'I am here on a matter of unavoidable business. I would not be here unless I was forced.'

Roger sat down on the bench. 'And what business would that be?' He glanced at his half-brother, but Will, true to form, was saying nothing and hanging on to the garment hem of his mother's dominant personality.

The lines around Gundreda's mouth deepened. 'You are involved in the King's investigation into the fines for all widows and wards, are you not?'

'It is my brief to investigate their status,' Roger agreed.

Gundreda took a deep breath. 'Then you will know I am bereaved of my second husband . . . and I would not be wed again – ever, and to that end I offer a fine of one hundred marks to keep myself in honourable widowhood.'

Roger gave her a puzzled frown. 'But that is indeed a matter for the courts, madam. Why come to me? I do not think anyone would dispute your decision or your fine.'

'Hah, I am not so sure,' she said bitterly. 'I would not want my goods and chattels distrained by the King's "officers" or have a marriage forced upon me because I was in default.'

Roger ignored her insinuation. 'I am sure the exchequer officers will find a fine of that sum in order,' he said icily.

Gundreda returned him a withering look that suggested she did not believe him. 'I desire to set my life in order and to do that I need to see myself and my sons settled. We must come to terms over the matter of your father's estates. You have the King's ear and it seems you always will. I cannot match you, but I can be a thorn in your side – a constant one, I promise.' She stood up straight.

'I have come to negotiate a settlement. My sons need something to live on – something out of the inheritance.'

Roger suppressed the urge to enquire why her sons were not old enough to sort matters out for themselves. Huon wasn't present and anyone would think that Will was a deaf mute. 'Then I suggest you do indeed stay to dine,' he said. 'It is going to be a long negotiation.'

Ida sat at her sewing in the upper chamber of the old hall. Birdsong rippled through the open shutters and late afternoon sunlight streamed over the swept floor. Outside, she could hear the children chasing about on the sward, Ralph the loudest as usual.

'I always knew Gundreda was a termagant,' Roger said wryly, 'but I never realised how much.'

Ida took several small, neat stitches while she composed herself. She hadn't told Roger about the fraught exchange between herself and Gundreda. Whatever hurt she had taken from it, she preferred to tend it in private. Besides, Gundreda's words about her forty years of struggle had pricked Ida's conscience. 'It is a shame that you could not reach an agreement,' she said after a moment.

Roger grunted. 'I will not give up lands for which I have paid a thousand marks, especially not to set up my half-brothers when I have the future of our own sons and daughters to think of.' His mouth twisted. 'I suppose she is hoping that I'll receive yet another fine and that it'll make me more lenient. That is why she told me she was paying a hundred marks not to wed again. It will put her in good graces with the new chancellor.'

Ida rested her needle. 'The dispute has been running for more than twenty years. Perhaps it is worth a little sacrifice to see it put to rest?'

Roger scratched the day's stubble on his jaw. 'I am

prepared to give some ground, but not yet. It is like buying or selling a horse. You bargain. She wants peace; I want to stop being milked of fees for lands that are mine by right.' He waved his hand. 'We can't go forward anyway until she brings Huon to the discussions and I think he would rather stick knives in his own face than negotiate with me, but we'll see.'

Ida resumed her stitching. Humming dreamily to herself, Marie came into the room carrying a bunch of cowslips, and purloined an earthenware cup in which to put them. Then she went to the cradle to coo over her baby sister.

Ida said softly so that Marie would not hear, 'Ranulf FitzRobert is rather personable.' She kept her eyes on her work, but her mind was picturing the young man who had accompanied Gundreda and her son. He had a pleasant mien, quiet, but self-assured and well-mannered. Had Ida been Marie's age, she would have been smitten.

'I liked him well enough,' Roger said.

Glancing up, Ida saw that he was watching her with quizzical eyes and a smile on his lips.

'A match with the de Glanville family would be very useful,' Ida said. 'It would be like stitching a loose thread into a garment so that it wouldn't bother us again. It would give us our own kinship with the Archbishop of Canterbury, and we still have two other daughters we can match elsewhere.'

'I had been considering either a Marshal marriage for Marie, or a de Warenne,' Roger replied, 'but Marshal will be looking to unite his heir with Aumale and Marshal has a daughter, so we can match the other way if necessary. I agree with you that young FitzRobert is worth consideration. By all means, let us welcome him again. Invite him for some hunting in the deer park. He's about

Hugh's age, so I dare say they'll make good companions and we can further think on the matter.'

Ida smiled over her sewing. 'I do not believe you will have to invite him very hard,' she said.

'You have done what?' At Bungay Gundreda's eldest son threw up his hands in disbelief. 'Jesu God, Mother, have you lost your wits? I'll never give up what is rightfully mine – never. Do you hear me?' Tears blazed in Huon's eyes.

Gundreda winced as he kicked a stool across the room, narrowly missing one of the dogs. 'I am totally within my wits,' she retorted stiffly. 'I weary of the battle. Your stepfather was the one with the lawyer's abilities. Longchamp is dead. What else am I to do? If you want to continue the fight then do so, but I will pay my hundred marks to live a widow and retire to the cloister.'

His voice cracked. 'I didn't endure the hell of Outremer for this!'

Gundreda shook her head. 'I know you did not, but there is nothing else to be done. Your half-brother is willing to negotiate, but he wants you to come to the table and talk with him face to face. I told him you would come to Thetford a week from today.'

He bared his teeth. 'Hell will grow icicles around its door before I do that, Mother. I still cannot believe you went to him. You are no better than a whore!'

Gundreda whitened and crossed her hands over her breast. Will rose to his feet and stood protectively in front of her. 'You go too far, brother.'

'I don't go far enough!' Huon snarled. 'She wants to sell our patrimony for a hundred marks. If that's not whoredom, I don't know what is! And you condone her, you gutless worm. You are no better!' Turning on his heel, he flung from the room.

In the dreadful silence that fell behind the hem of his cloak, Gundreda bent her head. 'All I want is peace,' she whispered. 'I have fought all my life for him and I cannot do it any more. How can he say such a thing to me?' The thought came that while he was of her blood, he was exactly like his father, who had called all women whores too, and like his father he knew how to hurt. Perhaps it was punishment too, for what she had said to Ida that afternoon – a rebound of her own cruelty.

Will awkwardly patted her shoulder, then without a word he too left the room. Gundreda covered her face with her hands and wondered how it had come to this.

Huon sat on the chair beside his bed. It had belonged to his father and he had brought it with him out of Framlingham in the days before they had had to leave. Sometimes he would sit upright, hands on the polished arms, and pretend he was the Earl, dispensing justice as he chose, exercising his power, advising kings. He had twice Roger's ability and felt sick to the core that his own mother and brother had betrayed him by trying to make a settlement behind his back. His fists clenched on the chair's finials, he swore he would never give up the fight. Huon still vividly remembered taking Roger's sword and girding it on when their father was alive. He still remembered how good the weight of it had felt against his hip. He should never have let Roger take it back. He should have run him through when he had the chance. Holding out his hands, Huon stared at them. His flesh was starting to show the spots and mottles of age like the mould on a dead leaf. There a scar where a Saracen blade had nicked him at the siege of

471

Acre and a fresh mark where he had dug out a splinter earlier. Would that he could dig Roger out in a similar wise.

He looked up and then scowled as Will entered the chamber. 'Get out!' he snarled.

An anxious frown furrowed Will's brows, but he stood his ground. 'You should not have called our mother a whore,' he said.

Huon's lip curled. 'Indeed you are right, brother,' he sneered. 'I should reserve that title for the Countess of Norfolk and all of her get – and call my half-brother cuckold and taker of other men's leavings.'

Will chewed the inside of his cheek. 'You should make amends,' he persevered. 'She does not deserve such words after all she has done for us.'

Huon didn't answer. In a far corner of his mind, he knew he was being unfair, but fairness had little worth to him. It was a weak value and now more than ever he needed to be strong.

'Will you at least come and listen next week?' Will extended his hand. 'See what he has to offer?'

'What, like a huckster bargaining at a market stall for cheap burel cloth?' It was an appropriate comparison, he thought, since burel was used to cover shrouded corpses on the way to burial if the weather was bad.

'You have nothing to lose.'

'And nothing to gain either. If we yield now, it makes a nothing of the entire struggle, don't you see?'

'But we are going to be left with nothing anyway. Better to settle for something now. Why don't *you* see?'

Huon gave his brother a look filled with loathing. Rising to his feet, he poked Will in the paunch overflowing his narrow leather belt. 'You've always been soft as spilled guts,' he snarled.

472

'Maybe so, but it's time to put a stop to the fighting – for all our sakes.'

'I'll never stop,' Huon said, and there was a bitter taste in his mouth.

Roger faced his brothers across a scrubbed oak trestle table in the guest house at Thetford Priory, territory more neutral than Framlingham and just as ancestral. Outside, the rain of the previous day had given way to a pale, sun-washed morning, redolent with spring and new growth. In the midst of it, Roger thought Huon looked like an old dead tree. The five years since the siege of Nottingham had done him no favours and Roger was uncomfortably reminded of their father. It was almost as if his ghost had stalked from the crypt to be with them at this meeting. Huon's features were hatchet-sharp and raddled. Broken veins threaded his cheeks and his mouth dragged down at the corners, while the petulant lower lip was a moist shelf of discontent. Will, dark-haired and carrying an excess of weight, leaned a little back from the trestle, the pose mirroring his general attitude to life and engaging with problems. They made an unprepossessing pair.

Sunlight rayed through the open windows on to the board where the brothers sat and gilded the documents and tallies lying there with warm, pale gold. A scribe perched a little apart from the brothers, his ink horn and quills to hand and a clean sheet of vellum at the ready.

'I am only here to humour my mother and set to right any misapprehensions she may have given you,' Huon growled at Roger. 'I'll fight you to the death for my patrimony.'

Roger raised one eyebrow and indicated the documents. 'You have no patrimony. This is the copy of our father's will, lodged here at the priory and you see that it names you nowhere.'

Huon bared his teeth. 'That will is not worth using as an arsewipe and you know it. It's invalid on two counts. You are bastard-born and it's a forgery. I don't recognise it.'

Roger remained calm. Indeed, now that the moment was here, he felt as detached as he did on the judicial bench. 'It bears my father's seal and it is witnessed by his knights, some of whom still witness for me.' He gestured round at Hamo Lenveise, Oliver Vaux, and Anketil. 'As you well know, an annulment does not convey bastardy on any children born of the marriage.'

Huon snorted. 'Then there is no point in me being here, is there?'

'Your mother wanted to negotiate a peace settlement and I am willing to do that.'

Huon leaned forward. 'The only thing that will satisfy me – brother – are the lands of my father that he gained after becoming Earl – as is rightful custom, and you know it. And I want Bungay too, which is my mother's in dower.' The light in Huon's eyes made them shine a bright, opaque grey against the yellowish whites.

Roger compressed his lips and tapped another document on the trestle. 'At the time of my father's marriage to your mother, it was agreed by all parties that Bungay would go to the heir that my father designated in his will.'

'So you hide behind parchments and steal my patrimony? You take it all and you wonder why I will baulk at sitting at a table with you, you bastard.'

Loathing coiled in Roger's belly. 'I steal nothing. I have come to an agreement with your mother over the estates which were hers in dower. I am prepared to offer you two estates in return for your quitclaim on the earldom.' He kept his tone impassive and signalled a squire to refresh his cup.

'I am not a beggar to be tossed a stale crust and expected to accept it with gratitude!' Huon spat with furious indignation. 'You insult me!'

Roger said with weary distaste, 'Tell me then, "brother", if our situations were reversed, exactly how much you would give me? At each turn, if you have ever thought you had the upper hand, you have sought to stamp on me. From the moment you learned how to steal you took my things and you broke them.' He set his jaw. He had not meant to say that and knew he was exposing his own bitterness. 'I grant you lands worth two knights' fees. Take them or leave them because that is all I will give to you and I know it is more than you would ever give to me.'

Huon jerked to his feet, his throat working. Out of long habit, he reached for his sword, but grasped thin air, for all weapons had been left in the custody of the Prior. 'I should have killed you when I had the chance.'

'You never had the chance,' Roger retorted, his own hands gripped in his belt. 'Do you want to take it to trial by combat now? Do you? Shall I have one of my knights fetch our swords and shall we fight across our father's tomb? Do you want to test me, brother – to the death?'

Huon glared at him, his jaw grinding as if chewing on words that he was unable to spit out. Picking up his goblet of wine, he dashed it in Roger's face and hurled from the room, flinging over the scribe's lectern on his way and shoving an attendant into the wall. The two knights who had accompanied him followed at a swift stride. Roger stayed his own men, making a calming gesture with the palm of his hand. Someone handed him a napkin and Roger mopped his face and throat. The scribe and one of Roger's knights picked up the lectern and the scattered writing materials.

475

'Close the door,' Roger said quietly to Anketil, then looked at Will, whose fleshy features wore an expression of stunned shock. 'Unless you are leaving too?'

Will shook his head. 'No, my lord. Where would be the point? He will expect me to follow – perhaps in a moment I will, but thus far we have done naught but trade insults, and that was not the purpose of coming here.'

The smell of wine filled Roger's nostrils, metallic, almost like blood. It was on his clothes, his skin, his hair. He sat down again as Anketil closed the door with great gentleness. 'The insults have not been mine.'

Will gave him a level look. 'My brother certainly considers two knights' fees an insult.'

'He was always going to consider whatever I offered him an insult,' Roger said with a shrug, and wondered about his youngest half-brother. Ten years separated them, and a gulf of bad blood and family strife. Roger had never known him except as Huon's shadow. But then Roger supposed that it was easy to overlook the drab bolt of fabric at the back of a mercer's booth, but drab did not necessarily mean unserviceable or weak. Sometimes the opposite. 'I have nothing else to offer,' he said. 'Huon has no sons, but I have five to provide for, and three daughters to find marriage portions. As matters stand now, his threats are nothing but bluster. I will not give him the wherewithal to make them more than they are.'

Will plucked at a loose thread on his cuff. 'There is no love lost between us, and between you and our stepmother, but were you to offer a little more, it might be easier to compromise.'

'Such as?'

'My brother desires to set up a fair for the borough of Bungay and collect tolls as a source of revenue. You could

476

use your influence to see it granted for a good price. You could see royal favours come his way now and again.'

Roger felt amusement and mingled with it a new respect for this drab, pasty half-brother of his. 'And what do you gain from all this?'

Will eased to his feet and straightened the creases in his tunic. 'My brother has no wife. He has had mistresses in the past but not one has quickened with a child. I am his heir and I have a wife and a small son. One day, in the fullness of time, that land and that grant to a fair will be my boy's . . . I am not as proud and bitter as my brother, nor as ambitious. What would I do with half an earldom?' He gave Roger a bleak smile. 'What would half an earldom do with me?'

Roger found himself returning the smile and it was a strange experience to have that kind of understanding and share the humour of someone whom he had considered his enemy for most of his life. 'Yes,' he said, 'I think I could do what you ask.'

'You think, or you are prepared to agree to bind yourself to do so?'

Roger's smile deepened along with his respect. 'I agree,' he said. 'Before these witnesses, yours and mine, I agree.'

'And you will promote my son among the men of your mesnie when he is old enough?' Will gestured in a slightly embarrassed fashion. 'If I am not ambitious for myself, then I want my son at least to do well within his means.'

Roger nodded. 'I will do so. He will be a knight.'

Their concord ratified, he and Will left the guest house together. The birdsong flourished around them, and the sun was almost warm. Side by side, they entered the chapel and paced down the nave, entered the choir, and stood before the tomb of their sire.

Roger grimaced as he gazed upon the incised floral motifs and the cross outlined in the centre of the tomb slab. 'My father and I will be united in bones and dust as we never were in the flesh,' he said.

Will too looked wry. 'It is strange, is it not? Huon and I stayed with him throughout his life, but we will not lie with him in death.'

'I do not suppose it matters where we sleep before the final judgement, as long as it is in hallowed ground.'

Will gave him a sidelong look. 'You were always the one he favoured the most, you know.'

Roger shook his head. 'He hated me.'

'He didn't like you, that I grant, but then he cared for no one anyway. He did respect you even if he never admitted or showed it.'

Roger exhaled down his nose. 'I doubt that. I lost count of the times he'd demand something of me and then castigate me for failing.'

'Mayhap, but it was the same with us. He thought it would toughen us to the world. But we obeyed his will. We didn't rebel and stand up for ourselves. You left him; you fought against him in battle and you won. You forged your own path and that was what made the difference to the will he left. You showed him you were the strongest of us all and the best man to take the earldom forward. I never saw it earlier, I just thought he was an unfair old bastard, but he knew what he was doing.'

Roger looked again at his father's tomb and had a sudden sense of understanding as subtle as the change in the angle of sunlight across the top of the slab. He still could not bring himself to like his father, but Will had illuminated a degree of understanding. It was easier to have compassion too, now that he was long in his grave. Wounds healed even if they left scars. Falling to his knees, he touched his forehead against the side of the tomb in grudging respect, and felt as if a burden had been lifted.

After a while, he rose to his feet, lit a candle for his father and went from the church. The monks were entering the priory for the service of nones and the sound of their chanting filled the space between the ground and God in an ethereal swell that was like sustenance.

Roger's knights waited beside the horses. There was no sign of Huon, but Roger had not expected to see him. Will's own escort consisted of a groom and a serjeant.

'I will talk to Huon,' Will said as they paused beside their mounts and clasped hands in tentative friendship.

'What I do, I do for your future, not his,' Roger said. He pushed his cloak out of the way to swing astride, then paused as he saw a messenger approaching the gatehouse on a blowing horse. Roger recognised William Marshal's messenger, Dickon, and took his foot out of the stirrup. A jolt went through him because he knew this must be grave news. Will gave Roger a questioning look and stayed his own mounting.

'My lord!' Swinging down from his horse, the man knelt to Roger and handed him a parchment closed with the Marshal's small equestrian seal. Roger broke the wax, read what was written within and looked at Will.

'The King is dead of a festered arrow wound at a siege in the Limousin. The Marshal bids us attend a council at Northampton a week hence.'

Will looked at him with shock-filled eyes. 'Richard is dead?'

'That is what is written and I do not doubt the Marshal's word. The King is being borne to Fontevrault for burial beside his father.' He turned to the messenger. 'I assume you are riding on?'

'Yes, sire. I've to bring the news to Earl Warenne at Castle Acre.'

Roger gave a brusque nod. 'Go to the kitchens first and get them to give you bread and wine at least. Take one of the priory's horses. I'll see to the reimbursement.'

The messenger saluted and left. Roger stood staring at the soft April day around him.

Will cleared his throat. 'Who is to succeed the King? He leaves no heirs of his body.'

Distracted, striving to pull his thoughts together, Roger turned. 'The Marshal says that John, Count of Mortain, has been accepted by the Normans as their Duke, and that he will be King of England should the barons support him.'

'What about Arthur?' Will queried. 'He's King Henry's grandson by a son older than Richard. His claim must be strong. Richard named him his heir when he was on the crusade – I know because my stepfather dealt with the correspondence.'

Roger rubbed his right foot over the gritty path under his boot sole. 'So, we have a boy of twelve in the pocket of the King of France and, set against him, a grown man who knows England well.'

'Whom do you favour?'

Roger considered his half-brother. While there was accord between them he was not going to trust him with a potentially damaging opinion, and besides, there was a deal of hard thinking to do between now and Northampton. 'We shall see what the Marshal has to say when he arrives, but there will be upheaval. When Richard came to the throne, he put everything up for sale and men flocked to him to buy offices and estates and pledge their support.' He sent Will a wry look, acknowledging without words that the Earldom of Norfolk had been one of those offices and estates. 'There has been plenty of dissent since the King's return from the Holy Land, but after Nottingham, only a lunatic would rebel against Richard in England. This changes everything. The new King, whoever he is, will be a supplicant this time. He will have to offer bribes for what he wants, not the other way around, and those who have grievances will not have a firm hand pinning them down. There is likely to be trouble.'

Will eyed him sharply. 'But what we discussed just now. Your word still stands, I hope?'

Roger swallowed a surge of irritation. 'I may not have sworn, but I do not go back on my promises – any of them. Yes, it still stands, but I will expect Huon to surrender all claims in return.' He adjusted his cloak and gave his bridle back into the care of his groom. 'I must go and tell the Prior. There will be candles to light and masses to be said for King Richard's soul.' He tightened his lips. 'The world has turned on its head.'

Will mounted his horse. 'I had better catch up with Huon,' he said and, with a stiff nod to Roger, rode off at a rapid trot.

Roger drew a deep breath and held it in his chest for a moment. The words on the parchment still dwelt on the surface of his mind, which was reluctant to let them seep into the deeper layers. He could still feel the sun on his skin and hear the confusion of April birdsong. Nothing in the vicinity had changed and yet everything was suddenly different because across the sea the King was dead and his successor undecided.

39

Northampton Castle, April 1199

Roger stood on the wall walk of Northampton Castle in the soft spring evening. Darkness had fallen but a sprinkling of stars and a gleam of moon shed some ambient light. The serenity of the sky soothed him and it was good to have this solitude before retiring, to assemble his thoughts and just dwell in the peace of the moment.

He was not alone for long, however. A sentry scraped his spear to attention, there was a brief exchange of voices and the soldier moved off to a post further along the battlements. The new arrival paused to rest his hands in the crenel gap. The guard hairs on the fur collar of his cloak glinted across his broad shoulders, and his stance was relaxed but spoke of quiescent power.

'My lord.' Roger acknowledged William Marshal.

The latter turned. 'I was settling myself before sleep,' he said. 'It's good to breathe fresh air after the smoke in the hall. That fireplace needs attending.'

'I am here the same,' Roger replied. 'There has been a lot of smoke one way and another today. If you would rather be alone . . .'

William gestured. 'No, stay. It is useful to have someone to whom I can speak openly, someone with a clear mind and no axe to grind.'

Roger leaned beside him. 'Everyone desires something, my lord, and I do not blame them. Arthur is the Earl of Chester's stepson, so Chester has a vested interest in the succession. The Earl of Derby wants certain lands returning to him and will sell his support highly. Many have grievances they will expect John to mend in return for their support, and all will demand favours. I never liked William Longchamp, but when he said everyone has his price, he was right. You cannot afford to support Arthur because you have little influence in his party. He is a puppet of the French King.' He looked shrewdly at William. 'I wager that the price of your loyalty to John is to be the Earldom of Pembroke.'

William stiffened for a moment, then gave a soft laugh. Roger saw the crease line in his cheek and the sudden gleam of his teeth. 'Ah, my lord of Norfolk, you are astute. My wife said the same thing and I told her we were treading dangerous ground. Isabelle says it is our right to have Pembroke because it was her father's in King Henry's day, but if one accepts the bribe of a king, then one is also beholden, no?'

Roger shrugged. 'What is the alternative?'

William looked over the battlements. 'My little daughter dropped her doll over the castle wall at Longueville just to see what would happen. It landed in the pig wallow and when she went to retrieve it, she became as muddy as the pigs themselves. It took almost an entire afternoon for the women to get her clean and the doll was ruined.' His voice held amusement at the memory. 'She learned from the experience though.'

'Not to throw her doll over the wall?' Roger was amused

too, reminded of his own daughters, but he was well aware that this was more than just a humorous non sequitur.

'No, not to drop it when there's a pig wallow underneath. By all means take the risks, but balance them with common sense and think of the consequences for all concerned.'

Roger stroked his chin, considering, and said after a long but not uncomfortable silence, 'So you advise us to take John for king? That is your notion of not falling in the pig wallow?'

'Hardly that, my lord Bigod, but the best we can do. If Arthur comes to the throne, I believe we really will be in the mire.' He pushed away from the battlements and faced Roger. 'What is your asking price, my lord? I noticed your reticence during the first round of negotiations. Chester remarked to me that you were keeping it all under your hat as usual.'

Roger smiled. 'My demands are modest enough. I want my lands guaranteed. I will pay no more fines to keep what is rightfully mine.'

William nodded. 'Nor should you, my lord.'

'I want royal recognition to all of my titles.' Roger reached up to stroke the padded brim of his hat. 'And I want confirmation that my scutage payment will be on sixty knights' fees – as it was in my father's time.'

William's brows shot up. Roger's stayed level. He waited for William to say that the Earldom of Norfolk was worth close to three times that amount when the Yorkshire estates were taken into consideration. 'That is a hard bargain, my lord.'

'I would call it fair myself,' Roger answered. 'I spent twelve years living on crumbs in a hall without defences while waiting for my case to find justice.'

William tilted his head in acknowledgement of the

484

point but Roger could tell he was thinking that the Earl of Norfolk was indeed fiscally ambitious. 'It is not for me to say, but I can offer you the same assurances that have been offered to Chester and Ferrers.'

'In that case, my lord – pending confirmation of my terms – you are assured of my support for the lord John.'

'Then I thank you. We have to make the best of the situation and there is no one I would better trust more to make fair and insightful judgements in the days to come.'

They gripped arms in a soldier's clasp and exchanged the kiss of peace, both bound by the words that went unsaid. Roger was content to have the matter settled, but still wary. He vowed to himself that as soon as this business was settled, he would draw in his horns and concentrate on his estates to make them secure and prosperous, and advance the work on Framlingham until the castle was impregnable. He trusted William Marshal, but he didn't trust John.

'I'm going to London,' Will told Gundreda and Huon, then braced himself for a tirade. As a small boy, he had covered his head with his hands or fled to hide in the undercroft whenever his father or Huon raged. But for the future, for the sake of his son, he had to stand up for himself. It was surprising how much the sight of a little boy running across the grass with a toy sword in his hand could strengthen one's resolve.

'You're going nowhere,' Huon snarled. 'I am head of this family and I refuse you permission. I'll not have you fawning over the dung-covered boots of the whoreson who calls himself the "Earl" of Norfolk!'

Huon had been drunk for the best part of three days – ever since agreeing to yield all claims in the earldom in exchange for two knights' fees. He seemed to think that pickling his senses in wine would make his consent go away. He couldn't face up to it; yet he must. John, Count of Mortain, was to be crowned in London and all business settled. Their half-brother was to have the Earldom of Norfolk and all his estates handed to him in perpetuity. Huon was supposed to ratify consent, but had retreated into a flagon instead.

'I am my own man,' Will retorted. 'I have accepted I cannot change what is to be and that I must make the best of matters. Fawning it is not.'

'You're not going,' Huon repeated and staggered over to the flagon to pour himself another measure of wine.'

'Huon . . .' Gundreda spoke up from the shadows by the corner of the hearth where she was sitting, an untouched piece of needlework in her lap. 'You need a clear head for this. You cannot think with all that wine swilling around inside your belly.'

Huon rounded on her. 'Perhaps I don't want to think, Mother. Perhaps if you had done more in the early days, we wouldn't be in this plight now.' Gundreda bowed her head and made a soft sound of despair.

Will eyed his brother with contempt. The scales had been dropping from his eyes for some time and now he could see him with all the clarity that Huon in his wine-wild state lacked. 'If you had done more in the early days to convince folk you were a viable candidate, then it might have made a difference too,' he said with disgust. 'There was never that much to choose between you and Roger when our father died, but Roger proved himself and you didn't.' These were enormous things to say and as they spilled out of Will, he felt them expand and fill the room.

Huon shuddered in response, his complexion growing dusky, as if Will's outburst had sucked the breath from his lungs too. He opened and closed his mouth, but no words came.

'I am done here.' Will strode to the door. 'I am going to London and let that be an end to all this.'

Huon lunged after him, seized his arm and spun him round. 'Do not turn your back on me, you spineless coward!'

Will shook him off with a brusque movement in which there was revulsion. 'I am not the one unable to face up to life,' he retorted. 'I've been your shadow for long enough! I'm going to stand in my own light now.' Borne up on a wave of determination, he raised the latch and stamped down the outer stairs to the stable yard calling for his horse. Behind him, he heard Huon curse, and then make a garbled choking sound. Will turned swiftly and saw his brother swaying at the top of the steps. Before his widening gaze, Huon staggered and clutched the centre of his chest.

'I will kill . . .' The threat never finished as he dropped on to the steps like a sack of cabbages and bounced down the first few before falling over the edge to hit the ground twenty feet below.

Will's own breath locked in his throat. For a moment, he was rooted to the spot, and then he was stumbling down the rest of the stairs to the bottom, shouting Huon's name, yelling for help. By the time he reached him, his brother's soul had gone from his body. Huon's lips were blue, his complexion livid, and there was a darkening stain on his hose and tunic as his slack bladder released a flagon's worth of wine into the dust of the bailey floor. Will's own heart hammered at twice its usual pace, making up for the one that had ceased to beat.

'Send for a priest,' he commanded raggedly of the witnesses as they gathered. Although he knew it was futile, he listened for the beat in Huon's chest and laid his fingers against the place in his throat where the blood should have throbbed under the skin and where there was nothing. Trembling, he closed Huon's staring eyes, and then the bared snarl of his jaw. God on the Cross. What an end to make of one's life, what a sordid, stupid, wasteful end. Tears of shock stung his eyes and he wiped them away with the fingers that had just closed Huon's lids. He removed his cloak, laid it over his brother's body, then climbed the stairs back to the solar to break the news to his mother – and finally to take charge.

40

Palace of Westminster, May 1199

Ida gazed at the subtlety formed from sugar, almonds and pastry. The craftsman had created an image of the Tower of London, complete with crenellations and turrets, and even banners on the battlements. Little marchpane boats with spun sugar oars sailed upon a wonderful depiction of the river Thames. Never had Ida seen such a confection, not even in her days at court as Henry's mistress. She wondered if she could commission one for the next feast at Framlingham.

The subtlety was the centrepiece of the women's feast in the White Hall following the coronation of King John in the great minster before the shrine of the Confessor. As custom dictated, the men were dining in the main hall separately from their mothers, wives and daughters.

Ida gave a surreptitious glance round then laughed at herself. She was the Countess of Norfolk and wife to a royal dapifer. What did she have to fear? Who was going to castigate her for appropriating a few pieces of sugar-work to take back to the children at Friday Street? Approaching the magnificent confection, a napkin at the ready, she noticed that Isabelle Marshal, newly created

Countess of Pembroke, was intent on a similar mission. Ida caught her eye and both women began to giggle.

'Whatever else may be thought of him, the new King certainly employs a fine craftsman when it comes to sugar sculpture,' Ida chuckled.

Isabelle purloined one of the boats on the river. Ida selected a couple of swans and a piece of turret including some cunningly fashioned arrow-slits. 'It reminds me of Framlingham,' she said as she neatly tied the pieces in her napkin. 'So does this rubble,' she added ruefully.

Isabelle's eyes sparkled with amused sympathy. 'That is soon going to be my lot since William has plans for a new keep at Pembroke.'

Ida rolled her eyes. 'I hear mason's hammers in my sleep and I swear I can still taste the dust from this last summer. Eleven years in the building and like London Bridge still not completed.'

'It will be a great castle when it is finished though, and a crowning honour to the earldom.'

'Yes,' Ida said, and managed to keep her tone light, although at best she was ambivalent about some of Framlingham's magnificence. 'The new hall is beautiful and the garden will be a pleasure when everything has grown.'

Ida and Isabelle enjoyed a detailed discussion about colours and furnishings, but once that topic had been explored, Isabelle changed the subject. 'Your older sons are both fine young men,' she remarked. 'You must be very proud of them.'

Warmth for Isabelle filled Ida's heart. She had such kindness and tact. 'Indeed I am, my lady, very proud.'

'One an earl, the other heir to an earldom. They do you great honour, and they are a credit to you. How old is Hugh?'

490

'He will have his seventeenth year day next advent.'

Isabelle's eyes widened. 'I had not realised how swiftly the time had passed. He is almost a man grown then.'

Ida felt wistful as she agreed to the last statement. She was both proud and sad to watch her boys becoming men. 'He's not officially of age but his father is going to settle ten manors in Yorkshire upon him so he can accustom himself to dealing with men and estates.'

'Have you had any thoughts on his marriage?'

Ida shook her head and drew back a little. 'There is plenty of time. My oldest son was married so young because the ideal lands and wife were available. With Hugh there is no hurry and he has four brothers.'

'I understand,' Isabelle said, smiling. 'My sons are still boys. I know my oldest will be matched with Alais de Béthune, but for the moment, he is mine. We have them for so short a time, don't we?'

Ida agreed wistfully that this was so.

'I look at my daughter,' Isabelle continued. 'I want her to be settled and content with the marriage we choose for her. We need to find someone who will be powerful in his own right and who will enhance our standing, but whom we can trust to treat her as we would – and whose family will welcome her with warmth. She is but five years old and a part of me is torn to be thinking of such things already, but they have to be considered.'

Ida wondered if Isabelle was casting gentle hints and decided that she was. There were many layers in the Countess of Pembroke's sea-blue eyes. She could choose to ignore the line that had been thrown, but knew that Hugh would have to marry at some point and William Marshal's eldest daughter would be an absolute coup. 'It is every mother's concern,' she replied. 'I hope to see my children settled well with suitable mates. My daughter

491

Marie will wed later this year, and we could not have found better for her in Ranulf FitzRobert. He'll be a fine addition to the family.'

'I think I saw him standing with your sons – in the blue tunic?'

'Yes.'

Isabelle's lips curved with remembered appreciation. 'Handsome,' she said.

'And with more between his ears than fleece.' Ida broke off another piece of the crenellations and nibbled. 'It's starting to look as if it's been involved in a siege,' she said with false grief.

'Who needs a trebuchet?' Isabelle laughed. 'Are you attending the water joust tomorrow?'

Ida gave her a puzzled look. 'Water joust?'

'On the river.' Isabelle gestured at the blue 'water' on the subtlety. 'They put a shield on a pole midstream and contestants try to shatter their lances against it from boats rowed by their friends. I've only seen it done once – when I was the King's ward and lodged at the Tower. More than half of the contestants end up in the water but it is good sport to watch. William's going to be adjudicating.' She made a face at Ida. 'Thank the saints, I say, because I wouldn't put it past him even now to get involved.'

'I know of the sport,' Ida replied, 'but I always managed to miss it when we were in the city. I've never seen one.'

'Then join us on the bridge.' Isabelle's expression brightened with enthusiasm. 'You're most welcome and I would enjoy the company. Bring the younger ones with you. I'll have Will, Richard and Mahelt with me.'

Ida thanked her and accepted and the women went their separate ways, each with her purloined hoard.

41

London, May 1199

From her vantage point on London Bridge, Ida had a fine view of the excited crowds lining the banks of the Thames three deep, waiting for the water joust to begin. The sky was clear and reflected on the river in a glittering blue, starred with sun sparkles of white gold. Colourful banners and bunting decorated the wharves and festooned the barges and boats at their moorings. Folk leaned out from the upper storeys and galleries of wharfside dwellings in anticipation of the sport to come; the air was one of celebration and festive enjoyment.

Cookshops and vintneries plied a brisk trade and all manner of hucksters wove through the throng, touting their wares: eels and whelks, meat pies and trotters, ribbons and laces, chaplets and posies, lead badges of saints, cheap brooches – all the sustenance and mementos demanded by Londoners in holiday mood.

The new King had come to watch the sport and was afforded an excellent view of the proceedings from his cushioned chair on a raised and canopied platform by the riverside. Beside him sat Hubert Walter, Archbishop of Canterbury, resplendent in white silk embroidered with gold, and surrounding them most of the court was present to enjoy the spectacle and a moment's frivolity before the serious business of government commenced.

Ida stood on London Bridge with Isabelle Marshal and several other baronial families. Isabelle had brought her two oldest sons, Will and Richard, and their sister Mahelt – a vibrant little girl with a plait of shining brunette hair and her father's deep hazel eyes. The doll she was clutching wore identical clothes to Isabelle, and sported two plaits of flaxen horsehair. Although thoroughly endeared to the little girl, Ida could not imagine her as Hugh's wife for she was still little more than a baby. Her two brothers aged nine and seven were of similar years to Ida's younger sons and the boys had teamed up in a chattering peer group. Will, the Marshal heir, had his mother's fine features and was surprisingly light of build. His brother Richard, on the other hand, was tall and robust with a shock of copper-red hair and freckles. Richard dwarfed Ralph who had been born the same year, but the pair of them had formed an immediate rapport.

Ida had brought gingerbread for the children and they pounced upon it with cries of delight. Ela, the young Countess of Salisbury, was also among their party, for as well as being Ida's daughter-in-law, she was blood kin to the Marshals. She nibbled her gingerbread daintily, her manners exquisite. She was quiet but not shy, which Ida thought made her a perfect match for her son.

'Here comes a boat!' shrieked Mahelt, pointing and jumping up and down with excitement. Her nurse shushed her, and her father's knight, Eustace, hoisted her on to his broad shoulders to give her a better view.

With everyone else, Ida peered over the bridge. A pole with a shield hammered to its top had been fixed in mid-river earlier that morning. Now a boat was surging

494

downstream on the ebb tide, crewed by several men all rowing furiously and using the power of the river to aid their endeavour. From her viewpoint on the bridge, Ida was reminded of an overturned beetle with flailing legs. Standing at the prow with a braced lance was a young man clad in shirt and braies, the wind from the river billowing his garments like small sails. Either side of the pole two boats with four men apiece rode the water, ready to pluck to safety anyone who fell overboard.

The youth took up a firmer stance as the shield approached. Ida's stomach jerked towards her spine in anticipation. She could sense everyone holding their breath. The young man made his strike. The impact wobbled the boat on its course, but the lance held true and shattered on the shield. The youth teetered for an instant then sprawled on his back in the belly of the boat, rocking it alarmingly from side to side. Laughter, cheers and loud applause rang from the crowd.

Another boat came shooting downstream, white scuds of water churning beneath the oars as the men hauled on them for all they were worth. Again, the strike broke the lance, but this time the jouster's stance was not as good and after a few seconds of frantic flailing, he tumbled into the water with an almighty splash. The roar from the crowd as he was hauled dripping into the rescue vessel was as great for him as it was for the youth who had succeeded.

Ida listened to Isabelle explaining to Mahelt that everyone in a particular boat had to take a turn at the shield and points were awarded for a strike, a miss and a fall. At the end of the proceedings, the King would present the winners with a pike on a silver salver.

'Papa doesn't like pike,' Mahelt said, wrinkling her nose.

'Well, he would probably distribute it to others who

do,' Isabelle replied, 'but since he's judging the event, he doesn't have to worry.' She smiled at Ida. 'He prefers to keep his feet on firm ground.' Her eyes suddenly widened and she pointed. 'Do your menfolk enjoy pike?'

Ida turned to stare at the boat hurtling downstream in a furious churn of oar strokes and let out a small horrified scream. She had thought her husband safely occupied at the wharf giving advice to the youngsters, but here he was standing at the prow of a rowing boat with a braced lance. She couldn't believe her eyes. Dear Christ, if William Marshal had the good sense not to get involved surely Roger, a sober judge and statesman, ought to know better.

The crowd was roaring like a sea. Hugh and Longespée were pulling on the oars for all they were worth, as were Anketil, Will Bigod, Goscelin and Ranulf FitzRobert.

Marie leaped up and down almost as vigorously as Mahelt Marshal had done. 'It's Papa!' she shrieked, although her eyes were all for Ranulf.

Ida clung to Isabelle Marshal for support as Roger planted himself, made his blow and shattered the lance against the target. He performed the move with neat precision and the cheers of the onlookers were loud enough for her to imagine it being heard all the way down at Greenwich. Clutching her midriff, Ida gasped and fought for composure as the boat came through safely.

'Dear sweet Virgin Mary!' she cried, shaking her head emphatically from side to side. She was both exhilarated and frightened. Through her relief, she felt a pang deep inside. Why should she not have thought Roger would do this? Beyond the implacable, steady judge weighing all things, beyond the measured calm, there still lingered a glimmer of the athlete and warrior who could twirl sword and spear like a professional tumbler; the adept sailor who could swarm aloft a ship's rigging in Ipswich harbour . . . The man who could still play like a boy if sufficient layers were stripped away.

'Papa did it, Papa did it!' Ralph exclaimed, his eyes shining with pride.

'Your lord is indeed a *preux chevalier*, my lady,' Isabelle Marshal said and there was respect in her voice amid the amusement.

Ida lifted her chin and returned Isabelle a proud, almost teary smile. 'Yes, he is,' she said. 'And I am well reminded.'

On the river, the rowers in the Bigod boat turned their vessel and hauled back upstream to the assembly of competitors at the starting wharf. Roger had not intended taking part, but somehow advice from the shore had become advice on the boat and before he knew it, he had become a vital part of the ensemble, not least because he had played this sport as a youth and young knight, and was adept on any kind of waterborne vessel. He glanced towards the bridge and gave a triumphant salute to the throng with his broken lance. Imagining the look on Ida's face, he grinned.

'We're going to win this!' Longespée panted, a competitive gleam in his eyes as he slowed his oars.

Roger considered the shattered end of the lance. 'It was a good clean break,' he said. He had felt tremendous exhilaration as he aimed for the shield and knew he was going to strike it true. The wind blustering through his shirt had been the breath of life. The sudden pounding of his heart, the fierce pleasure had made him feel young again and brimful of joy for the sake of joy. Daily life, by its very nature, dulled the lustre of such emotion, but now the shine was back, bright as a new coin.

497

The crew rowed alongside the wharf to collect a fresh lance. On the bank and the bridge, the crowd roared with laughter as a contender splashed into the water.

'That's de Warenne gone for a dunking!' Hugh cried in triumph. Roger tossed the new lance to Longespée. 'See if you can follow me, my lord,' he said.

The young Earl flashed Roger a look that said he would not only follow it up, he would do better. The men changed places, Roger taking Longespée's position on the bench beside Will. The half-brothers exchanged glances. 'I am glad you are here,' Roger found a moment to say. 'You row a steady oar.'

Will gave a self-deprecating shrug. 'It is not a great accomplishment. I used to take a boat out on my own when I wanted to escape – which was often.' He flexed his hands and gripped the smooth ash handle. 'Now it's time to turn for the shore.'

Roger clasped his shoulder and felt the solidity of muscle under the flesh. The gesture was one acknowledging that he understood what Will was really saying. 'But not quite yet. We need your strength in the current.'

Will smiled. 'You have it.'

To mutual nods, the half-brothers pulled into the first stroke, and, with their companions, worked the boat out into the current. They scudded downriver, driving towards the by now somewhat scratched shield on its pole. The cheering of the crowd was a distant roar in Roger's ears, noticed but an incidental because his focus was on holding their vessel true to course.

The lance braced, his fine silk shirt rippling in the wind, dark hair blowing at his brow, Longespée waited his moment. The lance head rammed against the centre of the shield, crunched and splintered. The impact of the blow sent Longespée reeling, but he tumbled into the well

498

of the boat, not overboard. For an instant the vessel swayed like a cradle rocked by an angry foot, but the rowers steadied it and with Roger directing, completed the course and turned back to prepare for the next run.

Roger handed the new lance to Hugh. Determination showed in the jut of the lad's jaw, but Roger could sense his tension and could well understand it. He and Longespée had both succeeded and the onus was now upon Hugh to continue the achievement.

'We can take the prize!' Longespée said as they sculled back out into the river. 'We're ahead on points!'

Roger cast a warning glance at his stepson.

'I don't need to be reminded,' Hugh said tersely.

'Steady, lad, steady,' Roger reassured him. 'Just fix your eyes on the centre of the shield. Become the lance.'

Hugh gave a brisk nod, swallowed, and readied himself at the prow. He wiped his palms on his shirt, gripped the lance and planted his legs as the others picked up the rhythm and began to scull downstream towards the shield. Roger's arms burned as he pulled on the oars. Will was hauling with steady strength. One stroke, two, three, four. He counted the distance down. Water glittered off the oar blades. Dip and pull, dip and pull, muscles straining, lungs on fire, giving Hugh as much speed as they could wring from themselves and their vessel. Hugh leaned into the strike and there was an almighty splintering sound as not only the lance shattered, but the shield, weakened by the battering it had taken, split and broke from the pole. Hugh teetered on the verge of spilling into the water. Roger let go of his oar, seized the hem of Hugh's shirt and dragged him back down into the belly of the boat.

Hugh lay on his back gasping, the broken lance clutched in his hand.

'God's blood, boy, you've split the shield!' Roger whooped. 'That has to take the prize!'

A beatific grin dazzled across Hugh's face. He laughed aloud and then flashed a triumphant look at his half-brother. 'I doubt anyone will beat that,' he panted.

Longespée inclined his head and gave him a thin-lipped smile. 'Not unless they have the luck of the Devil,' he said. 'Well done.' And then suddenly a brighter smile broke across his face because of the collective victory. 'Well done indeed, brother!'

Hugh flushed at the accolade and gave a brusque nod of acknowledgement – followed by a warm grin.

As they turned the boat back into the current, Roger realised that a barge was coming straight at them on the diagonal. The occupants – drunken youths intent on crossing the river to the Southwark side – were paying more attention to their singing and the women in the barge with them than they were to their steerage. Roger bellowed a warning, but there was no time to avoid the other vessel and the boats collided with a hefty smack. Roger was flung backwards and his head struck the prow strake. Numbness blossomed and radiated. A huge gulp of water filled the rowing boat as she rocked under the impact and then tipped over. As Roger hit the water, he was barely conscious.

As if from a great distance, he was aware of breaking the surface, of struggling for air and choking. His limbs refused to obey his will; his vision was a stinging blur; sounds were hollow echoes: splashing, shouting, the roar and gurgle of water. Someone floundered against him and pushed him under. He felt a kick and fabric trailing against his face. The world darkened, and through the darkness he felt a fierce grip on his arm and another on the back of his neck and, once more, his head broke the surface. He couldn't breathe. His limbs were useless lead weights. He heard Hugh gasping that he had got him and Longespée reassuring him the same from the other side. There was a sensation of being dragged through the water, then suddenly there was a hard surface under his chest, and someone was thumping rhythmically on his spine. 'My lord, Papa, in God's name!' He wondered what Hugh was in such a panic about. Lifting his head, he strove to answer. His belly heaved and he spewed half a gallon of the river Thames on to the jetty. Stars burst before his eyes. He dragged air down his raw throat and into his lungs and, coughing and spluttering, sat up. Hugh, white-faced and shivering, stood over him. Longespée had just taken a magnificent green woollen cloak from an attendant. He hesitated for a brief instant and then swept it around Roger's shoulders. 'Here, my lord,' he said.

Roger nodded his thanks and, still choking, looked round the wharf, which seemed to be filled with various dripping individuals, including two bedraggled women. Will was sitting with his feet dangling over the edge of the jetty, his head bowed and shoulders heaving as he coughed. Someone was doling out blankets. The side of Roger's head throbbed with hot pain as the chill from the water began to wear off.

He watched Hugh straighten up and grip his half-brother's arm, and Longespée return the clasp. The young men were still connected when Ida arrived in a flurry of anxiety. Ignoring them, she went to straight to Roger and dropped at his side, uncaring of the wet planks of the wharf under her gown.

'You fool!' she cried. 'You utter, purblind fool!' Her tone was so vehement and angry that her sons looked at each other askance.

501

'I'm all right,' Roger croaked, before starting to cough again.

She made an exasperated sound and glared round at the others. 'One of you have a litter fetched, don't stand there dripping.' She clapped her hands.

The members of the Bigod household, accustomed to her gentle way of doing things, stared at her open-mouthed for a moment, then Anketil came to his senses and hastened to do her bidding.

Through chattering teeth, Roger smiled at his wife. 'Despite all,' he said hoarsely, 'I think I can safely say we've won the pike. No one else will better this perform-ance!'

Epilogue

Framlingham, May 1199

In the spring sunshine, the Bigod family and sundry allies gathered in the embryo pleasure garden under Framlingham's west wall to dine in the fresh air. Trestles had been set up and the white linen napery draping the boards was adorned with platters of dainty fritters and pies, cold roast fowl, bream from the mere, custard tarts and honey cakes studded with raisins.

Leaning against the trestle, taking a momentary respite from socialising, Ida bit into one of the cakes and, as she tasted the golden sweetness on her tongue, allowed herself a moment's glow of contentment. More building work remained to be carried out on the fortifications, but the masons had downed their tools for the day and were holding their own feast in the ward. There was no dust and no noise. The new hall at least was complete and furnished with Flemish wall hangings and a fine permanent table on the dais. These were small causes for satisfaction, but what gave her the most joy was that all of her family were gathered under one roof. No one was quarrelling and the day was going to be a perfect memory to store away like a jewelled bead on a string, to recall when life was not so graced with delight.

Earlier, Marie had been betrothed to Ranulf FitzRobert in the castle chapel and the marriage was to take place before the winter. Roger had also officially granted Hugh custody of ten knights' fees in Yorkshire to give him an income of his own and the responsibility of governance. Hugh's elevation would take some weight off Roger's shoulders, which was a good thing. The grant meant that Hugh would soon leave Framlingham for Settrington, but Ida was not going to dwell on that today.

The shouts of children playing a boisterous game of chase drew her gaze to Ralph, who as usual was making the loudest noise as he fled from his cousin Thomas, the small son of Roger's half-brother. It was good to see that part of the past being mended. Roger had promised to advance his nephew and had been keen to have Will and his family included in today's gathering. Their presence was a sign of acceptance on both parts. The healing of old wounds could continue, even if the scars would always be visible. At least Gundreda's grandson was being given a platform to make his way in the world.

Juliana was deep in conversation with Longespée. Ida was delighted that her mother-in-law and her firstborn son socialised so well together. Juliana enjoyed William's court-liness and William was pleased to have attention paid to him by a dowager of finesse and elegance. Even Hugh and Longespée were managing to rub along in amity. The water joust had created a subtle shift in their relationship. They had worked together to save Roger from drowning when the boat capsized and Hugh's breaking of the shield had won them the prize. On both sides there was an atmosphere of wary tolerance that Ida hoped would mellow and strengthen as they matured; this at least was a start.

Roger strolled up to join her at the trestle. She bit the remnant of the honey cake in two, ate one piece, and fed him the other with a smile. If not the wiry, limber young man she had first seen at court more than a score of years ago, he remained handsome in her eyes and his hair still held all the seashore colours she loved, even if there was silver spindrift in it now. Today his brow was bound with the gold ceremonial coronet of the earldom.

He had been ill of a congestion of the lungs after his dip in the river, but had made a full recovery. 'Stronger than an ox,' the King had observed, visiting Roger's sickbed before setting out for Saint Albans. He had managed to make it sound as if it were a rustic attribute.

Roger linked her hand through his, raised it to his lips and kissed it. 'I thought we could bring some apple saplings back from the Norman estates and plant some trees over there,' he said with a nod towards the open space beyond the trestle.

'More mulching.' Ida gave him a teasing smile.

He laughed softly. 'I have always been fond of orchards for other reasons. Truly, mulching never entered my head.' He continued to hold her hand. 'There are going to be some uncertain times in front of us with this new King . . . not that there haven't been uncertain times before, but whatever happens, at least we have solid ground on which to stand, walls to protect us and a family on whom we can rely, every one of them.'

Slipping his arm around her waist, he led her away from the trestle to walk the ground where he intended to plant the trees. Ida felt the cool blades of new summer grass flicker against her ankles. She cast her glance to the great towers of Framlingham, shining in the sunlight, the shape reminding her of the coronet on Roger's brow. Her relationship with the castle and the earldom had been

505

one of light and shadow down the years, but in this moment, she was both elated and at peace. Everything she valued, everyone she loved was gathered here today and it truly felt like home, and a homecoming. No one could say their defences would stand for ever, but just now, it felt as if they would.

Author's Note

While writing two novels about the life story of the great William Marshal, I came across Roger Bigod, Earl of Norfolk, whose eldest son Hugh was later to marry into the Marshal family – a story I hope to follow up in the future. Roger is contemporary with William Marshal, and his life and career run parallel for much of the time, although Roger's remarkable story has not been so well documented.

Two things initially piqued my interest about Roger and Ida and made me want to write their story for a modern audience. The first was Roger's long struggle to win back the lands, prestige and honour that his father had lost in rebellion; the second was Ida de Tosney's relationship with King Henry and then with Roger, and the emotional repercussions involved for all concerned.

From the records one can piece together the first strand of the story, i.e. Roger's efforts to regain his lands. I firmly believe that Henry II was never going to give them to him. There was always the matter of trust and since Roger's stepmother and half-brothers were disputing the inheritance, Henry had a perfect excuse to keep the argued

507

territories in his own hands and milk their revenues. For Henry it was a win-win situation. However, he also knew how to employ useful men. Roger proved loyal (although sometimes I suspect he was gritting his teeth very hard!). As well as being an accomplished lawyer, Roger was a clear-minded and indefatigable administrator – not to say a man possessed of a very shrewd fiscal brain. He is first found working for Henry on the judicial bench at Westminster in 1187.

During Richard's reign, Roger was restored to the earldom and spent several years travelling the country hearing cases throughout numerous counties, dispensing justice and, importantly for Richard's empty treasury, levying fines on transgressors. For example, in 1195, Roger covered Northumberland, Yorkshire, Westmorland, Lancashire, Cumberland, Norfolk, Suffolk, Essex and Hertfordshire, with Warwickshire and Leicestershire following on.

Between 1189 and 1213, he rebuilt the demolished castle at Framlingham on a grand scale. Visitors to East Anglia can still see Roger's thirteen great towers standing today with the most complete wall walk of any castle in the United Kingdom. The hall where Roger and Ida first began married life no longer stands, but its Norman chimneys can still be seen, and the wall abutting the later building work. Some fragmentary remains of the new hall are still in evidence too, part of them housing the Visitor Centre.

Roger had several strings to his bow and was not only a competent lawyer and administrator, but also an accomplished soldier. The Chronicle of Jocelin of Brakelond, a monk of Bury St Edmunds, tells us that Roger bore the banner of St Edmund (perhaps the most revered saint in England in the twelfth century) at the battle of Fornham.

508

Roger was frequently found on campaign with successive kings of England, and we know he fought at the siege of Nottingham Castle in 1194. There is speculation as to whether he did or did not attend King Richard in Germany. Certainly, he is mentioned on the 'boarding' list, even if there is no charter evidence for his presence with Richard in Germany, so I took an author's decision to send him there.

The dispute between Roger, Gundreda and Gundreda's sons was acrimonious and both sides fought tooth and nail for what they considered their property rights. Huon was never reconciled to the loss of his patrimony and died some time before 1203, still battling for his right to his share of the inheritance. However, some kind of accord must have been reached within the family because Roger's nephew Thomas (Will's son) is later found in Roger's retinue, attesting charters. He also attested for Roger's son Hugh. Minor land disputes arose in the early thirteenth century between the two branches of the family, but they did not have the heat of earlier exchanges. Roger was indeed fined large sums throughout Richard's reign to retain his properties, but a new, final settlement was negotiated when John came to the throne.

Roger married King Henry's mistress Ida de Tosney around Christmas 1181. Not a great deal is known about Ida. There is neither a birth date nor a death date for her in the records, although it is known she died before Roger because no arrangements were made for her person following his death in 1221. Even her parentage is in doubt, although she is now strongly considered on good circumstantial evidence to be the daughter of Ralph de Tosney, lord of Flamstead, and his wife Margaret de Beaumont.

For many years her identity as the mother of William

Longespée, Earl of Salisbury, remained a mystery too, and it has only recently been solved by painstaking genealogical detective work. There remains much debate about the birth date of her son by King Henry and suggestions range from 1165 to 1180. For the purposes of the novel, I have chosen the later end of the spectrum. My reasons for this are that Ida's (probable) parents married in 1155 and her father died in 1162, so that gives us a rough window for the date of Ida's birth and means that the 1165 suggestion can be ruled out. My other reason for dating it at the later end is that Henry's mistress Rosamund de Clifford was supposedly the love of his life and she did not die until 1176. Therefore, I postulate a time after this date for Longespée's birth. This being a work of fiction I do have a certain leeway for speculation!

Some readers might wonder about Ida feeding her children herself during their early months and of being an involved mother, as it has been suggested that all aristocratic women handed their children over to wet nurses the moment they were born and had little to do with them. I consider this to be something of a blanket statement and believe that one size certainly didn't fit all. The Church preferred women to suckle their own infants and the cult of the Virgin Mary, with numerous images of the Christ child being suckled, always meant there were women, even of high status, who chose to nurture their own offspring.

Eagle-eyed readers who have read my other novels may notice some personalities have aged or suddenly grown younger, or minorly changed appearance. Sometimes this is down to authorial oversight, for which I apologise. Sometimes additional research on subjects less intensively studied for a previous work will shed new light. For example, in *The Scarlet Lion*, Roger and Ida's heir Hugh has his birth dated to early 1184. My research on the Bigods placed the more likely date as late in 1182, as his parents married around Christmas 1181, so in *The Time of Singing* he has gained a couple of years.

On the issue of the historical detail, the various human relationships and physical appearances, I have, as in my novels about the Marshals, used the Akashic Records as one thread of numerous sources of research. As mentioned in the author's note of my novel *A Place Beyond Courage*, this is a belief that each person leaves behind an indelible record of themselves impressed upon sub-atomic material and that this record can be accessed if one has the ability to tune in at that particular vibrational level. I have based the physical descriptions of Roger and Ida on those records. The records also pointed up such details as Roger's level determination and his fondness for hats, Ida's skill with a needle, her nurturing qualities, the trauma of having to leave her baby behind when she married Roger and the frictions between her two eldest sons.

For readers who are curious, here's a sample of the kind of material obtained from these records via the skills of Akashic consultant Alison King:

At a session early in 2000, I asked Alison to go to Ida de Tosney, Roger's future wife. I asked to see her when she first met Henry II, whose mistress she became. At the time she was an heiress in his wardship.

Alison: Gosh, what a lovely lady. She is so serene, so calm. I saw animals pulling something that looks like a sled. I think it's an illustration for an embroidery . . . Yes, I've got strong confirmation. She is thinking up pictures to sew. She's doing it in a calm way, like day-dreaming.

511

She is going to be taken to meet the King and is being got ready by older women who are helping her dress in her best. They're putting ribbons in her hair and draping a beautiful cloak at her shoulders – crimson, with emerald and blue trimming. Her dress is a peach colour with cream trimming. They're doing something to her eyes – putting on cosmetics to make her look more grown up. Brushing eyebrows into shape. She's not yet fully developed, perhaps about fifteen. They're not dressing her up with the air of making her attractive to Henry, but just so that she looks well groomed and her best. It will be of benefit to her if he likes her and it will make things better for all concerned.

She is brought to the room where the King is. She's quite excited and feels a bit tight in the chest. I can smell incense. I can sense her being brought in from a door in the corner. There are people in front of her. She is brought to the front row of a semi-circle of people being presented to the King. Henry is speaking to them individually in a loud voice. It's one of those public meeting and greeting things.

'Who are you? Tell me.'

Then it comes to her turn. Henry stands before her and touches her on her collarbone. 'Ah, de Tosney's little girl. It's long since I saw you. Just a babe in arms, and now by the look of you, old enough to have your own babe in arms.'

Ida blushes and curtseys. If he could, Henry would have his hand down the front of her dress right now. He would do it. He licks his lips and goes on to the next person, but he gives a lingering look back at Ida. She doesn't look at him; she feels terribly embarrassed.

Later, when he's talking to everyone, he pretends he can't arrange his footstool just right and gets her to do it, making her go this way and that with it. Then he gets

512

her to stand by him – just her. He engages her in conversation. 'Tell me what you've been doing today. Tell me a little story from the nursery.' Ida is very embarrassed again. 'I hardly know what to say, sire.' He sighs. 'It matters not.' But he doesn't want her to move from where he's put her. She's trying to watch what else is going on in the hall and is still embarrassed, trying to pretend this is not happening. She is frightened, but very aware of doing the right thing. Told to move the footstool, she has done her best to get it right. She is looking minutely at the décor. She's looking at the tassels on the cushions he is sitting on. Pale gold. She's getting a bit fed up and wondering when all this will end. She wants to go for dinner and hopes that he'll forget about her. People are leaving now to go for dinner. She has to go as well but the King pulls her back and says he needs someone to help support his cloak. He already has two small boys for this and she is even more embarrassed having to do this and being singled out. All the time she wants to escape. The next thing is that he wants her to sit with him, but his attendants are horrified and say no, a seat has been allotted for her. Alison says she feels that, even so, the allotted space is higher up the table than she would have at first been given, so that Henry can watch her . . . She's a bit relieved but still too close for comfort as Henry continues to smile and leer at her. However, she manages to get away after that.

The next day she receives a summons that 'The King wants to see you in his chamber.' Ida is very flustered and really quite worked up. Her ladies are dismissive of her fears. They say it's a great honour for her, but they are very worldly.

In the King's chamber he makes her undress the top part of her clothes and she's feeling extremely nervous, embarrassed and powerless. She doesn't know where to look. He starts touching her. [*We cut to the aftermath.*] Afterwards she's in shock, she's trembling. He is saying, 'Remember, it's a great honour I do you.' He's preening, getting himself ready for the next event. He chucks her under the chin. 'Lift your pretty little head.' She can't look him in the eyes and he's saying, 'No matter, no matter.' His attitude is that she'll come round. 'You're a sweet little thing, very sweet and it's to your credit.' He says, 'You are the King's virgin bride. You will do well.' And he brings out a fur collar and puts it on her. 'There, that will keep you warm for me . . . for tonight.'

Obviously this information can't be corroborated (and there is always the chance that it comes from the imagination) but there have been numerous other occasions in the course of this research when it can, and when it has been spot on with the known history. I leave it to the reader to decide. All I will say is that, braided together, the varying strands of research have illuminated for me the rich and tangled lives of people long gone, people very different from ourselves – and yet not so different at all, and, I hope in this small corner at least, not forgotten.

Elizabeth Chadwick

Select Bibliography

For readers wanting to read further on the matter of the Bigod family, their life and times, I enclose a short bibliography. This covers the most pertinent volumes and is by no means an exhaustive list.

Appleby, John T., *England Without Richard* (Bell, 1967)

Atkin, Susan A. J., *The Bigod Family: An Investigation into Their Lands and Activities 1066–1306* (University of Reading, published on demand by the British Library Thesis Service)

Brakelond, Jocelin of, *Chronicle of the Abbey of Bury St Edmunds* (Oxford University Press, 1998, ISBN 0 19 283895 4)

Brown, Morag, *Framlingham Castle* (English Heritage, ISBN 1 85074 853 5)

Brown, R. Allen, *Castles, Conquests and Charters: Collected Papers* (Boydell, 1989, ISBN 0 85115 524 3)

Brown, R. Allen, 'Framlingham Castle and Bigod 1154–1216' (*Proceedings of the Suffolk Institute of Archaeology*, XXV, 1951)

Eyton, Revd R. W., *Court, Itinerary and Household of Henry II* (Taylor & Co., 1893)

The Feet of Fines of the Seventh and Eighth Years of King Richard I (The Pipe Roll Society 1896)

Gillingham, John, *Richard I* (Yale University Press, 2002, ISBN 0 300 09404 3)

Gravett, Christopher and Hook, Adam, *Norman Stone Castles: The British Isles 1066–1216* (Osprey, 2003, ISBN 1 84176 602 X)

The Great Roll of the Pipe for the ninth year of the reign of King Richard I Michaelmas 1197, ed. by Doris M. Stenton (The Pipe Roll Society, 1931)

Green, Monica H., *The Trotula: An English Translation of the Medieval Compendium of Women's Medicine* (University of Pennsylvania Press, 2002, ISBN 978 0 8122 1808 4)

Harper-Bill, Christopher, ed., *Anglo Norman Studies XVII: Proceedings of The Battle Conference 1994* (Boydell, 1995, ISBN 0 85115 606 1)

King, Alison, Akashic Records Consultant

Landsberg, Sylvia, *The Medieval Garden* (British Museum Press 1995 ISBN 0 7171 2080 4)

Morris, Marc, *The Bigod Earls of Norfolk in the Thirteenth Century* (Boydell, 2005, ISBN 1843831643)

Sancha, Sheila, *The Castle Story* (Collins, 1993, ISBN 0 00 184177 7)

Stenton, Doris M., *English Justice between the Norman Conquest and the Great Charter 1066–1215* (George Allen & Unwin, 1963)

The Treatise on the Laws and Customs of the Realm of England Commonly Called Glanvill, ed. and trans. by G. D. G. Hall (Oxford Medieval Texts, Clarendon Press, 1993, ISBN 0 19 822179 7)

Tyerman, Christopher, *Who's Who in Early Medieval England* (Shepheard Walwyn, 1996, ISBN 0 85683 132 8)

Warren, W. L., *Henry II* (Eyre Methuen, 1977, ISBN 0 413 38390 3)

As always I welcome comments and I can be contacted through my website at www.elizabethchadwick.com or by email to elizabeth.chadwick@btinternet.com

I post regular updates about my writing and historical research at my blog at http://livingthehistoryelizabethchadwick.blogspot.com. The url is at my website. There is also a friendly informal discussion list at ElizabethChadwick@yahoogroups.com, which readers are very welcome to join.